GHOSTS
OF THE
GRIDIRON

Greg Lautenslager

*For my wonderful sons
Craig, Jeff, and Jared*

PART ONE

The Bomb

1

November 28, 2005

Jack Byrne couldn't write his own obituary without a momentary lapse of life. His eyes wandered from his computer screen across a valley of balding has-been sportswriters, preppy Pulitzer pretenders, and a chubby prick overlooking his flock from his glassed-in office to a high school gridiron illuminated by floodlights and a full moon.

A 14-year old boy breaks the huddle and marches through the fog to midfield in front of angry defensive linemen twice his size. He slides his shaky hands under the center's behind to the calls of "pussy" through the gray bars of his opponents' facemasks, wiggles his shoulder pads under his purple jersey, and hollers through the single white bar of his thin purple helmet, "D-d-down. S-s-set. H-h-hut one. H-h-hut–"

The boy glances left to a man in work boots, blue jeans, and a plaid shirt rushing from the sidelines. The man grabs the boy's facemask and pulls him toward his team's end zone to the mixed horrors and giggles of teenage players and their coaches and parents until the boy disappears into the fog.

Jack felt a claw on his back, this one from someone he detested more than the man who ruined his football career before it got started. The suited prick known to his staff as Dick Schwartz, Executive Sports Editor of The Dallas Star, and to Jack as the Sawed Off Stack of Shit – Soss, for short – was overlooking his shoulder and screen. Taking the advice of the jockeys he never covered, Jack never looked back.

"What's this shit?" Soss asked.

"The obit you ordered me to write." Jack kept tapping at his keyboard.

Soss kept reading while exhaling Cuban cigar breaths over Jack's desk littered with stacks of scribbled notepads, chewed pens, NFL media guides and scrunched PR releases, empty Dr Pepper bottles, Baby Ruth wrappers, donut crumbs, and a tangled phone cord. The phrases "star sports columnist" and "inspiring mentor" and "devoted husband" each elicited a "huh" from Soss. "Promising quarterback with Super Bowl potential" produced an all-out chuckle. Jack lifted his left hand off the keyboard and scratched his goatee but kept staring at the screen. "What's so funny?"

"In my wildest dreams," Soss said above the keyboard tapping and phone chatting from the surrounding desks of his sports tribe, "could I ever imagine you playin' football, much less in the Super Bowl."

"I played."

"What?

"Powder Puff?"

"High school. Briefly. I really don't want to talk about it."

Soss had assigned his scribe to write an obituary of a living sports star as punishment for his column following the Dallas Cowboys' 45-7 drubbing by the Miami Dolphins in the 2005 Annual Thanksgiving Day Game at Tom Landry Stadium. Soss arrived at his office suite post-Thanksgiving holidays to a flood of letters-to-the-editor, the least kindly calling Byrne "an insensitive horse-shit writer whom I'd pay a million bucks to watch his arms and legs and overly inflated head ripped from their sockets by two 350-pound linemen and then pissed on by their teammates."

Soss tacked that letter on the bulletin board above the water cooler and said he deserved it after what Byrne wrote for his lead:

Rex Fanning should give thanks to Dolphins' nose tackle Buck Bamford for knocking the Cowboys' seldom-maligned quarterback out cold in the fourth quarter of Thursday's abysmal turkey of an NFL game that sent his fans to an early Thanksgiving dinner. Fanning, if he ever wakes up in St. Luke's intensive care unit, should hope that the four interceptions and two fumbles he offered to the Dolphins will be a miserable memory erased by the jarring, helmet-first early Christmas present from Bamford to Fanning's chin.

Had Fanning's sleep turned eternal one minute before deadline that night, his obituary – complete with his bio, career statistics, and tributes from players and coaches – magically would have appeared in The Dallas Star only a few hours later. The newspaper staff routinely writes obituaries of famous living people in case their demise happens suddenly and on deadline. They use quotes from past features for tributes. All the duty editor has to do is write in the lead how, where, and when the famous bloke or bloke-ette died and, presto, you have an instant obituary.

This dull task normally is reserved for interns or general assignment reporters. Soss assigned one to a begrudged Jack and let him choose any famous sportsperson he wanted.

"I said somebody famous!" Soss' explosion made the keyboard tapping and telephone chatting cease. Unknowingly, Soss had the attention of his entire staff. Even Jack swivelled his chair around to see Soss' teeth clench and nose curl inward like an angry pit bull.

"I'm famous," Jack said, looking down.

"No, you're infamous. I want someone famous – and I mean famous-famous." Soss pointed a manicurist-groomed fingernail at Jack's forehead with the mention of every famed name. "Brett Favre. Peyton Manning. Michael Jordan. Jack Nicklaus. Wayne Gretzky. Andre Agassi."

Soss started his march back to his office, stopped, turned around, and shook his right fist.

"Not Jack 'Fucking' Byrne!"

JACK COULD HEAR Soss' office door slam from his desk a third and a mile away and, after a short pause, the return of keyboard tapping and phone chatting. Jack was too far into his own obituary not to finish it. He recounted what he thought were his most famous columns – like the one about Johnny "Wrong Way" Molinski, the Lone Star State University quarterback who recovered a fumbled snap and then ran into the wrong end zone – and all the famous players and coaches he had interviewed.

After tapping out the last line – "Jack Byrne, famous sportswriter, will be respected and remembered and loved for a long, long time" – Jack heard tapping from across the room.

Jack peered at the glassed-in office to see his boss motioning with his thumb. He didn't need to be a lip reader to know what he was saying: "Get your ass in here right now."

Jack's walk past gawking sportswriters and his weave around copy editors looking up from the sportswriters' stories they were butchering was more like a death march. Jay Verona, the Star's NFL beat writer, said, "Good thing you finished your obit, Jacko," just as Jack grabbed Soss's gold-plated office door handle and the eye level sign that read. "Dick Schwartz, Executive Sports Editor."

Jack lumbered past Soss' office mini-bar and sat on the leather sofa in front of the solid oak desk. Soss had just taken a phone call, leaving Jack time to look around at the office he had hated so much and grown so accustomed. His eyes wandered from the back office wall to Soss' self portraits and his framed certificates and wondered how someone who never graduated from college and never wrote or edited a story could be declared "Sports Editor of the Year."

"If I were a ghost," Jack thought, "I would serve this Sawed Off Stack of Shit a cup of his favorite cappuccino – with scalding water. As he sprays the hot lava onto his Armani suit, I pour Tabasco sauce into his water bottle and lace his blueberry muffin with Ex-Lax. I slither into his "private" bathroom, cover his toilet seat with Vaseline, and listen to his faint groan as he slams onto the linoleum.

"I sit in the leather passenger seat of his black Lexus as he drives to Feelin' Big Health Spa for his lunchtime workout and rub, expel a silent but deadly from my rotted bowel, and keep turning the channel of his 24-hour Sports Talk Radio to K-STAT – '24 hours of constant static.'

"As he jogs 15-minute miles on the treadmill and still manages to soak his white headband on his bald scalp while smiling at the blonde Pilates instructor in full body Lycra, I pull the power cord out of the wall and see him crash into the ESPN SportsCenter anchor on the eye-level television screen. While he is having an ice cold shower, I spray his underwear with heat balm and watch him spend the rest of the day backslapping with the good ol' boy managing editor and butt-tapping his well-endowed PA in absolute agony."

"YOU KNOW WHAT'S gotta be done," Soss whispered into the telephone before hanging up. He swiveled around toward Jack, leaned back in his leather office chair, and folded his arms. Then he grabbed a two-iron from his golf bag behind him. Jack was frightened that Soss, who spends more time at the golf course than at the office, might be able to connect with his balls.

"So you really think you're famous?" Soss gripped the two iron and held it upright.

"I've got a few fans and lots of friends," Jack said.

"How many you think will come to your funeral?"

Jack smiled, leaned back on the sofa, and spread his arms along the top pads. "They'd probably have to book Tom Landry Stadium?"

Soss returned the smile and leaned forward. "Nah, just the visitors' locker room."

Jack thought, "For you, they'd only need a ticket booth."

Soss stuffed the two-iron back in his bag and pulled a pile of letters-to-the-editor turned letters-to-the-columnist from his desk drawer and dropped it on his varnished desk atop Verona's weekly NFL injury report. "Here are your 'fans', Byrne."

Soss read several salutations. "Dear Pinhead. Dear Porcupine-face. Dear Tiny Snake's Penis. Dear Worst Sports Columnist To Ever Write for a Daily Newspaper."

Then he pulled out a piece of paper from his notepad with scribbled words and read, "You're not only an unskilled writer – or whatever they call you down there– but a bore. I'd rather read 'War and Peace' backwards than suffer through your dribble. The only saving grace is that your columns help cure my insomnia, and I can use them to line the cat's litter box. Signed, unsatisfied and former Dallas Star subscriber."

Soss snickered when reading the P.S. "Please pick up a loaf of bread and some milk on the way home."

Jack did not laugh along. He dropped his arms from atop the sofa and joined his hands. "I knew it was a joke before you read the P.S."

"You don't have a cat?"

"That and the fact my wife never reads my stories – unless they offer a tip from a pro on how to fade a three iron or blast a buried lie out of a fairway bunker."

"Does she like stories about third-string quarterbacks?"

"Huh?"

Soss picked up a fresh Cowboys' press release and handed it to Jack, who read the headline. "Cowboys sign emergency quarterback."

Fanning's knockout and unknown return made it necessary for the Cowboys to find another quarterback. The NFL requires a team to have an emergency quarterback but does not count him on their 45-man game-day roster.

Jack stared at the release. "Who the hell is Scott Hilfinger?"

"That's for you to find out."

Jack stood, crumpled the press release in a ball, and swished it into the small waste bin in the office corner. Soss, still fuming over Jack's self-obit, couldn't have found better punishment – making him write a story about the unknown stiff replacing the injured star quarterback trashed by the Star columnist.

"That's not a story, that's a note," Jack said. "Some hack wannabe getting his dream shot and then standing on the sidelines next to the offensive coordinator with a clipboard in his frozen palms and a towel over his shoulder pads, making himself look important while the head coach can't even remember who the fuck he is. Unless he's a faggot, he'd have a better chance running across the Dead Sea, er Red Sea – whatever you call it – than sticking his hands under a center's ass."

Soss stood from behind his desk, leaned over it, and brought back the pit bull pose. "I'll give you a choice, Byrne. You write the story or I'll pull you from your column permanently and stick you on the Demolition Derby beat."

The sound proof office kept the staff from hearing Jack's reply. All they saw were the two men pointing at each other and their lips flapping.

"This paper wouldn't survive without my column."

"The letters from the readers prove otherwise, Porcupine-face."

"Those just prove I have readers. Tons of 'em."

"Let's see if they read about the third string quarterback."

Jack looked down at the plush berber carpet under his worn blue Nike sneakers partly hidden by the shredded bottoms of his gray

Levi's. He realized his contract wouldn't make it economical for Soss to fire him and quitting wouldn't help his chances of his dream job – Sports Illustrated senior writer. SI editors rarely hire 42-year-old sportswriters from the Weekly Shopper. He said, "All right," stepped away from the sofa, and reached for the office door.

Soss read out loud with his usual condescension the words on the laminated sign glued-tacked to the door just before Jack opened it:

"Don't let the gold door handle get you in the ass on the way out."

2

No one noticed the lanky 6-foot-4 Deadhorse, Oklahoma native as he marched through the long hallways and the lumbering traffic of bulging biceps and Tungsten steel hamstrings at the Cowboys Training Center.

Scott Hilfinger, with a notepad and two Bic pins in his left hand and the Cowboys' playbook in his callous-covered right, looked like a student en route to his first day of college classes. He was the only player to sit in the front row of the Cowboys' monstrous meeting room after the door was slammed shut Monday at 1:55 p.m. Players sat as far back in the auditorium as possible to buffer them from what was about to come from the mouth of their head coach.

Ray Myles walked in wearing a gray Dallas Cowboys' T-shirt, blue coaching shorts, and a whistle. He began softly. "I hope everyone had a good Thanksgiving holiday with your family and friends. Played some golf. Had a few beverages at your favorite nightspot. Did some early Christmas shopping."

Myles panned the room of players, none cracking a smidgeon of a smile. His softness suddenly became a shriek. "You didn't deserve one mother fucking minute of it!"

Hilfinger sat back in his chair like he was watching a horror flick, which was what Myles compared the game film of the team's Thanksgiving Day massacre. "Missed tackles! Dropped balls! Stupid penalties! Missed blocks – including one that cost us our mother fucking star quarterback!"

Myles pointed at offensive tackle Shante Williams as he made his last lament, then put his hands on his hips. "You think you are a Super Bowl team? Give me a mother fucking break. You'd have better odds making it in there as a marching band."

The odds of Hilfinger making it on the Cowboys were much worse. He was the second string quarterback on the Manitoba Mooses of the Canadian Football Developmental League. When Mooses' starting quarterback Ian Dubois pulled himself out of the lineup because of frostbite late in the fourth quarter of the CFDL's scoreless championship game against the Saskatchewan Sled Dogs in Edmonton, Alberta, Hilfinger trudged through the ankle-high-snow atop the Eskimo Bowl turf ready to lead his team to its first title.

The snow swirled so frantically he couldn't see the goalpost from midfield. He warmed his hands under the center's butt and hollered the snap count over the blustery wind. Right as the ball was snapped, the referee blew the whistle. Game called because of blizzard.

Hilfinger bought a one-way bus ticket and a quart of whisky in Edmonton and spent the next four weeks thawing and drying out in his 92-year-old grandma's house in Deadhorse. He worked as a bartender at the Dead Horse Saloon and stayed in shape throwing a football through an old tire he roped onto a backyard tree and running along the country roads with what town folk called Scotty's far-fetched dream of playing in the Super Bowl. The town motto was: "Deadhorse: Want to know how we got our name? Come visit."

After Thanksgiving dinner and watching Fanning leaving Tom Landry Stadium via ambulance on Grandma's black and white portable television, Hilfinger re-packed his duffel bag and thumbed a ride to Oklahoma City. He slept in a chair in the Greyhound bus station and boarded the 6 a.m. express to Dallas.

Hilfinger snuck past the front desk receptionist at the Cowboys Training Center and into the office of Royce Heyward, general manager and son of Cowboys' owner Sterling Heyward. Royce, recovering from the three turkey drumsticks he ate and the seven Wild Turkeys he drank before releasing his latest Dallas Cowboys Cheerleader conquest from his bedpost, held an ice pack on his forehead and sipped a glass of Alka-Seltzer.

Royce barely could see Hilfinger from his hangover haze. "Who the hell are you, and what the hell do you want?"

"Ah, ah, ah...I-I-I'm Scott, ah, Hilfinger, a quarterback from the Canadian League and I used to play for OU, where you and your, ah, dad went to school. I see you need another quarterback and just, ah, I just wanted to know what would it take to make the team.

Royce put down his ice pack and grabbed Hilfinger's left wrist, feeling for a pulse. He nodded, "You're in."

Hilfinger signed a contract for $5,000 that afternoon to play out the rest of the season. In the unlikely event that the 6-5 Cowboys would make the playoffs, he would make another $5,000, but only if he got in for one play during the regular season. He would make $40,000 in the more unlikely event the Cowboys won the Super Bowl, but only if he played a down in the post-season.

ON MONDAY, Hilfinger was just happy to be dressed in a Cowboys' practice uniform with the assigned number "13" on his chest and throwing footballs to the wide receivers on the practice squad. Sterling had asked his son why in God's tarnation he signed this guy. Royce explained he was hung-over. "Besides, daddy, our guy on the practice squad just got picked up by the Raiders and everyone else around the circuit is either injured or in jail. No one gives a rat's behind 'bout the emergency quarterback, much less write about him."

Jack shared Royce's sentiment until he saw Hilfinger's first practice throw, a magnificently-lofted 60-yard spiral down the sidelines into the stretched arms of the receiver. It was the most perfect pass Jack had ever seen a Cowboys' receiver drop.

Soss, the Sawed off Stack of Shit sports editor, had thought the assignment was Jack's perfect punishment. Not only would Jack be subjected to a boring story but to the abuse of the Cowboys' players after what he wrote about their star quarterback. Soss, who had never been to a Cowboys' practice or interviewed anyone, did not know that most players don't read his column and many can't even read. None really cared about their star quarterback.

They called Jack DH – dickhead, for short – as he walked through the volley of linemen smacking into blocking sleds and running backs tap-dancing through old tires on the warm Monday

Ghosts of the Gridiron

afternoon. They called every reporter DH and didn't know one DH from another DH.

Watching Hilfinger, the sun glistening off the star on his Cowboys' helmet, drill bullets to receivers on every pass pattern in his playbook was delightful punishment. When Myles blew a long whistle, denoting the end of a long, painful practice, Jack walked with Hilfinger off the field toward the locker room.

"Pretty good shootin' out there, hoss." Jack clutched his notepad in his left palm and looked eye-to-eye at Hilfinger, who took off his helmet and dangled it alongside his padded pants.

"Thank you, sir."

Jack thought, "Sir? Not DH?"

Jack introduced himself, and Hilfinger offered to sit with him in the bleachers. He told Jack about the Eskimo Bowl and about his lifelong dream of playing in the Super Bowl. As he talked about his throwing for 4300 yards and 46 touchdowns in leading Deadhorse to the Oklahoma State Six-Man title his senior year in high school and walking on at OU, Jack stopped him. He knew Hilfinger had to go in for a team meeting, that he would be fined if he was late, and that his potentially remarkable story could not be told in the time it would take him to shower and shit.

Jack would have been willing to scrub and wipe him, if that was what he took for an interview. This is the kind of story that could elevate Jack to reach his dream. Sports Illustrated was the Super Bowl of sports journalism. The young man's politeness gave Jack the courage to make an offer of a bucket of chicken while watching Monday Night Football on his 50-inch plasma television.

"Oh, yes sir," Hilfinger said. "I would be much obliged."

He sure would, seeing that his signing check hadn't cleared and that he barely had enough money for a room at the Downtown YMCA and a pepperoni pizza. Jack said good-bye and caught Coach Myles just before he walked off the practice field.

"Hey there, DH," Myles said.

"So what do you think about Scott Hilfinger?"

"Who the hell is Scott Hilfinger?"

13

"Your new emergency quarterback. He's got quite an arm."

"Who gives a fuck. He'll only play if there's an emergency, like if everyone on the team but Hilfigger – Hilfucker, whatever-the-fuck-his-name – got dysentery and are pootin' all over the turf. I'd play the punter before I'd play him."

MYLES SLAMMED the locker room door and the next slam Jack heard was the passenger door of his red Mazda Miata. Jack removed the Dippity Donut box from the seat, threw it and Hilfinger's green Manitoba Mooses gym bag into the back, and put the convertible top down to give the quarterback and himself head room.

Over the next five hours – on the drive to his house via Chucky's Fried Chicken and the unbeaten Kansas City Chiefs' 60-3 romp over the Cleveland Browns on Monday Night Football – Hilfinger filled Jack's head with the most remarkable anecdotes and circumstances ever flung from an emergency or non-emergency quarterback.

Hilfinger was even polite enough to take interest in Jack's backyard sports cage, illuminated by a rusty, aluminium floodlight. "I throw footballs through the old tire and dream of winning the Super Bowl just like you do," Jack said. (After what Myles told him and not repeated to Hilfinger, Jack figured he would have just as good a chance.) "When my wife is home, she yanks the tire down and smacks a zillion golf balls into the net until the sun comes up the next morning."

"Where is your wife, Mr. Byrne?"

"Somewhere in North Carolina hittin' golf balls, but this time without a net. Quite scary."

Jack drove Hilfinger downtown to the Y, a 20-minute bus ride to the practice field, and looked over at his subject smiling as the cool breeze smacked into his face. Hilfinger thanked Jack for the interview – another first for a professional football player – before leaping over the passenger-side door with his green gym bag flung over his shoulder and sauntering into the distance.

Jack stared until the quarterback was out of sight and said quietly to himself, "So that's who the hell Scott Hilfinger is."

3

An empty Mountain Dew bottle, crumbs from a jumbo carton of Oreos, and a few NoDoz tablets lay amongst a yellow pad of scribbled notes and next to Jack's laptop – and Jack's face.

Jack's left hand rested on his keyboard with his index finger touching the last letter he pressed on the greatest story he had ever written. Sweat dripped from his forehead as the birds rose with the sun and the exhaustion from a hard night of writing knocked him out. He didn't even have the strength to turn off his desk lamp. The light shone on the final words of his masterpiece.

"Scott Hilfinger may never make the Hall of Fame. He may never take another snap. But he did the one thing many men fail to achieve.

"He made his father proud"

Jack passed out before pressing the period key.

At midnight Jack had pressed the first key and written his first sentence of the story, "Scott Hilfinger's unrealistic dream of playing in the Super Bowl began in Deadhorse, Oklahoma and will end there barring a miracle the magnitude of the parting of the Red Sea."

But the story was written in Jack's head by the time his red Mazda convertible slid into his driveway.

Over a bucket of Chucky's Chicken and two-loud mouthed announcers blaring above the noisy crowd from the big screen television, Hilfinger satisfied his appetite and spilled his guts. Jack scribbled every word on his notebook and looked up only when his subject stopped to pick up another thigh or drumstick or watch Marvin Mallard, the Chiefs' red-clad 357-pound sack machine, slam another quarterback into the icy tundra of Jim Brown Stadium.

"Uhhh," Hilfinger said, wiping the grease off his chin. "Too bad I'm not on the Browns."

"You'd get to play," Jack said. "But with a wimpy offensive line like that, for how long?"

Playing football was all Hilfinger ever wanted to do. His mother, Ruth, died of lung cancer when he was four. His father, Lou, raised Scott and his older sister, Martha, while working as a spot welder by day and a bartender by night at the Dead Horse Saloon. Somehow, he had enough energy left in his middle-aged legs to plod pass patterns for his miniature quarterback son with an arm that could knock over a mailbox with a football from 30 yards.

Hilfinger only grew big enough to see over the defensive line his junior year in high school. His senior year he was towering over them. He threw for 593 yards and six touchdowns in the championship game of Oklahoma Six-man Football. Lou never missed a game but retired in the third quarter of the title match when he realized the stinging pain in his chest was not from the mustard-lathered corny dog he gulped at halftime. Not wanting to disrupt his son's concentration, Lou snuck out the stadium exit and asked the paramedic assigned to the game to take him to the hospital with the ambulance lights and siren off.

The Deadhorse High coach informed his triumphant star quarterback of his father's heart attack while spraying Gatorade on his teammates in the locker room and rushed him to his father's side.

Hilfinger dropped a chicken bone on Jack's coffee table and wiped his eyes. "It was the best day and the worst day of my life," he said.

"What were his last words?" Jack said, simultaneously staring and writing.

Hilfinger looked away for a second and looked back at Jack. "He said, 'Follow your dream, son, and I'll always be with you.'"

Hilfinger wiped a tear from his eye. "He was the greatest man I ever met. You probably had the same with your own father, Mr. Byrne?"

Jack didn't look up from his notepad. "I'll ask the questions."

The final words from the elder Hilfinger never left his son. He eschewed a scholarship at Oklahoma Baptist and tried out at

Oklahoma. Head coach Shank Healy mistook him for the water boy, and that was Hilfinger's position his freshman year.

"The world's tallest water boy," as he called himself, was the last one to lock up and locked himself in every night and slept on a cot he kept hidden in a storage closet. He only had enough money earned from washing dishes at the Dead Horse Saloon for tuition. He ate scraps from the athletic dining hall and cold pizza the players failed to devour after home games.

He was the Rudy of the Oklahoma Sooners but a Rudy with a powerful arm used to fling water bottles to players from the sidelines. He tried out at quarterback every spring and finally made seventh string when two of the Sooners' blue chip quarterbacks were busted for armed robbery. His role on the practice squad was a live dummy for unblocked tackles and blitzing linebackers.

Hilfinger kept moving up the ladder with every torn ACL and busted probation from the QBs ahead of him. In the fourth quarter of the spring game before his senior year Coach Shank, not risking another injury to his starting quarterback, hollered, "Hey, Waterboy, go in thar and take a few snaps."

His first snap was followed by a perfect spiral to his split end over the middle for a 42-yard gainer, his second a bullet to his flanker for a 26-yarder, and his third for a beautifully lofted 21-yard touchdown toss to his tight end.

Hilfinger made third string and the travel squad the next fall for a Sooners' team that went 11-0 and with their number one and two quarterbacks handcuffed to Coach Shank until they took the field. No longer a sack dummy, Hilfinger honed his craft by playing the opposing quarterback versus the Sooners' starting secondary and watched with a smile as Coach Shank berated them with every completion.

Hilfinger moved to number two quarterback when starter Kareem Hartung stepped in a sprinkler hole and sprained his ankle two days before the Rose Bowl, which doubled as the NCAA Championship game.

"I didn't care that there were 100,000 people in the stands and television cameras were sending the game to millions across the world," Hilfinger said, clutching a chicken wing in his right hand. "I wanted one chance, just one chance, I would make the most of it. Make a name for myself and the NFL draft."

As the lights were turned on in the Rose Bowl, the lights were turned off on Sooners' back up quarterback Flynn Ramson after a vicious sack by Michigan's Leonard Robinson midway into the third quarter of a 20-20 game. Hilfinger, his helmet glued on his head since the opening kickoff, buttoned his chinstrap. He tossed a few balls on the sidelines while Ramson was being carted off the field. Hilfinger marched to the right shoulder of Coach Shank, who was looking over his left shoulder.

"Saunders, git in there and win us a title," he said, slapping the third-string quarterback on the butt and propelling him toward the huddle. Hilfinger took off his helmet.

At Jack's house, he tossed the half-mauled chicken wing back into the bucket. Saunders, a true freshman, threw three interceptions without being benched. The Sooners lost 37-20. Hilfinger marched – pads, red OU jersey, white cleats, black eye-paint and all – to the nearest liquor store, returned with a half-case of Corona, and awoke the next morning to leaf blowers gathering hotdog wrappers from the bleachers.

"A Mexican tapped me on the head with his leaf blower and said, 'Take Cervesa and vamoose, amigo.'"

Jack laughed. Hilfinger didn't.

HILFINGER TOOK A BATHROOM BREAK at halftime while Jack rustled up some Coronas of his own. Hilfinger passed on the beers. Instead he sipped a Coke, munched potato chips, and continued his story with him dropping out of college and asking his high school sweetheart back in Deadhorse to marry him with the promise of working at her father's hardware store.

A week before the wedding a letter with the strangest looking stamps and return address marked Dusseldorf, Germany arrived at the house now occupied by Hilfinger and his grandmother. The envelope was red with little footballs resting atop a fire. Hilfinger opened it and rushed to his fiancee's house like he was on fire.

"Look, sweetie, I've been asked to come to Germany to try out for the Rhein Fire, the only NFL Europe team or any other team around the world that looked at the film of the OU spring game I sent them. I have to leave right after the wedding, so we could go there for our honeymoon."

Ginger Huckabee never had been out of Oklahoma and never desired to leave Oklahoma. She said, "If you go to Germany, then it is auf Wiedersehen for you and me."

Hilfinger cashed in the wedding rings and bought a one-way ticket for one to Dusseldorf. He didn't make the Rhein Fire. Not throwing a football for four months of drinking in his off-hours of tending bar at the Dead Horse Saloon didn't help. He was placed on their developmental team, the Wurzberg Warriors.

It launched a seven-year sojourn that included stops on six European developmental teams, a fledgling Australian league, and summer semi-pro league stints throughout North America. Hilfinger's passing improved, but it was not reflected in the statistics. In Wurzberg his receivers were mostly converted soccer players, who weren't accustomed to using their hands.

The games took on a carnival flavor. Spectators cooked sausages along the sidelines and some carried kegs into the stands and offered beer to the players.

"I got so drunk during one game I didn't even remember throwing three touchdown passes and running for the winning score," Hilfinger said. "I didn't believe it until I saw the game film."

Jack pondered the improbability of this and then recalled the unrecalled brilliant columns he had written in a drunken stupor and the mornings he awoke with a hangover and no memory of driving home from after-deadline happy hours.

Hilfinger drank to forget his ongoing semi-professional career that was going nowhere. He was kicked off the Wurzberg Warriors for sleeping with the head coach's 17-year-old daughter. He broke his collarbone after being thrown from a bull during halftime of a Spanish Football League game between his Salamanca Salmons and the Madrid Matadors. The Salmons field was set in a bull ring, and halftime bull-riding exhibitions were written into his contract.

The field in the Australian Football League was on a cricket ground, and the middle of the field was roped off so players wouldn't tramp on the cricket pitch. The goalposts had extra tall rugby uprights, players kept lateraling the ball, and announcers called a touchdown a try. After a score, the referees shot their arms forward and pointed their index fingers like in Australian Rules Football instead of raising them overhead.

As the Monday night game started the fourth quarter, Jack gave Hilfinger another Coke and took his interview into the final stanza. "So did you make any money?"

Hilfinger took a sip and laughed. "Only enough to live on, but it sure beat working in a hardware store in Deadhorse. And it kept my dream alive."

Hilfinger shared apartments with ants and cock roaches above pubs, funeral homes, and massage parlors. He ran out of money while playing for the Dramen Dark Knights in Norway, so he hooked up with a Knightette only because she offered for him to move in. The Knightette lived in a strict all-women's hostel at the local university.

Hilfinger would put on a skirt, a wig, and makeup before leaving and entering the hostel every day. Knights' teammates discovered a skirt and blouse in his gym bag and told a local reporter, who followed him back to the hostel and wrote that he was the Scandinavian Football League's first openly gay player. His teammates started calling him "Hilfy."

"I didn't mind," Hilfinger said. "I got my own room on away games."

"That story could come back to haunt you," Jack said.

"Or the one about when I was accused of being a terrorist."

Jack pressed the mute button on his T.V. remote. "A terrorist?"

In August of 2004 Hilfinger was flying from Amsterdam to Athens to play for the Athens Antelopes of the Greek Football League. The plane stopped in Thessaloniki. Hilfinger, thinking the flight was non-stop, thought he was in Athens and got off the plane. When he didn't re-board, Uzi-toting security guards handcuffed him and brought him into a little holding room. With the Olympics on, security in Greece had been tightened and everyone was a suspect.

When Hilfinger showed him his letter from the Antelopes, a security guard called the head coach of the Thessaloniki Kings football team for verification. "I need a quarterback," Kings' coach Dimitri Poulas told Hilfinger at the airport. "If you agree to play for the Kings, I'll get you out of here."

Hilfinger played like a Greek god that fall, throwing for 4,130 yards and rushing for another 607 in the Kings' 12 games. His top receiver was Canadian sprinter Franny LeBlanc, whom Poulas persuaded to stay on after the Olympics. He came in handy in the Greek Bowl, played against the Antelopes on the narrow field in the old Olympic Stadium. Hilfinger just threw him bombs all game, and the Kings won 42-10.

Poulas thanked Hilfinger by getting him a tryout with NFL Europe's Scottish Claymores, who named him their starting quarterback for the spring of 2005 one day and the next day announced the team was folding. The following day Hilfinger and his bottle of whisky boarded a plane to Oklahoma. He swore he never would return to Europe.

Hilfinger played semi-pro football for the Tulsa Tornado and felt like he got hit by one every game. He took his bruised ribs to Canada, where LeBlanc got him on the Manitoba Mooses. He froze on the bench that early fall and contemplated an end to his football career and to his life. "Maybe I'll hang myself from the goalpost," he had thought.

He again got drunk instead and returned to Deadhorse, broke and disillusioned. He went to Dallas with nothing to lose that Thanksgiving night. Game films, faxed resumes, and telephone calls to NFL teams had all gone unreturned over the past seven years. Arena Football didn't even want him. The worst that could happen was a security guard could fling him out of the Cowboys Training Center like so many former Greco Roman wrestlers-turned-linebackers did on the makeshift football fields throughout Europe.

All along, Hilfinger kept hearing his father calling him: "Follow your dream, son."

AFTER THE CLOCK STRUCK 0:00 on another Monday Night Football clash, Jack drove Hilfinger back to the Y. As he cruised between the Dallas skyscrapers and into the Y's parking lot, Jack wished his subject good luck.

"This is my final shot, Mr. Byrne." Hilfinger shook his head. "If I don't make it–"

"If you don't make it, you don't exactly die," Jack said.

"I'm already dead." Hilfinger grabbed his green bag from the back of the convertible and stared into Jack's eyes. "The GM never really found a pulse and perhaps thinks a corpse for a third-string quarterback is sufficient. I just want one chance. One chance, and I can live again."

Hilfinger looked down for a second and back. "Football is all I've known, Mr. Byrne. All I want to know. Without it, I'm truly dead."

Jack patted the Cowboys' third stringer on the back. "Then get after 'em, Hilfy," bringing about a wry chuckle.

The next morning the telephone rang and moved Jack's face from his desk. It took four rings for him to realize he was awake. Then he picked up the phone.

"Get your ass to the office right now."

Jack hung up, wiped his sleepy eyes, and looked at his computer. He smiled but still didn't type the final period onto his story.

4

Jack didn't walk from the parking garage to The Dallas Star Building that warm Tuesday afternoon. He marched.

Past a random security guard who barely checked his badge. Past the waving wannabe writer and reference librarian Penny Pettigrew at the Morgue, where all the old newspapers are stored on microfilm. Up three flights of stairs. Down the hallway and between walls decorated by award-winning Star photographs and stories (none his). Into the sports department and to his desk. All with a computer disk tucked safely into his leather satchel that hung from his left shoulder.

Jack didn't care that he hadn't taken a shower in two days, that he was in the same clothes he had passed out in at his computer, that he stunk of old beer and chips, that his goatee was flaked with milk and Wheaties, that his hair could pass for a bird's nest. He had a story on a disk that was going to change his life.

As he slid the disk into his computer, he was interrupted by copy editor – a butcherette, in Jack's terms – Yolanda Lopez.

"Hey there, Yo-Lo," Jack didn't look up.

"I see your wife had a magnificent round yesterday in North Carolina." Yo-Lo smiled, showing her braces that made her look like a teenager.

Jack sat in his chair and tapped the keys of his computer. "Oh yeah? What'd she shoot?"

"You didn't read the paper this morning? Sixty-nine."

Jack stopped for a second and thought, smiling, "That's the first time she's had 69 in a while."

"Another two more rounds like that and she will make the Women's Tour," Yo-Lo said.

"Another two more rounds like that," Jack thought, "and I'll be eating Chucky's Chicken all next spring."

Yo-Lo's wife report was interrupted by a tapping on the glass walls of an office across the room. Dick Schwartz, that Sawed Off Stack of Shit sports editor, motioned Jack to his office. Jack tapped a couple of keys on his computer and marched to Soss' office. Soss held the door for NFL writer Jay Verona after another lengthy Tuesday afternoon meeting but didn't hold it for Jack.

"You stink," Soss said.

Jack sat on the office sofa and patted at the leather. "Sorry, I was up late working on my story."

"No, I mean you really stink."

Soss sat, then swiveled back in his leather office chair. "I order you to write a simple story on a third string quarterback. I look in the paper this morning and I don't see a story on a third string quarterback."

Soss gave Jack the pit bull stare. Jack smiled.

"Relax, Dick. I wrote the story last night. It was much too good for a six-incher or even a column. Have a look at it. You might want to run it on the front page Sunday before the Cowboys-Texans game."

Soss typed with his usual clumsy two-finger style on his keyboard and found the story Jack had just downloaded from his computer disk and sent to him. Soss didn't even read the lead. He scrolled the length of Jack's masterpiece in a few seconds and pressed one key – the delete key.

"That's what I think of your story."

"You killed my story?"

"Gone."

"You don't even want to read it?"

"Not me or anyone. You said it yourself, no one wants to read about the third string quarterback."

"That all changed once I heard his story."

"I don't give a shit how interesting you think he is. All I know is there is an empty space in my morning paper and a sports columnist in my office about to be a former sports columnist."

Jack's heart pounded to a tune of Taps for his fallen masterpiece. Dirty sweat dribbled from his forehead and down his face that tilted toward the plush carpet. "Soss can't fire me," he thought. "I've got a contact, and who would replace me – Penny Pettigrew?"

"One last chance, Byrne. I'm sending you to Houston tomorrow to cover the cowboys."

"The Cowboys don't play until Sunday."

"Not those cowboys. You're covering the Texas State Rodeo."

Jack's mouthed the word "RO-DE-O" and locked his lips on "O."

Soss continued. "You'll leave after work tomorrow night in a staff car with Yo-Lo and Lanny, the photographer."

"You're sending a copy editor on a trip?"

"I promoted Yo-Lo to assistant sports editor."

The "O" got bigger. It seemed to Jack like it was only the other week Yo-Lo was an intern serving him Alka-Seltzer to cure his hangover and only the other day butchering one of his columns. "Minority hire," he thought.

"She'll co-ordinate coverage of the rodeo and the Cowboy game on the weekend. If you don't fuck up the rodeo, you can write your game column."

Soss stood from his chair, planted his left hand on his desk, and pointed at Jack's head with his right forefinger. "But not one fucking word about the third string quarterback."

It was a deal Jack was in no position to refuse. Nor could he refute having to drive to Houston in the middle of the night with a rookie sports editor and a tobacco-chewing photographer in a white Ford Escort with silver Dallas Star logos on the driver and passenger doors. He had grown accustomed to flying on the Cowboys' charter plane, sharing martinis and pussy stories with owner Heyward and his staff of sons, and staying at the Four Seasons.

Now he would be staying at a Motel 60 in a bed with magic fingers overlooked by a miniature television attached to the wall. He would sit in an arena with an aroma of manure on a dirty bench next to a geriatric chewing tobacco and waving his cowboy hat with all the other hicks hollering, "Yeow," every time a goat roper stayed on an angry horse or bull for more than three seconds.

The greatest story Jack had ever written was stored on a disk he hid in the bottom drawer of his desk.

"It will never see the light of day," Soss said, as the executive sports editor's gold doorknob got him in the butt again on his way out of his office.

Yo-Lo met Jack at his desk with an itinerary of the next five days. She said she wanted to go over it with him and Lanny. Jack asked her to give him a couple of hours so he could stare into his computer screen and ponder what had become of his sportswriting career, why he was hated so much by the readers and ignored so much by the players and coaches, and what the newspaper would do without him.

Jack didn't walk from The Dallas Star Building to the parking garage as darkness set in and warm air gave way to a winter front blowing the Wheaties out of his goatee. He plodded.

A high-pitched call from behind stopped him as he put the key into the door of his Mazda convertible. Yo-Lo ran toward him with a piece of paper.

"Jack, about the itinerary."

Jack threw his leather satchel into the passenger seat, plunged butt-first into the car, and put his key into the ignition. "Just pick me up this time tomorrow."

"From where?"

Jack twisted the key and revved up the engine. "The Kazbar, of course."

5

Jeanine Pratt would have missed her eighth wedding anniversary had she sunk a four-foot putt on the final hole of the fifth round of the LPGA Q-school tournament. The ball slid to the left side of the hole and twirled around it before coming to a halt a half inch from the cup.

"Ya got Jesse Jamed," said Jeanine's older than them thar hills caddy, supplied by the local golf club.

"What does that mean?" Jeanine said, still staring at the ball in disbelief.

"Robbed."

Moments after learning she had missed the cut into the final round by one stroke, Jeanine slammed her clubs into the back seat of a courtesy car and ordered the driver to the airport. "Fucking four foot putt," she said, as the car hit the highway.

"Wud-ja say, miss?"

"Nothin'. Just drive."

Had the 34-year-old Jeanine made the putt, she would have been one of 24 players – most a dozen years younger than her – battling the next day for the 18 new spots available on the LPGA Tour. It was the fifth time she had qualified for Q-school and the first time she had made it this far in the six-round tournament.

The first round had started the day after Thanksgiving at Meandering Creeks Golf Club just north of Raleigh, North Carolina. The field of 84 international qualifiers from the four regional tournaments was whittled to 54 after the second round on Saturday and to 36 after Monday's fourth round. Jeanine's 69 put her into 25th place, and she figured an even par 72 would comfortably put her into the final round and give her a solid chance to achieve a dream that began when her father gave her golf clubs for her seventh birthday.

She awoke the next morning and went to her knees, praying to her father to "give me the strength, the courage, and a little luck to pull me through this round." It was the same prayer she said the morning of every tournament round since her father died of a brain tumor the day after she won the Texas Amateur Women's tournament the summer before her senior year at Caprock State University. She hadn't won a tournament since.

Jeanine ate half a banana and a bagel, all she could put down on that fateful Tuesday. She took her ritual pre-match shower and dressed into her white panties with little pink golfers, white ankle socks, white knee-length shorts, red golf shirt, and white sweater vest. She tied her auburn shoulder-length hair with a pink rubber band to make it fit through the back of her final accessory, the lucky white golf hat with her red alma mater mascot Tumbleweed on the front.

Jeanine checked her golf bag one last time to make sure her clubs, so sparkling she could use them for mirrors, were in ascending order from the two-iron to the pitching wedge in two sections. Her woods were nestled in the next section with the black woollen golf covers her late grandmother had knitted for her. The thin blade putter had its own section; Jeanine made sure the most important tool in her bag had plenty of breathing space. Not a spot of mud or a blade of grass were caked onto her clubs or the cleats of her lily-white golf shoes. Before tucking the red and white bag back over her right shoulder, Jeanine stared into the mirror and put her firm hands on either side of her faded tanned face, stretching them forward with every word.

"Focus and control," she said. "Focus and control. You are strong. You are powerful. You are, my dear, a winner."

The words taught to her by The Legend, her coach and mentor at Dallas' Forest Green Country Club, sent her out of her motel room to 18 golf holes, each flanked by thick forest and rock-filled creeks that ran along and sometimes through the narrow, soft-green fairways. Jeanine stepped up to her ball on the first tee, breathed in the aroma of the pine trees, told herself once more, "Focus and control," and then whacked a 265-yard drive into the middle of the forest. Sung-Ho Ko, her playing partner, helped her find her ball. It was so deep into the thick pine, she had to play a provisional and settle for a triple bogey.

Jeanine battled all day with her mind and kept telling herself, "Don't look back, only ahead. Focus and control." As she marched to the final hole, she looked back and ahead. She could not resist asking her caddy where she stood.

"Accordin' to da leaderboard, I'd say you needin' a bird," said the wrinkled, crooked-toothed man in the white overalls. "Take dis big ol' stick and knock the shit out of it."

There was no focus and control on the tee box of the 504-yard par five eighteenth hole – just pure adrenaline. She took a John Daly-like swing and put every ounce of her 128 pounds into her drive. The Titleist 1 ripped through the fairway and came to rest 12 metres in front of a fairway bunker.

The caddy took the driver from a grinning Jeanine and marched alongside her and down the fairway. "Never seen a skinnier lady hit a ball dat far before."

Jeanine looked up at the green, 218 yards in front of her, and the wide creek 30 yards in front of it. She picked up a few blades of grass and tossed it in the air and found a slight headwind.

"Lay up," the caddy said.

Jeanine stared at the flagstick barely wavering in the distance and a few spectators standing behind the green. "Give me the five-wood," she said without looking at him.

"You sure?"

"Give me the five-wood."

"Wow-K. You da boss."

Jeanine waited for Sung-Ho Ko to lay up, comfortably in front of the creek. Then she touched the bill of her cap, stepped up to the ball, waggled into her stance, and swung. The ball came cleanly off the five-wood and launched like a guided missile toward the green. Jeanine's eyes never left the ball. Her caddy was looking at the creek.

"Go ball," he said. "Go on and git."

The ball cleared the creek by five yards, bounced forward and found the front of the green. She was a 35-foot two putt from the final round of Q-school.

She stuffed the five-wood into her bag and looked at the caddy as if to say, "Lay up, huh? If I was payin' ya', I'd fire ya," just as he handed her the putter.

As Jeanine knelt and looked at the 35 feet of finely-mowed grass between her ball mark and the hole, her caddy said, "Further than it looks."

"Pull the flagstick," Jeanine said, and thought, "Then go play a duelin' banjo."

Jeanine slipped her putter blade behind the Titleist and swept it toward the hole. "Bite," she said and the ball obeyed, coming up four feet short. She marked her ball, watched Sung-Ho Ko sink her eight-foot birdie putt, replaced the mark with her ball, and focused on the slightly uphill putt.

"Firm and straight and you're straight into the finals," she said as she gripped her putter.

Jeanine tapped it firm and she aimed it straight. She nor her wrinkled caddy read a slight break that sent the Titleist around the cup. A half-pace slower and the ball would have fallen into the side of the cup. Instead, she was left to stare out the courtesy car window and ponder every one of her 75 shots as the car sped toward the nearest airport via her motel room, where she quickly stuffed her suitcase. Ko's birdie putt put her a stroke ahead of Jeanine and in 23rd place. A birdie in the group behind matched Ko's score and left Jeanine where she started the day, 25th place.

"Why did I miss that putt?" she thought. "Maybe I didn't practice enough on the greens. Maybe I need a more weighted putter. Maybe I need a more supportive husband. Maybe in the back of my mind I wanted to miss that putt, so I wouldn't miss my anniversary."

As the final boarding call for the non-stop flight from Raleigh to Dallas echoed off the walls of the passenger-filled departure lounge,

Jeanine pressed her cellphone and sent a cross country call to a bar in Dallas.

"Hello," Jack answered.

"Hey, it's me. I have got good news and bad news."

Jack took a swig of beer. "What is it?"

"I missed the cut, and we can celebrate our anniversary tonight."

Jack smiled. "Which is the good news and which is the bad news?"

The next sound Jack heard was a dial tone.

6

The Kazburger and fries did little to soak up the two shots of Johnny Walker Red and four Coronas that Jack consumed following what started as a warm, self-gratifying day and slowly turning, like the weather, into a cold, dreary night. The best story he had ever written sat rejected in the bottom drawer of his desk and its author at the neighborhood bar.

Milt Johnson, the Kazbar co-owner and bartender, wasn't helping the mood. He could pour drinks and run up Jack's tab, but he had no barside manner.

"You look like you're on death's door," he said.

"Feel like it," Jack said, looking at the small bandage on Milt's neck. "I haven't slept in my own bed since Sunday and I haven't slept with my wife in more than a week. You see, I got this asshole editor—"

Milt turned his back, and Jack said, "You're not interested?"

"Not really."

Jack figured Cathie, a former Dallas Cowboys Cheerleader-turned-barmaid, also wasn't interested nor were the three butchers who came to the Kazbar from their copy-butchering day shift at The Dallas Star. There was space at their table for Jack, but no one asked him to join them.

What Jack really needed was medicine for his pain, which is why he again turned to Milt.

"Doctor Milt, how about another Corona?"

"No thanks."

Jack didn't think being cut-off was fair treatment for one of the Kazbar's first patients, who had helped keep the place in business and once wrote a column about it. Milt started the bar in the early 1990's to honor his Cowboys' teammate Bill Kazmeer. The former Penn State fullback spent two years on the bench until an injury to starter Reb Stucky in the divisional playoff game gave Kaz his big chance.

Kaz knocked over tackles, linebackers, and safeties en route to a 227-yard, three-touchdown performance that led the Cowboys to a 35-14 victory over the Detroit Lions. Despite pleas from the assistant coaches and players, Kaz didn't play a down in the 24-3 loss to San Francisco in the NFC title game and then disappeared.

"Someone said he went back to Pennsylvania to mine coal," Milt had said. "I don't believe them."

Jack always thought Kaz would appear at the bar, and he likely would be there to see him – and write another column. Jack didn't know if he had spent more money at the Kazbar or Dippity Donuts, where he often staggered at 2 a.m. after the bar closed. A half-dozen glazed and a cup of hot chocolate alongside a few other drunks and a couple of bored Dallas police officers sobered him up enough to drive home.

There were Dippity Donut shops all over town, and Jack no longer needed the Dippity Donut map to find one.

"I can smell them," he told Cathie, after she served a pitcher to the butchers. "A Dippity cinnamon twist is better than sex."

"When did you have it last?" she asked.

"This morning on the way to work."

"You had sex on the way to work?"

"Oh, I thought you were asking about the donuts."

The waitress giggled loud enough for the butchers to look over from their table, curious enough for them to stare but not loud enough to hear the conversation.

"When was the last time you had it?" Jack asked.

"This afternoon before work on the bar."

"You had a donut on the bar?"

"Oh, I thought you were talking about sex."

Cathie professed to being a Dippity Donut virgin, and as Jack contemplated asking her to change her status after her shift, his cellphone rang.

Jack put the phone to his ear but could barely hear over the patrons' chatter and televisions' play-by-play coverage. Jeanine's voice cracked. "I'm calling you from one of these crappy airplane phones."

"What?"

"I arrive at 8:55 on American. Be there on time for a change."

Jack checked his watch as Jeanine hung up on him again.

"Who was that?" Cathie asked.

"My wife."

"When did she have it last?"

"About nine or ten weeks ago, on her birthday, and I'm not talking about donuts."

JACK ASKED CATHIE to bring him another Corona and walked toward the restroom. He stopped momentarily at the butcher's table. "Hi fellas."

"Hi Jack," Butcher Ed said. "Good column on the Cowboys' Thanksgiving game."

Butcher Phil: "Yeah, you sure gave it to Fanning. When do you think he'll be able to play again?"

"Maybe the Super Bowl."

Butcher Alex: "You really think they got a shot at the Super Bowl?"

Jack laughed and said, "About as much chance of them playing the third string quarterback," before continuing his journey toward the restroom. En route he looked on the wall at some old action photographs of Kaz and other Cowboys' grunts of football past and entered the restroom stall and locked the door. As Jack reached for the toilet paper roll, Butchers Ed and Phil came in and stood in front of the urinals without realizing the jeans pulled down to the ankles in the stall belonged to Jack.

"Great to see the Almighty Jack Byrne stopping to say hello to the little people," said Ed, unzipping his trousers.

"Without a doubt," said Phil, also unzipping and looking over to Ed, "he's got to be the most arrogant, conceited, self-serving prick to ever write for The Dallas Star."

"Did you know he wrote his own obituary yesterday?" Ed said.

"You kidding?" Phil said.

"No, and get this, he called himself a 'promising pro quarterback in his youth.' He said he had a great arm, speed, agility, and courage."

The butchers laughed as they zipped up. Jack pressed his ear against the stall to hear over the flushing urinals.

"The guy's a coward." Phil said. "He runs away from everything. You see how fast he ran out of Dick's office this afternoon?"

"I wanted to chase 'him' down after his chicken shit column on Thanksgiving," Ed said. "He sent it, as he always does, a minute before deadline."

Jack thought, "That's so you butchers have no chance to edit it."

Phil walked to the sink and washed his hands. "Did you see him flirting with Cathie?"

"His wife's playing her heart out for a spot on the LPGA tour, and he's putting the moves on a bimbo half his age," said Ed, drying his hands on a paper towel.

The butchers tossed their paper towels in the trash pail, patted each other on the back, and opened the restroom door. "Let's go, Ed. I'll buy you a beer and we can toast to Jack Byrne, the worst sports columnist in Texas."

"And maybe the world," Phil added just before the door slammed.

Jack stood up from the toilet and pulled up his pants. "Pussies," Jack mumbled. "Without me no one would read the newspaper, and they wouldn't have a job."

Jack returned to the bar and sipped his Corona. Finally, he checked his watch again and downed the remains of his beer bottle. He gave Milt a 20-dollar bill, told him to keep the change, and then walked toward the front door.

"Thought you'd be waiting around for Cathie," Phil said as Jack passed by the butchers' table.

"Nah," Jack said buttoning his coat. "I'm going home to get laid."
"What makes you so sure?" Ed asked.
"It's my wedding anniversary."

7

Jeanine strolled down the airline ramp at the DFW International Airport like she was strolling down the last fairway en route to victory. Instead of a putter, she was carrying a box of her husband's favorite chocolate peanut clusters she had bought and had gift wrapped at Raleigh Airport.

As the light shone from the airport lounge, fellow passengers waved to their loved ones whom they greeted with a hug, a kiss, or a handshake. Jeanine smiled in anticipation of Jack standing there with a dozen roses tucked behind his back and a warm smile giving way to, "Welcome home, Jeanie" or "Happy Anniversary, my darling."

Like at the end of so many tournaments, there was no one waiting for the beloved Jeanie. Her fellow passengers walked hand-in-hand or arms-around-shoulders en route to the baggage claim. Jeanie stood, alone, like a lost little girl, turning in circles, staring down the corridors, peering at faces seated in the departure lounge. Maybe Jack had to go to the bathroom. Maybe he went to the wrong gate. Maybe he is stuck in line at the gift shop. Maybe he is waiting at the baggage claim.

As her golf bag slid down the baggage chute and circled around on the carousel and soon followed by her heavy suitcase, Jeanie realized that Jack is Jack – even on their eighth wedding anniversary.

While Jeanie was shoving quarters into the slot for the rent-a-cart, Jack was screaming down LBJ Freeway in his red Mazda Miata.

"Oh shit, I'm late," he said, weaving through traffic and showing his middle finger to every honked car he cut off while somehow chomping on a Dippity Donut and listening to the Cowboys' Tuesday night talk radio show.

He cut from lane one to lane six within 50 yards of the airport parking ticket booth to get one car ahead. He screamed, "Come on," as he waited three seconds for the automatic ticket to be dispensed. He fled the parking booth like a drag car racer and searched upward at the large lit screen to find the correct terminal and gate while trying to think up the perfect excuse for his tardiness.

"Got stuck in traffic. No, she won't see any traffic jams on the way home."

"Car trouble. Nah, I haven't paid my AAA fee. I'd still be on the highway."

"Held hostage by aliens. Nah, I'll think of somethin'."

Jack whipped his black-roofed convertible through the terminal entrance and parked in the passenger pick up lane. As he started for the airport door he looked into the distance at a woman shoving her golf bag and suitcase into a shuttle van and slamming the door. The shuttle van sped off. Jack, his breath showing in the cold wind, chased the van. He waved his arms and hollered, "Hey! Come back!"

The van pulled away.

Jack sprinted back to his car and called Jeanie on her cellphone. All he got was her answering message.

"Damn." Jack pounded his steering wheel. "She's either out of battery or she turned it off on purpose."

Jack started his car but was boxed in by two taxis. He opened his window. "Get the hell out of the way, fuckin' camel jockeys!"

One of the drivers who was helping an old lady with her suitcase heard him and started toward him with a clenched fist. Jack drove over the curb onto the walkway and scooted about 30 yards before squeezing between two parked taxi cabs and pulling back onto the road. This time he was being chased by a man with a towel around his head and hollering, "Come back here, you sheet!"

Jack's heart was beating what seemed like 1000 beats per minute. He wasn't sure if that was for the Middle Eastern man chasing him or the pissed off golfer/wife he was chasing. His heart beat faster when he realized the condition of his house. Piled up dishes that hadn't been washed since Jeanie left for North Carolina. Dirty underwear strewn over the unmade bed. Pizza boxes and dripping beer cans lying on the coffee table. Potato chips and cookie crumbs mashed into the sofa. Jack pressed the accelerator harder.

Like a stock car driver, Jack drove to within inches of bumpers and bobbed through thin clearings and flew past cars already creaming the speed limit. He could see the shuttle van through his windshield and the flashing lights of a police car in his rearview mirror.

Jack pounded his steering wheel again as the police siren blared louder no matter how hard he pressed the accelerator. "Five beers and two shots. I'm goin' to jail – and maybe divorce court."

Jack steered from the fourth to the first lane and to the nearest exit ramp. He ran a red light and was almost bulldozed by a pickup truck. He turned into a strip mall, drove through a motor bank court, parked between two station wagons at the Bag 'N Save, turned off the motor and the car lights, and hid his head under the steering wheel as his heartbeat seemingly surged to 2000 beats per minute. The police officer drove his squad car around the parking lot and eventually abandoned his search.

Jack wasn't going to jail, but where he was going seemed only slightly more pleasant.

JACK FINALLY MADE IT to Magnolia Avenue and as he rolled into the driveway, he thought, "She's probably in there consulting her caddy, "Should I whack him with the nine iron or the pitching wedge."

Jack knew his wife could do the most damage with her mouth. He didn't help his case by walking into his house not with a gift wrapped present but a Dippity Donut box.

"Jeanie?" he called, his heartbeat surging once again.

There was no answer. Did the shuttle van get lost on the way home? Is she so mad or exhausted she went to bed? Did she have the shuttle van re-routed to her local caddy's apartment? Is she hiding behind the sofa with a two-iron? Is this the calm before the storm?

Jack heard a familiar sound coming from the backyard like someone chopping wood. Light crept through the den windows. He opened the backdoor, and there was Jeanie blasting golf balls into the net. Jack could always tell how angry Jeanie was by what club she was using. She was using the Big Bertha driver.

He let her whack a couple more balls before announcing his presence. "Happy anniversary, honey."

Jeanie glanced at him and then placed another ball on her plastic tee mounted on a turf mat and swung harder.

After a few more balls, Jack asked, "How did it go today?" and then watched her swing even harder. As he snuck back toward the door, Jeanie dropped the driver.

"Not so fast, mister."

Jack studied his golf wife from toe to head and in her same outfit she put on after her morning shower. "You must have played bad. You didn't even have time to change clothes."

"Pardon?" Jeanie said. "You look like you haven't changed clothes in two days. Obviously, you haven't washed anything in two weeks."

Jack stopped postponing the inevitable and turned his eyes away from Jeanie. "Sorry I was late. I was finishing my feature on Scott Hilfinger and had to get it in on deadline for the feature page."

"Who the hell is Scott Hilfinger?"

"The Cowboy I brought home for an interview."

"I thought they all called you DH."

"Not this one. He calls me Mr. Byrne."

Knowing that Jeanie never read his newspaper articles, Jack thought the Hilfinger story was his best excuse. As he talked about Hilfy, Jeanie walked up and took a whiff of his breath.

"Is it a new policy to let you booze at work?"

Jeanie didn't give Jack time for a "Well, ah..."

"I called you from the plane at exactly 8 p.m. That gave you 55 minutes to chug your last beer, burp, take a piss, and drive to the airport. You should be able to do that in 25 minutes, about as long as it takes to trash a quarterback on deadline."

"I had to stop off to get you a present."

Jeanie stared at the glazed donut crumbs on Jack's goatee and followed him into the house. She crunched stale Cheerios on the floor and bruised banana peels that missed the overflowing trash can in the kitchen. She sniffed the sour milk that spilled from an empty milk carton on the kitchen table. Jack looked around the den for something he might have gotten her. He picked up the Dippity Donut box on the coffee table and opened it. "Here, honey, happy anniversary."

Jeanie grabbed the jelly donut and fired it into the wall. The red filling splattered all over the den, even onto the ceiling. "You lying pig. All you care about is yourself. It was more important to feed your face than greet me at the gate."

"Well, honey, I was hungry and there was a long line at the drive-thru window. Besides, what difference does it make. I was only a few minutes late."

"You don't get it, Jack. You 'never' get it. All the spouses of the passengers on my flight get it."

Jeanie put her hands on her hips. Tears welled in her eyes, but she was determined not to let them run down her face.

"It's about missing someone so much that you can't wait to see them. But you 'can' wait. Then you make me wait. Like at our wedding eight years ago today, when the minister thought you weren't coming and almost walked out."

Jeanie's voice grew louder with every example of Jack's tardiness. "Like our wedding night when I had to wait until the end of the fourth quarter of the USC-Notre Dame game to consummate the marriage. Like my last birthday when we had to eat at Taco Bell, because the Monday Night Game went into overtime and that was the only place open.

"Like every fricking time I come home from a tournament and I sit there and wait by the baggage claim for you to finish a column or a beer or whatever is more important than your poor ol' wife who is still suffering from the triple bogey that made her miss another cut."

Jack put his hand on Jeanie's shoulder and she yanked it off.

"Don't you dare touch me. You don't care about me. You don't come watch me play. You don't call and ask how I did. You don't support me."

Jack now figured the best defense was offense. Hollering louder, he figured, might calm her. "Don't support you? For eight years, I been payin' for you to fly all over the country to whatever tournament will have you and then listen to you moan about all those damn Swedes, gooks, and dikes stealing all your prize money. Then I pay for this Legend guy to coach you, while his horny son, Chad, carries your clubs around and pats you on the butt at the local tournaments. All this to bankroll this silly dream of yours.

"Why don't you get a job at the Putt-Putt or teach old farts with stiff shafts at the driving range? At least it's steady income."

Jack's strategy failed. The volume only increased, and Jeanie's teeth clenched. "You don't go to my tournaments. You don't know my coach. You don't know my caddy. You don't know what I do at the golf club from dawn to dusk."

"You're right, I don't know. Maybe you're shacking up with a caddy."

"I'm what?" Jeanie's scream woke the neighbors, and those still sleeping were awoken by barking dogs. "I'm out playing my ass off so I can make the tour and have some money to rent a maid to clean up all your shit, and you accuse me of caddy shacking? You asshole."

Jeanie reached down at the leftovers from the bucket of balls she brought in from outside. Jack sprinted for the front door as every Titleist, Dunlop, and Maxfli in every number and every color flew at his head. Jeanie kept pelting him and his convertible until he backed down his driveway and fled down Magnolia Avenue, leaving skid marks and lights coming on in every house.

Jack's heart was racing again and even faster than the motor. There was only one thing he knew for certain about his eighth wedding anniversary. He wasn't getting laid.

8

A Bic lighter woke Jack in the wee hours of November 30, 2005. A shivering old man with wrinkles upon wrinkles, gray beard, black hoodie, faded Wranglers, old high-tops, and a skull and crossbones tattoo on his left wrist stared at Jack's eyelids as they slowly creaked open.

"Ya' okay, lad?" The old man's voice was strained and sounded like a Scottish undertaker. His breath smelled like he had swallowed a bottle of whiskey and probably had.

Jack barely could see his face beneath the black hood through blurred vision. He checked his own pulse to see if he was still alive. His head felt like it had been hit with a hammer, his stomach with a tire iron, and his calf muscles with a billy club. His breath smelled worse than the old man's.

Jack cupped his hand over his mouth as if he was going to puke for the eighth time – one for each year of his marriage. "Please sir," he said. "Let me die in peace."

Jack didn't know where he was and didn't care until he woke up again and saw light creeping through the barred window of his jail cell. He felt like he was sleeping on a tombstone. That's because the three cots were taken by the other loud snoring drunks, and he had passed out on the cold concrete floor. Jack pressed his nostrils together to keep from breathing in his cellmates' poorly aimed vomit and urine near the lone toilet.

The events that led him to this temporary hell were starting to come back, whether he liked it or not.

JACK HAD ESCAPED the golf ball barrage as he looked into his rearview mirror to see Jeanie launching one last grenade and hollering, "Run away, again, you coward!," her voice and body fading in the night.

Jack ran away – or, in this case, drove – right back to where he started the evening. He was reunited with Johnny Walker and mutual friends Jack Daniels and Harvey Wallbanger in a corner booth at the Kazbar. Cathie must have figured the drunker he got the bigger tip she would get.

After several shots of jet fuel with two diehard Cowboys' fans who were too drunk or too stupid to recognise the much-maligned Dallas Star sports columnist, the tip Jack wanted to give Cathie was pink, not green. One of Jack's newfound drinking mates stared at Cathie serving a drink to another inebriated fool and whispered, "She can shit on my Post Toasties any morning."

When Cathie returned to the corner booth, Jack invited her to Dippity Donuts and said, "Honey, as long as I got a face, you got a place to sit."

The comment earned him a face slap and a face-first crash on the outside curb delivered by Milt's bouncer. "Take that, DH," the goon said, wiping his hands.

Literally thrown out into the cold, Jack eventually picked himself up and zigzagged his way to Dippity Donuts. No matter how drunk he was, Jack always could find his way to the donut shop. He just followed his nose, which he wiped off on a paper towel. Blood also flowed from his forehead and onto the massive cream-filled donut he nicknamed, "Moby Dick."

Squeamish at the site of blood and overcome by an alcohol level that would have flunked the easiest DWI test, Jack fell face-first into Moby Dick. Two police officers at the counter walked over. One pulled him up by his hair and said, "This looks like that sports columnist fella who comes in here a lot."

The officer identified him by his mug next to the column he wrote on Rex Fanning from a newspaper that had been lying around since the early morning after Thanksgiving. "What should we do with him, Sarge?"

"Cuff 'im."

The officers dragged Jack out of Dippity Donuts, pushed him against the wall, yanked his hands behind his back, handcuffed him, frisked him, and then whacked him below the back of his knees with a nightstick. "That's what you get for writing that shit about Rex Fanning," the sergeant said.

THE CUT ABOVE JACK'S FOREHEAD was reopened after guards threw him into the drunk tank. He didn't care. He wanted that old man to dig through the tombstone and push him in. Instead, the old man was sitting next to him when he awoke the third time.

"Almost check out time, lad," the old man said.

"When does the buffet line open?" Jack asked. "Can we get hot coffee in those tin cups?"

"I take it, unlike me, ya aren't a frequent guest at the Dallas Hellton. Dis is over a woman? Usually is."

Jack cracked a glimmer of a smile at the old man's perception. Nothing – not his migraine headache, his sour stomach, his scraped forehead, his sore wrists, nor his sore knees – could compare to the pain he felt from the golf balls and insults Jeanie had landed upon him and his convertible.

Marriage, Jack had thought, would settle him down and make him less lonely. But Jeanie saw more of The Legend and his horndog son/caddy Chad than she did of her husband. Her home was the Forest Green Country Club, where Jack had his pay checks made out to. He figured she may as well sleep there and constantly wondered if she was at least taking pussy naps in the caddy shack.

Jack lived much of his life in NFL press boxes. Jeanie sometimes had to look at his mugshot on the front of the Star sports page to remember what he looked like, before finding the LPGA golf story and results buried at the bottom of page 11. Conversations over the seldom dinner for two at the country club revolved around Jeanie complaining about the lack of coverage of women's sports and a request for Jack to write human interest columns about top sportswomen.

"People don't watch women's sports, Jeanie, so they certainly aren't going to write about them."

"Title IX is changing that," she said.

"All Title IX has done is taken college scholarships away from deserving football players the starters need for blocking dummies."

The comment slammed the door on the conversation and the door to the master bedroom. The cell door opened for Jack that Wednesday afternoon. His cellmate's voice echoed down the corridor between jailed robbers, rapists, and murderers, "So long, lad. Hope you find the meaning of life."

JACK PAID HIS $350 FINE for public intoxication and was sent back into a cold world that didn't seem to want him. He limped back to his Mazda Miata, parked outside the Kazbar with three parking tickets stuck under his windshield wipers. He looked inside the bar window to see Soss munching a Kazburger and discussing something with a goon, likely the bouncer who threw him out of the bar.

Jack drove home and quickly noticed that Jeanie had picked up all the golf balls. The jelly donut was still stuck to the wall. No dishes were done, and the place was just as he had left it.

There were no tissues by the bed, leaving Jack to conclude she lost no tears or sleep over the war. Her concern was getting to the club early to meet The Legend and preparing for her next competition, the Dallas Women's Christmas Classic, a tournament Jeanie always wanted to win but never came close. As usual there was no apology note, no remorse for the lumps the golf balls raised on her husband's scalp or the jabs that pierced his already deflated ego.

Jack showered, packed his bag, and drove back downtown to meet his traveling party – an over-prepared rookie assistant editor and a well-worn and well-fed photographer – to Houston. First, he stopped at the drugstore. He bought Alka-Seltzer and Advil and asked the pharmacist if they sold any over-the-counter cyanide.

"Nah," he said. "But thar's a gun shop down the road."

"Thanks," Jack said. "I gotta feeling this trip is gonna be a real blast."

9

Dallas lights up the week after Thanksgiving. Bulbs colored in red, green, blue, and white are strung across roofs and chimneys, around buildings and light poles, along sidewalks and patios. Even those plastic Santa Clauses and reindeer and nativity scenes have lights on them. Lights also are wrapped around the real and fake Christmas trees glowing from living room windows.

On this night no light could be seen through a thick fog that blanketed Texas. Not even the huge lit ball of Ritz Tower was visible from the parking lot of The Dallas Star Building.

"Rather eerie out here," Yolanda Lopez said right before the start of her maiden out-of-town assignment in a Dallas Star staff car.

Lanny, the photographer, looked around just before putting the key in the door. "Kind of like a graveyard."

Their bodies were about as cold as fresh corpses as sleet was turning to snow flurries and wind pushed old newspaper and plastic cups around the parking lot like a squib kick.

"Is he coming?" Lanny said as he turned the key in the ignition and put the heater on full.

"He'll be here," Yo-Lo said. "He was in the Morgue looking up an old article he wrote about a Lone Star State game and some quarterback, ah, Mulinksky?"

Lanny put a glob of chewing tobacco in his mouth. "Molinski. He'd have better luck finding him in a real morgue."

"How about the Internet?"

"Too long ago. You won't find him anywhere."

They finally found Jack, trudging through the fog with his leather satchel slung over his left shoulder and his clothing bag over his right. He was wearing a long navy blue overcoat, ski gloves, jeans, a white turtleneck, plaid pullover sweater, a white bandage above his left eye, and a frown. Jack shoved his bags in the trunk and slipped into the backseat behind Lanny, his back resting against the backdoor and his legs stretched out like he was relaxing for another Monday Night Football game in his living room.

"Ya' look like death warmed over," Lanny said, staring at Jack from the driver's seat. "With that bandage, you'll fit in real well with the bull riders you're about to interview."

"Just drive."

JACK WANTED TO SLEEP all the way to Houston but had too many things on his mind after what had transpired during the past 28 hours. Story rejection. Alcohol injection. Domestic dispute. Bar dismissal. A night in detox.

Alka-Seltzer and Advil only could relieve his physical pain. His front-seat traveling companions, one handing him a five-day itinerary with little rodeo horses and football players on it and the other spitting tobacco into a coffee can while driving, did little to soothe his emotional scars.

"It's hotter than hell in here," Jack said, taking off his gloves and coat and sweater and looking out the side window at whatever he could see of the highway. "I know it's like Siberia outside, but do you have to turn the inside into Nigeria?"

Lanny tried singing, "On the road again. Just can't wait to get on that road again..."

Yo-Lo tried conversing. "Sorry to hear about Jeanine not getting her Tour card. She came so close, maybe next year."

Jack sang nothing, said nothing, just kept staring out the window as they put Dallas behind them and cruised down the four lane-highway divided by a grassy brown median strip and flanked by small lit billboards and road signs hidden by the fog and flurries and a night that was becoming darker and colder with every lugy Lanny dropped into his makeshift spittoon.

"The rodeo will be really exciting," Yo-Lo said, offering Jack some M&Ms and then getting waved off. "Lanny should be able to get some tremendous photos, and you should be able to get a fantastic

49

story on a bucking bronco rider, a calf roper, or maybe a rodeo clown."

"Yee-hah," Jack said, pointing his right thumb downward and stretching his legs on the backseat. He thought of all Cowboys – rodeo and football – as clowns. Whatever they said, it came down to, "I feel good."

Jack then pictured himself as a rodeo clown. "I would be perfect," he thought. "I run away from the bull just like I run away from my wife, my boss, my family. Maybe I should keep running, see how well they go without me."

"We goin' straight to Houston?" Lanny asked

"We'll stop halfway to get gas," Yo-Lo said. "You know of a good place?"

"Gilmer's Gas and Grub," Lanny said. "That's dead smack in the middle. The guy comes out and pumps your gas; you don't even have to get out of the car."

Yo-Lo wiped her fogging up side window with her shirt sleeve and peered at the side of the highway at a tall, skinny man with a beard running next to the highway like he was being chased by a wild bore then stopping and holding up his right thumb.

"Stop!" Yo-Lo said.

Lanny eased his foot off the accelerator and steered the car to the side of the road. Jack raised up from the backseat and stared out the back window at the man hurrying toward their taillights.

"You're not gonna pick this guy up, are you? I was just getting comfortable back here."

"We can't just leave him out there," Yo-Lo said. "He must be freezing to death."

The man opened the back door. Jack reluctantly moved his legs and sat up as the man sat beside him. The man clasped his shaking hands and huddled his shoulders and knees together. His long black overcoat, similar to Jack's but a tad more worn, had done little to protect his bony ribs and arms from the frigid wind. The flecks of snow on his beard made it look like it was going gray. His long brown hair extended from the base of his Cowboys' toboggan hat to the bottom of his collar. The man untied his backpack, which had been tied to his matted hair, and set it at his feet. He took a long look out the back window and then turned around and leaned back.

"Sh-Sh-Shore is nice of you f-f-f-folks to pick me up." The man didn't have a stuttering problem. He was just cold.

Lanny drove the staff car back onto the highway and looked back at the man who appeared to have had less sleep recently than the man beside him and smelled like Jack did before his shower. "Where to, bud?"

"Wh-Wh-where ya'll goin?" he asked.

"Houston." Lanny turned his eyes back to the highway.

"Wh-What a coincidence, that's where I'm goin."

Yo-Lo poured a steaming cup of coffee from her thermos and handed it to the man. "What's your name, sir?"

The man took a gulp of coffee. "Gr-Gr-Graham."

Yo-Lo introduced herself, Lanny, and Jack and told him they were journalists traveling to Houston to cover the rodeo and the Cowboys-Texans game. "Do you like football?"

"Y-Yes ma'am, I used to play."

Jack laughed. "Quarterback, right?"

The man took a longer gulp, which cured his stammering. "Yes sir. I had a real strong arm. Yip. My teammates said I might play in the NFL someday."

"Hey maybe you could play for the Cowboys on Sunday, and maybe even in the Super Bowl."

"Take it easy, Jack," Lanny said.

Yo-Lo opened a Tupperware container and offered homemade brownies to the men in the backseat. Graham stuffed two in his mouth. He looked as if he hadn't eaten in three days and probably hadn't.

Jack waved off the brownies as he had the M&Ms. "Unless they have marijuana in them, no thanks."

Lanny took a brownie and slid an Oldies Country Western CD into the dashboard. His passengers were treated for the next hour to Hank Williams, George Strait, Johnny Cash, Willie Nelson, Waylon Jennings, and George Jones as the headlights deflected off the thick fog. The music and the coffee warmed Graham's soul and his frail body. He took off his coat and put it on top of Jack's coat.

Jack stared out the window with his chin resting on his right palm and watched the quiet road and the few cars, pickup trucks, and 18-wheelers seldom pass by them. The fog lifted only enough to see a lighted-billboard that read, "Gilmer's Gas and Grub two miles" and a road sign that had pictures of a gas station, bed, and food and the words, "Next exit." Jack looked ahead to the dim lights in the distance as a guitar, harmonica, and George Jones' soft words filtered through the darkness.

He said I'll love you 'til I die
She told him you'll forget in time
As the years went slowly by
She still preyed upon his mind...

Lanny guided the car toward the exit sign and took his foot off the accelerator. The car slowed as it started down the slick exit ramp.

Ya'll awake?" Lanny said.
Everyone nodded but Jack.
"I'm awake," he said. "But I wish I was dead."
George Jones' voice grew louder as the chorus began.

He stopped loving her today
They placed a wreath upon his door
And soon they'll carry him away
He stopped loving her today

10

The warning "Flammable Liquid" in bold black letters shone off a silver cylinder-shaped tank truck as it rolled through the fog of the Central Texas highway. Just above the words on the red diamond-shaped sign was a black symbol of a flame shooting skyward.

Silas McCormick bounced on the driver's seat along with a cowboy hat atop his bald head, gripped the steering wheel with his right hand and a Budweiser can with his left while singing in unison with Kenny Rogers and the intermittent wipers that swept the occasional snow flurry off his windshield.

You've got to know when to hold 'em
Know when to fold 'em
Know when to walk away
And know when to run

Silas took a swig of beer and finished the song with Kenny.

There'll be time enough for countin'
When the dealin's done

For 15 years, Silas had driven his rig back and forth solo from Houston to Dallas three days per week. He had driven through thunderstorms, dust storms, gale force winds, torrential rain, and even a tornado. So to him, what was a little snow and ice.

"I could do dis blindfold," he told his third wife SueBeth at breakfast that Wednesday morning.

What Silas didn't prepare for was what happened as he approached the exit for Gilmer's Gas and Grub and pressed the sole of his right cowboy boot on the brakes. There weren't any.

"Oh Lordy." Silas let go of his Budweiser and death gripped the steering wheel with both hands. He pressed harder, then pumped the brakes up and down. Nothing.

"Lordy, Lordy, Lordeee!"

The exit sign appeared through the fog. Silas slammed his left foot on the clutch and tried shoving the stick into a lower gear. It wouldn't move. The runaway truck flew down the exit ramp past shops and cafes and took dead aim on Gilmer's Gas and Grub. Silas pulled the horn and screamed, "Oh God, I'm a goner!" while turning the wheel with all the might from his bulging tattooed biceps.

The truck jack-knifed, and the large cylinder tank tore off at the neck below the cab. The tanker slid down the icy road without losing speed, spun, and then cart-wheeled toward the gas station.

Gilmer Jenkins, who had just stuck the nozzle of the unleaded gas hose into the fuel tank of The Dallas Star staff car, heard the truck's horn and glanced at the tanker hurling at him. His eyes turned the size of silver dollars and his mouth flew open, dropping his lit cigarette onto the payment. He sprinted toward the pond behind the gas station like he was already on fire without a hint of a warning to the car's occupants whose fogged up back window blocked their view of the steel monster tumbling toward them.

Sparks flew from the tanker as it somersaulted atop the slick road, took one last leap and crashed sideways atop the staff car and the fuel pumps.

Boom!

Within a finger snap the gas station exploded into a ball of flames, an inferno of oil and gas skyrocketing into the heavens and spilling the air with noxious fumes of tar and metal. The impenetrable heat melted the tires and the painted stars off the staff car. The flesh on the bodies inside roasted into skeletons. Their bones disintegrated with another explosion that sent flames and ashes soaring even higher into the night sky.

The few customers in nearby shops fell to the shaking ground and covered their ears as the blast cut the power from the buildings.

Ghosts of the Gridiron

Cars and trucks on the adjacent highway were stopped for a look at the burning wreckage below, their headlights barely piercing the dark dust. For a few minutes only the roaring flames broke the eerie silence until a fire engine sounded in the distance.

The fog was now mixed with smoke so dense nothing was visible within a few feet, not even the ash that fell alongside snow flurries and crumbled to the road. Suddenly, a silhouette of a man in a long black overcoat shone through the smog. It drifted from the darkened Dippity Donut shop toward the blaze as if through a cloud, and stopped.

Jack Byrne stared at the inferno. He scratched his goatee and shook his head as he looked down at the worn black fabric on the sleeves and felt the hole in the lining of the left pocket. He mumbled to himself, his cold breath showing in the fog.

"That son of a bitch stole my coat."

PART TWO

Cellar Dweller

II

There is nothing better than waking up from the dead. There are no bills, no taxes, no house or car maintenance, no nagging spouses or bosses, no dirty dishes or laundry, no telephone calls, no computers, and no story deadlines.

Jack Byrne had no care in the world when he awoke on Thursday morning, December 1, atop a fluffy white pillow and between the soft white sheets and a warm blanket in a quiet room in the middle of nowhere with a simple black and white sign outside that read, "MOTEL." Several moments passed before the tragic events of the previous night crept through his peaceful bliss.

The fog had lifted and gave way to sunshine. There was not a cloud in the sky, and the only cloud on the ground came from the gray smoke billowing off the smouldering remnants of what used to be Gilmer's Gas and Grub and a Dallas Star staff car with three people trapped inside. There were pieces of charred metal lying in the large crevasse made by the explosion but not a particle of human remains – no hair follicle, tissue, membrane, or cell of any kind. Nothing.

Silas McCormick and Gilmer Jenkins miraculously survived. Silas suffered a broken leg after the cab of his truck tore away from the tanker and slammed into an embankment. He called his wife, SueBeth, on his cellphone. "Oh good Lord, my darlin', I'm alive," he said as paramedics loaded him into an ambulance in the glow of the nearby blaze.

Gilmer's back was singed as he sprinted for the pond behind the gas station and dove in. The freezing water immediately extinguished the flame and protected him from the random sparks that flew from the wreckage. Gilmer swam to the edge of the pond, pulled himself ashore, and sat on the bank. He used the heat from the fire to thaw his frozen body and was still shaking as police interviewed him next to the pond.

"Th-th-thank God for f-f-football," he said.

Gilmer was an all-state receiver in high school. His coach had told him how important the game was and said, "Someday, it might save your life." The fast-twitch fibers in his aging body propelled him to safety just in time.

Jack was saved by Dippity Donuts. He had not planned to leave the car and brave the freezing conditions until he smelled the soft dough from the shop at the bottom of the exit ramp, about the length of a football field from Gilmer's Gas and Grub.

"They probably sell donuts at the gas station," Lanny, the photographer, said right before spitting a final glob of tobacco.

Jack laughed. "Stop the car and let me out here."

Jack did not realize the hitchhiker, Graham, had laid his overcoat atop his overcoat and didn't notice any difference on the dark road or in the donut shop, where he had ordered a half-dozen glazed and a hot chocolate to go. The clerk was fumbling over the change when the explosion rocked the building, broke the store front window, and knocked both of them and the donuts to the floor. Jack reached for the donuts but could not find them in the darkness caused by the power outage.

He stepped through the broken glass and drifted outside through the fog. After mourning the loss of his laptop and the coat and the clothes he had stuffed in his bag, Jack turned his attention to his fallen co-workers.

Experts say it can takes survivors of such tragic circumstances months, even years to overcome such an ordeal. It took Jack about 20 minutes. He mastered the five stages of grief in about the time it takes him to shit, shower, and shave. News reporters are supposed to be immune to tragedy, not sportswriters – although Jack had been covering the Cowboys the past 10 seasons. He was just happy to be standing there watching the fire instead of roasting in it.

Jack enjoyed the convergence of firefighters from all over the county spraying hundreds of thousands of gallons of water from their big hoses onto the inferno and the police officers frantically closing the highway and moving bystanders back into the fog. He could have grabbed a pen and paper from the donut shop and interviewed the truck driver and the gas station attendant but thought, "Fuck it, it's not my beat."

Jack meandered toward the pond and heard Gilmer identifying The Dallas Star staff car and telling a police officer that there were three people in the car. He was adamant that there were a man and a woman in the front and one man in the back.

Immediately, Jack pulled his cellphone from his pants pocket. He needed to call his newspaper office and tell the news reporters that the person in the backseat was a hitchhiker, not him. Otherwise, they would assume that all three Dallas Star staffers were in the car and the headline on the front of the newspaper the next morning would read, "Star sports columnist killed in explosion."

"Jeanie will think I'm dead," he thought.

Jack pressed the area code and the first six numbers of the office telephone number. He did not press the seventh. He slipped the phone back into his pocket and walked back toward the exit ramp, scratching his goatee and thinking.

"Jeanie wanted me dead last night. She didn't come looking for me or phone me. She didn't care that I didn't return home. My passing out and spending the night in jail would be none of her concern. She's taken me for granted for as long as we've been together and doesn't appreciate me."

Jack wandered back toward the donut shop. "Does she love me? Does she really love me? We are about to find out?"

Jack snuck back into Dippity Donuts and used the light on his cellphone and his nose to find dust-free donuts on the shelf behind the counter. He helped himself to another half-dozen glazed to replace those that fell to the floor and poured hot chocolate into a paper cup.

He strolled past the blaze, still roaring despite the firefighters' efforts, to the motel along the highway entrance ramp. He gulped his hot chocolate and devoured his final donut as he reached for the motel office door. The motel clerk did not respond when Jack pressed the buzzer on the counter, so he left a note explaining that he grabbed the key for room 5 off the rack and would pay for it in the morning. Jack giggled as he put the key in the door. "Probably not a concierge at this place."

He turned the heater to full, took off the smoky coat and his pants, tucked himself into the bed, and turned off the lamp. He took off his watch, placed it on the bedside table, and looked at the digital time 11:59 p.m. glowing in the dark. He thought again about calling Jeanie, who likely had been notified by someone at the newspaper about the explosion, and wondered whether she deserved going to bed thinking she was a widow. Jack closed his eyes and went to sleep before his watch struck midnight.

JACK'S WATCH was showing 11:59am the next time he glanced at it. The exhaustion of two sleepless nights had overwhelmed the excitement of one monumentally eventful one. He was literally dead to the world in that cozy bed, and the only thing that made him get out of it was the complimentary Dallas Star newspaper that lay outside one of the rooms.

He didn't even take time for his regular two-minute morning pee. Sunlight poured into his dark room as he opened the door. Traffic from the re-opened highway roared in either direction and the scent of smoke from the smouldering fire overwhelmed the lingering cigarette smell of the room. Jack grabbed the newspaper, slid back the window shades, and lay on his bed.

A color photograph of the blaze covered the top half of the page. The bold headline below The Dallas Star masthead read, "Massive explosion leaves three dead." The sub-head, in smaller letters and less bold type, read, "Dallas Star staffers perish in blaze."

"That sucks," Jack said out loud to the motel room walls. "My name didn't even make the sub-head."

Nor the first five paragraphs of the story, a combined effort from a Dallas Star reporter and an Associated Press writer. The lead, which Jack read silently, was "A runaway tanker collided with a Dallas

Star staff car last night at a Central Texas gas station and exploded, sending flames soaring into the heavens and killing three people."

Jack read the next sentence aloud. "Police on the scene said the blast was likely caused by fuel aboard the tanker crashing into the car being gassed up and the adjacent gas tanks, the sparks flying off the road, and an attendant's lit cigarette errantly dropped on the ground."

"Sure, blame it on the grease monkey," Jack said.

He grew more angry with the first named victim in the fourth paragraph. "Lanny Pickett, a longtime Dallas Star photographer, was identified as the driver of the car. Pickett was one of the top sports photographers in the country and won a handful of awards."

Then came the fifth paragraph. "Yolanda Lopez, an assistant sports editor, was sitting in the front passenger seat. Star sports editor Dick Schwartz said Lopez was a rising star on his staff with a bubbly personality and would be greatly missed."

Jack threw the paper against the bedpost after reading the sixth, which was located on the jump page at the bottom of page 13. "Sports columnist Jack Byrne also died in the blaze."

"That's it?" Jack said. His voice could have been heard in the next room had someone been staying there. "Where's my obit I wrote Monday?"

Jack flipped to the sports section to find game stories on the Dallas Mavericks and the Dallas Stars and other NHL and NBA teams, college basketball highlights, high school features, NFL notes, and the results of the final round of the LPGA Q-school tournament. But no tribute to the writer of hundreds of – what he wrote in his obit - the best sports columns ever published in this newspaper.

"Not even a picture of me," Jack said. "I'll bet that Sawed Off Stack of Shit had something to do with this. Or maybe those two butchers."

Jack stood, paced the room, and continued his conversation with the motel walls. "After all I've done, that's what they think of me. They want to bury me in the sixth paragraph and on page 13 below a hack photographer and a snot-nosed editor. I'll show them."

Jack desperately wanted someone to talk to. Someone to express whatever remorse he had for his fallen colleagues and the unknown hitchhiker and his pure good fortune of surviving the massive explosion.

As he stood there in a small, basic room in a generic motel in the middle of nowhere in his tighty whities hidden by a wrinkled white turtleneck, he realized he was all alone.

12

When he was a boy, Jack always dressed like a Dallas Cowboys' player for Halloween. Never a ghost, like most of his friends.

But he had to act like one to sneak out of a household that banned trick or treating and most other extra-curricular activities.

He waited for his parents to go to bed before doing a disappearing act, vanishing from his bedroom, slithering downstairs through the den, and out the backdoor and over the back fence without the slightest of a peep. He was back in bed by midnight without anyone noticing he was gone or the miniature Snickers bars and lollypops he hid in his closet. No one also seemed to notice him on his Halloween run through the neighborhood, favoring the spooks and headless creatures to the blue taped 13 on his white home-made jersey, pillowed shoulder pads, silver pants, black cleats, starred helmet, and black paint strips under his eyes. The candy simply was dropped into his sack without anyone saying, "So what are you suppose to be?"

If someone had asked why number 13, Jack would have answered in his prepubescent voice, "Because it's the only number never worn by a Cowboys' player."

No one asked.

He felt like a ghost and, 30 years later, he was one. He again found an empty front desk at the motel at checkout and the unopened note he had left on the counter the night before. He stuck his room key back on the rack but left no money. Ghosts don't pay for motel stays.

Jack exited the motel lobby. The outside air cooled his freshly showered skin. Jack smelled the embers of the previous night's blaze and barbecue brisket sizzling from the same direction. He followed his nose to a catered barbecue for the firefighters and police officers who were recovering from a long night and longer morning. No one noticed Jack, who had not had a meal in 24 hours, take a plate and load it with beef, potato salad, and baked beans or his second and third helping.

Jack felt that his ability to go unnoticed was an asset to his newly acquired non-existence. Ghosts have the freedom to travel when and where they want and do whatever they want. They can haunt their enemies and spy on their loved ones. Knowing this was enough encouragement for Jack to remain dead through the weekend.

The problem, Jack would realize, was that he couldn't cash a check or use one of the credit cards from the wallet he had kept in his back pocket. He would have to rely on the per diem money Yo-Lo had given him and whatever cash was inside the hitchhiker's coat.

Ghosts really don't need money. That's what Jack found out as he overheard a firefighter with barbecue sauce slobbered on his face telling someone he was driving his fire truck back to Houston that afternoon. Jack always had wanted to ride on a fire engine and he was in no rush to return to Dallas. To honor his fallen colleagues he wanted to complete the trip, and watch the Cowboys – the football Cowboys – without having to cover them. No responsibility is a ghost perk.

While the firefighter was stepping into the driver's seat, Jack snuck onto the back and crawled into a space on top under the ladder as they sped away from what should have been Jack's fiery grave. He lay there atop the fire engine like a corpse and felt as cold as one after the two-hour journey. He jumped off just before the truck was driven into the downtown fire station and walked four miles to the Executive Hotel and Suites, where for the next three days he would do what he had wanted to do for a long time. Nothing.

Yo-Lo had told him not long before she perished that she was joking about the Motel 60. Yo Lo had booked and paid for three rooms at the Executive and was now not alive to cancel them. No one knew where she had booked, and the newspaper would have to pay for them whether anyone stayed there or not. Jack wrote "Dick Schwartz" on the register, rode the elevator to the 18th floor, and floated down the red-carpeted hallway to his suite. No bellboy asked to carry his bag, because he didn't have one.

Jack hung the hitchhiker's black overcoat in the closet and slipped into the white hotel robe, his sole attire for a peaceful three days in a king size bed. He watched on the 50-inch flat screen television a pro football game on Thursday night, college games on Friday and Saturday, and movies, sports talk shows, and the Playboy Channel in between. He ordered room service every meal – bacon and eggs and waffles and orange juice for breakfast, cheeseburgers and fries and milkshakes for lunch, and filet mignon and shrimp for dinner.

He cleaned out the snacks and drinks from the mini-bar. He left the bed only to take a spa bath or stare out the window at the massive Earl Campbell Stadium in the distance.

After waking up from one of his midday naps, he thought, "Maybe I did die in that explosion and went to Heaven."

Everyone else can go somewhere much further south, he thought. Soss and his readers would yearn for his columns. Jeanie would crave his midnight back rubs and pillow talk about the 20-foot birdie putt she had sunk in the Pro-Am. The mourning must have been well under way. Funeral arrangements were being made, and all he had to do was snap open another can of Coke and press the remote to ESPN.

But even ghosts can't hang around forever. After his Sunday morning pancakes and sausages, Jack had one last spa bath and dressed back into the clothes he had an attendant launder. He yanked the black overcoat from the closet and a faded black wallet fell out of the pocket. Ghosts can get curious, also.

He counted 37 dollars and found 38 cents in a little change pocket. He glanced at his driver's license only noting the man's name, "Graham Repert." The only other items in the coat pockets were an armadillo-shaped key ring with a rusty, worn Volkswagon key and an apartment or house key and a newspaper clipping with the NFL odds for Week 12.

Jack slid his arms into the dead man's coat and walked out of the suite, out of the hotel and back into the cold. Somehow he knew his life as a ghost would never be the same. Halloween, at least for the treat, was over.

13

The afternoon sun shone through Earl Campbell Stadium and reflected off the Dallas Cowboys' number 13 as it waited in the tunnel in front of a mob of other sky blue numbers. Like the number 2 of new starting quarterback Jarmelle Beezley, the number 89 of star receiver Delarius Tromane, and the number 76 of mountainous offensive tackle Colby Zeller.

Number 13 Scott Hilfinger had been waiting all his life for this moment and nominated himself to lead his team onto the field.

Hilfy peered around at the 83,000 spectators nestled into their seats, the television cameras lining the field, the Texans Cheerleaders forming a V from the tunnel on the other side of the end zone, and the three-story press box filled with print and broadcast journalists ready to bring this game to readers and viewers all over a world he had encircled to arrive here. He had played in a Spanish bull ring, an Australian Rules Football pitch, a Greek Olympic Stadium, and bleacher stadiums from his hometown Deadhorse, Oklahoma to Edmonton, Alberta. The only comparable stadium, the Rose Bowl, was almost forgotten in a career he thought was finished less than 10 days before.

Jack watched from the auxiliary press box on the other side of the stadium as Hilfy bounced up and down in the tunnel as Houston's offensive starters and head coach were introduced with a roar and Dallas' defensive starters and head coach introduced with boos.

Then as the announcer's voice echoed off the stadium, "And now the rest of the Dallas Cowboys," Hilfy pointed to the sky, likely to his father, and snapped his chin strap across his helmet. A stadium official said, "Let's go."

Hilfy charged toward the field, took one step onto the artificial turf, and was clothe-lined by the Cowboys' defensive line coach. "No turd string quarterback gonna lead my team onto da field," said Alvin

Baines, as the storming herd trampled Hilfy. "No sir. Specially not one wearin' unlucky number 13."

Hilfy lay there in a fetal position after the final cleat dug into his rib cage. He thought he might be the first NFL player carried off the field following the player introductions. No one seemed to notice but Jack. Not even the Cowboys' mascot, who caught him with a spur as he hurdled him.

"Has to be the shortest career in the history of NFL football," Jack thought.

As Merle Howard crooned the Star Spangled Banner, Hilfy slowly got up on all fours and crawled to the bench. He grabbed a towel and wiped blood off his elbows. He took off his helmet and applied an ice pack to his chin with his right hand and massaged his bruised chest with his left. He couldn't have played in the game even if he was called to.

NO ONE SEEMED TO CARE but Jack. He had kept his media pass in his wallet but eschewed the luxurious main press box for the modest auxiliary press box, where he was not known by the Mexican radio announcer and small town newspaper reporters who were banished to other side of the stadium. While sports reporters – like Cowboys' beat writer Dave Noonan and whatever last-minute columnist Soss found to replace Jack – in the main press box were served wine coolers and prime rib, Jack and the other minions in the auxiliary box had to fetch warm cokes from a broken refrigerator and week-old popcorn stuffed into little red boxes.

Jack was just happy to be there. No one said anything to him. He sat with an Executive Hotel and Suites notepad and pen but didn't write a word. For once, he was able to admire the game instead of figuring out what aspect or player he would write about.

From Jack's high perch the Cowboys' players looked like ants in football drag as they took the field for warm-up. Some stretched while others tossed the ball around, kicked field goals, punted, jogged around the field, practiced blocking, did short sprints, or stood and watched everyone else. One unknowing would have thought Hilfy to be the starting quarterback. Through the lenses of the binoculars Jack borrowed without asking the press box attendant, Hilfy looked even sharper than he did at his first Cowboys' practice, lofting 40-yard missiles into the outstretched arms of reserve receivers and firing bullet passes to the rookie tight end who had no hope of being thrown one in the game.

Beezley, replacing the injured star Rex Fanning, was showing his nerves in the pre-game. His balls were either drilled at the starting receivers' shoelaces or a full two yards over their heads. One ball on a sideline route smacked the head of a member of the chain crew.

Still, Jack favored Beezley over whom he had nicknamed Rex "The Robot" Fanning. About The Robot, Jack once wrote that he had seen "mobility scooters move faster."

Fanning's only escape from a blitzing linebacker was to throw to the peanut vendors. What Beezley lacked in arm strength he made up for in agility. He had rocket legs that could propel him from any pocket collapse. He could scramble up and down the field, long enough to find an open receiver or tuck the ball under his sturdy elbow and weave around defensive backs for a big gainer. At least, that's what he showed in the pre-season.

Suddenly, the Rex Fanning Show had been pre-empted and the rookie quarterback from UCLA was now center stage. Should he also fail, the Cowboys were in deep manure. Their new backup QB, Brody Guthrie, hadn't played a down in three years. After once quarterbacking the Jacksonville Jaguars to an 0-16 season and then the next season winning a Super Bowl ring as the San Francisco 49ers emergency quarterback, Guthrie was happy to sit the rest of the season out. He couldn't wait for the final gun of his final game, so he could take his NFL pension to his ranch in New Mexico. He would be happy to give his spot to the over-ambitious Hilfy, whom he watched in warmup. No one else noticed Hilfy, not even the trainers who walked past the puddle of blood that dripped under Hilfy's elbow as

Cowboys' kicker Agberto Gerrone booted the opening kickoff through the uprights.

"Bravo, Señor Gerrone," the Mexican play-by-play announcer yelled through his on-air mike.

That was about the only play he praised in the first half. Three and out became the ritual for both teams, and each team's punter limped to the locker room at half time with a sore right foot amidst the boos from the masses. Ray Myles led his team back onto the field with a voice much hoarser than before he left it. Whatever expletive he hollered at his "herd of losers" didn't seem to make a difference in the third quarter. The Texans recovered a fumbled punt snap from Cowboys' punter Colin Flanders on the Cowboy 23 and broke the scoreless tie with a 32-yard field goal.

Hilfy finally found the sidelines in the fourth quarter as another Cowboys' drive stalled. Myles paced the sidelines past Hilfy and then said, "Where's Guthrie?"

Myles found Guthrie hiding behind a Gatorade cooler and said, "Get warmed up. You're goin' in if this fuckin' Jig can't move us down the field next time."

As Guthrie tossed balls on the sideline, Jack said out loud from the press box, "Oh no, Guthrie is warming up. The Cowboys are doomed."

The Cowboys got the ball at midfield with five minutes to play and immediately went backwards. On a third and 27 Beezley dropped back to pass, and the Texans sent in everyone but the water boy. Like a scared housewife wielding a rolling pin and running away from burglars, Beezley eluded the hungry blitzers and escaped to the sidelines. He got a block from tight end Heath Garrett and cut back to the center of the field. He stiff-armed a safety and carried two cornerbacks to the 18-yard line. Myles told Guthrie to stop warming up.

Two plays later Cowboys' running back Theunis Adkins plunged to a first and goal at the Texans' five-yard line, but his team never came closer to the goal line. As the ball on the field goal attempt split the uprights to tie the game and the Mexican announcer yelled, "Bravo, Señor Gerrone," the Cowboys retreated to the sidelines for Myles' instructions for the kickoff.

Myles grabbed Gerrone's single bladed facemask and gritted his teeth. "Kick the fucker out of the end zone, amigo."

Gerrone looked up at Myles, pointing toward the goal line and said, "Como?"

Señor Gerrone lined up for the kick alongside the special teamers and trotted toward the ball. As he planted his left cleat on the artificial turf, he slipped. He swung his right toe at the ball and drilled a worm burner downfield. The ball looked like a Mexican jumping bean as the Texans' special teams players attempted to recover it. Several Cowboys dove at the ball. It took officials three minutes to dig through the dog pile and discover through a call of 83,000 boos that the Cowboys were in business with the ball on the Texans 31-yard line with 1:27 left on the clock.

Myles grabbed Beezley's facemask. "Houston's only got one timeout. Take a knee three plays, call timeout with five seconds left, and maybe this greaser can slide one through there."

Gerrone trotted onto the field, lined up the 49-yard field goal, made the sign of the cross and looked upward as if to say, "Por favor, Dios. Por favor."

The ball was snapped and placed. Gerrone took two steps and aimed his foot at the ball, just below the fingers of the holder, the punter Flanders. The ball floated end over end into the waning sunlight at the goalpost. Myles stared. So did Hilfy, Beezley and all the Cowboys' players, coaches and spectators hoping to avoid overtime and end their nasty three-game losing streak and another tongue-lashing from the head coach.

Jack stared also from the auxiliary press box but didn't need to wait for the signal from the officials or hear the crowd's reaction to discover if the ball had whistled through the uprights.

He looked over to the Mexican play-by-play man.

"Bravo, Señor Gerrone. Bravo."

14

As far as party buses go, nothing could compare to the Cowboy Express. The converted school bus had been painted Cowboy colors – blue, silver, and white – and had stars and star players, past and present, sketched around the outside. The tires were dyed blue with whitewalls, and the hood ornament was a miniature Cowboys' football helmet.

The inside had some of the most loyal fans and heaviest boozers in Cowboys' history. They drank on the way to the game; they drank on the way from the game. It didn't matter if the Cowboys played in Houston or Seattle or in Buffalo, they drank. The farther away the game, the drunker the passengers. The drunker they became, the louder they got.

No tickets were needed. You just stuck $10 into the life-size Cowboys' helmet held by the bus driver and climbed aboard. The bus seated 40 and had room for another 10 standing-room-only passengers and another 10 in the overhead luggage rack.

Jack had thought a few years before about writing a column, but that meant he would have had to ride in it. The bus stories were legendary. Like when the air conditioner broke coming back from the season opener in Phoenix and everyone kept cool by opening all the windows and doors and taking off all their clothes. Like when the heater broke on the way back from a playoff game in Chicago – in January – and someone piled twigs in a beer cooler and started a fire. Like when the fan belt broke en route to Atlanta and a new one was constructed from the panty hose from female passengers.

The Cowboy Express must have had a half-million miles on it and shook like the Runaway Mine Train at Six Flags. With no other way back to Dallas, Jack had no other choice. He must have looked out of place as he stepped onto the bus. He was the only passenger not wearing a Cowboys' jersey, sipping a Budweiser, and yelling, "Yee-haw."

Most wore Rex Fanning Number 7 in the white, blue, or throw-back jersey. There were a few 34's with "Adkins" on the back and 84 with Heath Garrett's name. Many had blue and silver face paint. These were the masses, the people who carry signs of a "D" and a fence at games or in this game, "Mess with Texans." These are the kind of people who would go to the airport to welcome the Cowboys before they would go there to welcome their own son. People who had a Cowboys' pennant and a Cowboys Cheerleaders' poster, instead of family portraits, on their living room wall. These people read Jack's column during their Monday morning dump. Oh, how they must have hated him.

One diehard entering the bus hollered, "Wonder what that asshole Jack Byrne's gonna write tomorrow" without anyone responding, "Nothin,' that sumbitch is dead."

Jack snuck to the very back of the bus and hid into the dark left corner in the hope that no one recognized him from his column mugshot. If he didn't die on the way *to* Houston, he certainly would die on the way *from* Houston. With the bus well over the passenger capacity and nearing a Guinness Book record, the driver fired up the engine. Jack didn't know what was louder the engine or the screaming fans. Breaking that three-game losing streak was a good reason to celebrate.

"Who are we?" a chubby man wearing middle linebacker Muta Falusa's Number 50 shouted.

"Cowboys," everyone but Jack screamed

This was repeated three times, and became louder with every scream.

IT WAS DEFINITELY LOUDER in the bus than the visiting locker room, where the Cowboys were relieved to be spared another postgame rant from their head coach. The only injury was suffered by the third string quarterback during the player introductions. Scott Hilfinger sat in the corner of the locker room with an ice bag on his sore ribs, while the sportswriters filtered through the locker room with their notepads and tape recorders and talking to seemingly every player but him. What would they ask Hilfy? "How does it feel to get clothe-lined by the defensive line coach and make a total ass of yourself in front of 83,000 people?"

It sounded like there were 83,000 people on the bus as it rocked north up I-45 and smelled of beer, sweat, and nachos. When the incoherently drunk man next to him dropped his iPod, Jack picked it up and stuffed the ear pieces into his ear holes. He scrolled down the artist list on the lit screen to the only non-country and western group – Simon and Garfunkel. He turned the volume to full to silence the crowd noise and pressed the play button.

Hello darkness, my old friend
I've come to talk with you again
Because a vision softly creeping
Left its seeds while I was sleeping
And the vision that was planted in my brain
Still remains
Within the sound of silence

Jack looked out the window at the roadside billboards that lit the dark four-lane highway. Soon the bus crept past the burial site of The Dallas Star staff car and its three passengers. It was now a ghost stop without a gas station and shops with boarded up windows. Jack thought of Yo-Lo and how he would never again see that bubbly smile of wired teeth. How Lanny would no longer spit another wad of tobacco. How their families must be missing them and welcoming their friends who had arrived in town for their funerals this week.

He thought about Jeanie. What it must be like going to bed alone and wondering what the future holds for her. How many golf balls had she hit since learning her husband had been charred beyond recognition. Did the nightmare of his burning flesh overcome the nightmare of missing the Q-school cut?

And what of Graham Repert? Was anybody missing him? Or was he just another ordinary schlep who had never done anything and wasn't going anywhere – although he did look like he was running away from something. Then again, no one but Jack knew he was dead.

Several miles later, the bus pulled to the side of the highway. Was it the radiator? The fuel pump? The back and front doors opened and passengers scattered into the woods. This is what happens when there is no on-board toilet and an endless supply of Budweiser. A five-hour drive to Dallas could turn into a nine-hour drive with frequent urinating and/or vomiting stops.

Jack didn't want to take that long, and Simon and Garfunkel no longer could drown out the bus party. He walked down the road 100 yards and realized this was where Lanny had picked up Graham. "I remember that old farmhouse there," Jack mumbled.

He walked another 100 yards and saw a rusted yellow Volkswagon van stranded in the ditch on the other side of the road. Jack dug into Graham's long black overcoat and pulled out the VW key. "Could it be?" He thought.

Jack sprinted across the highway and opened the door o the Volkswagon. He put the key into the ignition and twisted it. The fuel gauge read empty.

"That's why he was hitchhiking." Jack said to no one. "But why did he abandon his car? Why Houston?"

Jack looked up, and the Cowboy Express rolled back onto the highway. Jack didn't bother chasing it. He had his own bus. He just had to find it a drink of gasoline. He jogged back up the highway, likely in Graham's footprints. He stopped at the farmhouse but didn't knock on the door. All the lights were off. The garage door was open, and Jack noticed a one gallon gasoline can.

Within seconds, Jack was pouring the contents of the full can into the VW van fuel tank and left a drop for the carburetor. He tossed the empty gas can into the ditch and jumped into the driver's seat while sniffing old beer, sweat, and nachos. It took several ignition twists and accelerator pumps, but the VW started. He drove a U-turn across the median strip and onto the highway. "Big D, here we come," he said, steering a wheel bigger than the one on the Cowboy Express.

The old VW van had more miles than the Cowboy Express bus, but it had more zip. After a quick stop at an all-night gas station, Jack gunned the VW back onto the highway. He honked at the parked Express passengers doing their business in the bushes and zoomed toward Dallas. Soon he could see Ritz Tower in the distance and the rest of the Dallas skyline.

Jack drove past The Dallas Star parking lot, finding it difficult to believe that barely four days had passed since he left on the fateful trip to Houston. He parked on the street and whirled past downtown bars well past their curfew and the leaves and paper debris that swirled about the sidewalk toward another Dippity Donut feast with a hunger in his stomach and the song in his brain from the iPod he abandoned on the Cowboy Express.

In restless dreams I walked alone
Narrow streets of cobblestone
'Neath the halo of a street lamp
I turned my collar to the cold and damp
When my eyes were stabbed by the flash of a neon light
That split the night
And touched the sound of silence

15

For all of his life, the first section of the newspaper Jack flipped to was the sports page. But as he sat in the back corner booth at the Dippity Donut shop in downtown Dallas dunking a glazed donut into his hot chocolate, he went straight to the obituaries.

"Looks like everyone died in alphabetical order again," Jack joked to himself as he opened the Sunday newspaper left on the counter. The other three customers were either passed out or semi-conscious. The Arab donut clerk, who probably knew Jack's face from previous visits but not his name, didn't notice him talking to himself and couldn't have cared less if he was dead or alive.

According to The Dallas Star obituaries, he was still alive. There was an obituary notice for a Jack Burne, not for a Jack Byrne.

"Those idiots," Jack said.

Those idiots also posted his wrong birthdate and didn't include a photograph. Jack bit into another donut. "How hard would have been to simply use my column mug?"

The four-line obituary likely was written by an intern on deadline and likely from information Jeanie had sent to the funeral home. The formula obit was not much different from the 86-year-old granny in the next column. "At least the wrinkled old prune got a photo," Jack said.

All Jack got was "... died suddenly on November 30 at age 42. He was a sports reporter for The Dallas Star. He is survived by his wife Jeanine, a women's golf professional and his sister, Katherine. Services will be held noon Tuesday, December 6 at St. Blaise Catholic Church in Geburtville."

"Geburtville?" Jack shook the newpaper. "Is she crazy?"

Jack couldn't understand why Jeanie chose a hometown he never considered home to stage his final send-off. He hadn't been there since the night of his high school graduation and hadn't been to St. Blaise since his baptism. The town was an hour's drive northeast of Dallas, and the church, as Jack remembered from the outside, was not nearly big enough for a celebrity funeral. "Pretty inconvenient for all my co-workers, friends, and readers," he thought.

Jack had to excuse Jeanie. Where they would be eulogized or buried in case of sudden death never came up in conversation, which rarely centered on anything other than football or golf. He told her little of his family. All she knew was that Jack hadn't seen or heard from Katherine, a neurologist somewhere in the Northeast, since their parents were killed in a car accident in 1990.

Jack read down the alphabet of the deceased until he came to Lopez, Yolanda. There was a lovely picture of her bubbly smile and an obit column that stretched down the page. Her survivors' list included her parents and grandparents, five sisters and three brothers, aunts and uncles, nephews and nieces, and her longtime boyfriend, Hector. The obit read that the "The Lord has called this gentle soul and loving servant to be with Him in Heaven. Her earthly life will be dearly missed by the many lives she touched. Her soft-hearted appeal, her care-free attitude, her caring nature were the memories she has left her survivors and the lesson on how they should live."

"Saint Yo-Lo," Jack mumbled.

Jack then read that the funeral Mass was slated for that evening at the Santa Maria Catholic Cathedral. "They should have had my funeral there," Jack thought. "That place is huge and it's about two football fields from here. People could have come here afterwards to eat donuts and share their stories about me."

Jack took his last donut, a cinnamon twist, and bit into it as he went further down the alphabet to Pickett, Lawrence. Lanny had left behind a loving wife, two daughters, a son, and his beloved basset hound, Rolph. A memorial service would be held for him at noon Monday at Shady Shores Park, on the banks of White Rock Lake, where Lanny spent much of his leisure time.

"Time chewin' tobacky and chewin' the fat," Jack thought.

THE FRONT DOOR of Dippity Donuts swung open. A cold draft preceded the entrance of a chubby bald man with a smug smile and a hot-off-the-press Dallas Star in one hand and Fort Worth Express in the other.

Jack hid behind the newspaper from his booth. "That Sawed Off Stack of Shit," Jack whispered as the Executive Sports Editor marched to the counter.

"Mr. A-Rab, two cream-filled donuts and a cup of hot coffee. Make it snappy."

Soss sat three booths in front of Jack, his back facing him. He opened The Dallas Star first with the intent of soaking in his team's splendid coverage and later the Fort Worth Express to mock and belittle their amateurish writing and blown coverage.

Jack wanted so badly to sneak a peek over his shoulder and read the Star's Cowboys' coverage and do his own smirking for how much the relief writers screwed it up. Soss gave no hint of a problem. He sipped his coffee and nodded with every column word from Jack's replacement. He browsed through a few more pages before walking to the restroom behind Jack's booth. Jack ducked behind his newspaper as Soss breezed past him, giving off a scent of bourbon he likely consumed at the Kazbar before nabbing the first newspaper off the conveyor belt at The Dallas Star press room.

As soon as he heard the restroom door shut, Jack sprinted to Soss' table and grabbed the Star sports page. He rushed back to his booth and stared in shock at the mug on the front of the sports page of the new Dallas Star columnist – Penny Pettigrew, the assistant librarian from the Morgue.

Jack figured Soss offered her the column in return for a game of hide the salami, to prove a point that anyone could replace him, or to make himself a bigger man for finding talent in unusual places. Perhaps, all of the three.

Jack read Penny's column to himself, his lips curling into more of a smirk the more he read.

The pigskin was held by a finger tip on the bright green turf in the late afternoon of a Sunday gridiron thriller in a Houston stadium with 83,000 pairs of eyes staring at it. Agberto Gerrone, a man with a star on his helmet and a fire in his heart, stared also. But not for long. He had a job to do or else he would be out of a job.

Jack gripped either side of the paper, "What the fuck?"

He read on:

Agberto took three steps, planted his left leg, and then flung his right toe at the ball. Suddenly, the ball launched over the hungry, hulking defenders like a NASA space rocket and shot toward the steel poles being held by a crossbar and a stand.

"It's called a goalpost, honey." Jack said, then kept reading.

The pigskin flew magnificently end-over-end and perfectly between the posts, its flight interrupted by a screen that kept it from going into a crowd that would soon go home disappointed. Agberto jumped and prayed and slapped his teammates and soon would say to all of the reporters who surrounded him in the locker room, 'Mi siento bien.'"

Translation: "I feel good."

Jack's smirk turned into a frown. "What a crock of shit."

He couldn't believe his column would now read like a romance novel, full of adjectives and adverbs and descriptions of every movement. Jack would have written about Jarmelle Beezley's first NFL start, about the Cowboys stubborn defense, or about Hilfy being clothe-lined before he would write about a former Mexican soccer-star-turned-NFL-kicker which has been done to death. Sports columnists on deadline don't have time for interpreters.

Jack stuffed the sports page in the garbage bin. He marched toward the front door but stopped as he passed Soss' table and stared at his half-empty coffee cup. Jack snuck behind the counter, grabbed the coffee pot roasting on a hot plate, and filled Soss' cup with the boiling caffeine. Jack made it back to his table just as Soss came out of the restroom.

Jack peered atop his booth as Soss frantically looked around for his sports page. Then he took a long swig of scalding coffee, slammed the cup on the table, and sprayed the hot lava all over the walls of the donut shop. As a bonus, the cup broke and the ungulped coffee burned his right hand.

"Yeeee-ow!" Soss woke up the other customers and likely the Arab, who rushed a glass of water to him. "Who the fuck filled my cup?"

Jack snickered to himself and thought, "That's for the time you cut my story on the blind high school football player to make room for a feature on freestyle skateboarding."

Soss walked around the shop searching for the culprit. When he came to the back corner booth, it was empty. Jack had escaped out the back door, leaving donut crumbs and a hot chocolate mug and Sunday's newspaper. Everything but the obituary page.

16

The sun broke through the clouds and the dirt-caked windows of the Volkswagon van to wake Jack in time for Lanny's memorial service. Jack wouldn't have to travel much farther from where he had parked under a grove of trees within several van lengths of White Rock Lake.

Too late and too dark to find Graham Repert's apartment – or to find out if he even had one – Jack opted for a World War II sleeping bag atop a rat eaten mattress in a space where there used to be three rows of seats. The black overcoat that kept him from freezing to death now caused him to sweat as the sun's rays heated the van like a blow torch.

Jack's stomach growled, and he wished he'd have grabbed a half-dozen Dippity Donuts to go before filling his boss' cup with a boiling potion that likely burned the roof off his mouth. Jack wondered how far away the memorial service was. The bagpipes blaring in the distance provided the answer.

He followed the sound to a grassy area next to the lake where attendants were setting up chairs and caterers were bringing plates of food to a nearby tent. "Lunchtime," Jack thought.

He used his nose to sniff out the funeral reception and helped himself to a ham sandwich and a fistful of potato chips. The attendant went on about her business without noticing the uninvited mourner stuffing his face or telling him, "The food is for after the service."

Jack waited for the attendant to turn around, before grabbing another sandwich and sliding it into his overcoat.

He walked back to the van and munched on the sandwich as the guests arrived. From Jack's distant vantage point it was quickly evident there weren't enough chairs. Friends, family, and admirers came from every direction around the lake. About every Dallas Star writer and editor he knew was there – including Soss, who had a bandage on his right hand and likely some burn medication on his lips. "No coffee for him at the reception," Jack thought.

Lanny's wife and his two daughters and son marched down a makeshift aisle as the bagpipes signified the start of the memorial service. They were accompanied by Rolph, Lanny's beloved basset hound, who lay down in the front and cried with the rest of the mourners.

Jack snuck closer and hid behind a big oak tree. A preacher said a few prayers and spoke of Lanny's life, which seemed to be surrounded by the lake. He grew up not far from the lake, and his father often took him fishing on his boat. He played little league baseball on an adjacent ball park and he and his friends often came to the lake for a cookout. He took his first photographs at the lake, at dawn, of white swans gliding across the glassy waters. He proposed to his wife and married her on the very spot the preacher spoke and bought a house with a lake view.

Lanny took his own son out onto the lake just as his own father did with him. He and his family and friends would take long walks along the lake, shared stories and spit tobacco on the ground, and always accompanied by Rolph.

"If any of Lanny's ashes would have been found," the preacher said, "they would be spread around this lake."

"Or stored in his spittoon," Jack whispered to himself.

The preacher said Lanny is no longer strolling along this lake, but "I know his spirit still does." The preacher was followed by eulogies from 18 friends and some family members, often having to pause to wipe their eyes. Bagpipes signified the end of the service as the guests retreated to the tent for warm hugs and whatever ham was left.

Jack retreated to the van and drove away, careful not to run over Lanny's ghost on his afternoon stroll.

JACK TOOK A LATE AFTERNOON NAP in the back of the van and when he awoke it was dark. He wiped the condensation off the window and saw lights coming from Santa Maria Cathedral and people in black suits and dresses filing into the church. He had been the first guest to reach the parking lot and the last to enter the church. He snuck up to the balcony, hid behind a curtain, and saw the photographs of an always smiling Yo-Lo flashed on a large screen and to the piped-in music of Sarah McLachlan's "I will remember you."

Handkerchiefs were out in force even from the sports staff which was spread throughout the church. Soss sat near the front with his wife, who did enough crying for both of them.

"I'd cry a lot too if I was married to Soss," Jack thought.

The music stopped, the lights were turned off, and candles were lit and held by the packed congregation which stood and sang as the organist played Amazing Grace. The candlelit Mass suited Jack, because it eliminated the possibility of being caught by a wandering dry eye. Much kneeling, standing, and sitting preceded the Bishop's passionate eulogy.

"Death does not discriminate between young and old, black and white, men and women, or good and bad." His voice echoed off the tall stained-glass windows. "It can come after a long struggle or like, in Yolanda's case, a flash in the night."

The Bishop paused and his voice resounded from the pulpit. "That's why you live each day, each moment, each breath to the fullest. No one did that better than Yolanda Lopez."

He said Yo-Lo lived the way a person should live – constantly caring for those around her and making everyone feel wanted, accepted, loved. He said she kept a calendar of birthdays of her parents and grandparents, brothers and sisters, nieces and nephews, and close friends and never missed sending them a card with a special note inside. She had taken a packet of Christmas cards and her address book with her to Houston.

Jack tipped-toed down the balcony stairs and out of the cathedral, while thinking, "I've got to get out of here before the canonization."

Ghosts of the Gridiron

He crept next door to an empty room where Jack helped himself to a paper plate of enchiladas, refried beans, and brownies the deceased's sister made from Yo-Lo's favorite recipe. "Saint Yo-Lo would want me to do this," he thought.

Jack grabbed two Coronas from behind the bar and walked to his van in the corner of the Cathedral parking lot. He sat in the driver's seat with Graham's overcoat raised over his head and sipped the glass bottles as the mourners walked past with their arms around each other, some still sobbing.

Whatever thoughts he had about being the featured guest at his own funeral multiplied by the time he downed the final drop of Corona. Curiosity had now consumed him. How many family and friends would make the trek to Geburtville? Who would give the eulogies? How would he be glorified, remembered? Would Jeanie say a few words or would she be too overcome with grief, sadness, and guilt to utter a word about her beloved husband?

Jack wrapped the overcoat around him and rolled himself into the old sleeping bag. He did not sleep. He was too excited about crashing his own funeral. So excited that at dawn he swept the Corona bottles out of the driver's seat, revved up the engine, and drove the VW van back to the highway via a Dippity Donut stopover for a dozen glazed. The funeral march to Geburtville had begun.

17

Geburtville wasn't the ghost town Jack expected as he steered Graham Repert's rusted yellow VW van through the small downtown stretch on the morning of his funeral. The town looked much the same as in his youth, except that most of the stores had changed names and there were more people milling around.

Oliver's Department Store, where Jack spent most fall Sundays watching Dallas Cowboys' games through the storefront window, was now Ollie's Electronics. The cathode ray tube television was now replaced by a large flat screen, but the price was about the same. The Geburtville Library, where Jack told his parents he was headed every Sunday, was conveniently still located next door.

Jack opened his driver's side window and sniffed fresh meats from the former Sal's Butchery, now called the Sausage Grinder. Bryson's Bakery, where Jack acquired his taste for donuts, was now Bryson's Bagels. There were similar looking dress shops and shoe shops and stationary stores. Marvin's Sporting Goods, where Jack bought his first football cleats, was now Run and Sun. Quaint outdoor cafes with small, round tables were still there and the root beer still hadn't been replaced by real beer. Other than the town's name, Geburtville never really adopted its German heritage. Not much sauerkraut sold, and Octoberfests were non-existent.

Jack looked out the van window for a pub but couldn't find one. "What's a German town without beer?" he thought.

The town now had flower-filled baskets hanging above the sidewalks, and Christmas lights strung over the store windows. Everything was different but it was the same. "Maybe you *can* go home," Jack said as he drove away from the town center.

Jack thought Geburtville would have deteriorated to a state of dystopia, like many of the small towns in Northeast Texas. What saved Geburtville was the rapidly-growing housing industry north of

Dallas. Builders relied on wood from the Geburtville Sawmill, where Jack's father and so many other fathers worked. They never lost their jobs, only their fingers. Also, Geburtville was far enough from Dallas not to become a suburb like many closer towns that were over-run by the big city.

The one casualty of the town's success was Jack's old high school, which Jack drove by just past the town square. A new high school was built, and the old red brick building stood there waiting for a wrecking ball. Jack shook his head and stared straight through the van's windshield. He refused to look at the old Gebbie Bowl, where his football career suffered a cruel and humiliating death. Jack found it too painful too even peek.

He pressed the accelerator, turned left down a gravel road, and looked straight ahead at a tall structure he had not seen since his baptism – the St. Blaise Church steeple. He parked the van at the side of the church and walked inside. Jack snickered, "Smaller than I remember."

He scratched his head. "How are they going to fit all the people in here for my funeral?"

He counted 15 wooden pews on either side of the middle aisle leading to the altar rail, estimated 12 mourners per pew times two, equals 360 people. "They're gonna need a bigger church."

Jack gathered some chairs in the lounge next door and put them in rows in the vestibule. He moved the holy water font to the side to make room for more chairs. Jack looked around at the chairs and recalculated the seating capacity. "Still not enough, but it will have to do," he mumbled. "Some people will have to stand. You can't rely on Jeanie for anything."

Jack retreated to the VW and daydreamed about his funeral and about how he might present himself. He lay on the mattress in the back and closed his eyes.

"Maybe I pop out of a casket?" Jack thought. "When the priest asks for volunteers to give a tribute, I walk to the pulpit and start eulogizing myself. Or why not just sit amongst the congregation until someone recognizes me and screams?"

He kept thinking until he ran out of steam.

JACK AWOKE TO CHURCH BELLS he thought tolled for he. He looked at the digital numbers on his watch, "Eleven-thirty?"

Jack peered out the back window of the van and saw an empty parking lot. No hearse. No cars. No early arrivals in black suits and dresses and soggy white handkerchiefs. He rechecked the newspaper to make sure he had the right time and place.

"Probably so many cars that they got backed up on the highway," Jack said.

Then an old black station wagon appeared in the distance, its tires kicking up dirt from the gravel road. The station wagon, with the gold letters that formed "Geburtville Funeral Home," entered the parking lot and stopped at the front steps of the church. Two men in black suits got out, opened the back door, and carried a western-style wooden coffin up the church steps.

"Rent-a-coffin," Jack said. "They must have put a lot of my memorabilia in there. My best columns, feature stories, my old Tandy computer, my Dallas Cowboys' toboggan hat, my old football cleats, some birthday cards, perhaps a sentimental letter Jeanie wrote me after I died, maybe a Dippity Donuts' box."

Jack was too big for the coffin, so he snuck into another box – the church confessional in the back corner of the church. It was pitch-black in that little room, and the doors were properly oiled. He could crack open the door without anyone hearing or seeing him and he could hear perfectly. The tires of cars leaving the gravel road and coming to a stop in the parking lot. People whispering as they entered the church. Microphones tested. Candles being lit and sending smoke fumes into the air. The organist cranking up Pachelbel's Canon in D major.

"A little loud and scratchy but I like it," Jack thought as he pressed a button on his watch to see the glow-in-the-dark numbers 11:47 on his watch. "I think this is what they played at my wedding."

The music played for a full 15 minutes and drowned out what Jack speculated a herd of footsteps and sobbing moving into the church and mourners settling into the pews. Suddenly, the music stopped.

Jack cracked open the confessional door and saw his wife standing at the entrance to the church. He had imagined her wearing a long black gown and black veil covering the black tears streaming from her eye-liner. Instead, she wore a sky blue mid-thigh length dress with no sleeves. Her hair was tied in a pony-tail, the same way she wears it for a golf tournament. She walked toward the front pew like she was strolling down a fairway, her white purse dangling from her right shoulder. The purse was too small to carry a handkerchief.

Jack looked around at the church and counted the people. "One-two-three-four-five-six-seven-eight-nine-ten-eleven-twelve."

They spread out around the church, but they could have fit into one pew. "So much for those fucking chairs I put out," Jack thought. "You get more people at a pet funeral."

There were no flowers on the altar, just a coffin sitting on a metal stand that Jeanie didn't think to place her hand on as she reached the front pew and sat down. The mourners were mostly elderly people, likely locals whom his parents knew when he was growing up and came for the post service refreshments that Jeanie also didn't organise. His sister did not attend. The only person from The Dallas Star was a high school sportswriter whom Jack had never met.

"A token from the sports department," Jack thought. "Soss probably sent him, because he's covering the high school basketball game here tonight."

The organist interrupted with the opening song, "How Great thou Art," a good choice if the song was about Jack and if anyone knew the words. No one bothered to make programs.

A priest who looked and talked like an old Leprechaun walked up the center aisle and turned around in front of the altar table. He smiled and barely waited for the final mourner to sit down before rushing through the intro like he had to catch the first boat back to Dublin. He needed an interpreter who spoke English.

"We gatter dis mornin' – ah, aftanoon – to pray for da repose of da soul of Jack Byrne, a gud man who led a trilling life of a sport writer. He was baptized in dis church on da turd of August, nineteen hunderd and sixty-tree and died tragically on November Tirtieth."

His three bible readings were delivered with a similar down-tempo and were as difficult to comprehend. Some tuned out mourners looked around at the stations of the cross on the church side walls. Another checked his wrist watch, and another read a text message on his cellphone.

"Didn't Jeanie audition this guy before she booked him?" Jack thought, still peering from inside the confessional.

Mercifully, Father O'Malley or O'Reilly or O'Shaughnessy, O'Something, did not give the eulogy. He invited anyone to come forward and share a story about Jack's life. There were no takers. Everyone looked at each other and the priest said, "Anyone?"

The confessional door opened wider but Jack stayed put. A wrinkled man in a plaid sport coat and fresh pressed pants walked to the pulpit, looked around at the audience, took out a piece of scribbled paper and a handkerchief, and leaned into the microphone.

"Jack was a great man, a wonderful human being who treated everyone he met with respect. He was kind, lovable, giving, and always thought about others."

Jeanie looked up at the pulpit, as if to say, "Are we talking about the same Jack Byrne here?"

Jack clenched his fist. "Must be one of my loyal readers," he thought.

The old man continued. "He meant so much to me in the short time we knew each other. He was my friend, my mentor, my hero, and, and, and."

"And what?" Jack thought.

"And my lover."

Jeanie opened her mouth in shock. The others whispered to each other. Jack almost rushed out of the confessional.

"We first met in boot camp at the end of the second World War, me a lonely buck private and he a spunky sergeant. Little did we know how much our friendship would grow."

Father O', recognizing the quizzical looks from his audience and the illogical time frame, walked to the pulpit and whispered in the old man's ear. The old man turned redder than the priest, "Jack 'Byrne?' Oh, I thought it was Jack 'Burns' that died. Thank God."

Everyone chuckled as the old man shook his head and marched out of the church. Father O' walked back to the altar. "Now dat we got tat straight, we say a final blessin' for Jack Burns, I mean Byrne, and wish him a fond farewell."

Father O' made a rapid sign of the cross gesture, and the funeral was over. Not even a closing song. The dry-eyed Jeanie followed the priest down the aisle, thanked him, shook some of the others' hands, and marched out of the church.

JACK WAITED FOR EVERYONE ELSE to depart before sneaking out of the confessional and into the vestibule and hiding behind a large statue of the Virgin Mary.

Jeanie marched from the parking lot with a gym bag, re-entered the church, and slipped into the restroom. Within three minutes she had changed into her normal golfing attire – red slacks, pink sweater atop a white polo shirt, red golf hat, and white spikeless golf shoes – and strolled out of the church with her dress and high heels stuffed in her gym bag.

Jack emerged from the statue and stared out the glass door as Jeanie sat behind the wheel of his red Mazda Miata with her golf clubs resting upright on the passenger seat and sped out of the parking lot and down the road like she had a 1:30 tee time back at the Forest Green Country Club.

"Can't believe she's driving my car." Specks of spit flew out of Jack's mouth and onto the glass. He walked out of the church to the VW and returned when he realized he had left Graham's black overcoat in the confessional. He didn't stop for a last look at his funeral setting or the rent-a-coffin that sat before the altar, waiting for its ride back to the funeral home. He wanted out of Geburtville more than he did as a teenager. The confessional door shut behind him as he felt around for the coat in the tiny dark box.

His search was interrupted by the soft words of a deep-voiced orator that floated out of a screen on the wall and echoed around the room. "In the name of the father and of the son and of the holy spirit. Amen."

In contrast to Father O', every syllable was pronounced.

Jack shook and looked around for the voice. "Who's there?"

"I am here for your confession."

Jack snickered. "My confession? You might be in here for a while, pal."

"You can take as long as you like, my son."

There was nowhere to sit, so Jack knelt on the padded kneeler in front of the screen. "Look, Padre, I just came in to retrieve my coat and scram. I got no time to confess any of my sins. Besides I'm not Catholic. I mean I was baptized here, but I never went to church."

"Does not matter. God is always present to hear what is inside your heart."

"I don't believe in God."

"You must believe; otherwise you would not be here."

"I told you I just came in to get my coat. Besides, what's God ever done for me?"

There was a brief pause. "Breathe, my son."

"What?"

"Just close your eyes and take a nice long breath."

Jack, still mesmerized by The Voice, obeyed but with a short quick breath. "Ok, can I go now?"

"Sure, and go with God."

"I just told you, I don't believe in him."

"If simple breathing is not enough, then what would it take to believe."

"A miracle."

There was another short pause and then The Voice again, "You mean like a parting of the Red Sea."

"Yeah, that would do it."

"Well, my son, I hope you find a Red Sea parting. But remember you are always welcome to come back and talk about anything, whether you believe in God or not."

"Sure thing, Father." Jack opened the door and put on the black overcoat. He walked toward the vestibule and looked back at the coffin and wondered what remarkable memorabilia of his life Jeanie had placed inside. He walked down the aisle and placed his hand on the coffin. He opened the lid and peered inside.

Empty.

18

Jeanine Pratt marched onto the Forest Green Country Club driving range an hour after her husband's funeral, dropped her golf bag in a tee box, pulled out her Big Bertha driver, pushed a tee and ball into the cold, yellowish-brown turf, took one practice swing, planted her driver behind the white Titleist, swaggered her hips, lashed at the ball, and sliced it so badly it cleared the barrier net on the right side of the range and the adjacent four-lane roadway and skidded into a creek.

She hooked her next drive into the practice putting green. She topped her next ball and sent it skidding atop the grass and killing winter worms. Her next shot was a pop up with a hang-time twice as long as a fair-caught punt in the NFL.

Her local caddy, Chad, stood at a ball washer, staring at Jeanie from the first tee while moving the same spotlessly clean ball up and down on the mud scraper.

"Jeanine's lookin' hotter 'n ever," Chad told the bespectacled greenskeeper Bernie Ross. "Look at the way her titties bob up and down like jello after every drive."

"Her ass looks pretty nice in those tight slacks too," Bernie said. "Too bad she's married."

Chad stopped washing the ball and looked at Bernie. "You haven't heard? Her ol' man got fried in a car explosion last week. You are starin' at one fine lookin' widow."

Bernie also stared and had watched and heard from Chad about how chummy Jeanie and her caddy had become over the past year. Now there was nothing standing in Chad's way of Chad's version of "a hole in one."

"Man," Bernie said, "if you don't fuck that you're crazy."

Jeanie pressed another Titlest into the ground, took her eyes off the ball upon impact, and stubbed the turf. The ball dribbled ahead of the tee box before dying 35 yards in front of her.

Jeanie dropped the club and her butt to the ground, sat cross-legged, and put palms to her eyes. The tear drops that never came the night of November 30th finally spilled like the rapids down her pink sweater sleeves.

JEANIE WAS SNUG in her bed and reading her mentor's "Golf: The Legend's Way" for the 47th time at 11:45pm on the last day of November, when the door bell rang. It rang three more times before she shouted, "Did ya' lose your key again, Jack, or are you too drunk to fit it into the door?"

The doorbell rang twice more before she threw off the covers and marched to the door, mumbling, "It's about time you slithered back here to apologize."

She unlocked the door and peered around it to an African-Amercan in the blue Dallas police garb and all the bells and whistles – gun, billy club, badge. He tipped his hat. "Ma'am, can I come in?"

"No. Just say whatever and let me go back to bed. You're letting a cold draught into my house."

"All right," the officer said. "The Dallas Star vehicle your husband was traveling in tonight was hit by tanker at a gas station in Central Texas and exploded. No one in the vehicle survived."

Jeanie death-gripped the door. "Are you sure it was my husband?"

"Jack Byrne, ma'am. He was traveling in the backseat of the vehicle. Confirmed by the gas station attendant and the sports department."

Jeanie said nothing, just kept staring at the porch light shining off the officer's badge and not believing a word of it.

"Sorry if you don't believe me, ma'am. But your husband has been confirmed dead."

Jeanie looked down at her pink slippers and started laughing. She swung open the door, pushed the police officer aside, and wandered around the front yard in her pink silk pajamas. "Where are you, Jack? The joke's over. Come out, please. I'll forgive you."

She turned to the police officer. "Who are you, one of Jack's drinking buddies? Where'd you get the fake uniform?"

"Not fake, ma'am. Unfortunately, this is for real."

"Oh yeah? Where's your police car?"

"Back at the station. I'm off-duty and was just making this call on my way home."

Jeanie walked back to the front door. "You can go on home now, and tell Jack this has to be the stupidest trick he's ever tried to play on me."

Jeanie walked to the practice tee at Forest Green at 10 a.m. the next morning amidst the stares from the pro shop. The Legend, armed with the front section of The Dallas Star, greeted her as she loosened up.

"What in God's sake you doin' here, Jeanine?"

"Warming up for my practice round, whattaya think I'm doin'?"

"No one's told you?"

"Told me what?"

The Legend showed her the newspaper. Jeanie read the headline, "Massive explosion kills three."

She took out her golf glove and stretched it over her left hand. "So you are in on the gag, too."

"What gag?"

"Oh come on. Jack works for a newspaper. He can rig up a front page just like that, easy."

The Legend walked back to the clubhouse as Jeanie whacked balls down the middle of the driving range. Chad stared at her out the window. "You done tell Jeanine that her ol' man just bit the big one, Daddy?"

"That lady is in denial, son. Deep denial. It will hit her, and it will hit her like a ton of bricks."

It would have taken a brick to shake Jeanie. Television and radio news reports of the crash. Friends calling and coming by to console her. Funeral director calling to arrange a service. Obituary notice. On the Sunday, the Legend's wife drove her to the crash site. Jeanie looked down at the big hole and said. "Nah, Jack's not down there."

"How do you know that, dear?"

"I just know it; I just feel it."

Jeanie referred the funeral director to Jack's sister, who made the arrangements in Geburtville but was either too busy with her hospital work or too snowed in to head south or she just didn't care.

Jeanie went to the funeral fully expecting Jack to pop out of the coffin or give his own eulogy. She figured her driving his Mazda Miata would force him to come raging back from the dead. But, even though she felt his presence, he never showed up.

As she drove onto LBJ Freeway, she turned on the radio. A voice echoed off convertible roof.

How long will I love you
As long as stars are above you
And longer if I can
How long will I need you
As long as the seasons need to
Follow their plan

Jeanie easily recognized the Waterboys' song, the same song that Jack played on the boom box next the bed in his messy apartment as the two first made love. He sang to her as he gently touched his lips against hers and applied little kisses down on her neck to her firm breasts and to her hard nipples.

How long will I be with you
As long as the sea is bound to
Wash up on the sand

Jack stopped singing. He slid his warm hands down Jeanie's back to her buttocks and gently rolled on top of her as she spread her legs and dug her heels into his soft thighs. The words barely could be heard over the panting, moaning, thrusting, loving.

How long will I want you
As long as you want me to
And longer by far.

    Jeanie steered the sports car into the parking lot of the country club, stared down at the steering wheel, and lightly touched her breasts. She remembered what Jack told her after the music stopped and they lay, naked, holding each other in absolute bliss.
    "Are you happy?" he asked.
    "I will always be happy if I am with you, Jack."
    "Then you will always be happy."
    Those words opened the floodgates in Jeanie's eyes as she sat slumped in the tee box, her palms covering her eyes and her body quivering.
    Chad, still staring from the ball washer, looked over at Bernie.
    "Ya' think she's ballin' over her dead husband or all those crummy shots she just hit?"

19

Jack couldn't get out of Geburtville fast enough. After miles of yellowish brown farmland leading to Dallas, an area known as the dead zone, it seemed as if he had gone nowhere.

An earlier escape led to journalism school at Lone Star State, the sports editor's post on the university newspaper, an internship and eventual hire at The Dallas Star, and a daily column he thought had touched the lives of thousands of readers. The sadness of his funeral was not that someone had died, but that no one seemed to care that he lived. Not even his wife.

Jack stared at the flat desolate road as his thoughts spun around in his head like a hamster wheel. "I know we had our problems, but that's all she thinks of me? Sure, we drifted apart, my going from game to game and she going from tournament to tournament, but we had some good times."

Jack tried to think of one but couldn't. Perhaps his mind was clouded by his last memory of Jeanie, running down the street firing golf balls at him like they were grenades. "She wanted me dead that night, so why should she show any remorse a night later when she found out I actually was dead. There was no guilt, no fond memories, no longing for what she once had. Just relief that the bastard was finally out of her life."

Jack tapped on the steering wheel. "So how do I get her back?"

The Dallas skyline finally shone through a VW van windshield covered with dirt, bugs, and bird poop. Had there been a grave, Jack would have fallen into it. The next best thing was a bed, somewhere he could lay in a fetal position and not move for three days. Low on Yo-Lo's per diem money, Jack's best option was to find Graham Repert's place – if he had one. The only other key on the silver Armadillo key ring he hoped belonged to an apartment.

Jack stopped at the downtown Dippity Donuts, but not even a half dozen glazed could improve his mood. He searched through the van for a clue and all he found was a ripped up envelope with the real estate company Dumas, Inc. in the glove compartment. It was addressed to Occupant at 1313 Beacon Road, Apt. 1b.

Jack stared at the envelope and shook it. "Beacon Road. I'd never be caught dead on that street. The only people who go down there are pimps, crack heads, and junkies."

Realizing most vehicles were stripped within minutes of abandoning it on Beacon Road, Jack left the VW in the Dippity Donuts' parking lot and walked to seedy side of downtown.

JACK'S ENTRANCE onto Beacon Road is what he expected – an old man in a gray coat passed out on the sidewalk with a whiskey bottle in his right hand, black birds pecking at garbage that stunk like old hamburger meat strewn along the road, and buildings with broken glass and rusted framed windows that were filthier than the VW's windshield.

Jack walked briskly and followed the street numbers falling off the building until he came to 1313. He walked down some steps and almost fell on the loose concrete. He pressed on the doorbell but heard no sound. He knocked on the door, and the only response was from some old brown paint that fell down his black overcoat. He slid the rusted key into the rusted lock. "Hope it doesn't work," he thought.

It didn't, at first. He twisted a little harder and could hear the bolt releasing inside the door. He twisted the wobbly knob. The door creaked open. He ducked under cobwebs to enter an abode lit only by an afternoon sun ray that crept through the soiled, white curtain that covered the lone, rectangular window from atop the door.

The room was about as big as Jack's master bathroom on Magnolia Avenue but still big enough to have accommodated, as that Saw Off Stack of Shit of a sports editor predicted, the guests at his funeral. Jack tripped on the bare floor mattress the occupant likely confiscated from an alley. He flipped a light switch but no light came on. He opened the old thin refrigerator that stretched only from the floor to his waist and felt the melted water that spilled onto his sneakers.

Jack turned the rusted silver faucet and watched only cold, brown water drip from atop plates and bowls and a pot with caked on remnants of past instant meals. Crunched Bud Light cans and empty TV dinner trays were stacked in the corner on the cold tile floor along with some loose papers that included an eviction notice. He sniffed gas that likely leaked from the last time the stove was used.

The only other room, the bathroom, stunk like it hadn't been cleaned in weeks and probably hadn't. Jack couldn't summon the courage to open the toilet lid. There was an old bathtub, no shower, and a half piece of white soap. Hairs, mostly from Graham's beard, clogged up the bath and sink.

The only sign of life came from a Dallas Star sports page and a portable black and white television atop three milk crates Graham likely used for a dresser and night stand. Jack's mug and story about the Thanksgiving blowout was on the front of the sports page and the words underlined with a black pen, "I wouldn't bet on the Cowboys winning another game this season."

Jack twisted the knob on the television and another light entered the room. "Huh, the batteries still work."

He adjusted the rabbit ears atop the television in time to get a clear picture of Cowboys' coach Ray Myles, whose voice broke the deathly silence of Graham's apartment. "People done wrote us off, but our win last week showed we have the resolve to win it all."

Jack laughed and then squinted above Myles' head at the practice field to the only player still at work. Scott Hilfinger tossed bullet passes at blocking dummies "likely," as Jack thought, "because all the other lazy dummies were in the shower."

Jack switched off the television and fell on the mattress. He took a heavy gray blanket on the floor beside him, wrapped it around the black coat, and curled into bed for three days. All he heard were cars passing by and the occasional winter rain slamming onto the adjacent road.

He only got up to use the toilet or buy a six-pack of Coors Light or a meat pie or pizza heated by a microwave oven at the corner convenience store, "Bill's Beer, Bread, and Bail Bonds." He didn't waste a half-dollar on The Dallas Star, especially Friday's issue in which Penny Pettigrew lauded the Cowboys' offense and predicted a "triumphant outing" in the big Monday night home showdown against the Chicago Bears.

Jack wrapped himself back up like a corpse in a Taco and lay in his squatter's nest the rest of the day. That night a full moon lifted above the clouds and shone through the soiled curtains.

Suddenly, another sign of life – a knock on the door.

20

Jack could not see Jeanie, but he could feel her spirit flowing through his body as his coffin was lowered into a grave marked "Dickhead" on the 50-yard line of Tom Landry Stadium. The frigid cold of the foggy air above the grave was replaced by a heat wave beneath it.

Sweat poured from Jack's forehead, and the fright of being buried alive overcame him. An eerie silence gave way to the cheering of 90,000 spectators. He could hear shovels digging at the artificial turf and a chuckle from Soss as dirt poured into the grave. Jack went to push open the coffin with his arms and legs, but he couldn't move. He tried to scream, "Help, Jeanie! Help me!" Nothing came out.

Jack could still feel Jeanie and felt never closer, though he couldn't reach her, physically or kinetically. The dirt kept falling, and the diggers' laughter and the crowd noise grew louder. Jack still couldn't move or scream and he gasped for whatever oxygen remained in the cramped coffin.

Then he heard a knock. Then a louder knock. Then an even louder knock. "Jeanie?" he thought.

Jack opened his eyes. He looked up at the moonlight that broke through the fog and crept through the lone window of Graham Repert's apartment. He wiped sweat off his forehead and pulled the gray blanket off his warm body. He heard another knock, this one so loud, the walls shook.

Jack lumbered to the door and opened it. It wasn't Jeanie. This face was big and round and looked like it had been hit with a crowbar. The giant goon wore a brown leather jacket over a beige T-shirt printed with a sketched dinosaur named Grog. He let himself in and knocked Jack to the floor in the process.

Big brown Cowboy boots are what Jack saw when he opened his eyes. Grog looked even more like a giant from Jack's floor angle. "Who are you and what do you want?" Jack said.

The answer was a big brown Cowboy boot – likely steel-tipped – planted into his gut. Jack held his stomach and gasped for breath as the goon raised the other boot and ploughed a heel-first strike into his lower ribs. The heel also may have been steel-plated. Jack blacked out for a second and hoped this was another nightmare. It wasn't. His next hope was that this was the landlord's goon wanting back rent before tossing him out on the street.

Jack coughed up blood as he struggled to his side. The black overcoat wasn't much of a shield but likely kept Grog from breaking his ribs. Jack wiped blood off his goatee and struggled to his feet. He put his arms on his knees and looked up at the smirking goon. "Whattaya want?"

The goon also sounded like he was hit in the face with a crowbar. "Forty thousand big ones."

"Scratch the landlord," Jack thought.

"We wudda just broke a rib or two if you'd kept winnin'," Grog said, "but you done bet it all on the Texans."

Even in his broken state, Jack realized that Graham Repert was a bettin' man – and not a very good one. He remembered The Dallas Star column on the floor of the apartment and how he advised not to bet on the Cowboys. "Why did I write that?" Jack thought.

Grog scraped his hairy knuckles into his hand. "So what about the 40 thou?"

Jack calmly took off his coat. "I beg your pardon, sir, you must have me mixed up with someone else."

Grog clenched his fist, his teeth, and Jack's collar. "This is Graham Repert's apartment and you're Graham Repert."

"No, sir, I'm Jack Byrne."

Grog let go of Jack's collar, started to walk away, and then threw his big meaty fist at Jack's face, "Fuckin' liar!"

Jack ducked, and the fist flew over his forehead. He countered with a knee to Grog's groin, threw the black overcoat over the goon's head, and sprinted for the door. He bounded up the steps and burst down the sidewalk. He looked back at Grog chasing him through the fog and didn't see the clothe-line formed by the long log-like arm of the goon's partner, who had been waiting outside in a parked car.

The concrete broke Jack's fall but not his neck. He played unconscious for a moment, then shot to his feet and fled just before the goon in pursuit arrived. Jack turned the corner and sneaked into "Bill's Beer, Bread, and Bail Bonds." He hid behind the bread aisle and silently begged with a finger on his lips to the short Indian man behind the counter. Grog told his partner – nicknamed "Hog," perhaps – to go on, while he checked the convenience store. Grog said to the clerk, "You seen a guy with a goatee rush in here."

The clerk pointed toward the bread aisle.

Jack pushed over the bread shelf and fled out the back door and into an alley that stunk of rotten eggs and lit by light coming from windows of the fleabag apartments above. He charged down a garbage-cluttered lane between old buildings – some containing gambling hangouts, some crack houses, some whore houses. Stray cats meowed, and rats scrammed as Jack ran for his life. He blew frost from his lungs and panted with every stride as more fog and darkness separated himself from the slower but persistent goon.

Jack didn't see the wooden milk crate and flew chest first through broken beer bottles. He could hear Grog's breathing getting closer and Hog rushing in from the other direction. He pushed himself off the glass and snuck into the first backdoor he saw. He heard Donna Summer's "Hot Stuff" blaring from speakers. He ran down a hallway and up some steps. He opened another door and ran out onto a well-lit runway where a topless woman with folded dollar bills tucked into her G-string twirled around a pole.

The two goons followed Jack onto the stage. Jack jumped off between two old guys concealing their boners and beaming up at the talent onto a table where another patron was receiving a lap dance and ran for the front door. He dodged topless waitresses and carved between tables, knocking long-neck beer bottles from rednecks' palms. The bouncer gave chase with the two goons. Jack reached the door first.

He dodged cars on the road with three men now in pursuit. He jumped over the curb on the other side of the street and sped down that sidewalk. He dodged drunks – including a department store Santa – staggering out of their regular watering hole. They sped past bums curled up on the sidewalk. One he recognized by his voice, "Way to go, lad," from the night he spent in jail.

The harder Jack ran, the harder he breathed and the more distance he put on his pursuers. Sweat poured into his eyes, and he tripped on a homeless man he didn't see lying on the concrete. He got up only in time to duck into an x-rated theatre. He flew by the ticket taker and rushed down the theatre aisle between rows of perverts. He turned around the screen and out the backdoor and into another alley.

He ran in the other direction and quicker yet. This time the goons had surrounded him. He couldn't go forward. He couldn't go back. There was no manhole, so he couldn't go down. He went up.

He climbed a steel ladder attached to a three-story building, a warehouse of some kind. He reached the top of the building and looked down to see Grog climbing up. He looked over the edge for a ladder or a ledge to climb down. There was none, and he couldn't climb down the brick wall. He saw a trap door on the floor and started for it. But Hog crashed through it. Grog reached the top followed by the bouncer, and they marched toward Jack. He looked at both goons and the bouncer and then trotted to the side of the building and jumped.

The goons peered over the side. Their view to the ground was blocked by the dense fog. They rushed to the street, while the bouncer ran back to his strippers. Where they expected Jack to be sprawled out in a pool of blood was a large opened dumpster, lit by a street lamp. Jack's fall was broken by newspapers, egg shells, beer cans, milk cartons, food wrappers, and leftover meat. But where was Jack? Nothing moved but a mouse that crawled out.

"He's either dead or buried in shit," Grog said.

Ghosts of the Gridiron

The goons heard some rustling at the bottom of the dumpster. Jack picked his way through the trash and rose to the top of the dumpster with a Dallas Star sports page clenched in his right hand. "Here," Jack said, still puffing. "This proves who I am."

He pointed to the column with his mug beside it and his name in bold letters and illuminated by the street lamp. "Jack Byrne." The goons looked at the photo and at Jack and back and forth. Grog looked at his partner and said, "He's right; he is Jack Byrne."

The goons walked away with Hog saying, "What we gonna tell the boss?"

Jack climbed out of the dumpster and shook cookie crumbs out of his hair and wiped potato skins off his sleeves. His voice echoed off the brick buildings to his amazed audience, consisting of cats and rats. "Tell him Jack Byrne is back in town."

21

Jack awoke Saturday morning in Graham Repert's bed thankful he was alive, but more thankful he wanted to live. For all he had discovered about his empty life since his co-workers and staff car went down in a ball of flames, he wondered if there was any reason to live. He could have just as easily lay there and let Grog stomp his steel-plated Cowboy boots into him until he stopped breathing.

A flame remained inside and was stoked in a dramatic chase that ended in the bottom of a dumpster. Jack figured by coincidence, not by miracle, the dense fog had cleared momentarily to allow him to spot the dumpster three stories below and that the old newspaper he pulled up contained his column mug.

He figured the next time he would see his mug was in the morning's newspaper, after the goons' discovery of his resurrection. Or at least some speculation. They still run stories about UFO and Elvis sightings, no matter if the source is a crackpot or on crack. Word got around quickly in Dallas circles.

Jack would not be able to get to a newspaper, because he couldn't get out of bed. Every time he rolled over, he felt like someone was sticking a broom handle into his ribs. Every time he tried to raise up, his stomach felt like it had been whacked with a rolling pin. His feet were still stinging, though the garbage had broken his fall. "I'd never make it as a stuntman," he said, wincing.

He had staggered several blocks from the dumpster without anyone offering to help. He was simply pegged as another staggering drunk. Besides, he stunk so bad from the dumpster that no one dared go within a first and 10 of him. He collapsed onto Graham's bed like he had just finished a marathon.

For all his pain, Jack looked back at the previous night's chase with pride. He never felt more alive – sprinting down streets and sidewalks, weaving between bums and barmaids, climbing onto and diving off buildings. It was an adrenaline rush, like what a quarterback feels when he is scrambling away from 300-pound linemen. Like what Jarmelle Beezley did in setting up the tying field goal in the win over Houston. Jack felt he proved from that chase with the goons that he had the agility and the strength to play in the NFL had he been given the chance.

BY LATE SATURDAY AFTERNOON Jack mustered the courage to sit up, which he did with a "Uggh" that echoed off the apartment walls. It was even louder when he stood up. He had smaller eruptions with every step to Bill's Beer, Bread, and Bail Bonds. He bought a newspaper and cans of soup to hold him over until he was able to eat solid food. The same Indian man served him but didn't even notice him. Jack was likely not the store's only fugitive that week.

Jack poured the soup in a pot and heated it on the gas stove while searching unsuccessfully for a story about him in The Dallas Star. He found Penny Pettigrew's column about punter and Sydney native Colin Flanders and how he traded a promising career in Australian Rules Football to become a punter.

"Whooppee," Jack said.

Jack wrote a column in his head. It led, "Jarmelle Beezley could escape from a bunch of slow, poor tackling goofballs in Houston to keep the Cowboys season alive, but in Monday night's shootout against an angry Chicago Mob the only thing that could save him would be a bullet-proof vest."

Jack figured he'd also need one once word spread about his death escape. He lay in bed the rest of Saturday and Sunday waiting for a knock on the door. A reporter. A police officer. Soss. Jeanie. Maybe he could use his lead after all when his column reappeared on Monday morning before re-claiming his seat in the press box at Tom Landry Stadium.

But all that smacked the door was a wind gust.

JACK WOKE UP Monday morning smelling blueberry muffins. He was daydreaming of his first visit to Jeanie's apartment and how she greeted him with a sweet smile and a fresh batch. She had found Jack's heart through his stomach.

As Jack braved a cold shower and dressed for his shock reunion with his beloved wife, he wondered if this time he would be welcomed or pelted with the muffins. The cool, clear afternoon did little to calm his nerves as he meandered back in Graham's black overcoat to the VW van parked at Dippity Donuts. He was so nervous and had so little cash he didn't even spring for a glazed and cinnamon to go.

He had made this drive from downtown to Magnolia Avenue hundreds of times but never more slowly than this. Afterall, he was about to walk back from the dead and back into Jeanie's life. Then again, knowing the word of his false demise had likely spread to her, the shock would have worn off by now. But why hadn't she come looking for him?

These thoughts spun through Jack's head as he exited the freeway and was soon driving down North Dallas streets with houses fronted by large naked oak trees and plastic Santas and manger scenes. Jack's heart beat out of his shirt as he started down Magnolia Avenue and looked around and saw a stray golf ball lying atop a curb. "That's two football fields from the house," he thought. "She can throw it farther than she can hit it."

Jack cruised to within one football field and stopped as soon he saw his house. Out front was his red Mazda Miata with a "For Sale" sign and a note below saying, "Hail damage, make offer."

"Golf ball size hail," Jack thought.

In the driveway where his Miata normally sat was a Ford pickup truck with a golf bag in the back and the license plate, "Legnd2." Jack drove past the house, down the street and back through the alley. He parked the VW and climbed over the fence into his backyard. There were no signs of his footballs or the old tires he used as imaginary receivers. The Big Bertha was there and a zillion golf balls Jeanie likely had driven into the back of the golf net since the funeral.

Jack crept along the back of the house and peeked through a back window at Jeanie serving Chad, her caddy, a blueberry muffin and coffee. She nodded to his "Thanks, babe" and they sat across from the dining table and exchanged smiles and laughs. Jack felt like bombarding them with golf balls. Instead he snuck back over the fence, jumped into the VW's driver's seat, and drove down the alley.

"That fucking hard dick is eating my muffins," Jack said.

JACK COULDN'T MAKE a statement at home, so he drove towad his second home back downtown in half the time it took him to reach his house. He parked in front of the Dippity Donuts and walked across the street to The Dallas Star. He wondered what kind of reception he would get from his co-workers. A "welcome back, Jack." A "glad to see you alive." Perhaps someone would utter, "Your death was greatly exaggerated."

He got silence.

Jack was always at the stadium when the Cowboys played on Monday night football and didn't realize everyone was gone by 6pm. The butchers would arrive at 9pm to prepare the front page of the sports section and game sections and sharpen the knives they would use to slice Jack's column. He walked into the building, showed his I.D. to a new security guard, and wandered the empty halls to an empty sports department.

Jack walked to his desk, where his computer had been replaced by a water cooler attached with a receptacle of plastic cups. No one bothered to clean out his drawers. Jack picked up some loose coins, his address book, and a Cowboys' media guide in the top drawer. He didn't open the bottom drawer that contained the disk he had used to store his story on Scott Hilfinger. Jack grabbed a black permanent marker from the top drawer and walked over to the large framed picture of the dictatorial sports editor in Napoleon garb standing at attention as if looking down at his bowing pack of scribes.

"I always hated this picture," said Jack, as he sketched a Hitler moustache above Soss' lips.

Jack marched toward the exit, turned and did a "Heil, Dick" salute to the altered picture of his old boss, and hurried out of the room before the door handle got him in the ass.

Within a few minutes his ass was planted on one of the donut-carved stools along the counter of Dippity Donuts. Jack ordered the variety pack – two glazed, two cinnamon, and two cream-filled donuts - and hot chocolate. He scarfed down the glazed as the hot chocolate arrived.

Jack took a sip, curled his lips, and turned to the Arab attendant. "That's not hot chocolate; that's 'scalding' hot chocolate."

The front door opened, and Jack heard footsteps behind him as someone planted his cheeks in the next seat. A large meaty hand reached into Jack's donut box and grabbed a cream filled donut. Jack spun around to see cream splattered on the man's big lips. He held the donut with his left hand and Jack's throat with his right.

"Hello again, Repert."

22

It was Grog's version of a chokehold, a grappling claw driven into Jack's throat that had his victim gasping for air. Jack was lucky the sight of the whiskered lard-ass goon made him instantly swallow his cinnamon donut. Otherwise, he would be begging for a Heimlich Manuever.

Jack grabbed the meaty hoof but it was swatted away by Grog's other meaty hoof. Jack struggled to speak. "I'm Jack Byrne," he said in a croaky voice.

Grog half-giggled. "I done heard dat before."

"Ask the clerk." Jack's voice was even more scratchy.

Grog looked at the Arab clerk, whom Jack had ordered thousands of donuts over the years. The clerk shrugged and walked to the back room.

"My boss tole me dat Jack Byrne crashed into a fillin' station and got blown to smithereens. You might look like the dude, but you sure ain't the dude."

Grog pressed harder on Jack's wind pipe. Jack turned white, then blue, then purple. His hand shook as he reached for his hot chocolate, no less scalding than before Grog's arrival. Jack let out a little grunt and heaved the cup. The steaming liquid splashed off Grog's face and dripped down his whiskers, instantly melting the cream on his lips. He hollered, "Uhhhh!" while letting go of Jack's throat.

Jack was out the door before Grog finished his "Uhhhh!" He regained his breath before Grog regained his sight. The next door Jack opened was the driver's side door of the VW van, which he fortunately parked on the street. He pressed the clutch and turned the key and the motor hesitated. "Start, you mother fucker." Jack's voice was still scratchy.

He pumped the clutch and turned the key again and nothing. He shoved the gearstick into neutral, hopped out of the VW, pushed it down a small incline, jumped back in, and pumped the clutch harder. The VW started, and Jack smashed down on the accelerator. As he sped down Young Street toward Graham's apartment in the waning sunlight he glanced in the rearview mirror and looked again to see a red Chevy pickup with two goons in hot pursuit.

Jack pressed harder on the gas and shot through a red light and between a U-haul truck and a Toyota. He looked at the mirror, and the truck was gaining. Jack swerved the VW into the same alley he had been chased on foot a few nights before. Cats and rats scattered, and puddles splattered as the two vehicles sped between the backs of buildings.

Jack swerved left on the first big road and quickly realized from the honking and swerving cars and oncoming headlights that he was going the wrong way on the one-way Commerce Avenue. So were the goons. Jack steered the van onto a sidewalk, knocked over a plastic Santa, and careened back onto a clearing on the one-way street and turned right down Houston Street, also going the wrong way on a one-way. He looked ahead at the Texas Schoolbook Depository and another car coming at him. He jumped the curb on Dealey Plaza and drove over the grassy knoll and heard gunshots. These were from the goons' pickup, not the sixth floor window.

Jack Byrne was luckier than Jack Kennedy. He dodged bullets and cars and leapt down a steep bank onto the dry Trinity River bed, splashed through a creek, and powered up a hill and down a gravel path. Somehow he had managed to turn the radio to the Cowboys' pregame show.

Jack found the road again and then an entrance ramp onto Tom Landry Expressway. He drove even faster and wilder than he did before laptops, when he had to make it to the office to beat a deadline. He weaved in and out of the traffic of four and eighteen wheelers, oblivious to the honks and middle fingers and hopeful not to hear a siren. All Jack heard was the roar of his engine, his heart pumping faster than the VW's pistons, and the radio announcers explaining what Dallas' offense needs to do to break Chicago's tenacious 4-3 defense.

Quick rearview mirror glances showed he had pulled away from the goons but hadn't lost them. Another glance at the fuel gauge showed the needle on the E. He looked in the distance at Tom Landry Stadium and a road sign that read, "Sports Stadium exit 1/4th of a mile. Jack maneuvered the VW through four lanes of traffic to an exit and a queue of cars filled with men and women in Cowboys' jerseys and excited to attend the Monday Night Football Game.

Jack hid the VW in the row of cars and followed the fanatic fan procession down the road toward the massive parking lot. He knew he couldn't hide once he went into general admission parking. He would be like a duck in a shooting gallery. As he approached the gate he drove out of the queue and down a street fronted with restaurants and fast-food joints.

The goons spotted him and immediately chased him through a McDonald's drive-through. Jack accelerated down another familiar road and to a back gate with the sign, "Official Parking Only." He drove up to an attendant, pulled out his wallet, and flashed his Dallas Star press parking permit. The attendant waved him into the parking lot and waved off the Chevy pickup, whose occupants had no such pass.

Jack also had a season pressbox pass and he used it to enter Tom Landry Stadium. On the way to the pressbox, the goons spotted him on an escalator. "How'd they get tickets so fast?" Jack thought.

The goons rushed up the adjacent stairs and knocked down spectators and their popcorn boxes while yelling, "Come back here, Repert!"

Jack beat the goons to the top and sprinted down a hallway to the luxury boxes. He opened the first door he came to, and walked inside. A large, plump man with a gray beard, plaid orange blazer, brown western shirt, Levis, black Cowboy boots, and beige Cowboy hat met him at the door.

"Howdy, pardner."

23

The Cowboys' third string quarterback looked bigger in the high-powered binoculars Jack borrowed from his newfound drinking buddy, R.B. Dinwoody, than from his naked eye in the auxiliary press box. When Jack asked what the R.B. stood for, he said pointing to the diamond gold rings on his fingers and the Rolex strapped around his wrist, "Rich Bastard."

R.B.'s luxury box also contained his three sons – U.B. (Ugly Bastard), D.B. (Dumb Bastard), and C.B. (Cheap Bastard) – and their wives and children and some friends from his ranch within 50 miles of Deadhorse, Oklahoma and some friends he met while walking from the stadium parking lot.

"None of der kids are bastards, though," said R.B., sipping his smooth Scotch rocks.

Like his wife, R.B. had his gray hair dyed blond. Like her husband, Mrs. Dinwoody also was an R.B.

"Rich Bitch," R.B. whispered in Jack's ear. "She kept her maiden name. She's a bit liberal; she's from Tulsa."

Jack's sudden intrusion into R.B.'s luxury box only made him more welcomed. R.B. slipped a Coors Light in Jack's palm before he could utter, "Graham Repert."

"Unusual name, pardner. Where you from?"

"Tom Landry Stadium, born and buried."

R.B. laughed and clinked his glass on Jack's beer can. Jack didn't have to ask about R.B.'s roots. He offered.

His father D.B. – Dead Bastard – discovered oil outside their trailer home. Soon they had oil wells all over the county and the biggest ranch in the state. R.B. treated his family to a Cowboys' luxury suite every year and had the same box rented for the Super Bowl. Jack asked R.B. if he brought his family to the game to watch Deadhorse native son, Scott Hilfinger.

"Who da hell is Scott Hilfinger?"

Jack filled R.B. in on the third string quarterback and pointed him out on the binoculars.

"He throws a perty pass," R.B. said. "Better than that jigaboo they got startin.'"

Jack dismissed R.B's racial comments, because his life depended on it. Two goons were wandering the hallways looking for him and had not seen him slip into a box in which the guests were treated to barbecue beef, chicken, beans, cornbread, and an open bar. R.B. had one too many Scotch rocks to realize he had invited an uninvited guest to sit next to him in a leather swivel seat and watch the Cowboys make Monday Night mincemeat of the Chicago Bears.

Jack was thankful his pre-game column remained in his head. Jarmelle Beezley would have made a fool of him. On the first play after the opening kickoff, everyone on the field – the Cowboys, the Bears, the officials – but Beezley rolled right. Beezley was at midfield before anyone in the stadium realized he had the ball.

R.B. leapt and spilled his Scotch onto the tips of his Cowboy boots. "He's at the forty. He's at the thirty. He's at the twenty. Look at that black sonuvabitch run!"

Beezley kept running. The more he ran, the more the Cowboys ran, the more R.B. drank, and the more chance Hilfy had to play. With the Cowboys up 48-14 with four minutes left in the game and Beezley sucking oxygen from a sideline tank, Ray Myles had no choice but to relieve his spent quarterback.

"Where the fuck is Guthrie?" Myles yelled.

The backup quarterback could not hear the coach from a broom closet under the stadium, where he stuffed his head inside Dallas Cowboys Cheerleaders' pom-poms and chanted, "Give me a B! Give me a L! Give me an O!..."

Hilfy put on his helmet, rushed over to Myles. "If you can't find him, Coach. I'm ready."

Jack watched in R.B.'s binoculars with a chuckle Myles calling time out, tearing off his headphones, and pushing players out of the way in his search of his backup quarterback and with Hilfy following him around like a schoolboy and pleading, "Can I play? Can I play?"

Myles finally stopped, looked at Hilfy as he locked his chin strap in place, then ran over to Beezley, and ripped the oxygen mask off his face.

"Get your butt back in there," Myles said.

"But Coach," Beezley said between heavy breaths.

"Just hand-off or take a knee. We're up by five touchdowns."

Hilfy took off his helmet and threw it at the bench.

As the scoreboard clock struck 0.00, Jack waited for the masses to pile into the stadium foyer before making his escape. He thanked R.B. turned D.B. – Drunk Bastard – and fled for the exit. Goons Grog and Hog were waiting outside, right where they had lost sight of him.

Jack turned back into the luxury box, climbed out the window, and fell feet first into the lower stands. He dodged one-way fan traffic down an aisle, climbed over a rail, and let go. The next thing he felt was the artificial turf of Tom Landry Stadium. Suddenly goons and security guards were chasing him down the field with R.B.'s imaginary call whizzing through Jack's brain.

"He's at the forty. He's at the thirty, He's at the twenty. Look at that dead sunuvabitch run!"

Jack didn't stop at the goal line. He sprinted into the stadium tunnel to the locker room, whipped out his Dallas Star press card to the security guard, and snuck inside as Grog and Hog were denied entrance.

Reporters on deadlines already had done their token interviews and scribbled all the variations of "I feel good" on their notepads. All who were left were naked football players and sweaty coaches. Jack walked through them, mostly ignored, but to a submissive volley of "Hey D.H."

"Hey D.H."

"Hey D.H."

Then came a faint, inquisitive call from the far corner of the locker room.

"Mr. Byrne?"

PART THREE

Home Field

24

Scott Hilfinger thought he had seen a goat, not a ghost. The last time he had seen Jack Byrne was when he leapt out of his red Mazda Miata following a night he had told his life's story and poured his heart out to a complete but welcoming stranger.

Now Jack was hiding in the Cowboys' locker room behind 300-pound linemen and without a pen or a tape recorder.

Hilfy was not surprised Jack didn't answer his call of "Mr. Byrne?" No other reporter had gone near him since he stepped foot on the hollowed Cowboys' grounds. He felt more like a ghost than Jack. No matter how many bullet passes he rifled at Cowboys' receivers or how long he stayed in the weight room after practice, no one paid any attention.

Hilfy wanted his story told to a sympathetic public who might demand he get a few snaps, and the only man who showed any interest disappeared.

"Where the hell have you been?" Hilfy's question bounced off the luxury lockers and almost struck the ducking lone reporter.

Jack glanced at the corner of the locker room to a man with his arms folded and sitting in his blue jockey shorts on a padded chair. Jack looked around at the number 13 Cowboys' jersey, shoulder pads, and pants hung over two hooks on the wall above the man's head.

"Hilfigger," scribbled in black permanent marker on athletic tape, was stuck to the wall above the hook. His green gym bag and the rest of his gear was scattered on the floor beside him.

Jack half-smiled, "No locker yet, Hilfy?"

"That's your fault, Mr. Byrne."

"My fault?" Jack sat on the luxury locker seat next to the third string quarterback.

"I spent a night over at your house, watching football, eating chicken, drinking beer, and giving you the best interview you will ever get from a professional football player and I don't get one word of ink from you."

"Have you been reading the newspaper?"

"The sports page."

"Seen any of my columns since we talked?"

"No sir, matter of fact I haven't. You get fired?"

"No, killed."

"Beg your pardon?"

Hilfy put on his jeans and a plain white T-shirt and followed Jack into an adjoining office lit by the light of a PC. Jack logged onto The Dallas Star website and searched for a front page December 1 story with the headline, "Massive explosion leaves three dead."

Hilfy looked over Jack's shoulder and read down to the sixth paragraph.

Jack looked up to see Hilfy's mouth open and his skin whiter than his Cowboys' jersey. Jack could forgive Hilfy for not reading the story when it came out. Many of his teammates can't read, and those who do only read the sports page. They wouldn't have the patience or the interest to fiddle onto the jump page to see what other poor sucker went up in a ball of flames.

Hilfy slouched onto the office sofa and looked at Jack's face illuminated by the computer screen.

"I don't get it," he said. "Y-y-you're dead. How did you, what did you, how come you..."

Jack walked to Hilfy and made him grab his left wrist. "If you feel my pulse, you will see that I am very much alive. But if I don't somehow get out of here in the next few minutes, I am going to be very much dead."

"Huh?"

"These two goons have been chasing me all over town. Apparently the real dead guy whose identity I have taken placed a very large bet, and these dudes have been ordered to either collect the debt or cream him to death."

Hilfy didn't say "Huh" again. His expression said it for him.

"Come on, help me sneak out of the stadium and I'll tell ya' the whole story."

Hilfy had nowhere else to go. Third string quarterbacks rarely are invited to celebrate with their teammates they pat on the back and clap for as they juke and weave or drive their helmet into an opponent's midsection. Besides, his curiosity was spilling over.

Hilfy opened the locker room door and saw Grog and Hog waiting outside and pounding their fists against into their palms.

"You seen a tall guy with scraggly hair and a goatee go in there?" Grog asked.

"Yeah," Hilfy said. "He's right inside."

Hilfy told the security guard the goons were his friends and he let them in. Hilfy escorted the men to the office, where he said the man was hiding. Hilfy closed the office door as soon as they entered and motioned to Jack, who was hiding behind a whirlpool tub. Jack sprinted out the locker room.

"Not in there," said a red-faced Grog, who looked meaner than a bulldog who couldn't find his bone.

The goons sniffed around the locker room for a couple of minutes. Grog shoved Hilfy to the floor – his only sack of the night – said, "Fuck you very much," and exited the locker room.

The goons looked up and down the tunnel and only saw the Cowboys' mascot, wearing the big plastic face with the white-toothed grin and the big foam cowboy hat and holster.

"You seen a guy with scraggly hair and a goatee run up and down here?" Grog said.

The mascot pointed his large foam finger at the field, and Grog and Hog ran down the tunnel. Jack took off the costume he had borrowed from the real Cowboys' mascot and ran up the tunnel to the nearest exit.   Hilfy got up off the locker room floor, grabbed his green gym bag, and went to meet a dead man in the bar.

25

Jack didn't know if it was the seven glasses of Bud Light and the two Boilermakers Hilfy poured down his throat or the story of his fake death – the explosion, the assumption of a dead man's identity, the attendance at his own funeral, and the lucky escapes from two goons who almost killed him for real – that made the third string quarterback call him something other than Mr. Byrne.

"Idiot," Hilfy said loud enough to be heard over the crowd of Cowboys' celebrators at The Bar in Arlington.

"Whataya mean idiot?" said Jack, filling Hilfy's glass and motioning the waitress for another pitcher from their corner booth.

"You totally fucked yourself," Hilfy said. "Where ya' think you go from here?"

"Back home. Back to the newspaper. Back to being Jack Byrne, the hated columnist and the neglectful husband."

Hilfy took a swig and laughed. Like most OU football players, he majored in football and went only to classes like Hair Grooming 101 and Toe Nail Clipping 204 or to the occasional class, like criminal justice, that interested him. He recalled one lecture about a Fort Worth man whose boat capsized in the middle of Benbrook Lake in the middle of the night. All 12 of the inebriated guests aboard his vessel swam back to shore, but there was no sign of the captain.

"He went down with the ship?" Jack asked.

"Nah, he swam to the other side of the lake and walked to a motel. They dragged the lake for a week, never found him, and declared him dead. Then he pops up at his memorial service a couple of weeks later."

"He was just playing a joke on his friends."

"The joke was on him. He spent 10 years in the Huntsville State Prison for fraud. His wife never forgave him and married someone else."

"What's he doing now?"

"Dead. It's hard to fake your own hangin'."

Jack took a long swig of Bud Light and stared at the back wall, thankful his back was facing anyone who might recognize him. The man whose own life was at the crossroads and had saved him from the clenches of a death claw was now serving him with the cruel taste of reality.

Jack not only had assumed the name of Graham Repert but his life as soon as he put on his black overcoat and watched him burn into ashes and absorbed by the cold night sky. One press of the telephone button would have retained his life and left him hope that his wife be thankful for his survival and to ponder the fluke of his existence.

Jack didn't say anything, just fiddled with his beer glass and stared at the third string quarterback.

"What are you thinking about? Hilfy asked.

Jack planted his elbow on the table and rubbed his goatee. "How 'bout if I said I never got in the staff car and was so depressed about the blow up with my wife and how Soss was treating me that I hitched a ride to the mountains to get away from it and was unaware of the explosion."

Jack shook his head, "Nah, that wouldn't work. Yo-Lo had called someone at the office on her cellphone and told him I was in the backseat."

Jack thought for another second and looked back, wide-eyed, at Hilfy. "I got it. I was kidnapped when they dropped me out at the Dippity Donuts and they just now let me out."

"Nah," Jack said, continuing the self-dialogue. "Too far-fetched. Who would kidnap me in the middle of nowhere with no ransom note?"

Jack went on with possible scenario after scenario to the patient listener who became drunker and more impatient with every ridiculous scenario. Jack may as well have been sitting there talking to himself. Not once did he thank Hilfy for saving him from the goons or ask about the quarterback's own dilemma. He was stuck on the sidelines of a team struggling to make the playoffs and with a coach who didn't want him on the sidelines and unsure if that coach would even play the emergency quarterback in an emergency.

Hilfy had no degree and no skill other than throwing a football. His last shot was more remote than the Cowboys making it to the Super Bowl. Jack only seemed to care about Hilfy's life when he was writing about it and banking on the story getting him to his Super Bowl, Sports Illustrated.

"I've got it." Jack chugged the remains of his beer glass and held the sides of the table. "Amnesia."

"What?"

"Amnesia. I got knocked out by the explosion and I've been wandering aimlessly around Texas the past couple weeks with no clue who I am."

Hilfy slammed his fist on the table hard enough to topple Jack's empty beer glass. "You don't have amnesia."

"Why not?"

"You watch too many movies. Nobody'd ever believe ya."

"Yeah, let's say my wallet dropped out of my pants. I lost Graham's coat and some old spinster took me in and told everyone I was her husband and made no attempt to find out who I was and then suddenly my memory came back."

Hilfy's mouth was ajar. He waved to the waitress for another boilermaker and a pitcher and then stared at Jack's smile that would soon turn into a frown. "Why don't you just say you were abducted by a rock band and forced to become their drummer?"

"What's wrong with my idea?"

"The police would make you turn in your made-up spinster for not finding you help. Doctors would do a brain scan and see that there was no amnesia. Face it, Jack, you're fucked."

"Fucked?"

Hilfy spelled every letter, his teeth shining in the dimly lit bar. "F-U-C-K-E-D. You can't go back to your job, you can't go back to your wife, you can't go anywhere in public, you can't use your cellphone, you can't even go on the fuckin' Internet. If you're spotted, you're either killed by the goons or rotting in jail. Not only are you fucked, you fucked yourself."

Hilfy downed his newly arrived boilermaker and poured himself and Jack another Bud Light and continued. "The way I see it, you're gonna have to go hide somewhere near here until you figure something out. And I wouldn't wait until dawn. You're a DH to my teammates and coaches, but not in this bar or outside it."

Jack lowered his head, already trying to hide his face from the crowd, and then stared up at Hilfy. "There's only one place I know they won't look for me."

26

Darkness, Jack's old friend, re-emerged on that void of life between Dallas and Geburtville. All he could see out the windshield of Graham Repert's VW van was fog. All he could hear was the squeaking of loose wheel joints. All he could taste were the remnants of his final Dippity Donut, the cheap of thrill of torment over his tormentor, and the bitterness of a life he was leaving behind.

Scott Hilfinger had left behind the final swallow in the pitcher and the beer and nachos he deposited in the toilet of the The Bar in Arlington.

"Never been much of a drinker," Hilfy said, after Jack's third spew stop on the Tom Landry Expressway.

Hilfy was too drunk to remember what he had said to Jack earlier that night. Jack remembered every syllable. The Bud Light was a truth serum and it was shining through him. He no longer was Jack Byrne. No longer a Dallas Star sports columnist, and no longer the husband of aspiring pro golfer Jeanine Pratt.

Suddenly Jack felt like he was being chased by a helicopter with a spotlight hovering over him. He had to get out of town. First, he had some details to take care of – like sobering up his newfound drinking buddy and getting him home, his corner room at the Downtown Y.

The VW headlights showed Jack the way off the freeway and to the 24-hour drive-through window of the downtown Dippity Donuts. "This will soak up the alcohol," he said to his nearly comatose passenger as he pulled up to the window.

Jack looked past the Arab clerk into the dining area to the same booth inhabited by Soss after the last game. Soss was there again with his hot coffee, chocolate covered donuts, and fresh copies of The Dallas Star and the Fort Worth Express sports pages.

"I'll have a dozen donuts – 10 glazed, one cream filled and the longest chocolate twist you have on the shelf. Put the chocolate twist into a separate white sack. And two hot chocolates and four toothpicks."

Hilfy briefly came out of his coma, "What 'er da toot-picks for?"

"You'll see."

Jack opened his wallet to another reality. He barely had enough money to pay for the donuts. The Arab gave him the donut box, and Jack quietly backed up behind the building. He crawled like a chimp under the drive-through window to Soss' prized black Lexus, parked on the street the opposite side of Soss' booth. Jack scooted from wheel to wheel, poking the toothpicks in the valve stems and letting the air out of all four tires. Then he shoved the cream-filled donut in the tailpipe before sprinting back to the van.

"That's for your attempt to get me fired by telling the publisher that my award-winning story on the Columbian soccer player who overcame an abusive father and impoverished upbringing was racially motivated and a fabrication," Jack said while staring through the van windshield.

Hilfy said nothing – just munched on a glazed donut and giggled.

"The only sad thing," Jack said, driving the van back onto the road, "is I won't be here to see Soss' reaction when his fucking car blows up."

JACK DROPPED HILFY at the Y and watched him and his green gym bag stagger away from the VW like he hoped to be staggering to the sidelines after a hard sack.

"Bless his heart," Jack whispered. "Hope he gets his chance; he's a good quarterback and for all he's been through he deserves it. Otherwise he'll have a life of drinking and donuts."

Hilfy's life looked more hopeful than Jack's. At least Hilfy had a life. Jack hinged his hopes on what Hilfy told him was the beer talking. He drove to The Dallas Star and showed his employee badge to the newest trainee security guard, who didn't question what was in Jack's white sack. Unable to log onto the Internet in fear of being caught, Jack went to the Morgue and did an old-fashioned search of people who had faked their death.

He looked through an index in a folder and then scrolled through several reels of microfilm. He found a Vietnam MIA who was declared dead, assumed the identity of another MIA who *was* dead, and later was discovered by authorities. He was sentenced to 10 years in a federal prison in Shelby, Alabama, raped by inmates, beaten by guards, and worked as a supermarket checker under the supervision of his parole officer.

Jack located a California flight attendant who was supposed to be on an airplane that blew up in the sky. She tried to escape her abusive boyfriend by taking the name of the flight attendant who had replaced her on the flight. She handed in her resignation and spent the next five years as a gypsy, eluding the authorities and old acquaintances. She finally was discovered by her teenage daughter at a traveling circus, where she performed as a fire swallower. Her punishment was she had to stay in the circus but demoted to elephant excrement remover.

Jack found a couple more cases and then the man who supposedly drowned in Benbrook Lake. Every word from Hilfy was true. As Jack Byrne he was subject to being beaten up and dying in prison. As Graham Repert he was subject to being beaten up and dying in a dark alley.

Jack walked to the sports department for one last look. He stared at his desk and the water cooler dripping into a plastic drain where Jack once dropped his bombs on failing quarterbacks with a few strokes on his computer.

Before the final exit, Jack broke into Soss' private bathroom for a farewell pee. Not only did he decide not to flush it, he took the long twisted donut from the white paper sack, wiped chocolate on the lid and around the bowl and left the donut sinking, chocolate side up. He wiped the excess chocolate from his hands onto the sink, the walls, the mirror, and the door handle and made sure it didn't get him in the butt on the way out.

Ghosts of the Gridiron

"That's for giving the large office across the hall I was promised to the staff cartoonist and giving me the smallest, crudest desk in the overcrowded sports department," he said.

JACK WAS OUT of The Dallas Star, but as he headed north he had one last stop before leaving Dallas. After all, Magnolia Avenue was sort of on the way.

He knew Jeanie had no reason to change the locks, and he had kept his house keys. He parked again in the alley, leapt over the back fence, and slid his key into the backdoor lock. Jack crept to the kitchen and pulled out his flashlight from under the sink. He followed the light through a dark hallway to the master bedroom.

There was no wife in his warm king size bed, just his clothes in neatly sorted piles waiting to be stuffed into plastic garbage bags and donated to the Salvation Army. Jack turned on his night stand lamp and stared at the sweaters, shirts, jackets, and jeans that frequented press boxes from San Francisco to New York. Jeanie hadn't touched his underwear drawer, which was good because that is where he hid his spare cash. Atop the dresser was a pile of sympathy cards from friends and relatives. He read a few. All said how sorry they felt for Jeanie, but no one mentioned what a great guy Jack was or how much he would be missed. One was a Christmas card with letters, photos, and a "P.S. – Sorry to hear about your hubby."

The biggest sympathy card came from Chad, who wrote, "Just wanted to let u know I'm here for u, babe."

"I'll bet you are," Jack whispered.

Jack picked up Jeanie's cellphone next to the cards. The light flashed through the darkness. The inbox showed several messages from Chad. The most recent read, "Gr8 round 2day, babe. Ur reddy for the Xmas tourney next week."

Jack took a large plastic grocery bag and stuffed a couple of shirts, a sweater, blue jeans, and his Nike sneakers. He looked around for some special memorabilia – a trophy, an award certificate, a photo of Jeanie and him on their wedding day. There was nothing like that.

Had he looked under the bed, he would have seen the scrapbook Jeanie had started. It contained his best columns she had saved, his first press pass to a Dallas Cowboys' game, and a middle school term paper on Tom Landry with a red-marked A+ from his English teacher. Jeanie had planned to present it to Jack on Christmas morning.

Jack took the cash and some underwear and socks from his dresser and a blanket and pillow from the hall closet and headed for the kitchen. En route, he put down the bag and flashlight and slowly opened the door of the guest room, where he had been banished many nights. He heard the soft breathing and smelled the clean body of a woman who likely had a bubble bath before sliding on her silk pajamas and slipping under the warm covers. Jack stared at her angelic face, her moist lips, the tender skin above her partly covered breasts and recalled the nights in their early wedded bliss, when his beloved lay on his chest with her arm draped around his stomach before nodding off to sleep. She often called Jack her big Teddy Bear.

Was she dreaming about those nights or the night she smacked Jack with golf balls? Perhaps she was simply dreaming about smacking balls into the middle of the fairway.

"I do love you, Jeanie," Jack whispered gently as he lowered his head and walked out the door toward the kitchen.

Jack went through the kitchen cupboards and found the only blueberry muffins Chad hadn't devoured. He made himself a ham sandwich and grabbed a bag of chips, a banana, and some stale Oreos. He shoved them into a large baggy and into the plastic bag. He put the flashlight back under the sink and tiptoed out the backdoor without looking back.

About an hour later he was looking ahead for a glimpse of the road through the thick fog and trying to stay awake by searching for a radio station that played anything but modern Christmas Carols, like "Grandma got run over by a reindeer."

He found it when the fog broke and the van's headlights shone on the simple white sign with purple letters that spelled out "Welcome to Geburtville."

"Joy to the world, the Lord has come…" Jack hummed along with the music, filtered through the radio static as the van passed colorful Christmas lights on the houses leading to town and their front lawns dusted with snow.

"And heaven and nature sing, and heaven nature sing. And hea-a-ven, and heave'n, and nature sing."

27

That one place no one would look for Jack was the last place he thought he would ever go.

The humiliation, fear, resentment all resonated through Jack's bones as the VW van headlights shone on what used to be the 50-yard line on a field where his dream ended what seemed a lifetime ago.

Following a cliché the Cowboys' beat writer likely wrote in a game story, desperate times call for desperate measures. Hard to imagine that his birthplace and funeral place was the one place no one knew him. Geburtville felt a world away from Dallas, but it would take only one sighting of his van or his person for the cops or the goons to pluck him back to Earth.

Jack steered the VW through the town in the waking hours of Tuesday, December 13. The streets were empty. The only light came from Bryson's Bagels, whose baker was likely too busy rolling dough to notice the VW's rustling muffler fading into the distance.

The wrecking ball still hadn't crashed into the former Geburtville High School building, which prompted the weary VW driver to meander his vehicle through campus. He pulled around the gymnasium and drove down a narrow walkway to what used to be the Gebbie Bowl. The worn, wooden bleachers had been torn out from the banks that surrounded the field that now looked more like a goat pasture than a gridiron.

Jack stopped the VW atop the bank where the press box once sat and shone the lights in hopes of finding some lines and hash marks. All he saw was dirt and yellow grass. Beyond where the rusted and white goalpost marked the end zone stood the field house, a façade of broken red bricks also in the queue for demolition. Jack stared at the field house, snapped his fingers, and drove toward it. He drove the van in back of the field house and into an empty carport, which once housed the team bus. Perfect hiding place for the VW.

Jack buttoned the long black overcoat and put his hands in his pockets as he walked around the field house to the back door. He reached atop the door frame and dragged his fingers against the brick until he found what he was looking for.

"I knew you would still be there," he said, staring at a rusted key. It was the same key the equipment manager hid for him and other players who wanted to use the weight room during off hours. Jack often snuck out of his house after his parents went to sleep, climbed the stadium fence, and let himself into the weight room for a midnight workout.

"Come on, work, you bastard," Jack slid the key into the lock and twisted a doorknob that looked as old as the key. It wouldn't open. He twisted the key back and forth. "Shit. Come on, come on."

Finally, the key turned and the door opened. Jack flicked the switch on the wall and, to his amazement, the room lit up from old flood lamps that dangled from the ceiling. Jack walked around the footlockers where players once hung their jerseys on the hook above them and sat down on them to discuss the day's workout or the night's game.

He sat on his old locker and sniffed the lingering smell of Mentholatum Deep Heating Rub before walking out of the locker room down a hallway to the weight room. The weights were gone and a high jump pad, likely being stored there until the new track was opened, covered most of the tattered carpet floor. Jack walked into the old coaches' office which had been swept clean of whistles, clipboards, and playbooks that were once stacked on the coaches desks still attached to the wall. Not removed were a refrigerator, a microwave oven, a hotplate, and a floor heater – everything he needed for the perfect hideout.

Jack also was extremely exhausted from a day and night that seemed would never end. He turned on the floor heater next to the high jump pad, took his clothes bag and blue Cowboys' blanket from the van, and stuffed them into his old footlocker. He didn't bother to change clothes. He dove onto the high jump pad with the black overcoat and the blanket wrapped around him. When he woke up 14 hours later, it was dark again.

IF HE HADN'T BEEN so hungry, Jack may have rolled over and slept another 14 hours. The barbecue from the Rich Bastard's luxury box, post-game Dippity Donuts, and ham sandwiches and blueberry muffins he smuggled from his house had long been digested and soon be discarded in the locker room latrine.

Jack strolled into town – a ghost town at 9 pm on a Tuesday night. Geburtville was the anti-Dallas. No bars or strip clubs. No homeless people lying on the sidewalk. No 24/7 supermarkets or fast-food joints or gas stations. No scent of alcohol or late-night burgers. No squad cars patrolling the empty streets. Jack could hear his shoes squeak on the sidewalk and could see his breath fogging the cool, clean air as he toured the store-front windows whose Christmas lights had retired for the evening along with everyone else in town.

Jack's shout of "Damnit, I'm starving and there's nowhere to eat" were for his ears only.

He stared at his reflection in the Ollie's Electronics' storefront window illuminated by a quaint street lamp. He saw scraggly hair and a goatee that was sprouting into a beard. He looked more like Graham Repert than Jack Byrne and acted more like him, wandering through an alley looking for leftovers. The least dangerous was a plastic bag of Bryson's day-olds. He ripped it open and devoured a cinnamon-raisin bagel as he walked back to his new home.

He sat on the bank of the Gebbie Bowl, slowly chewing the assorted bagels from blueberry to poppy seed to chocolate chip. He looked at a sky full of a zillion stars and turned off his brain. He wanted to enjoy the peace that had eluded him since the last time he set foot on the field below. There was no thought of the goons who wanted him dead or cops discovering his identity or what had transpired in his youth on that 50-yard line. He just wanted to be.

Ghosts of the Gridiron

    Jack maintained his peace for another 12 hours and amidst the hustle and bustle of townspeople scurrying off to school, work, and shops. By noon, he had curled himself back onto the high jump pad-turned-bed and into a deep sleep until the sunlight filtering through the field house windows again turned to dusk.

28

A single beam of light flashed from atop the Gebbie Bowl and into a dusty window of the field house. A second beam followed a moment later, then two more, then four, and eventually Jack's new home was no longer hidden in darkness. Men's voices on the adjacent field disturbed the silence of this death row building.

Jack stirred on the high jump pad but his eyelids remained shut as if fastened by Super Glue. The lights kept flashing outside and inside Jack's head.

Red, blue, and white lights were followed by police sirens. The high beams of a pickup truck spotlighted cab passengers Grog and Hog and a dozen angry goons crouched in the back. A spotlight illuminated the field house from two military helicopters hovering above. Torches held by Dallas Cowboys' players and coaches and police officers and goons and irate readers and Soss, the Sawed Off Stack of Shit sports editor, and Jack's father were marched from midfield of the Gebbie Bowl to within extra point range of the field house. Jeanie wasn't holding a torch, just her Big Bertha.

Jack's father shouted into a bullhorn from midfield, "Come out with your hands up or I'll pull you out by your hair, kicking and screaming."

The lights grew brighter, the footsteps louder. Jack pleaded with the oncoming rush of Jack haters for it all to be another horrible nightmare. Then he heard a whistle.

Jack's eyelids cracked open, and the light remained. So did the footsteps, but they were heard from a distance along with the men's voices. Jack pulled the blanket over his head like he was trying to protect himself from bullets, punches, and clubs. He slowly pulled the blanket down to his chin and looked around at the illuminated weight-room-turned-fugitive's bedroom. He slid off the high jump pad and tip-toed into the locker room. Lights shone off the locker hooks and the stencilled numbers on the lockers. Jack stepped up on a footlocker and peered out the window.

The next lights he saw were headlights. They shone from pickups and cars surrounding the banks of the Gebbie Bowl and onto the field. Jack looked at the orange cones marking the goal lines and sidelines and middle-aged players running, passing, and tackling. One team's players wore white jerseys and the other wore red, blue, green, and purple jerseys – likely from the last high school or college game they had played. Their jerseys fit over their shoulder pads and beer guts like bologna, and their rust-stained chin straps stretched from one helmet ear to the other. They waddled like penguins back and forth from the huddle.

"Oh, wow," Jack said as he planted his fists on the window sill and pushed his forehead against the cold, cracked glass.

This field he remembered as a nightmare was now a field for players whose dreams ended decades ago. They didn't run fast; they didn't throw or kick far. There was more shirt-tail tackling than clothe-line tackling. But they juked and faked and dove for passes just as they likely had in their prime. There were hugs and high-fives after every touchdown and towels to wipe off their bloodied elbows and the knees beneath their padded pants.

Jack smiled along with them and wanted more than anything to join them. "What if one of them recognizes me?" he thought. "The nightmare could become a reality."

Still, a curiosity resounded from this fleeing reporter. Who are these has-beens, these ghosts of the gridiron? This was a story not even Soss could reject.

Jack hopped off the footlocker and ran down the hallway to the coaches' office. He looked through every desk until he found an old notebook and a pen. He marched toward the door. Then, suddenly, the voices faded. The lit field house slowly darkened as cars and trucks pulled away from the field, the roar of their engines fading into the distance.

Jack opened the door and started for the field, now deserted and dark. The final pass had been thrown, and the cleats and pigskins had been stuffed in the trunk or the truck until the next game.

Head down, Jack retreated to his high jump pad. He wrapped himself and his black overcoat in his blanket and closed his eyes. He fell back asleep with the wonderment of whether what he witnessed was a weekly or one-off game, a figment of his imagination, or a dream that overwhelmed a horrible nightmare.

29

Two nights later, Jack again was looking at the 50-yard line in Geburtville. This field at crosstown Gebbie Stadium was not lit by cars and pickups.

There were more bulbs atop the light poles on either side of the new stadium than the headlights at the Gebbie Bowl. They lit up the grassy turf, the purple uniforms of the Geburtville Gebbies and the whites of the Steuberville Stallions, the cheerleaders bouncing on the red track, and the blanketed, heavily dressed fans in the aluminium bleachers.

The smell of popcorn and the blaring of trumpets from the Gebbie's marching band brought a smile to the freshly shaven and bespectacled former sportswriter hiding in the corner of the one-story press box.

Jack had realized that he did not dream about the ghost-like football game upon waking up early Thursday morning. Still, the nightmare before it lingered. He had no clue how he could extricate himself from his predicament, but he wouldn't be able to figure it out from a prison cell or a grave following a Jack Byrne or Graham Repert sighting.

Jack marched into town and waited for the front door to be unlocked at Joe's Barber Shop, where he first purchased a haircut at age 13. Joe had saved him from the nicks and cuts of his father's clippers and the teasing of junior high classmates who called his haircut a "shavee-atal." Jack often had worn a Cowboys' toboggan hat until his hair grew out.

Jack thought Joe was 80 years old when he last cut his hair. He either wasn't as old as Jack remembered or maybe this was Joe, Jr. Either one didn't recognize him.

"What'll it be, mister." The old man in the white coat grabbed his scissors and started plucking away at the bird's nest atop Jack's head. "A little off the top?"

"All of it off the top," Jack said. "And off the sides and off the face."

Joe's crinkled fingers went to work as he cut and clipped and shaved Jack to look like a Marine recruit or one of the local high school football players whose heads he had shaved the day before.

"Goin' to the big game tonight?" Joe said, as he lathered shaving cream on the stubble on Jack's face.

"What game?"

"You're not from around here, are ya? The Class A State Semifinal game at the new stadium with our beloved Gebbies against the Steuberville Stallions. We haven't been this far in the playoffs since 1983."

"You made the finals?"

Joe grabbed his razor and started shaving Jack's face. "No, No. Got beat 42-zip to that same school. They had this quarterback who threw for 450 yards. He was unbelievable. His name was Molinski, I think."

Jack pretended not to know who he was talking about. "Whatever happened to him?"

"After he won Steuberville the state title, he went to Lone Star State. Lost track of him after that. Man, he sure was good. Everyone said he was destined for the NFL."

Jack closed his eyes for a moment and reopened them as Joe stroked the razor across his face. "So what are your chances tonight?"

"Not so good."

"Why not?"

Joe paused from the shaving and stared at Jack. "Our startin' quarterback was diagnosed with some kind of strange blood disease this week. He's still gonna play but don't know how effective he'll be. His daddy was in here yesterday and told me in confidence. Don't mind tellin' you, 'cause you a stranger. Who could you blab it to?"

Joe wiped the loose shaving cream off Jack's face and handed him a mirror. Jack stared at his bare head and his smooth face, beardless for the first time since Joe last shaved him in high school. "No chance of someone recognising me," Jack thought. "I don't recognise myself."

Ghosts of the Gridiron

Jack made double sure. He paid Joe $22.50 for the shaved head and face and $10 to the clerk at the next door Two Dollar Shop for a pair of thin black rimmed glasses with non-prescription lenses.

He bought himself a breakfast omelette at Val's Coffee Shop, while reading Tuesday's Dallas Star sports page inclusive of Dave Noonan's game story.

In a David and Goliath clash between two titans, the Dallas Cowboys gave it everything they had in their continual and unlikely climb toward the Super Bowl and turned what appeared to be a bitter battle into a cakewalk.

Jack's chuckle turned to laughter when he read Penny Pettigrew's column lead.

As cameras flashed bountifully off players' helmets and into the cool, crisp night air, the Dallas Cowboys' players darted aimlessly about the gridiron pitch toward a remarkable victory over a fierce Chicago squad before a warmly smiling home crowd.

His laughter stopped when he read a letter to the editor in Thursday's sport page:

Penny Pettigrew again captured the Cowboys' victory in her elegant and reverent style – a breath of fresh air from the dull, dopey prose of the former columnist.

Jack slammed the newspaper and a two-bit tip on the table and marched to Geb's Supermarket, where he bought two bags of groceries and carried them back to the field house. The supermarket clerk, like the other clerk, waitress, and barber substituted "Have a good-day" for "Merry Christmas."

"Yeah," Jack said without looking at them.

His shave, shop, and chow spree cost him nearly $100 and cut his life savings to $212.50. "What am I going to do for money?" Jack said to himself as he stuffed a milk carton and a plastic bologna tin in the field house refrigerator. "I'd knock off a liquor store, if this town had one."

JACK SAVED $20 and received free press box pizza and Cokes by flashing his Dallas Star press card at the front gate at Geburtville Stadium the next night. Jack knew the Star wouldn't send anyone there. Soss would have one of his butchers call the Geburtville Gazette and ask their reporter to send a brief story and stats.

Jack hid his new face under a writing pad as he walked up the steps of the stadium, likely filled with former teammates and classmates and teachers who probably didn't remember his name much less his face. He felt safer in the corner of the press box next to the Gazette reporter, a bleach blonde Barbie who didn't look like a sportswriter and wasn't. Certainly, none of the other men in the press box were looking at him.

"Hi, I'm Molli with an I." She smiled her pearly whites and slid her manicured pink-painted fingernails into Jack's right palm. "Molli Glass."

Jack didn't have to explain who he was. Molli with an I was too busy talking about herself. Before the Gebbies' players broke through the painted "Tame the Stallions" paper banner on the goal line and sprinted to the sidelines, he would learn that Molli was a former cheerleader and homecoming queen at Geburtville High and a journalism major at Berrington College. She would graduate in June, but only if she completed a required internship. Her father's friend was the newspaper's managing editor, who set up the internship during the winter term of Berrington's tri-semester system.

Jack knew Molli knew nothing about football when she asked who was the man in the striped shirt holding a coin.

"I thought you said you were the head cheerleader?" Jack said.

"Yes, but I always had my back to the field and my face to the stands."

"You didn't date the starting quarterback?"

"Once. Football is all he talked about over his Big Mac and fries."

Molli was assigned the game when Blaine Rainey, the Gazette's only sportswriter long before Jack went to school there and about as old as Joe the Barber, suffered a mild heart attack after the Gebbies' overtime win in the quarterfinals. Like Jack, the managing editor must have assumed football cheerleaders knew something about football.

Molli pointed to the line of scrimmage before Gebbies' quarterback Kody Keimer took the first snap. "Why is that guy putting his hands under his teammate's butt?"

Jack stared at Molli. "How are you going to cover this game?"

"I don't know. You want to cover it for me?"

"You serious?"

"I will pay you half what they are paying me to cover it and half of what The Dallas Star pays me to send them a story."

Molli didn't think to ask Jack who he was or why he was in the press box, and didn't care. In the middle of the first quarter she revealed she didn't even want to be a writer.

Molli showed no excitement for Kody's courageous effort in leading the Gebbies. She just sat there brushing her hair with her fingers and watching the cheerleaders yelling, "Give me a G, give me an E..." while Jack kept track of the statistics and jotted down some notes. She sat in the press box sipping her third Coke while Jack interviewed Kody and his father and the Geburtville coach, Jerry Grimes, after the game while explaining that he was " just gettin' some quotes for the beat writer who had a tight deadline."

Molli drove Jack to the Geburtville Gazette office in the white, black-topped Chrysler Sebring convertible her father bought her for high school graduation and scrolled through her emails from her sorority sisters while Jack batted out the stories. The story in the next day's Gazette under the headline "Keimer's inspirational victory" and Molli's byline read:

Geburtville's Kody Keimer stared at the Gebbie Stadium scoreboard to see the final score of Friday's Texas Class A State Semifinal clash with Steuberville –Home 28, Visitor 12 – flashing into the night and seconds ticking off on the historic victory. But now, Keimer wonders, how much time does "he" have left?

Jack detailed the symptoms that led to the mid-week diagnosis of Keimer's rare blood disease and the emotional and physical struggle he faced to propel his team to victory. The story included inspiring quotes from his parents, coaches, and teammates that must have left tears on newspapers all over town. It was the best story Molli never wrote.

There also was a story about the game in The Dallas Star, which Jack sent via Molli's email address at the stroke of deadline:

The Geburtville Gebbies came to play at the Texas Class A State Semifinals Friday night before a packed house of faithful followers, whom they rewarded with a resounding 28-12 triumph. The team, led by the pin-point passing of Kody Keimer, played on all cylinders like a well-oiled machine and by midway into the last stanza it was all over but the shouting.

30

The Dallas Cowboys seemed to be going down in flames like The Dallas Star staff car after losing their third straight game and their star quarterback on Thanksgiving Day. Twenty-four days adrift from the November 24th turkey, the Cowboys' captains approached the midfield star at Tom Landry Stadium and their burgundy and gold-clad rival Washington Redskins with a chance to take the NFL East lead.

No one knew that better than the sportswriter sitting uncomfortably crossed-legged in his press box seat and wearing a blonde wig, red lipstick, padded bra, pink silk blouse, gray skirt, dark panty hose, and black high heels.

Molli had gone from high school reporter to NFL feature writer in two days, thanks to the story Jack wrote for her about Geburtville High's inspirational quarterback.

Soss called her the next afternoon after the Star publisher/playing partner F. Morgan Rothchild interrupted his Saturday afternoon golf game to show him the story. He called Molli on his cellphone while waiting to tee off on the eighth tee at the Forest Green Country Club.

"Why did you write this incredible story for your shithole paper and send The Dallas Star four crappy paragraphs?"

"You get what you pay for, Mr. Schwartz," said Molli, who should have majored in marketing.

"Huh?"

"I gave the Gazette their sixty dollars worth and I gave the Star their forty dollars worth."

The Star gave her 240 dollars for reprinting the Gazette story on the front page of the Star's Sunday Sports Edition. Molli gave their butchers an earful after they changed the byline from "Molli" to "Molly."

"What are you pissed about?" Jack said Sunday morning as Molli applied a deep layer of mascara to his well shaven cheeks. "You didn't write or re-write the story."

The Gazette editor was so thrilled with the story that he assigned her a feature on Redskins' offensive tackle Fritz Gonnert, who started his football career at Geburtville Intermediate School before his family moved to Dallas. Molli had told Jack, who had dropped by the Gazette late Saturday afternoon to collect his $50 take from the two stories, she had no interest in writing the story or going to the game and wouldn't pay him until the newspaper editors paid her. Jack said he would take her place even if it meant going in drag.

"Who are you, Graham Repert?" Molli said as she stroked an eyebrow pencil above his right eyelid.

"I'm either poor, desperate to write, or can't miss a Cowboy game."

"Or all of the above?"

Jack didn't answer. He put on the blouse, skirt, panty hose, and wig and looked at himself in the full length mirror in Molli's bathroom. What Molli did not know is that this was the perfect costume to hide him from the goons and anyone who might recognize him from his Dallas Star column mug. He figured if the haircut, shave, and fake glasses wouldn't elude the goons, the women's makeover definitely would. He could even sit in the press box.

JACK DROVE Molli's Chrysler convertible from her parents' house to Tom Landry Stadium on the warm winter morning. He kept the black roof up in fear of his wig blowing off. Jack showed his press pass to the gate attendant and walked to the elevator. Out the corner of his eye he caught Grog, who was looking from side to side but took no notice of him. Jack figured there were other goons looking for him – a him, not a her.

Because women sportswriters were not a rarity anymore in press boxes or even locker rooms and the fact that he was a little too muscular to attract the male sportswriters, Jack went unnoticed from his seat on the 20-yard line in the press box that extended the length of the field. He missed his 50-yard line seat but enjoyed a pre-game barbecue feast while watching the Cowboys' number 13 rifling bullet passes to Cowboys' receivers.

"Wow, he can really zing that football," said Jack, testing his high-pitched voice.

"Who?" the sportswriter next to him said.

Jack pointed into the glass. "Scott Hilfinger."

"Who the hell is Scott Hilfinger?"

Jack doubted Hilfy would get a chance against the defending NFC East champions, who were tied with the Cowboys for the league lead at 8-5. The Redskins took the kick-off and marched 80 yards on 14 plays for a 7-0 lead. It was 21-3 by the end of the first quarter. Boos rang from the crowd as petite PR ladies with smiles, short skirts and freshly shaved legs flooded the writers' desks with statistics and notes.

Jack looked around at the other writers, whom he had shared this press box for many years. Most already started typing the Cowboys' game obituary, especially when Jarmelle Beezley was helped off the field in the second quarter and Ray Myles was penalized 15 yards for unsportsmanlike contact. Jack read Myles' lips on the massive screen that hovered over the playing field.

"That was a late hit, you Zebra-dressed cocksucker."

While Brody Guthrie was throwing his only completion to the Redskins' cornerback and then being dragged down the sidelines by the interceptor's facemask, Beezley was being escorted to the X-ray room to see if his ribs were broken, and Myles was having another go at the head referee.

"Put that fuckin' yellow handkerchief back in your pocket or I'll wipe your ass with it."

The referee turned on his microphone and announced through a roar of jeers from Cowboys' fans and players that their head coach had been ejected from the game. Myles called the ref a "whistlin' pussy control freak who oughta be shovelin' horse shit at the rodeo" and jogged to the locker room while waving to the crowd. Minutes later, he was rushing Beezley in his Cowboy blue Ford Explorer to the nearest hospital, in downtown Dallas, after the quarterback told him the X-ray machine was broken.

Down 28-3 on the last play of the half, Guthrie heaved a Hail Mary pass from midfield to the end zone. Guthrie grabbed his right arm with his left and fell to the turf with a private but vocal prayer. "Oh God, I haven't thrown a ball that far in two years."

As trainers escorted Guthrie to the locker room with an ice pack on his arm, confusion consumed the press box and the locker room. Writers batted out their Cowboys' demise stories, while Jack snuck a peak over Dave Noonan's shoulder at the words on his laptop: "The Cowboys self-destructed in the first quarter and the wheels started falling off in the second quarter. The Redskins couldn't wait until the third quarter to deliver a knockout punch."

Then he peaked over Penny Pettigrew's shoulder and read with a silent chuckle: "The blue sky above Tom Landry Stadium on a warm winter afternoon was laced with threatening storm clouds that needed more than a Cowboys' rain dance to keep them from being scalped."

Jack retreated back to his seat as Soss, that Sawed off Stack of Shit sports editor, slithered over with a cocktail to pat his Star writers on the backs.

The real debate was happening in the radio booth.

"Now who's going to play quarterback?" KSTR play-by-play man Murray Stark asked halftime guest Rex Fanning.

"I'd come off the disabled list right now if the NFL would let me," Fanning said. "Guess they'll have to go with the emergency quarterback – whoever that is."

That was Hilfy, who sat in the corner of the locker room as the Cowboys' coaches argued over who was in charge and took a sip from his whiskey flask to calm his butterflies. They decided on defensive line coach Alvin Baines, because he had been with the Cowboys the longest and he was the meanest.

He told the players to "get ya'lls white and black asses back on dat fuckin' field and play some football."

The last player to leave was Hilfy, who was worried Baines would clothe-line him like he did in Houston. Instead, Baines put his arm around him.

"Yous get yo dream shot, Number 13. Don't fuck it up."

Hilfy took another shot from his whiskey flask, charged to the sideline, and fired warm-up passes to the water boy along the sidelines and took some snaps.

He would have realized his NFL dream had Antonio "The Rocket" Crocket not returned the second half kickoff 105 yards to cut the deficit to 28-10 or had the Redskins not responded with another 14-play drive to the Cowboys' one-yard-line or had the game not been stopped for two injuries and three challenges. After the Cowboys stopped the Redskins on fourth down on the one-foot-line, Hilfy snapped on his chinstrap and strolled to the Cowboys' huddle in the back of the end zone.

As the announcer's voice echoed off the stadium, "Now playing quarterback for the Dallas Cowboys, Scott Hilfinagger," spectators looked at each other and said, "Who the hell is Scott Hilfinagger?"

They were about to find out as Hilfy looked at the blue painted turf in the huddle and said, "Q-q-quarterback sneak on one, break."

Hilfy looked around at the massive stadium, the television cameras, the snarling Redskins' linemen, and looked at the sky. "This is for you, Dad," he whispered.

His next words were shouted. "Blue. Forty-seven. Eighteen. S-s-set!"

"Set" was interrupted by a whistle. "Timeout. Cowboys."

The head referee's voice was amplified by his microphone and echoed off the stadium.

Hilfy ran to the sidelines and could hear a police siren in the background. He wrinkled his forehead and stared at Baines. "Why did you call timeout?"

"Just got a text from Coach Myles. Beezley's X-rays were negative. The doc wrapped tape around his ribs, and Myles is rushin' him here behind a po-lice escort."

The siren grew louder as Hilfy sprinted toward the huddle, but Beezley beat him to it. Myles skidded his Ford Explorer to within a yard of the tunnel exit and pushed Beezley out the front door.

While Beezley was sneaking to the Cowboys' five-yard line behind a wall of blockers, Hilfy was retreating to the sidelines. While Beezley was leading the team on a 99-yard touchdown march, Hilfy was taking a long swig from his whiskey flask. He took a swig for every Cowboys' interception, fumble recovery, and Beezley touchdown pass en route to the Cowboys' 38-34 victory.

No one noticed Hilfy staggering off the field through the hugs and high-fives of his teammates and coaches toward his makeshift locker. He looked back at the field as he stepped through the end zone and said, "I could have done that."

31

Scott Hilfinger thought he had gone to the whiskey well once too often when he was approached by a female sportswriter who looked like Jack Byrne.

"It's me," Jack whispered.

Hilfy sat on the chair of his makeshift locker staring at Jack's legs. "Why didn't you get the see-through panty hose, Mrs. Byrne?"

"Trying to hide the hair on my legs. I would have shaved, but Molli wouldn't let me borrow her razor."

"Uncomfortable?"

"Hell, yeah. The hose itches my legs, the bra is chafin' my nipples, and the eyeliner keeps drippin' into my pupils. Sure am glad I'm not a woman."

"You just like to dress like one."

"It's a long story."

Hilfy took another swig. "By the way, who's Molli?"

"I'm Molli."

"I'm confused. One week you're Jack Byrne, the next week you're Graham Repert, and now you're some ugly chick."

"The real Molli's quite hot."

Hilfy took another swig and continued staring at Jack from the base of his black high heels to the top of his blonde wig. Jack said he would explain at The Bar in Arlington. First he had to get a few "I feel good" quotes from Redskins' lineman Fritz Gonnert for the feature he was writing for Molli. None of that seemed to register with Hilfy.

Jack waddled like a runway model between naked linebackers and safeties out of the Cowboys' locker room and returned twenty minutes later. Hilfy hadn't moved and seemed able to move nothing but his lips. "How was he?

"One of the best I've had as a male or female reporter. This guy even remembered the name of his high school coach."

"Better than me?"

Jack winked and spoke in his best Mae West voice. "Honey, nobody's better than you."

Had he been any other player or had he not sipped his whiskey flask dry, Hilfy likely would have thrown Jack across the room like a shovel pass. Instead, Hilfy was being escorted out the door by a cross-dressing ex-sportswriter without one catcall from his teammates. It was the first time Jack left the Cowboys' locker room without being called a DH.

JACK ESCHEWED The Bar in Arlington and drove straight to the downtown Dippity Donuts in an effort to drown Hilfy's whiskey and sorrows in coffee and soak them up in donuts. The frustrated quarterback was crying in his cinnamon twist.

"That was my chance, my one fucking chance."

Jack sipped his hot chocolate and bit into a glazed donut. Hilfy continued and with a glazed look on his face.

"One rib, just one rib, why couldn't that fucker have broken one rib. At least a hairline fracture."

The whiskey wasn't wearing off, so Jack tried a different strategy.

"The problem with you Hilfy is that you're not a team player."

"Huh?"

"You should be ecstatic that your team is a win away from the playoffs. You haven't lost since you arrived. You're a lucky charm wearing an unlucky number. The Cowboys aren't going to get rid of you as long as they are winnin'. You should be doin' shots with your teammates at The Bar in Arlington and not donuts with a has-been sportswriter, declared dead, living in an abandoned locker room, ghostwriting for a dumb debutante, and reincarnated as Marilyn "Fucking" Monroe."

Jack's reach for Hilfy's whiskey flask was rejected.

"What are ya' gonna do?" Hilfy asked.

"Fuck if I know. I've got to find out who I am, why these goons are chasing me, and how to reconnect with my widow who only needed a bucket of balls to overcome her grief."

Jack heard the glass front door open and peeked over his shoulder in the booth. "Sawed off Stack of Shit warning," he said.

"Who?"

"The asshole who rejected the story I wrote about you."

"The asshole whose car you tried to blow up?"

"Right."

Soss sat with two butchers and started reading The Dallas Star's early, early edition and Dave Noonan's rewrite which led with, "The Dallas Cowboys snatched victory from the jaws of defeat." Penny Pettigrew's column lead was unchanged.

Soss looked over his newspaper, whiffed Jack's perfume in the next booth, and stared at his soft shoulder-length wig. After Hilfy went to pee whiskey into the nearest unrinal, Soss sauntered to Jack's table. "Excuse me, Miss. Could I buy you a cup of coffee?"

Jack hid his face with his left hand and disguised his voice with a deep bass. "Fuck off buddy. I'm already spoken for."

Soss turned redder than a hot tamale and fled the donut shop as the butchers giggled at their boss' embarrassment.

Jack thought, "That's for the time you transferred an irate reader's profanity-laced call about one of my columns from your office answering machine to my home answering machine on Christmas Eve."

Jack and his date followed. Their path to the car was interrupted by a bum who was eating discarded donuts from the trashcan behind the shop. "Where's your coat?" Jack said. "It's getting cold out here."

The bum with a liquor breath harsher than Hilfy's did not recognize his shivering former cellmate. "T-t-tall, sk-sk-skinny bloke took it from me awhile back."

Hilfy's whiskey breath could be seen in cool night air. "Come on, Jack, it's freezing.' Get me home.'"

It was an ironic request in the presence of three men who didn't have a home. Within the next 90 minutes Hilfy would be asleep at his corner room at the Y, the bum on nearest street corner, and Jack in an abandoned locker room – all dreaming of the loves and the lives that had abandoned them.

32

Jack woke up Tuesday before Christmas in a small town on his converted high jump pad that could sleep 10. There was no one else he wanted to share his giant purple pillow but an aspiring female golfer in the nearest big city.

Jack and Jeanie never saw much of each other during the days leading up to Christmases. Jack was either traveling with the Cowboys to the next game or too busy writing another obituary for a losing season. Jeanie was practicing for and then playing in the Annual Dallas Women's Christmas Classic on her home course.

Jack picked up the newspaper he bought in town on Monday and flipped to a story about the Classic, buried beneath the Cowboys' coverage. Jeanie was not mentioned in the story, only her name in tiny print in Thursday's opening round pairings of the 54-hole tournament.

Jack had fond memories of the Classic, because this was the tournament where he and Jeanie met and on the golf course where they were married. Ever since the explosion that spurred his fake death, Jack dreamed nightly about Jeanie. Now he was having a daydream.

It was Christmas 1994. Jack had been elevated to columnist that fall and was assigned to the Christmas Classic's final round. The crusty veteran columnists hogged the Cowboys' and college bowl games, leaving a need for columns on a local angle.

Protesting his assignment, Jack decided to write a column on the last place golfer instead of the first place golfer. Also, the last place golfer would tee off first, giving him enough time to bat out his column and return to his apartment in time for the Cowboys' kickoff.

He staggered to the first tee at dawn, following a night covering another Dallas Mavericks' downing and a Kazbar drowning, with bloodshot eyes and a box of glazed Dippity Donuts.

"Want one?" Jack held the open box before the only other person on the tee, a petite woman with tight red slacks and matching sweater with a tumbleweed on the corner.

Jeanie waved off Jack's breakfast with her gloved left hand, pulled out her Big Bertha driver, and took practice swings. "I'm just here to play golf."

Jack stared at Jeanie from her spotless white golf spikes to her clean white Caprock State cap. "You look more dressed for prayin' than for playin'."

Jeanie kept swinging. "Yeah, I'm praying to Saint Babe."

"Babe Ruth?"

"Babe Didrikson, the greatest women's golfer of all time. You don't follow women's sports, do you?"

Jeanie stuffed the driver back in her golf bag, loosened her back and neck, and stared at Jack as he stuffed a donut into his mouth and licked his fingers. "Are you my caddy?" she asked.

Jack laughed and shook his head.

"The way I have been playing this week, you look like the kind of caddy I'd get."

Jack wiped his right hand on his faded jeans and shook Jeanie's hand. "I'm Jack Byrne, columnist for The Dallas Star. You don't mind me following ya' around today?"

"You must not know anything about golf, either. The higher the score the worse the player."

Jack wiped donut crumbs off his goatee. "I played golf once and hated it. I kept hitting that damn windmill."

Jack detected a smile creasing the right corner of Jeanie's smooth lips. "I could interview your opponents," he said, "but there's no Korean interpreter out here."

The left corner of Jeanie's lips creased and moments later, there was a full blown grin. Jeanie stuck a ball and a tee into the cold brown turf, took the Big Bertha back out of her bag, positioned herself alongside the ball, waggled her hips, and swung as hard as she could. She squinted into the morning sun but couldn't see the ball. Jack could.

"It's a bird, it's a plane. No, it's a pop fly to the second baseman. Did you get the hang time on that tee shot?"

Jeanie would get a bogey. Jack, a bird, not the first from a lady but the first from a gloved middle finger. Jack and Jeanie strolled together down the fairway alone – Jeanie carrying her heavy golf bag and Jack his Dippity Donut box. The odd number of players in the field assured she would have no playing partner. The only other spectator was an 85-year-old golf official who followed along in a golf cart.

Between tee shots and bunker shots Jeanie told Jack about growing up on a golf course in Midland, her love of the only game she has known, her late father, and her aspiration of making the LPGA Tour. She had just graduated from Caprock State and came to this golf tournament hoping to meet The Legend and hopefully to be coached by him.

"I'm not making much of an impression," said Jeanie, replacing a large divot in the 13th fairway.

"More like a dee-pression," Jack said.

Jack's comebacks received more frowns than grins but finally a giggle when he replied with a Happy Gilmore answer to a question about why he doesn't like golf. "Golf requires goofy pants and a fat ass. You should talk to my neighbor the accountant, probably a great golfer. Huge ass."

"I hate to admit it, but that's one of my favorite movies," Jeanie said, marching to the 14th green and igniting a banter of Happy Gilmore quotes.

After her fairway shot on the par five 15th, Jack said, "That's two, Shooter" to which Jeanie replied, "Good, you can count."

"And you can count on me meeting you in the parking lot."

After airmailing the green on the par three 16th, Jack said, "I can't believe you want to be a professional golfer. You oughta be working in the snack bar."

Jeanie smiled, grabbed Jack's shoulders, pinned him against the old official's golf cart, and pretended to punch him in the stomach. "You're gonna get it, Jacky."

The comedy routine loosened up Jeanie, who saved par on the 16th and birdied the seventeenth. She whacked her final drive 250 yards down the middle of the 18th fairway and knocked it four feet from the pin. Jack clung to the back of the golf cart like a chariot driver as the official drove past her toward the green.

"Jeanie, Shooter's gonna choke. The gold jacket is yours."

Jeanie's voice carried in the cool breeze. "Gold jacket, green jacket. Who gives a shit?"

Jack held the flagstick for Jeanie as she sank the birdie putt. She pumped her fist, gave Jack a peck on the cheek, and whispered in his ear as he stuck the flagstick back in the hole. "You better write a good column about me."

Jack did more than that. He found her a coach, a job in the Forest Green pro shop, and renewed hope in her golf career. He did it not by anything he said on the golf course or to The Legend but by what he wrote on his laptop in the clubhouse while Jeanie was smacking a large bucket of balls on the practice range after her round of 78 managed, by one shot, to keep her from finishing in the cellar.

Legend has it, there is a new kid in town. She doesn't wear goofy pants and she definitely doesn't have a fat ass. What she does have is what most golfers with more grind and grunt don't have – a determined grit and a youthful grin that she carried around the Forest Green golf course in yesterday morning's solitude and destined to carry her around the world's finest golf courses in absolute glory.

Jack's words were followed by Jeanie's words on a homemade card with smiley face golf balls and golf club letters that formed the words, "Thank you," that she mailed to him at The Dallas Star sports department.

Jack hugged the pillow he had taken from his house and smiled as he lay on the high jump pad remembering what she wrote in a pink marker pen at the end of the note. "In case you are interested, here is what I shot on my last 10 holes on my home course in Midland the other day – 624 555 3445."

It had taken Jack a few days, but he finally got it. She had sent him her telephone number.

33

Jack knew that Molli Glass knew nothing about sports. A quick read of her advance on the State Class A Championship football game made him realize she knew nothing about writing.

Geburtville High really wants to win the state title on Friday night in front of their home crowd, and no one wants to win it more than Gebbies' Coach Jerry Grimes.

"I really want to win it," remarked Coach Grimes. "It would mean so much to me, my family, my players, our fans, and this community."

"How bad is it?" Molli looked over Jack's shoulder as he stared at the computer screen and sipped a cup of leftover eggnog from the afternoon's staff Christmas party.

"Not as bad as Penny Pettigrew's dribble. Why did you major in journalism?"

"Because it's the only thing easier than P.E."

Jack figured Molli was more interested in an MRS degree than an MS and he was right. As he dismantled Molli's story, she showed him her promise ring from Cullen Abernathy III.

"That's cute," Jack said, turning his eyes back to the screen.

"We met freshman year at Berrington, and he's now in his second year at Harvard Law School."

Jack interrupted the future Mrs. Abernathy III before she went on about how they met at a fraternity-sorority mixer, decided to go steady, met his parents at their Highland Park mansion, and received her ring on Valentine's Day. "I'll rewrite this for you, but you're gonna need to call Grimes again and get more quotes."

"I just called his house and his wife said he was at the office, but he wasn't there either."

"Have you tried the cheerleading coach?"

"Why in the world would I call the cheerleading coach?"

"That's where most high school coaches spend their Wednesday nights. When I covered high school football in Dallas way back when, if the coach wasn't at home we usually could find him at the cheerleading coach's place."

"Didn't he get mad?"

"I didn't give a shit who he was screwin;' I just wanted some quotes."

Jack hurried Molli, so he could get back to the field house in time to see if the gridiron ghosts would return to the Gebbie Bowl for their Wednesday night game, even though it was pouring outside. The cheerleading coach answered and handed the telephone to Grimes.

"How did you get this number?" Grimes said.

Jack listened on the other line and sent directions via email. Jack wrote, "Just tell him, 'Sorry but I had a couple more important questions I forgot to ask you at practice?' You're a pretty blonde, he won't hang up."

Grimes answered each question Jack kept passing to Molli. Jack typed everything Grimes said and then filled in the narrative to make up the best football advance Molli also never wrote.

Jerry Grimes remembers sitting on the 30-yard line after the 1983 state semifinal game and watching the opposing team carry off the field their star quarterback Johnny Molinski, who would carry Steuberville to the championship a week later.

The Geburtville coach has waited 22 years for redemption and nobody wants it more than him. "I can't tell you how much it hurt," Grimes said. "(Winning the title) would mean so much to me, my family, my players, our fans, and this community."

A mountain stands in front of Geburtville in the form of undefeated two-time defending state champion Porterfield. But the Gebbies have some climbers as tenacious as Sir Edmund Hillary.

When Molli had asked Grimes, per Jack's request, whatever happened to Molinski, the coach paused and said, "Who the fuck cares about Johnny Molinski?"

Jack left that quote out of the story.

Molli didn't thank Jack for writing her advance and refused to give him an advance on the money she owed him. He was down to the $42.50 he shoved under the high jump mattress. Molli didn't even offer him a ride in the pouring rain. She only said, "I'll see you at Gebbie Stadium on Friday night."

Jack raided the staff lounge refrigerator, stuffing a large turkey drumstick and dressing and two pecan pie slices into a Tupperware container. He stuck two full beer bottles into his black overcoat and grabbed from behind the receptionist desk a navy blue umbrella with the words "The Gazette, Your Hometown Newspaper" in white letters on the vinyl top.

"They owe me," Jack said as he shut the door and stepped into a downpour.

JACK WALKED QUICKLY toward the Gebbie Bowl carrying his dinner in one hand and holding the umbrella with the other. His blue sneakers splashed water on the sidewalk with every step as rain slid off the umbrella. "They won't be playing in this shit."

Ghosts of football seasons past, he figured, were fair weather players. Unlike in their youth, football was supposed to be played on crisp winter nights on a field carpeted with soft green grass that felt like a sponge when you topple onto it.

It was so damp, homeowners didn't bother turning on their Christmas lights. Plastic shepherds and wise men were taking a bath on front lawns. It was so dark, Jack only guessed he was walking in the right direction. A few drenching steps farther he looked ahead and saw a light glimmering in the distance. He followed it like the real shepherds and wise men followed the Star of Bethlehem. Then there was another light and another and another. The more he walked the more he soaked his sneakers, the more lights he saw and the more evident that football was being played at the Gebbie Bowl.

Jack arrived atop the bank to a field surrounded by car and pickup truck headlights and full of mud and players covered in mud.

Ghosts of the Gridiron

They slipped and slid like children who had never played football in the mud before. They giggled and grunted as they sloshed down the sidelines, slithering through tacklers while cradling the pigskin they would lose as soon as they slammed into the mud and to the mob dog-piling each other in absolute splendor.

Finally, a score. A receiver hauled in a pass shot-putted from the quarterback. He wiped mud out of his eyes, side-stepped two defenders who fell backward, and fled the others. As he reached the goal-line designated by orange, mud splattered cones, he dove and slid belly first through the end zone.

Jack watched from the passenger seat of a white, mud splattered station wagon in which he took refuge. Rain dripped down his coat and landed on the floorboard. He chomped on the turkey drumstick as the men continued playing in the Mud Bowl. Every jersey and face was black and no one could tell what college or high school they played for and even what race they were. And they didn't care.

For a moment Jack forgot what transpired the last time he attempted to play on this field, which didn't look the same in the mud. "Boy, that looks like fun," Jack said between turkey bites.

The rain eventually stopped and so did the players. Jack snuck out of the station wagon. He hid himself behind the umbrella and marched to the field house. He looked back at the players still laughing and patting each other on the back, wondering how they would explain their appearance to their wives and how good a hot shower would feel.

Jack felt a good story coming on. He was overcome by temptation and rushed to the final remaining headlights atop the bank. A gentleman sat in the driver's seat of his pickup and wiped mud off his wrinkled face with an old towel. Jack tapped on window. The man was reluctant to talk to someone not covered in mud, but he opened his door. Ghosts are allowed to talk to other ghosts.

"Whaddaya want, Bub?"

"Just passing by, and wondered what was going on out here."

The man said, "Nuttin,' just playing a little football with my pals."

He went on to explain he once played for Geburtville and at his high school reunion the past summer, a few of his old teammates decided to start the ghost league and play at the now-defunct Gebbie Bowl. Word got around to other former players from other schools, and they decided on the secret Wednesday night games.

"You're not gonna blab it to the press are ya'? If word gets out, the cops will throw us out of here."

"Nah, I won't say anything. I was just looking for a former Lone Star State quarterback, Johnny Molinski, and thought one of ya'll might know what happened to him."

The man scratched mud out of his graying locks.

"Ya' mean Wrongway Molinski?"

"You know him?"

"No but Jerry Grimes, the Geburtville coach does."

"You sure?"

"Yeah. Jerry was his college roommate."

34

Geburtville High School will never know if it won the 2005 Texas Class A State Football Championship.

That was the lead under Molli's byline that Jack wrote in the darkness of Gebbie Stadium and soon lit up the Geburtville Gazette and Dallas Star sports pages.

It was ironic to be writing in the dark after two of the most well lit days and nights in the town's history. Geburtville mayor Willard Schiebler decided to light the Gebbies' passage to victory by declaring the Thursday and Friday before Christmas, "Light up Geburtville."

The sun showed up at dawn Thursday and dried up the puddles in the town square and the mud in the Gebbie Bowl, leaving only faint cleat-prints from the previous night's game. Students dug a hole on the 50-yard line and surrounded it with large rocks. They piled twigs, branches, wood, logs, and newspaper atop the pit and hung a pirate doll with a Porterfield football jersey from the goalpost.

Students, staff, and fans assembled on the field and the banks of the Gebbie Bowl. They whooped and hollered when a player lit the bonfire, sent flames shooting into night sky, and yelled, "Incinerate the Pirates!"

Seemingly the whole town followed the flame for the impromptu pep rally. Jack could smell the embers, feel the heat, and see the fire through the windows of the otherwise pitch-black field house. It reminded him of the blaze that should have taken his life only a few weeks before. He walked outside and watched the boys in the purple jerseys parade before the bonfire to the claps and hollers of their fellow townspeople.

Coach Grimes spoke of the boys' season-long commitment and how they had dedicated themselves to fulfilling their dream to bring a state title to Geburtville. He mentioned how a quarterback named Molinski stopped them his senior year in high school, but it would take more than an undefeated Pirates' team to keep him from it this time. "We will make them walk the plank."

"Arrr! Arrr! Arrr!" the Gebbies fans yelled.

Mayor Schiebler quieted them down as he announced his "Light Up Geburtville" campaign. He drew a big cheer with, "Let's shine our way to victory."

Watching the flames shooting atop the 50-yard line was ironic for Jack, who felt he could have led the Gebbies to a state title until his flame was extinguished on that very spot.

The bonfire eventually burned out over the night but not the Christmas lights atop roofs, trees, bushes, porches, and balconies of seemingly every home in Geburtville. Christmas tree lights were left on, and the town sparkled in red, green, and white.

THE LIGHTS were turned back on at dusk the next day, three hours before kickoff. Not only Christmas lights, but house and porch lights and lights inside and outside of shops and stores in the town square.

The Porterfield fans could see the lit up town as they approached from 20 miles out. No place was better lit than Gebbie Stadium. The multiple lights atop the steel poles blanketed the field and stands with their powerful rays.

The only dark spot was the Gebbie Bowl. Jack used a flashlight to find his way out of his makeshift digs and almost smacked his head on the Pirate doll still hanging from a rope on the goalpost. He didn't need the flashlight as he followed the stadium lights to the front gate, where he flashed his Dallas Star press badge while covering his name with a frozen finger. His profile was illuminated upon his trudge up the stadium steps toward the press box. He wore his fake eyeglasses but still hid his skinned head under the bill of his black overcoat on an evening so cold that fans left their home heaters on high for an immediate dethaw when they returned.

Every light was on in the press box and so was the television set and radios. Jack enjoyed a pre-game chicken feast while watching the Channel 7 sports report – mostly Cowboys' coverage, updates on

Jarmelle Beezley's sore ribs, and the team's chances of clinching the division title on Christmas Day in New York should the elusive quarterback not play.

Jack stared into the screen as second round highlights of the Christmas Classic golf tournament were shown and turned his ear toward the set to hear the announcer amidst the press box chatter and the tubas and horns tuning up from the marching band section.

"As usual, a Korean is atop the leaderboard. But a surprising and inspired local golfer is challenging for the title."

Then flashed Jeanie in her neat white slacks, white golf shirt and red sweater, and Tumbleweed cap rolling a 20-foot putt and fist-pumping as the ball fell into the side of the cup. The gold bracelet Jack had given her the last Christmas dangled down her right wrist.

"Pratt's birdie finished off a four-under par 68. She is only two strokes behind going into tomorrow's final round in her quest for the biggest victory of her life."

Jack clenched his fists. "She's playing for me."

"Who is?" Molli's voice called from the seat beside him.

"Oh, nothin.'" Jack looked away from the screen and to the reporter whom he was about to ghost-write the biggest game in Geburtville history. The only words she would write would be those to her Harvard Law boyfriend on the texts she would send throughout the game.

"Got my money?" Jack asked.

"Sorry, Graham. No check yet."

Jack piled more drumsticks and mashed potatoes on his plate and settled into his seat beside Molli. Jack asked the Porterfield Press writer why they aren't playing at a neutral site.

"Pirates hadn't lost in three fuckin' years and don't figure losin' anywhere they play," he said. "They may have lost a fuckin' coin toss, but they sure as hell ain't gonna lose this here game."

The Pirates lost another coin toss unbeknownst to Molli, who tapped away on her cellphone with long purple fingernails.

"She can pay a manicurist $95 but can't front me up a dime," Jack thought. "I should walk out now."

Had he walked, Jack would have missed one of the best comebacks in high school football history. With Kody Keimer in the hospital getting a blood transfusion and backup quarterback Braden Edwards unable to push the ball past midfield, Grimes decided to put at the helm a player off the junior varsity with his team trailing 30-0 at halftime.

Shon Runnels was likely the Scott Hilfinger of Geburtville High School football. He hadn't played a down his first three years but finally made the most of his chance in leading the J.V. team to an undefeated season. He was rewarded by sitting on the varsity bench for the playoffs. Unless he got a football scholarship, Runnels would join his father in the sawmill after graduation. This was his only chance.

Runnels played as if going to the sawmill would be like going to hell. He rifled passes through the smallest creases between defenders. He twisted and juked away from tacklers. He faked a pitch to a tailback and sprinted down the sidelines like he was being chased by an axe murderer. Runnels rallied the Gebbies to 28 unanswered points in front of a crowd so loud his linemen could barely hear him stammer the plays in the huddle.

"That could have been me," Jack thought.

Molli kept texting even as Runnels rambled 35 yards to midfield on a quarterback draw with 32 seconds remaining and no timeouts with the Gebbies trailing 30-28. By the time he spiked the ball, there were only 17 seconds left.

"Wish these people wouldn't yell so loud," Molli said, staring at her cellphone. "It's hard to concentrate."

Runnels had lit up an offense from a fully lit town and needed another big play to get into field goal range. He told his receivers between breaths to run as fast and far as they could. He dropped back and sidestepped two blitzing linebackers, ducked under the blind side end, and dodged a defensive tackle. As the entire Pirate line pursued him Runnels sprinted up the field, faked out a safety, and swept to the Pirates' sidelines. He dove for the out-of-bounds marker at the 25 yard line. The numbers 0:03 flashed off the scoreboard.

Helped up by his receivers, Runnels limped across the field to the applause of the home crowd. He patted Gebbies' kicker Luther Mobley on the shoulder pads, "You can do this."

He could, but Luther's longest field goal was 35 yards and this would be from 42 yards. Luther looked at the ball between the center's legs and then to the holder, who stretched his hands and shouted, "Hut!," and then corralling the snapped pigskin.

Everyone in the stands stood and screamed. Gebbies' fans and players held hands. Every light in town seemed to be shining on the goalpost. The ball was placed on the cold turf. Mobley took two steps forward, dug his left cleat into the brown grass, and swung his leg at the ball. The kick was like a torpedo firing straight for its target. The ball lifted over defensive linemen and soared end-over-end and just as the towering boot descended over the end zone, the stadium lights went out.

The crowd silenced. All those lights and heaters left on in Geburtville caused a county-wide power failure and left Gebbie Stadium in darkness. The only light was from Molli's cellphone. The two referees in back of the end zone heard the ball land. But they had no idea if it went over or under the crossbar.

Everyone was confused until the head referee made an announcement 30 minutes later over a bullhorn. Grimes, hoping for the wind to die down, had lobbied for a postponement for the lights to come back on or until the next morning. The head ref denied the request, saying that the visiting team was driving home after the game and there was no certainty when and if the power would be restored. He instructed everyone parked behind the end zone on either side to turn on their headlights. Six school buses were driven onto sidelines and shined their lights on the field. The lighting in Gebbie Stadium was now no different from the Gebbie Bowl. Mobley sat on the bench with a blanket wrapped around him.

"That's one way freeze your own kicker," the Porterfield Press writer said to Jack, who batted out his assumed game story as deadline loomed.

Mobley marched back to the field and lined up for his second attempt. He stared at the headlights flashing onto the goalpost. The crowd noise quieted as the ball was snapped, players crashed into each other, and Mobley swung his leg even harder than on his first attempt. As the ball sailed like an out-of-control bottle rocket, Jack was typing the final words of his lead he crafted in the dark as Molli shined her cellphone on the keyboard.

Geburtville High School will never know if it won the 2005 Texas Class A State Football Championship.

Luther Mobley will never know if his 42-yard field goal try into a shivering North Texas breeze flew gloriously over the crossbar or a miserable few inches below it. What he and his teammates will remember was how a miscalculated Light Up the Town scheme left them in darkness and how a frozen kicker's final re-boot at glory didn't even reach the goal line.

35

Christmas is about hope.

Hope for a good family and friends. Hope for a loving partner.

Hope for a special present under the Christmas tree. Hope for a life of contentment and joy and a life after life.

Without hope, there is only darkness.

Jack Byrne studied the darkness in the field house early Christmas Eve before the sun rose and gave hope for a new day and for the seniors on the Geburtville football team whose final game they would relive as ghosts at class reunions and on pickup football games on a field lit by headlights. Jack's only thought was of the gold bracelet dangling from Jeanie's wrist.

She kissed him exactly one year ago, on Christmas Eve, when the Byrnes traditionally exchanged gifts in their warm white robes. Jeanie rubbed her soft fingers over the gold plates and sat the tiny golfer medallion in her palm. She put the bracelet back in the white box and led her husband back to the bedroom.

Jack never saw the bracelet again until the sportscast he watched in the press box. The more he thought about spending Christmas without Jeanie the more he knew what he had to do.

The bracelet appeared again along with a photo of the fist-shaking Jeanie and ironically right above Molli's championship game story on page 12c of The Dallas Star Saturday newspaper, which Jack bought along with five gallons of gasoline at the first lit filling station found on the Dallas outskirts.

Jack didn't consider the VW van starting after hibernating behind the field house a Christmas miracle, though it took seven twists on the key and several pumps on the accelerator. By now, Jack assumed a large network of goons were on the lookout for Graham Repert's rusted out van. He had to arrive at the Forest Green

Country Club before the bagpipes signified dawn and the first group on the number one tee.

Jack drove through a field behind the country club and parked in a weed grove between a thicket of oak trees. There were more trees there than on the course. There was no forest, and the winter grass on the country club was brown, not green. There wasn't much green in his wallet either. The gasoline, newspaper, and the dozen glazed at a Dippity Donuts dropped his savings to 13 dollars and 12 cents, and he only had enough gas to make it back to Geburtville.

There was plenty enough energy for Jack to follow his widow around the golf course and enough spectators to hide behind. First he found another player who intrigued him – Dick Schwartz, that Sawed off Stack of Shit sports editor.

Soss was playing his normal Saturday golf game with three other Dallas Star backslappers on the adjacent Lakes course, which had a few ponds but no lake. Jack had spotted Soss' black Lexus, with a cracked tailpipe, through his fake eyeglasses on the road leading to the clubhouse and heard the loathsome foursome walking up the fairway in front of the oak trees. He heard a chuckle that sounded like a Chihuahua with a chicken wing stuck in his throat.

"I know that fucker's laugh anywhere," Jack thought as he scooted along the fairway, peering around a tree as Soss lined up his shot with a fairway wood and sliced it into the woods.

Soss located his ball and flipped it back into the fairway with his "hand wedge," not knowing that Jack was the only one watching. "Incredible luck," Soss said as he pulled the Cuban cigar from his lips and blew smoke at his golfing buddies. "The ball must have caromed off a tree and into the middle of the fairway."

Soss thought his next shot landed in the fairway, but he found his ball buried in the green-side bunker.

"That's for the humiliation I felt when you replaced me with a cock-sucking intern at the Cowboys' training camp two years ago," Jack said, wiping sand off his hands and watching from behind a bush as Soss took three shots to blast out of the bunker after being hidden in a sand cloud.

His next tee shot ended up in a creek, his recovery shot in front of a tree, and his approach shot in the thick weeds behind the green. Jack put on a greenskeeper's black overalls so no one would notice him, in ghostlike fashion, relocating Soss' balls. Following his fourth swat at his ball in the tall weeds, Soss swung his pitching wedge into a tree and bent it in half. As a bonus, Soss was bombarded by a sparrow with loose bowels hovering from above.

Jack laughed inwardly. Soss' playing partners laughed outwardly. "You can't get a birdie, so the birdie got you," one of them yelled from the golf cart.

They all got the bird as Soss yanked his golf bag from the cart, marched to the parking lot, slammed his golf bag into the trunk of his Lexus, and sped off.

"Good riddance," Jack said.

THE NEXT SHOT Jack saw was a long, wonderfully arced beauty that flew from the practice tee to the center of the practice range. The only thing more beautiful was the player who hit it.

Jack walked around the range to get a better look at the golfer with tanned legs on a winter's day warm enough for a white skirt and a tight red sleeveless shirt shaded by the white cap with Tumbleweed logo. The gold bracelet dangled down her bronzed right wrist as she clutched her Big Bertha and flung her hips toward the fairway. It was a more powerful sounding whack than Jack recalled from his backyard. There was no net stopping this towering white speck that soared through the blue sky and seemingly stayed airborne forever. Jack kept staring at the bombs set off by a woman, his woman, with the pearly white golf spikes and ankle socks and the look of a determined champion. She wouldn't notice Jack if he ran naked down the practice range.

Still he remained inconspicuous in his greenskeeper's overalls, peering through the gallery at this angel in golf garb sauntering up and down the fairways striving for a victory that had eluded her all her married life. Jack barely noticed Chad, her caddy, handing her club after club or Chad's daddy, the Legend, whispering words of wisdom in her ear as she battled for the Christmas Classic trophy and $40,000 first prize.

The gold bracelet flapped back and forth on her wrist after her fist pump celebrated the 20-foot birdie putt on the par 4 16th hole to tie three-time LPGA tour winner Kyung Ho for the lead. Jack was close enough to see a tear running down her right cheek as her five-iron shot on the next tee splattered into the front bunker on the par 3 hole but not close enough to hear Jack's whisper, "You can do this, honey."

Jack did his own little fist pump when her bunker shot stopped a foot from the hole. It was easier to stay hidden on the 18th fairway, where the gallery had gathered two-rows deep to cheer the local girl. Their applause reached a crescendo as her towering drive split the fairway and rolled to a stop 130 yards from the green. Ho stepped up to the tee, and with Jack whispering to himself, "Shank it, shank it," hooked her ball into the rough. Her recovery floated over the green, hit a television camera, bounced between two bunkers, and rolled 45 feet from the hole.

Advantage golfing beauty. Chad handed Jeanie her trusty eight-iron, the club that had not failed her all week. She looked at the flagstick fluttering lightly in the late afternoon sun. She approached the ball, jangled the bracelet on her wrist, took one last glance at the flagstick and a short breath, and swung hard. She pointed her club at the flagstick as the ball dove from its ascent. Jeanie and everyone on either side of the fairway and behind the green stared as the ball dropped onto the green seven feet from the hole. She handed her club back to her caddy and waved her gloved left hand to the cheering crowd.

Jack peeled off the overalls, stuffed his glasses in his pants pocket, and arrived at the green before Jeanie did. He peeked between two heads from the second row around the green and "ahhhed" with the crowd as the Korean's downhill birdie putt lipped the cup.

Jeanie knelt behind her ball and used her putter as a guide to where she should aim her uphill birdie putt on a slight slope. The crowd grew silent as Jeanie stood, rubbed her fingers over the gold bracelet, and slid her hands down the putter's shaft and the silver blade behind the white dimpled ball. She stared back and forth from the hole to the ball without thinking about the silver golf trophy and the big check that waited in the club house or the invitation to four LPGA events in 2006.

"C'mon, Jeanie, drain it," Jack whispered.

Jeanie pulled the putter back and smacked the ball like she was tapping a nail with a hammer. The crowd started yelling, and the noise grew to a crescendo as the ball spun around the hole and dropped into the cup.

Jeanie dropped her putter, knelt, and put her hands over her eyes. Jack squirmed through bodies to the edge of the green. Tears seeped down Jeanie's cheeks onto the bracelet. Tears also formed in Jack's eyes. He took one step onto the green as Jeanie, sporting an ear-to-ear smile stood and turned in Jack's direction. But Jack's path to Jeanie was blocked by a caddy with his arms spread wide. Jeanie lunged into Chad's arms. They jumped up and down in unison as they embraced and kissed long enough for a crowd's wave of "W-o-o-o-o-a!" to finish echoing off the 18th green.

Jack didn't wait for their lips to unseal or hear them exchange, "We did it, we did it." He was off the golf course before player and caddy, arms clasped around each other's shoulders, strolled off the green. He was peeling the rusted out VW van onto the road, beating his fist three times atop the steering wheel, and hollering "F-u-u-u-ck!" about the same time Jeanie was signing her winning scorecard.

Christmas, Jack thought, was about hope. All he felt was despair.

36

If he hadn't been down to his final 13 dollars and 12 cents, Jack would have spent Christmas Eve guzzling whiskey in the corner booth at the Kazbar. Instead he spent it guzzling a 12-pack of generic beer in the darkest corner of the Kazbar parking lot.

After pouring the last drop of each white can down his throat, Jack crunched the can that read "Beer" in his hand and tossed it in the back. "Bitch, fucking bitch."

A cold northerly rocked the VW van from side to side and forced Jack to bundle in his black overcoat to keep from shivering. What he would have given for just one shot of whiskey or a shot of morphine. He didn't even have enough money for a glazed donut and only enough gas in the tank to make it back to Geburtville.

He shot-gunned his final "Beer" smashed the can against his forehead and fired it into the back window faster than a Scott Hilfinger bullet pass."Bitch, mother fucking bitch."

Jack burped an awful stench from his lungs. Blood dripped from the gash he had just put in his forehead above his right eye. He shook the van key like a Parkinson's patient and after several misses, found the key hole. He would have turned on the heater, but he couldn't figure out how. The van lights shined onto the Kazbar and his former cellmate whom he almost ran over. The shivering bum still without a coat staggered past in search of a warm street corner to spend Christmas. He squinted into the VW headlights, "Merry Christmas, lad."

Jack figured by now the goons were on a Christmas break; otherwise he might spend Christmas curled up with his old cellmate. All he wanted was to curl up in a warm bed with his beloved Jeanie just as he had the past eight Christmases. He turned on the radio as he drove through the dark downtown Dallas streets to Bing Crosby singing "I'll be home from Christmas."

Ghosts of the Gridiron

Jack sang along as he swayed the van from one lane to the other on the desolate North Dallas Expressway – the cops, he figured, also were on Christmas break – before steering from the inside lane to the exit and aiming his vehicle toward Magnolia Avenue. The street would have been darker than downtown had it not been for the Christmas lights that adorned every rooftop – even on Jack's house.

"Who the fuck put those up?" said Jack, who never put up a Christmas light.

Jack drove past his house and down the alley to his normal spying spot along the backyard fence. He stepped out the driver's side door and fell face first in the alley, making a dent on the other side of his forehead. Then he got his black overcoat caught in the fence as he climbed it and fell back-first into his backyard. "Bah, humbug," he grumbled.

He started for the backdoor but was stopped by the multi-colored lights shining from a perfectly groomed and decorated Christmas tree sparkling in the den.

"Who the fuck put that up?" said Jack, who never put up a Christmas tree.

Jack peered through the window and saw the Christmas Classic trophy glimmering off the mantel piece and several empty coffee mugs that likely had been filled with spiked eggnog for guests of a victory/holiday celebration. There was one guest remaining, and he was kissing Jack's wife even though there was no mistletoe in sight.

"I'll be home for Christmas still stirred in Jack's head" and it may have been playing in Jack's den. But Jack wasn't coming home. He was back in the VW van, heading for the freeway faster than Santa Claus could fall down a chimney.

The van set a new personal land speed record as Jack smashed his foot on the accelerator and hollered, "Now Dasher, now Dancer, now Prancer, and Vixen. Get me the fuck out of here," while imagining Chad giving Jeanie a new putter for Christmas.

THE DETOUR to Magnolia Avenue and the increased speed into a cold northerly wind used up the remaining gas in the VW's tank. Jack paid no attention to the fuel gauge nor the speedometer and wished he had crashed into the tree off the side of the dark highway at the 100mph he was driving the van instead of the 1mph he was pushing it to the tree after running out of gas.

The temperature was also about 1 and felt like minus-100 as Jack zigzagged toward Geburtville into a wind that must have come from the North Pole. He would have solicited a ride from someone not minding a drunken passenger on Christmas Eve, but there were no cars. Jack walked over a bridge and looked down at a raging creek until he realized no Clarence the Angel was coming to his rescue. Jack had seen what life was like without him, and it seemed everyone was much better off.

He didn't jump. He pushed on, shaking more than staggering but not exactly sobering. His eyebrows were frozen and he barely could make out the Welcome to Geburtville sign or smell the chimney smoke from the homes of sleeping children awaiting their stocking surprises. The Christmas lights of Geburtville, now restored by the power company, greeted Jack. But he didn't have enough energy to make it across the old high school campus to the Gebbie Bowl field house, which was like an icebox on this frigid night.

What kept Jack going was the faint chorus of, "O come all ye faithful, joyful and triumphant, o come ye, o come ye to Be-eth-lehem..."

Jack followed the call which grew louder and louder until he recognized the road on which his hearse had carried his empty casket a few weeks before. Jack weaved up the gravel road, while humming with the chorus, "Come all ya' fateful..." and feeling the warmth the closer he staggered to St. Blaise Catholic Church. The parking lot, filled with cars and pickup trucks, was like the homestretch of a marathon. The finish line was the church foyer.

Jack still shook as the midnight mass goers in their sweaters, sport coats, and long dresses prayed and sang from their packed pews adorned with sweet smelling Christmas fir. He looked out of place in his long black overcoat, jeans, sneakers, and gashed forehead and sought a hiding place warmer than the freezing foyer. As the congregation walked up the aisle for communion, Jack snuck into the same confessional in which he had hid during his funeral.

He was warmer and more sober by the time "Joy to the World" finished echoing off the church walls and the parishioners exited the foyer for the warmth of a hot chocolate and cinnamon roll in front of their home fireplace. Jack curled up in the pitch-black confessional, which felt much cosier than his downtown jail cell. He was about to fall asleep, when the little screen door of the confessional slid open. A call, the same call of a great orator he had heard at his funeral, broke the silence.

"Merry Christmas. Can I help you?"

Jack sat up and pressed his back against the wall of the confessional while propping his sneakers on the kneeler. "*Now* what the fuck do you want?"

PART FOUR

Hang Time

37

A stray football lies frozen on the 50-yard line of the Gebbie Bowl. Its nose points to the goalpost where the stuffed pirate still hangs from a rope.

Beyond the goalpost a body lies stiffer than the hung pirate beneath a blue Cowboys' blanket and cuddled in a black overcoat atop a high jump pad in a frigid field house. Every drop of generic beer has been spewed into the locker room toilet, and Jack somehow crawled to what appears to be his final resting place.

Darkness eventually gives way to dawn and the light flickering through the filthy window stirs Jack from his coma. Several seconds go by for Jack to recognize where he is and several more for him to process the pain of a stomach that feels like it's been speared by a linebacker's helmet at full speed. His head feels like a defensive tackle crunched it with a forearm. Jack wants to fall back asleep but realizes he may never wake up again. Besides, the Cowboys are about to kick off to the Giants.

Jack trudges through frozen grass, icy streets, and surviving snow flurries that qualify Geburtville for a white Christmas. He whiffs the smoke from chimneys and glances through house windows at families opening presents, laughing, hugging, and drinking eggnog. He hears nothing, which allows him to remember the early hours of Christmas 2005.

JACK PROBABLY would have spent Christmas passed out in the confessional had it not been for the voice that resounded off the wooden walls of the small room. Saying "fuck" in the confessional didn't seem to faze the man whose calm voice rang out from the other side of the wall.

"I saw the little light above the confessional and thought perhaps someone needed guidance on this Christmas morning."

"I just needed a place to get warm," Jack said, his head still propped against the back wall and feet resting on the kneeler.

"Ah, I recognize your voice. You're the one to whom faith requires a miracle. Have you seen the parting of the Red Sea since we last spoke?"

"I don't believe in miracles, not even on the football field. Why don't you go save some other poor soul and let me rot in peace."

The man's voice grew softer. "OK, my son. But if you ever want to talk, feel free to pop by Tuesdays from four to five pm."

"I told you before, I don't believe in God.

"That is not a requirement."

The little screen closed and so did Jack's eyes. But only for a moment. Church was the last place he wanted to spend Christmas, and he would spend it stretched out in his own vomit in a little box. He staggered back outside barely noticing the snow flurries as he zigzagged back down the gravel road toward the Gebbie Bowl.

AS JACK WANDERS away from the field house toward the town center and the bells that clang noon, all that is rotting is his stomach. There are no cars and no people. All the shops and restaurants are closed, much like the Sundays in his youth. Jack arrives at Ollie's Electronics just in time for the kickoff. He stares through the storefront window at the players running around on the large screen. The only differences from his youth are that this television is a flat screen and in color, unlike the black and white images from the cathode ray tube sets.

Jack doesn't need to hear the announcer tell him the importance of this game for the 9-5 Cowboys versus the 4-10 Giants at New York's Y.A. Tittle Stadium. If the Cowboys win, they clinch the NFC East even if they were to lose their final regular season game and the Redskins win out. The Cowboys are unbeaten in division play. The Redskins have lost twice to the Cowboys.

From the opening kick-off the Cowboys don't play like they are competing for a title. Agberto Gerrone slips on the icy turf and boots a knuckle ball to Giants' return man Rashid Elmore, who corrals it at his 20-yard line and breaks four arm tackles en route to his first touchdown of the season.

The Cowboys' opening drive starts at their own 10 and goes backwards. Jarmelle Beezley's sore ribs are protected by a helmet-proof vest so heavy he barely can run or throw. The mobile quarterback is immobile. He is sacked seven times in the first half, fumbles twice, and throws three interceptions. Coach Ray Myles, back in charge following his ejection the previous week and a $30,000 NFL fine, refuses to relieve Beezley even though the Cowboys trail 35-0 going into the fourth quarter.

The television camera pans to the Cowboys' bench. Scott Hilfinger sits alone. He is draped in a long black sideline cape with the hood fitted over his helmet. He can't see over the players and coaches standing along the sidelines, and doesn't seem to care.

Jack walks away in the middle of the fourth quarter south of town to what is now called the Geburtville Ghetto. He stares at a front yard planted not with flowers but an old pickup truck jacked up on cylinder blocks, rusty car parts, and a Doberman chained to the porch. He shakes his head at the white chipped paint on the exterior of his boyhood home, which he visits for the first time since he ran away as a teenager from a father not in pursuit.

Jack strolls down the block back into Geburtville, up a large hill and through a forest and stops when he comes to a clearing, his former field of dreams. It was here he threw his first touchdown pass to his next-door neighbor, Ronnie McLain, in one of the hundreds of after-school pick-up games he played.

When there was no game, Jack would throw the NFL-brand football, which he bought at Marvin's Sporting Goods from the money he earned for the glass bottles he found and returned to Geb's Supermarket, through the old tire that still hangs from the massive oak tree. He would pretend he was the Cowboys' quarterback, leading the team downfield in the Super Bowl to the winning touchdown. The more he threw at the old tire the better passer he became. By the time he ran onto the field for his first real game as a Geburtville High freshman, it seemed nothing could stop him.

Jack looks out over the hill, a view he recalled that he could see forever. He closes his eyes and breathes in clean, crisp air. This was his special place, one he named Jack's Home Field, where he could tune out the horrors of his world beneath.

Jack meanders down the other side of the hill, through a thick of trees over a wooden bridge beneath a clear water stream to a cemetery. He stops when he comes to a row of tombstones. One has Keith Byrne sculpted on one side and Rosemary Byrne on the other. The tombstone next to it is blank. Jack presumes that is for him. His sister hasn't gotten around to paying for the engraving of his name yet. Unlike the next door graves, nobody is buried beneath.

Jack chuckles. "Here lies Jack Byrne, whoever he was. They should just leave it blank."

The elementary school and middle school interrupts Jack's walk down memory lane to the Gebbie Bowl. The ice has melted and turned the field to mud. He walks to the goalpost and stares at the noose wrapped around the stuffed pirate's neck. He stands for several seconds, thinking. Then he marches to the 50-yard line. He picks up the stray football, carries it to the goal line, and stops.

Jack takes off his black overcoat, puts a death grip on the ball, and glares at the pirate hanging from the goalpost. Jack cocks the ball behind his ear and pauses. He takes one step forward and fires the ball like it has been shot out of a pistol. The ball smacks the pirate in the head so hard it unravels from the noose and falls to the ground.

Jack smiles and puts the overcoat back on.

38

The first day of the rest of Jack's life ended at a funeral.

He woke up the day after Christmas, starving but somewhat relieved he was still breathing. He didn't know what he was living for but wanted to hang out long enough to find out why. Out of food and out of money, he took a cold shower and marched to the Geburtville Gazette and begged Molli with an I to pay him.

"And how was your Christmas, Graham?" she said. "Mine was great. My boyfriend called me on Christmas morning and we opened our presents on the phone. He got me a beautiful scarf. My daddy bought me a new laptop and then took us to a champagne brunch at the Ritz Plaza in downtown Dallas."

Molli never waited for her ghostwriter's reply. He just stood there with his hand out.

"You're in luck," she said. "The Dallas Star check came in the mail today, and I will get a check from the Gazette this afternoon. I'll cash these today or tomorrow and get you what I owe you."

Molli didn't look up from her sparkling silver laptop to see Jack's gaunt face or his sunken eyes. She couldn't see his ribs sticking out beneath his black overcoat. Jack looked like a begger, but now he was demanding.

"Pay me now or your next story really will be written by Molli Glass." Jack glared at Molli until she finally looked at him.

"Graham, you look like shit. You been a bad little boy this Christmas?"

Jack kept glaring. Molli opened her purse and pulled out a 20 dollar bill among a crisp stack of greenbacks and credit cards. "Here, take this. I'll pay you the rest tomorrow but only if you cover this funeral for me tonight."

"Funeral? The Associated Press covered the Cowboys' game for ya.'"

Molli chuckled and handed Jack the Monday Dallas Star sports page. "The Cowboys are alive and well."

The headline read, "Cowboys in, despite Giant thrashing."

Dave Noonan's lead read, "Humiliation turned into jubilation on the Cowboys' plane ride back to Dallas after their loss to the Giants on Christmas Day."

The pilot had relayed the news that the Redskins had lost to the Eagles, thus ensuring the Cowboys of the NFC East title.

Jack browsed the color photo of the Cowboys jumping up and down on the tarmac in front of their charter jet at DFW International Airport. He did not see Hilfy. "He probably got bombed on airplane whiskey and passed out in coach," Jack thought.

He looked inside the sports page to see a mugshot of Jeanie and the little headline that read, "Pratt commits to LPGA opener in Vegas on Super Bowl weekend."

Molli interrupted. "Some assistant football coach over in nearby Westerville died of a brain aneurysm last week. I hate writing about dead people."

"Or live people," Jack thought.

Molli handed Jack the Sunday's Star and told him to look for the coach's funeral notice in the sports briefs. He found it next to a large black and white photo of a wildly smiling Jeanie leaping into Chad's arms, her hands grasping his meaty shoulders and her legs grappling his wide hips. The two-line headline next the picture read, "Jeanine jumps for joy after Classic victory."

Jack tossed the newspaper in the trash can. He did not read the story in which Jeanie said she was playing the tournament for her deceased husband, whom she had met on the same course 11 years ago. "I could feel his presence," Jeanie was quoted in the story. "It was like he was with me the whole way, and not like watching me from above. More like from the sides of the fairways and greens."

Jack ripped the twenty out of Molli's fingers and scratched his palm on her long pink nails. Half the money went to the diner and the other half to the gas station.

JACK WAITED UNTIL DUSK to jog three miles down the highway with his borrowed gas can to where he pushed the VW van. He fist-pumped when he found the van and fist-pumped again when it started.

"This story is a slam dunk," Jack said, as he looked for a parking spot amongst the cars and pickups lined up in rows and along the sidewalks in front of the Westerville Methodist Church. "Old codger who inspired a bunch of kids kicks the bucket and leaves behind his bawling former pupils and a shitload of broken trophies."

No one was crying. The old codger was only 32, and those who eulogized him were merely thankful he came into their lives. Jack was more stunned than saddened when he left the church and at a loss for words when he tried to type on Molli's old keyboard.

"How can I write about this guy?" Jack said, studying the walls of the lonely Gazette newspaper office and the clock that read midnight. "I never knew him."

Immediately, Jack typed his first sentence. He was finished writing by 12:30 and was asleep on the high jump pad by 12:45. His story, with Molli's byline, in the next day's Geburtville Gazette read:

I never knew Kevin Foster.

He passed through this Earth touching the lives of everybody who knew him. He talked with them. He laughed with them. He worked with them. He coached them. He loved them.

He died of a brain aneurysm last Wednesday at age 32. I never knew him. But after listening to those he coached, taught, listened to, helped, played with, kidded, and loved, I wish had known him. I wish everyone had.

39

The little screen door on the St. Blaise confessional opened one minute until 5pm. A warm voice rang out, "In the name of the Father and of the Son and of the Holy Spirit."

No one answered.

There was a long pause. Jack pressed the button on his watch that lit up the numbers "5:00."

"Sorry," Jack said. "Confessions are finished. I'll come back another time."

The Voice kept Jack from walking out the door. "I don't keep office hours, my son. My time is your time. Take all the time you need."

Jack's return to the confessional was sparked by the funeral he attended the night before, the absolute loneliness he felt the next morning as he lay alone on the high jump pad, and his strong desire to talk with an impartial person who might help him instead of judge him. And not over a round of drinks with a bitter, inebriated emergency quarterback.

Jack was more bewildered in death than he was in life. The coach in Westerville lived only 32 years, but he greatly affected the lives of everyone who crammed into the Methodist church. The only lives Jack affected were those angered about the awful things he wrote about their heroes. He was so forgotten that his gravestone was blank.

There also was guilt – a positive sign, because Jack rarely felt anything. Perhaps a good confession could clear his mind and put him on a better path. The confessional had a musty scent – the priest didn't seem to get much business amongst the devout parishioners. Still, it was a good place. He wasn't required to believe in God, and it was free.

"Okay, how do I start?" Jack assumed the position from Christmas morning – sitting against the back wall with his legs propped up on the kneeler, but this time sober. "Is it like, bless me Father, I've sinned? Show me the way? Something like that?"

"No formalities here, my son." The Voice was never more calm or clear. "Just tell me what is in your heart."

"It's more on my chest, and I want to get it off my chest."

"Proceed."

Jack rubbed the stubble on his face with his left hand and felt once more like running out the door. "Okay, but whatever I say you won't repeat to anyone. You have the same vows as a shrink?"

Jack detected a soft chuckle from the other side of the screen. "Yes. Whatever you say will not leave these sacred walls."

"I'm sure you've heard a lot of bizarre things in here, but never anything like this."

"Try me."

"Here it goes." Jack took a breath. "I died four weeks ago, and I've come back to life."

There was a pause and another soft chuckle from the screen. "You are correct. I have never heard anything like that unless I had heard Jesus Christ's confession."

"Let me explain," Jack said.

Within the next five minutes Jack talked about the car explosion, his faked death, his assumed identity, his flee from the goons, the haunting of his former sports editor and his wife, his escape to his former home of Geburtville, and his current ghostwriting."

A light bulb went on in his listener, but the confessional remained dark. "So that must have been your funeral the first time we talked."

The Voice sounded more intrigued than ashamed, so Jack went on.

"Look, Father. Can I call you Father?"

"Yes, my son."

"I know I've done a stupid thing. But I just want my life back. I want my wife back. I want to know how to get it back. And don't tell me to go kneel down and ask that statue bolted onto the cross to help me."

"The statue cannot help you, God cannot help you. I cannot help you. The only person who can help you is you."

Jack squinted his face. "Huh?"

"Let's just leave it at that for now. Reflect on it and come back next week."

"Next week? That's an eternity."

"Eternity is an eternity. That is what we are all after."

Jack stood up and put his hand on the confessional door. "You talk crap, Padre. This ain't what I came here for."

"What did you come here for?"

"A quick fix."

"That would take something you don't believe in, my son."

"What's that?"

"A miracle."

40

The ghosts of the gridiron were lost in a cloud. The Wednesday night fog that rolled into the Gebbie Bowl prevented Jack from seeing the ball, the goalposts, and the one man he had hunted all day.

Jerry Grimes hadn't been seen all week. The Geburtville High coach hadn't been at home or the cheerleading coach's house. Jack sought his whereabouts from a reliable source.

"What'll be, mister?"

"Just a little more off the top, and a shave."

Jack didn't worry about Joe the barber recognizing him from his youth; he didn't recognize him from two weeks ago. He seemed to know Grimes' whereabouts, though.

Joe lathered Jack's face. "He's been up at Lone Star State interviewin' for a coaching job. Defensive backs coach, I thunk. They want 'um there first thing tomorra mornin'.'"

"He'd just leave town without a warning?"

"Yup," said Joe, scraping Jack's whiskers with a shiny silver blade. "That's Jerry."

A FRESHLY SHAVEN JACK batted out Molli's story at the Geburtville Gazette as she was doling out the money she owed him and then, as directed by Jack, calling the Lone Star State football office. Staff refused comment. Molli called Grimes' house and all she got was "He's out."

Jack prodded Molli to ask Grimes' wife if he had taken a coaching position at Lone Star State. "He's out," she said.

"Is he still the Gebbie's coach?"

"How many times am I going to tell you?" Donna Grimes said right before slamming down the telephone. "He's out."

Calls to Coach Grimes' cellphone only got re-directed to his answering system that said that he was out. Jack had enough for the story after Molli staked out Grimes' house and watched real estate agents walk in and out like the home had a revolving door.

The whereabouts of the winningest football coach in Geburtville High history are unknown this holiday season, and a source close to the team is saying that Jerry Grimes is taking his talents to his alma mater.

Lone Star State officials refused to confirm Grimes' new position as the new defensive backs' coach. But Grimes had a tee time with the head coach at a golf club near the Lone Star State campus.

When asked if her husband was still the Gebbies' head football coach, Donna Grimes said, "He's out."

Jack relieved Molli on the stakeout, so she could write her name on the byline of the next morning's story that would read, "Grimes 'out' as Gebbies coach." Jack didn't care about getting a confirmation from Grimes before the story ran, but he couldn't let him escape Geburtville without knowing the whereabouts of Grimes' college roommate.

JACK'S OBSESSION with the disappearance of Johnny Molinski, the most promising quarterback in Texas history, led him to stowing away beneath blankets and pillows on the floorboard of Grimes' pickup after the ex-Gebbies' coach shrugged him off in the dark fog of his driveway.

"I'm in a hurry," he said, stacking a suitcase and a duffel bag into the back of his truck.

Grimes pecked Donna on the cheek and sped down the road to the home of the cheerleading coach. He said good-bye to her with a pecker, instead of peck, which Jack recorded outside her bedroom window. Jack dove back into the truck just as the coach had completed his two-minute drill.

"Next stop, Lone Star State?" Jack thought, snuggling in his black overcoat.

Ghosts of the Gridiron

The coach's engine died a few minutes later. After hearing the door slam, Jack crawled out of the truck in darkness and fog without realizing he was home.

Grimes' farewell stop was the Gebbie Bowl and a football game he had been promising his old teammates he would play. He wore number 27 on his old Geburtville High School jersey and floated around in the cloud with the other ghosts of football past. Jack stayed hidden in the fog and waited till game's end and for Grimes' final good-byes to say hello.

He met him on the 50-yard line, where most reporters met him after the wins and losses of so many high school games. His fellow gridiron ghosts had driven away, their headlights no longer shining through the fogged-in field. It was so dark that Grimes didn't recognize Jack from the Kodi Keimer interview.

"My name is Graham Repert. I'm writing a story on Johnny Molinski."

"Don't want to talk about it." Grimes marched up the bank to his pickup but stopped after Jack pressed the play button on his tape recorder.

"Oooh. Aaah. Oh yes. Oh yes. Give it to me one last time, Coach. Oh-h-h-h, y-y-yes!"

Grimes walked back to the midfield stripe and pointed at Jack's face. "Gimme that tape."

Jack smiled. "You give me a story, and I'll give you a tape."

Grimes looked around at the field swallowed by the fog. "I'll give you five fucking minutes, but let's get out of the cold."

Jack thought, as the coach disappeared into the fog. "That's more 'fucking' minutes than you gave the cheerleading coach."

41

Coach Grimes led Jack to the field house and felt above the door for a key; he too knew of its hiding place from the many late nights in the weight room. Jack simply opened the door.

"No need to lock it," Grimes said. "They'll bulldoze it soon."

Grimes sat on the bench in front of a locker, and Jack sat in the corner of the dark locker room with his tape recorder. He put in a fresh tape and pressed record. "So Johnny was your roommate?"

"More than that," Grimes said. "He was my best friend."

The coach inhaled and exhaled a couple of cold breaths. "And the best damn quarterback I ever saw."

Grimes said he never saw someone throw that hard or that accurate, on or off the field. He recalled him throwing tennis balls through the stadium exit ramp at Armadillo Stadium and hitting runners in stride as they sped down the track and later chunking snowballs from his ninth floor dormitory window and hitting a police officer in the face as he wrote out a parking ticket by a car at the far end of the lot.

Molinski's record-breaking passing performance for Steuberville in Geburtville's heart-breaking loss in the state high school semifinal game was Grimes' first glimpse of Molinski's greatness. Grimes was shocked when Molinski walked into his dormitory room at Lone Star State and began transferring his clothes from his dark gray Samsonite to the drawer beneath his bed.

"I thought you'd go to a more prestigious college like Oklahoma or Alabama or USC," Grimes said.

"Got a book scholarship offer at Notre Dame," Molinski said, hanging his high school letter jacket with awards patches down the sides into the closet.

"You mean a 'books' scholarship," said Grimes, sitting on the bed on the opposite wall.

Molinski stopped and glared at Grimes. "No a 'book' scholarship. I mean one frigging book."

Grimes was more shocked when Molinski was red-shirted his first year.

"They had a senior who had started for three years and had a chance to set some school records," Grimes said, his white teeth showing in the darkness. "He didn't get a record, and we barely got a win that season.

"Johnny worked his butt off all off-season. He was up at six every morning throwing footballs through the tires on the practice field and in the weight room until six every night. He threw for 300 yards and three touchdowns in the spring game and won the starting job for the first game of the season – against TCU."

"What happened?" Jack put his hand on his chin and looked up at the ceiling, not disclosing that he was at the game.

Grimes was quiet for a moment. Jack couldn't see the warm gleam that came over Grimes in the dark room.

"Johnny woke up at dawn on game-day, put on his gray sweats, jogged to the stadium, and looked around at the empty seats. He imagined his father sitting up there, his high school coach, all his old teammates. A few hours later he was running through the tunnel with the rest of us, throwing warm up passes, and getting last minute instructions from the head coach.

"Then came that first play, that awful first play."

Jack also couldn't see Grimes' frown in the dark, the one that looked like someone remembering his beloved beagle being put down.

"What happened?" said Jack, who already knew what happened but wanted his memory refreshed.

Grimes recounted the events like he was recounting the events of a train wreck. Molinski called the play in the huddle, marched up behind his offensive linemen in his lily white Lone Star State jersey with the red number 13 and little Armadillo on the sleeve gleaming in the sunlight. He looked at the massive defensive linemen in their all purple uniforms, grabbing the turf with their huge paws and digging their size 15 cleats into the midfield stripe.

"Come on, you pussy," the Horned Frogs' middle linebacker said. "You ready to get your skulled cracked open?"

Molinski backed up a yard, looked away from his linemen squatting alongside the ball, and stammered through the signals. "F-f-forty s-s-six, tw-tw-twenty one!"

He stepped forward and slapped his hands under what he thought was the center's butt. "S-s-set. Hut."

Molinski did not know he was under the left guard. The center hiked the ball and launched it between the running backs. Molinski sprinted back, picked up the ball, ducked under a monstrous purple tackler, and spun around his fullback. He looked up and saw daylight and a clear path to the end zone.

"He ran like he was being chased by a million hornets," Grimes said. "If he had just looked back, he would have seen that he was being chased by men in white singlets, not purple ones.

"I got off the bench and sprinted after him down the sidelines."

"Come back, Johnny, come back," Grimes had screamed, as did the coach and the players and his father and the 40,000 spectators. "You're going the wrong way."

Molinski raised the ball as he crossed his own goal line and spiked it in the end zone. He was surprised none of his teammates patted him on the back and couldn't understand why a TCU player dove on ball, why the other buffoons in purple were laughing, or why the crowd was booing.

Jack couldn't see the tears welling up in Grimes' eyes as he sat still on the locker room bench.

"He suddenly realized what he had done," Grimes said. "He walked over to the sidelines with his head down, trying not to look at his teammates' glares and not to hear one of them yelling, "Dumb-fuck."

The coach pointed to the bench, where Molinski sat the rest of the game mostly with his hands over his eyes. After the 42-0 loss,

Molinski didn't even shower. He grabbed his gear, ran to his dorm room, packed his Samsonite, and disappeared.

"I brought back a quart of his favorite Haagan Daz chocolate chip ice cream to try and comfort him," Grimes said. "But he was gone; everything was gone but his high school letter jacket."

"Why didn't he come back?" Jack asked.

"He would have come back, if it hadn't been for that damn newspaper article."

Grimes was referring to the next day's game story in the Lone Star Daily Ledger with the headline, "Wrong Way Molinski leads the Armadillos in Wrong Direction."

The lead went like this:

Johnny "Wrong Way" Molinski doesn't know the ass of a donkey from the ass of a center. The red-shirt freshman not only botched the snap of the Armadillos' season-opening play, but he picked up the loose pigskin and ran 40-yards in the wrong direction for a Horned Frog touchdown en route to a 42-zip drubbing.

The story was picked up by the Associated Press and ran in about every newspaper in the country. Molinski's tragic miscue was played over and over by seemingly every local sportscast in the world. The ESPN SportsCenter anchor called it the "top bonehead play of the year."

Lone Star State University declared the ensuing Monday "Wrong Way Molinski Day", and everyone walked backwards across the campus. People all over town were walking backwards. At practice that afternoon, the coach announced the new depth chart. When he came to quarterback, he said, "Molinski is now third string. Looks like he is going the wrong way."

Everyone was laughing but Molinski, who snuck out of the locker room without anyone realizing he was there.

"I know Johnny." Grimes' voice cracked and he sounded like someone who lost a brother, and he did. "He was too proud. He couldn't face the humiliation. Or even his father, whose whole life was about watching his son succeed on the football field. Their goal was playing in the Super Bowl.

"If it hadn't been for that damn newspaper article, Johnny could have come back. He would have made it. He was too talented not to make it. But whoever wrote that not only destroyed his dream. He destroyed him."

Jack pressed the stop button on the tape recorder. Grimes said he would like to get his hands on the guy who wrote that story. He could, easily. The writer was sitting three feet away on the locker room bench across from him, in the dark.

42

Jack was having another nightmare, and not about him. It was about a man standing in his underwear on the 50-yard line of the Gebbie Bowl, which on this sunny day was the Super Bowl.

He wore a white wife-beater T-shirt with the number 13 painted in blue only on the back and a unrecognizable name scribbled above in red crayon. A gray chinstrap slid across his throat and was snapped to the other side of his leather football helmet. He had a lineman's facemask but no face.

There was no one on the bench, and the only people in the stands were Jeanie and Chad. They were holding up red traffic signs with white letters that read, "Wrong Way."

A dark cloud appeared in the background followed by Grog and Hog and 20 other goons, all with tomahawks clasped in their right hands. They were led by Soss, that Sawed Off Sack of Shit sports editor who pointed a Big Bertha driver and yelled, "Charge!" as a bum, likely the one Jack met in jail, walked to midfield in a black overcoat and blew a whistle.

The mob sprinted toward the man who tried to run toward the goal line but couldn't. The harder he tried to run, the faster the mob approached and the louder their grunts echoed off the banks of the empty stadium. The man looked down at his bare feet driving hard into the cold, hard ground and propelling him nowhere.

Then a football appeared in his arm and he began moving forward and away from the mob. He had a clear field in front and was sprinting effortlessly with the goalpost coming nearer. The announcer's voice was the same as the one from the confessional, echoing like a broken record, "He's at 50. He's at the 50. He's at the 50."

As the man was about to speed away from the 50-yard line, Jack's father appeared in referee garb and clothe-lined him. The man exploded into a ball of flames. The ground opened up, and the man was falling and falling down the dark hole while still holding onto the football.

Jack's father hollered "Four!" as he kept falling and falling and falling until Jack woke up.

IT WAS DARKER in the field house than it was in the hole. Jack was sweating and panting as if he was the one who had been running nowhere. "Someone is in trouble, someone is dying," Jack whispered. "And I can't do anything about it. Or maybe I can?"

He lay on the high jump pad like a corpse with his eyes open until dawn broke the silence and until he gave up trying to interpret his nightmare. A quarterback with the number 13 was falling down a hole. The only quarterbacks he could think of who wore that number were Johnny Molinski, Scott Hilfinger, Dan Marino, and himself."

"Scratch Marino," Jack said. "He's in the Hall of Fame."

He decided to look first for Hilfy, because he was easier to find than Molinski. Or was he?

Jack strolled to the rusty old pay phone attached to the field house wall with an old telephone book from an old office desk, dropped in a quarter, and dialled the Dallas Cowboys Training Center. The receptionist, who first asked, "Who the hell is Scott Hilfinger," said she had not seen him all week nor had the receptionist at the YMCA. Perhaps, he was the one falling and falling into a dark hole.

On to Molinski, Jack didn't have enough quarters and it was too cold to stand outdoors. He marched to the Geburtville Gazette and waited in the cold for Molli with an I to come to work. She peeled into parking lot in her Chrysler convertible and led Jack to the newsroom sporting a new blonder perm and a fresh manicure and a stack of bridal magazines.

She was greeted by "Great scoop on Grimes" from the editor and a reporter, who did not notice her ghostwriter trailing like he was her lackey. She sat at her desk and opened her fan mail that she read and handed to Jack. The letters that once berated Jack's work for bashing their heroes turned into nothing but praise for his tender prose about a high school quarterback suffering from a blood disease, an inspiring coach spelled by a brain aneurysm, and several others in between. A note in need of editing was attached to a cheque from Soss.

"Touching peece on the Westville coach, Molly. Your the best writter I've come across in a while. You could've taught my last columnist a thing or too, but the prick died before I could fire him."

Jack found Soss' note the most gratifying. Molli was more interested in reading her bridal magazines. She didn't ask Jack where he learned to write like that, but he answered anyway.

"I was always a good writer but I wrote bad stuff about people, because that's what got me ahead."

No bigger example was the Wrong Way Molinski story, which Jack wrote his senior year at Lone Star State. It earned notice from sports editors from all over the country. Jimbo Conrad, The Dallas Star sports editor at the time, offered him a staff position. Jack quit college, moved to Dallas, and quickly earned the college football beat. Soon he was ridiculing quarterbacks from Stanford to Purdue to Boston College. He never considered what damage words did until his talk with Grimes.

"I have to make it up to him," Jack said, thinking about Molinski.

"To who?" Molli didn't look up from her bridal magazine.

Jack reversed subjects. "Why are you looking at those?"

Molli finally looked up and flashed her perfectly straight teeth. "I'm getting married," she said.

"Not like Cullen to pop the question in an email," Jack said.

"No, silly, he called this morning and said he is flying to Dallas on Sunday, New Year's Eve, and taking me to Ritz Tower for dinner. He said he has something he wants to talk to me about."

Molli flexed her left hand and stared at the simple promise ring that would be replaced by a much grander engagement ring. Jack thought, "The doorknob of a diamond will probably push Cullen's suitcase over the weight limit."

Molli offered Jack a ticket to the Cowboys' season finale if he would drive her to Ritz Tower where she would meet Cullen and his rock.

Jack nodded. Molli went back to her magazines, and Jack went to the phones. He spent five hours looking up Molinski on the Internet and calling various athletics departments and old teammates and relatives in search of the quarterback he disgraced. Someone said he was a bum, another a monk, another an alcoholic, another a drug addict, another an Elvis Impersonator, and another said he was in prison.

Jack didn't believe any of them. Molinski simply vanished into football obscurity like so many quarterbacks before and after him. It would take one of those miracles to bring him back from the dead, for one last interview, for one last pass, for one last chance for Jack to make it up to him.

Molinski, Jack figured, was still falling and falling into a dark hole.

43

Molli with an I not only almost knocked Jack over with her fragrant perfume. She was killing him with her looks.

Molli stood on her parents' front lawn on the warmest New Year's Eve in North Texas history talking on her cellphone while sliding her perfect pink fingernails along the narrow dress strings atop her bare shoulders and wiggling her permed locks. Jack stood by Molli's polished Chrysler Sebring convertible. He would drive blondie to her date with destiny, but he was too busy gawking at her perfect cleavage and the outline of her nipples that protruded from a thin strapless bra to be in a rush.

His eyes started at the base of her shiny black high heels and worked their up to the clean shaven calves to the well-toned thighs barely covered by the red silk dress so short Jack could see the start of her soft buttocks. This ensured him that she was wearing a G-string – likely black silk, he figured, and snuggled against the blonde hairs clinging to her wet vagina.

Her pearl necklace bobbed down her front and her silver bracelet strapped loosely on her slender left wrist matched the round earrings that dangled from her lobes. Her skin glistened in the sunlight, assuring the wide-eyed Jack that she wore no clothes at the local tanning salon.

Molli slipped her cellphone into her the designer purse that matched her dress and strutted toward the car. Jack didn't move. He stared at her lips, lightly painted with pink lipstick just waiting to purr the words her beloved wanted to hear. Jack figured she was not just dressed to say, "I want to marry you." She was dressed to say, "I am going to fuck you."

It had been several months and too many lonely nights since Jack had heard those words, and still eye-balling Molli as she opened the passenger door, he wondered why he never looked at her before with bedroom eyes.

It was warm enough to put the convertible top down. But Jack did not want to be spotted by a goon or cop or anyone wondering why a luscious blonde would be out with a geek in a Dallas Cowboys number 17

Rex Fanning jersey that he and 10,000 other lunatics would be donning along with a red-striped popcorn box and a plastic beer cup in the fold-down seats at Tom Landry Stadium. Borrowing the jersey from Molli's father would help him blend in, stay unrecognizable, and enjoy the game. For extra precaution, he painted his face blue and silver.

No one would recognize him with the blonde bombshell, whose only view of the stadium was from atop Ritz Tower.

"So who are the Cow-pokes playing?" Molli asked.

Jack didn't take his eyes off the highway. "Eagles."

"Where are they from?"

"Philadelphia."

"Big game?"

"Final game of the regular season; means nothing."

"Then why are they playing it?"

"Good question."

Jack wondered out loud if Scott Hilfinger had surfaced, and if this worthless game might give him a chance to fulfil his NFL dream. Certainly the Cowboys would give Jarmelle Beezley's ribs a chance to heal and preserve backup Brody Guthrie late in the game by giving Hilfy a few snaps.

"Any relation to Tommy Hilfiger?" Molli asked.

MOLLI WAS SOON looking at Tommy Hilfiger jeans and also wedding dresses in the Forest Green Mall, while Jack spied on his former beloved at the nearby country club. He wasn't the only one watching Jeanie bending down to pick up golf balls on the practice tees, peeking at the white panties under her short skirt.

Jack wasn't just observing her putting stroke from his distant view in the parking lot. He saw her chatting with the old club players, likely encouraging them and wishing them luck and a hole in one on their next round. She smiled and seemed more interested in their game than her own.

Chad had a better view from the ball washer. The more Jeanie bent over, the faster Chad slid the golf balls up and down. Then he strolled over to the green. Jack heard him say, "Let me show ya' how, babe."

The caddy clasped his arms around the back of Jeanie as she stood in her putter's stance and joined her hands on the putter's shaft. In unison they whacked the ball toward the hole and giggled when the ball fell into the cup. She kissed him on the cheek. He put his arm over her shoulder and escorted her off the green.

Jack backed the convertible out of the car space and left the parking lot and two skid marks. He picked up Molli and didn't say another word until he reached downtown. Molli was meeting a friend for lunch and a few wines to calm her nerves before her date. Not even a half dozen Dippity Donuts could calm Jack. He drove around the downtown Dallas streets like a Grand Prix driver with the image of Chad grappling Jeanie stuck in his mind until he spotted the car of the only person who could make him angrier.

Soss drove his black Lexus with a cracked tailpipe from The Dallas Star parking lot and was headed toward Tom Landry Stadium. Jack gritted his teeth at the memory of Soss turning the press box into a luxury box. The writers plugged away on deadline while he drank martinis and ate caviar with Cowboys' PR sweeties.

Jack wheeled Molli's Sebring into oncoming traffic and pushed ahead of the Lexus and braked in front of a yellow traffic light, causing Soss to wait behind him. Jack ignored the honks from the Lexus when the light turned green and as he crept down the two lane road at 20 miles per hour. Soss liked arriving two hours before kickoff for the pre-game barbecue and bullshitting with Cowboys' executives, and Jack made sure he missed it, stopping on yellow at every light and stalling in front of the highway entrance ramp.

Soss laid on the horn and shouted out the window, "Move your piece of shit."

Jack moved the convertible top just enough to raise his middle finger as he steered the car onto the highway. Soss stuck his finger out the window and flew past the Sebring. He was followed by the flashing lights of a police car. The officer chased down the flabbergasted Sawed Off Stack of Shit sports editor and pulled him off onto the noisy shoulder. The officer was writing a ticket as Jack strolled past, honked, and again waved his middle finger.

"That's for killing my 100-inch masterpiece on the Arkansas quarterback's experience in prison, because you said you didn't feel sorry for him."

Jack laughed in the silent air permeated by the lingering perfume from a beautiful woman.

44

Scott Hilfinger's journey to the NFL was about as long as his journey to the Cowboys' last game of the 2005 NFL regular season.

He was about to board the team charter flight from New York City the night of the Christmas Day massacre by the Giants when Royce Heyward, the owner's son, yanked him out of line.

"Need your seat, pardner," Heyward said.

Heyward explained that his daddy, Sterling Heyward, promised his little step-niece a seat on the plane. Since there was none left, a seat had to be made available. The only seat left was a seat on the Cowboys' equipment truck. Instead of taking three hours to get to Dallas, it would take three days.

The equipment truck wasn't exactly first class nor was the driver, Charlie Ray Anderson. Hilfy bounced up and down on the front seat and kept hitting his head on the cab ceiling while enduring the shriek country songs of Travis Tritt, Kenny Chesney, and Merle Haggard and Charlie's echoing sing-along. Hilfy wasn't much of a country western fan, not even growing up in Deadhorse, Oklahoma.

Charlie spit tobacco into a coke bottle he kept between his crotch and didn't notice it overflow onto his bluejeans. He insisted on keeping the window open and breathing Arctic air mixed with the combustion from a loud muffler. Dinner was all-you-can-eat and puke burgers at truck stops and sleep was sitting in the same seat at highway rest stops.
Hilfy refused to follow Charlie into the brothel in Normal, Tennessee but agreed not to tell his wife.

Hilfy had a lump on his head, an earache, and a 102-temperature when Charlie dropped him off at the Downtown YMCA late Wednesday. Hilfy didn't wake up until Friday morning and didn't report to practice until late Friday afternoon.

To his surprise and his dismay, no one noticed Hilfy was missing. Or at least no one asked where he had been. Hilfy thought the club owed him after giving up his plane seat. He lumbered to Sterling Heyward's office after practice and told him of his three-day ordeal and how he wanted and needed to play in the final regular season game without reminding him that he needed to play a down to be eligible for the Cowboys' $5,000 playing bonus. "Sir, it would mean so much to me if you could ask Coach Myles if I could play one down."

Sterling Heyward sipped on a martini. "Who are you again?"

"Hilfinger, the third string quarterback."

"I'll see what I can do."

BY GAME TIME, Hilfy thought it was a moot point. Myles decided to rest Beezley. The unfit and unmotivated Brody Guthrie would start but hadn't played a full game in his worthless NFL career. How long would Guthrie go before pulling a hamstring? How long before Myles would lose his patience with his team losing a million to nothin' to the league-leading loser, the Philadelphia Eagles?

Jack posed that question to Hilfy as he motioned him over to the stadium rail in the pre-game warmup. Hilfy stared at Jack's Rex Fanning jersey and the blue and silver face paint he had applied before marching again, incognito, into the stadium.

"Last time you're a woman, now you're a fan," Hilfy said. "What next?"

Jack shook Hilfy's hand. "Make it look like we're close friends," Jack said. "I just bet the guy next to me in the blue Heath Garrett jersey twenty bucks that I know one of the players."

A smile crept under Hilfy's facemask. "I'm not a player until I get a snap, but I got a good feeling about this game."

The feeling grew with the Cowboys trailing 52-0 early in the fourth quarter, all the Cowboys' starters on the bench, and Guthrie barely rising to his feet after every sack. Hilfy stared up at the president's luxury suite and raised his hands as if to say, "Did you ask Myles if I could play?"

As Guthrie limped to the sidelines following another incompletion late in the fourth quarter, Jack started a chant among the remaining fans, "We want Hilfinger! We want Hilfinger!" The verbal wave slowly spread around the stadium, although it sounded more like, "We want 'Hee-figger'."

"Who?" Myles asked defensive line coach, Alvin Baines

"I think they wants Hilfinger," Baines shouted over the crowd.

The chant and the boos grew louder after Philadelphia scored again to make it 59-0. Guthrie lay on a massage table unable to move as the Eagles booted the ball out of the end zone with 47 seconds left in the game. Hilfy buttoned his chin strap and stood next to Myles, who looked at his comatose back-up.

Myles turned and stared into Hilfy's hopeful eyes and called out, "Flanders!"

True to his word, Myles played the punter before he played the third string quarterback. Two snaps and 47 seconds and a few more boos later, Hilfy was out his $5,000 bonus and any hope of playing in the NFL. He took off his helmet and bounced it off the turf. The only person who noticed was the one who retrieved it.

"Hold onto this; you might need it," Jack said, his grin cracking his face paint. "You've got one quarterback with bruised ribs and another with a pulled hamstring.

"In the meantime, let's go get fucked up."

45

There couldn't be a more appropriate place to spend New Year's Eve than atop the world's tallest penis.

Ritz Tower stands erect, almost two football fields high. A restaurant and bar revolves inside the massive round head, and patrons can see clear to Oklahoma on a clear day. On this night couples only stare into each other's eyes as the countdown begins to a new year that promises a promiscuous beginning.

Jack rose to the top of Ritz Tower for the New Year's countdown, because he had nowhere else to go, and the eight Coronas and three shots of Johnnie Walker he consumed while obscured by the more inebriated Cowboys' third string quarterback at The Bar in Arlington did little to steer him in any direction.

Most of his New Year's celebrations had come atop football stadiums in the aftermath of college bowl games or NFL regular season finales. Jeanie never hated Jack's job more than on New Year's Eve. She normally stroked golf balls into the backyard net from one year to the next. Jack figured that was precisely where Jeanie was as he ascended in the glass elevator to the top of the Dallas Skyline.

Hilfy did not accompany him. The Coronas and shots he had shared with his face-painted drinking buddy only did what they intended – fucked him up. "You better not go up there," Jack said after smacking Molli's convertible Sebring into the curb at the Y. "After what Myles did to you, you might jump off."

Hilfy did not disagree.

Jack sobered and cleaned himself up with four glazed and a hot chocolate and face wash at the nearby Dippity Donuts. No one could see him, wrapped in the long black overcoat in the darkness of the Ritz Tower bar. He was wondering if it was the fake glasses or the impending hangover or the altitude that caused him to see things.

Molli sat in the corner, alone, with a shot glass in one hand and a beer glass in the other.

Jack slid next to her in the brown cushioned booth. Her eyes were watery, and streaks of eye-liner ran down her cheeks. "I thought the only glass you'd have in front of you would be a champagne glass."

Molli hid her face on Jack's shoulder. His black overcoat absorbed the tears that flooded down her face. Jack stared at Molli's bare ring finger. Two hours ago, Jack was consoling one friend at The Bar in Arlington and now another at a bar above Arlington.

Through sobs, Molli told him that the purpose of Cullen's meeting was to propose a break-up not a marriage. He said there was too much distance between them and not just geographically. He said she was a distraction from his studies, that he wanted to focus on his career, and that she should concentrate more on writing good stories than cute little texts.

After Cullen descended back to Earth, Molli sent him a farewell text: "FU."

She said the same to a dozen or so male visitors of the WTP (World's Tallest Penis) but not until after they bought her drinks. She barely could be heard over the large crowd and the music that blasted over the dance floor, but the would-be suitors could read her lips. Jack would have asked Molli to dance but after they clinked glasses, toasted to "Cullen, Harvard's biggest and brightest asshole," and downed double-Scotches neither could stand up.

So they ordered another drink and watched the patrons who could stand, count down 2005 in a loud unison. "10 – 9 – 8 – 7..." When they got to "4," Jack wanted to call a time out. The woman he thought would be counting down with a Big Bertha was screaming "3 – 2 – 1..." with a bottle and a Bubba. Moments later she was smiling, screaming "Happy New Year," throwing streamers, and wrapping her arms and her lips around her date as fireworks lit up the city. Jeanie wasn't wearing a golf sweater; she was wearing a golf caddy.

Jack couldn't recall the last time he saw Jeanie in a dress, her hair done, finger and toenails painted, or smiling. Jack was sitting within a long putt of her but could imagine the sweet perfume that replaced her normal bent grass scent. Jeanie couldn't have seen Jack even if he wasn't seated in darkness. She was too busy staring into Chad's eyes and singing with the other celebrants:

Should old acquaintance be forgot,
and never brought to mind?
Should old acquaintance be forgot,
and days of long ago?

Molli came up for air from her Scotch and said in slurred English, "Now that's a pretty lady."

"That's no lady," Jack said. "That's my wife."

"Well, your wife's gettin' laid tonight."

Now Jack felt like leaping off the tower. Instead he sat there gawking and frowning as Chad and Jeanie held each other and swayed on the dance floor. Jack wondered how a grieving widow could throw herself into the arms of a lesser man while her beloved's ashes – or whoever's ashes they were – were still simmering in a deep hole.

The Jeanie sighting sobered Jack. He never looked down at his glass – kept sipping and staring at Chad's hands sliding up and down his wife's ass. An overwhelming urge to splash the urinal overpowered his urge to slash the horny couple in broad moonlight.

When he returned from the bathroom, the pretty lady and her caddy were gone. Jack turned 360-degrees and found them in the descending glass elevator. He grabbed Molli's hand and dragged her from the booth. She fell over her high heels. Jack dragged her on her bottom to the elevator door and pushed her inside when the glass elevator finally made its round trip.

Jack held Molli's hand only to keep her from falling over again as they zigzagged back to her car parked at Dippity Donuts. Jack didn't even stop for a dozen glazed to go and stiff-armed his more inebriated former cellmate who grabbed at his black coat. Soon Jack was zigzagging through downtown Dallas and the North Dallas

Expressway. Molli lay her blonde locks on the headrest and said, "W-e-e-e-e-e!" before nodding off.

CHAD BEAT JACK to his house. Jack parked across the street and spied from the driver's seat. The light came on in his bedroom. Jeanie's and Chad's silhouette shone through the window. They embraced, and soon Chad was kissing Jack's wife from her forehead down to the base of his neck. Then the light was turned off.

Jack ran to Chad's white Ford pickup, parked in the driveway, and jiggled the door handle. The car alarm blared off the neighborhood, which quickly lit up. Chad ran out the front door, wearing nothing but unzipped blue jeans. He opened the car door and turned off the alarm only to be summoned minutes later before he could get out of his jeans. The third alarm woke up Molli. She waggled over to Jack, who was hiding behind a tree.

"I feel sick," she whispered.

Jack escorted Molli to the driveway and back to her car just before Chad came out in his saggy underwear wielding a five-iron. "OK, you bastard, who's out there?"

Chad marched to his truck and whiffed an awful stench. He looked in horror to see a one gallon spew of beer and whiskey streaming down the truck bed. Jack sped down the street in the Chrysler convertible with Chad and his five-iron in hot pursuit and, moments later, a police car in pursuit of Chad.

Jack and Molli laughed. "You stand corrected," Jack said. "My wife is not getting laid tonight."

"No, but her husband is."

46

"Bless me father for I have sinned. I slept with another woman."

Jack whispered into the confessional screen at 4pm on Tuesday like a child confessing to stealing a bike. He cringed, expecting a hand to crash through the screen and grab him by the throat. He received only a soft reply.

"Yes, my son, what else?"

"What else? I committed adultery. What else do you want? I faked my own death. I tried to blow up my boss' car. I got drunk off my ass four times and thought about hanging myself from a goalpost. Is that what you want to hear?"

The pause from the other side was brief. "I don't want to hear anything. I want you to tell God, so He can help you help yourself."

"So you're kind of like the middle man?"

"You could say that."

"How much you get? Ten percent?"

"Twelve, but who's counting."

There were slight chuckles from each side of the confessional. It released Jack's tension and allowed him to tell the story he wanted to get off his chest. He loved the priest's soft voice. More important, he loved and needed his ear.

He told him how he and Molli celebrated their crummy lives with a six pack on the drive back to Geburtville. They were both so drunk neither could remember where Molli lived. He parked in the end zone of the Gebbie Bowl and they walked while trying to keep upright and singing "Auld Lang Syne" to the field house door.

Jack eventually figured out how to put the key in the lock and soon they were fast asleep on the high jump pad, clasped into each other's arms. Jack woke up and peered under the covers.

"We were both, ah, naked," Jack said. "I don't know if we did anything. I was so drunk I don't remember doing anything."

"Does your friend remember any of it?"

"Don't know. She got dressed, got into her car, and drove home. Haven't seen her since."

There was a pause long enough for Jack to put his lips up to the screen. "Father, are you all right? What's the verdict?"

"I'm a priest, my son. God is the judge."

"If there is a God, what would he tell you to say?"

"That if you feel in your heart you have committed a sin, then it is a sin."

"Even if I was unconscious, Padre?"

"It is what is in your heart, my son. If you are dead, as you have stated, you have not committed adultery."

"Quite confusing and vague."

"What can I say? God pays minimum wage."

"Well, what should I do? Do I get a penance or something. Please no Hail Marys."

"Simply ask God for forgiveness."

"But I told you, I don't believe in God."

"Then ask Molli for forgiveness, or your wife, or yourself."

"Do you forgive me, Father?"

"Already have."

JACK WAS MORE confused after leaving the confessional than before going in. He didn't know if he wanted the priest to tell him it is all right to have sex with other women because he was declared dead or admonish him because he's not. Feeling guilty for something he may or may not have done was a good thing. That's because he felt something — guilt. That meant he was alive and that he really did want his wife and life back. But how? A miracle?

He pondered it all as he sprinted up the hill to Jack's Home Field at dusk and threw a football through the tire hanging from the big oak tree. He ran down the hill in the dark to the Geburtville High School gymnasium, where Molli had ordered him the previous week to cover and ghost-write the basketball game for her.

The first person Jack saw as he entered the packed gym was Molli sitting at the scorer's table in a purple pullover sweater, black slacks, and brown loafers. She wore little make up and no earrings or fingernail polish. She looked more like a sportswriter than a sorority sister.

Jack walked around the gym floor first before approaching her. He couldn't look her in the eyes.

"What's nice girl like you doing in a sweaty place like this?"

"What do you 'think' I'm doing, Graham? I am covering a basketball game."

"I thought you wanted me—"

"You thought wrong. I'm covering my own games from now on and writing my own stories. Come by the office tomorrow, and I'll pay you what I owe you."

Jack almost chuckled at the thought of Molli writing her own sports story. He started to walk off but turned back to the scorer's table. "Hey, Molli with an I. When the referee holds both hands up in the air, he's signalling for a jump ball not a touchdown."

Molli threw a cup of ice at the giggling sportswriter while yelling, "Fuck you, Graham."

"You already have."

47

Jack's miracle wish was for Johnny Molinski to spring out among the flock of football forgottens onto the Gebbie Bowl turf, cold smoke blowing out his lungs and a fire brewing in his belly. He would furl bullet passes at ghostly receivers as they broke over the middle and loft floating bombs into their outstretched arms as they flew down the sidelines

The unearthing of the missing Molinski would flash from every sports page in the United States and give rebirth to the man who defamed himself and relief to the man who scorned him. Jack didn't even try for a "I don't feel good" quote after Molinski's last game but would relish an exclusive interview after his next one.

Jack waited outside the field house as every player filed his car headlights around the frigid field on the Wednesday night and slinked to the 50-yard line in the football jersey they donned in their glory years. There were several numbers from Molinski's former teams at Steuberville High and Lone Star State U. But no number 13s.

The only number 13 was worn by Jack. That was the number on the only old faded purple Geburtville High School jersey Jack could find in the field house. He also found some baggy padded football pants and a helmet with the "G" partially scraped off and cleats two sizes too big. There was no helmet chinstrap, and the facemask had a single bar across his chin. He barely could fit the small jersey over his shoulder pads. Perhaps it was the same jersey he wore that fateful night his freshman year.

Jack waddled to the sidelines and threw warm-up passes to players who didn't mind playing catch with someone who looked like Jerry Lewis.

"You throw pretty good, Gramps," the player draped in the red Steuberville High School jersey said. "When did you play for Geburtville?"

"Late 70's."

Jack tossed the ball back. "When did you play for Steuberville?"

"Early 80's"

"Did you play with Johnny Molinski?"

The man caught Jack's pass and held the ball at his side. "Best damn quarterback I ever saw."

Jack wandered up to the man after catching a pass. "Where did you see him last?"

"Um-m-m, at a bar in downtown Dallas. The Kazbar, I think. He was drunk off his ass. He was so skinny and looked like he hadn't shaved or taken a bath in years. Couldn't believe it was him. Someone said he was living on the street."

"Didn't he have family to turn to?"

The man twirled the ball in his hands. "Nah. His 'ol man sort of disowned him after he dropped out of college. I think 'ol Johnny's been wanderin' around for a while, a shadow of his former self."

"Why didn't you or one of your teammates try to help him?"

The man didn't answer. He flipped the ball back to Jack and in mid-air and asked, "Why do you give a shit?"

Jack caught the ball, tossed it back and walked to the sideline. "Just curious."

The game went on without Jack, despite offers for him to play. "Bum hamstring," he kept saying.

Actually, Jack didn't have time. He walked the sideline like a detective asking any player in a Steuberville or Lone Star State jersey if he had seen Johnny Molinski recently.

They all shook their heads but the information Jack gathered between the grunts and groans on the field made him feel Molinski was there that Wednesday night and wondered how he missed the story as the beat writer for Lone Star State football.

Molinski's grandparents immigrated from Poland early in the 20th century. They lived in Baltimore, where Molinski's father, Jozef, became a huge Colts' fan – particularly Johnny Unitas. He called his only child, Jan, nicknamed him "Johnny", and had him throwing miniature footballs in his crib and real ones through a tire in the backyard as a toddler. Father and son shared a dream of playing in the Super Bowl.

Johnny's mother died of breast cancer when he was age 10. Jozef and his son formed a closer bond and moved to Texas, where they heard football was king. They watched film of Johnny Unitas, and Johnny Molinski emulated the great quarterback right down to his black high-top cleats. He dropped the high-tops at Steuberville High School, because he claimed they were not cool. He chose number 13 instead of Unitas' 19, because he had learned in bible class that the number 13 meant "the promise of new life."

Johnny started on varsity his freshman year, after Jozef bribed the coach. This infuriated Johnny, who wanted to win the starting role on his own merit. He worked even harder to prove himself and was setting state Class A passing records his sophomore year. Johnny wanted to move to Dallas and set Class 5A records, improving his chances for a scholarship to a major university. Part of the bribe, though, was that Johnny never leave Steuberville.

Jozef's's obsession with his son's football career made Johnny want to put distance between him and his Tiger Dad. But Lone Star State was the only school that would gamble on a Class A phenom. Former Armadillo players speculated that Jozef's badgering of the Lone Star State staff played a role in Johnny getting the starting role, and the embarrassment Jozef suffered from the fateful play led to the estrangement from his humiliated son.

The *last* person who would know of Johnny's whereabouts was Jozef Molinski.

Johnny's former high school teammates wished they did know where Johnny was and that he would reunite with them on the field where he propelled them to the state finals. Every player said the same thing as he strapped on his helmet and retook the field.

"Best damn quarterback I ever saw."

48

Tremont Jones said on the Thursday, January 5, 2006 Around the NFL show on ESPN that the Dallas Cowboys' chances of beating the Carolina Panthers in the Wildcard playoff round on Saturday were about as remote as a snowman being built in Brownsville, Texas.

The "Clownboys," as the columnist for the Charlotte Observer had penned them, had lost 104-3 in their last two regular season games while the Panthers closed with seven straight victories to win the top Wild Card spot. The only writer crazy enough – or in this case naïve enough – to pick the Cowboys was Penny Pettigrew.

She wrote that the Cowboys' home crowd would "rally" them to victory without mentioning that only 50 percent of playoff tickets had been sold. There would be more fans' donning Panthers' jerseys than Cowboys' jerseys.

"What planet did dis Pettigrew person come from?" said Tremont, the former Giants' defensive end-turned-television analyst. "Dallas ain't even got a quarterback. Beezley's banged up, Guthrie's a has been, and they got so little faith in their third string quarterback – whoever that is – that they'd rather play the punter."

Pettigrew's ridiculous comments finally got people to read her column. But the former reference librarian at The Dallas Star's Morgue had been so ridiculed by the broadcast media and in the letters to the editor Jack figured the editor still refused to publish that a change was imperative. The only worse writer in Dallas-Fort Worth area was the interim sports editor of the Geburtville Gazette.

Jack laughed at Molli's story about the Gebbies' basketball victory on Tuesday that didn't appear until Thursday because she missed the deadline. "Writer's block," she would say when Jack plopped into a chair next to her desk to receive the money she owed him for his recent ghostwriting. Jack re-read her lead out loud.

"Hoop magic sprang from the locker room last Tuesday evening as the Geburtville Gebbies took the home floor for their big basketball shootout with their District 5 rival Stark City, who needed to pull a rabbit out of the hat to pull off a victory over a team that would have made Houdini proud."

Jack kept reading to himself until Molli interrupted. "What's so funny?"

"The Gebbie musicians practically made the Sharks disappear in the third quarter."

"What's wrong with that?"

"It's 'magicians', not 'musicians.'"

Molli leaned over her desk and hid her face in her sweater sleeve. "I know, I know. I suck as a sportswriter."

"Wouldn't worry about it. Only people who probably looked at the story were the basketball players, and most of them can't read."

Molli leaned back in her chair. "Fortunately Dick Schwartz didn't read it."

"How do you know that?"

"Because he asked me to be the Star's fill-in columnist for the Cowboys' game on Saturday."

Jack laughed even louder.

"What am gonna do?" Molli said.

"Don't know. You fired me as your ghostwriter."

There was a long pause before Molli asked the inevitable question. "Would you write it for me, Graham. P-l-l-lease."

"You mean go in drag, again. My nipples are still chafing from wearing your bra."

"Pretty please. I'll pay you the whole 300 bucks Mr. Schwartz offered me. I'll even go spy on your wife again for ya'."

Jack sat up and stared at Molli. "You remember that?"

"That's about all I remember. I woke up somewhere with a splitting headache and found my car in a field. The next thing I recall was waking up in my bed the next morning and telling my parents I had the flu."

"You missed all the New Year's Day bowl games."

"And the parades."

Jack was so relieved at the prospect that he may not have cheated on Jeanie that he agreed to write the Cowboys' column. He also figured it was the only way he could watch likely the Cowboys' last game of the season and comfort Scott Hilfinger, who likely would be heading back to Deadhorse, Oklahoma with a one-way bus ticket and a bottle of whiskey when the final gun was fired.

Also fired, Jack figured, was Penny Pettigrew.

"Oh, no." Molli said. "She got promoted."

"Promoted?"

"She's now the *head* librarian."

49

The guy in the wig, lipstick, and women's sweater and slacks wondered in the press box of Tom Landry Stadium what it would be like being hit by a Mack track.

Below, Jarmelle Beezley didn't have to wonder. The Cowboys' quarterback scrambled from the backfield on the first play of the Wild Card Playoff Game and attempted to take refuge on the Dallas sidelines. Just as he arrived, the Panthers' mountain-of-a-nose tackle, Methuvius Ruck, drove his 320 pounds into the elusive play-caller and piled on top of him before he reached the bench.

"Ohhh!" Jack said in a high voice, making sure the others along press row would not question his gender.

The Panthers' agenda was clear and likely formed from Tremont Jones' comments on ESPN. Take out the Cowboys' starting quarterback, and maybe even the second string. That would leave only the third stringer – or the punter – to save their team.

The Panthers needed more than one good hit to expel Beezley. They followed with a clothe-line, a forearm to the jaw, and a few more body blows. Each time, even when they drew blood, Beezley got up and staggered back to the huddle.

The Panther thugs, as well as Scott Hilfinger, looked on in dismay every time Beezley rose to his feet. Brody Guthrie, the backup who wanted to stay that way, was the first one to greet Beezley with an ice pack and a trainer on the sidelines. When the team doctor asked Beezley how many fingers he was holding up, Guthrie whispered in Beezley's ear, "Three."

Three was also the temperature. A cold front swept down from Canada and turned Texas into an icebox. Snow flurries were spotted as far south as Brownsville.

Jack snuggled in his black overcoat with the wide collar covering his face, more to hide from The Dallas Star sports editor than to stay warm in the well-heated press box. He scrunched in the corner seat and pretended to be concentrating too much on the game to greet Soss, that Sawed Off Stack of Shit sports editor, who came over in the first quarter to introduce himself.

Even with thick makeup and fake nails and the fake glasses, Jack worried Soss would recognize him. Jack's perfume drew Soss closer. Jack had a contingency plan. He poured liquid Ex Lax into Soss's Texas chilli when he was looking at the field instead of his fake breasts. Within minutes, Soss excused himself and never was seen the rest of the game. Fortunately, Soss was wearing brown pants.

"That's for the time you assigned a female intern, who asked if a linebacker plays on offense or defense, instead of me to cover the Cotton Bowl," Jack thought.

The game here was equally crappy, and Beezley looked ready to shit himself. Somehow, the Cowboys found themselves only down 6-3 with 90 seconds left in the fourth quarter and a third down and 10 at midfield.

Ruck dug his cleats into the frozen fake grass and grumbled, "I gonna finish you off fo' good, nigga," as Beezley called an audible that was quite audible over a crowd that only half filled the stadium. Ruck plowed through three blockers and was on top of Beezley seemingly milli-seconds after he yelled, "Hut." Ruck could have been mistaken as a pro wrestler – Methuvius the Magnificent, perhaps – body slamming his opponent into the hard ground.

Beezley didn't move. The only finger he could count was the middle one Ruck showed the referee after he was flagged for a personal foul. He received another penalty for unsportsmanlike conduct, giving the Cowboys a first down on the Panthers' 20-yard line. Cowboys' coach Ray Myles grabbed Guthrie's facemask while trainers helped Beezley off the field.

"Take three snaps, kneel down each time, and call timeout with three seconds to go," Myles said.

Guthrie didn't question Myles' strategy, which did not include kicking a field goal to tie the game. "We're gonna fake it," Myles said, loud enough for Hilfy and special teams coach Ari Lazzari to hear.

"You don't wanta try to win it in overtime?" Lazzari, the native Italian, asked as Guthrie bobbled the first snap.

"You wanna rely on that bumblin' idiot?"

Myles' tactic was to have the punter, Colin Flanders, who holds for the placekicker, roll around and lob a pass to the end zone.

"You a kiddin?" Lazzari said. "He hasn't thrown a pass since a playin' Australia Rules Football."

Hilfy interrupted. "I'll do it, Coach. I was a holder in Europe, and I guarantee you I can zing it to the end zone."

Myles watched as Guthrie knelt a second time."Nah. If they see a quarterback in there, they'll suspect somethin'."

Hilfy took off his helmet and returned to the bench as placekicker Agberto Gerrone and Flanders jogged to the field for what everyone but the Cowboys' field goal unit thought was for the tying field goal. "Sudden death?" a reporter lamented from the press box.

"More like a slow, lingering death," Jack said in a female voice.

Flanders took the snap and stood up as Gerrone booted at an invisible football. Ruck chased Flanders as he fled toward the sidelines. Just as Ruck grabbed Flander's jersey, the punter shoveled a desperate Aussie Rules-style pass into the night. The ball floated over the defense to the back of the end zone. All but Heath Garrett lost the ball in the lights. The tight end lunged at the back pylon, dragged his feet on the blue painted turf, and hauled in the sweaty football.

Half the team mauled Garrett in the end zone and the other half lifted a wobbly Flanders on their shoulders and carried him off the field.

Hilfy still sat on the bench and watched, "Could have been me," he mumbled.

HILFY SAT THERE for an hour, pondering it all while Molli's ghostwriter batted out her first column for The Dallas Star. Jack re-applied his lipstick and snuck to the parking lot. The only one who spotted him was a football player still wearing his white number 13 jersey and carrying a green gym bag.

Jack eschewed The Bar in Arlington for the Kazbar, where he would search for clues for his long-sought mystery man Johnny Molinski. The Kazbar was the last place Molinski was spotted, and Jack figured the bar staff would be more receptive to a less-than-attractive female.

They were greeted outside by Jack's former cellmate who grabbed at his black overcoat and begged him to bring out a bottle. Jack took a dollar from his purse, told the man in his normal deep voice to buy some breath mints, and escorted Hilfy into the bar.

Hilfy drank whiskey, thankful he was drinking it in a bar instead of on a bus headed for Deadhorse. Royce Heyward actually had found another backup quarterback off the Jaguars' practice squad but forgot to sign him before Tuesday's deadline for acquiring players off waivers. "Too busy trying to find fans than football players," the GM explained to Myles before the coach slammed his fist through Heyward's office wall.

Jack took out an old photograph he found of Molinski on the Internet.

"Why you so damn obsessed with this guy?" Hilfy asked.

Jack took a sip of beer and pointed at the photograph. "If I can find this guy, I can write the most incredible story. So incredible that the writer will be so sought after that he can come back from the dead, forgiven for his deception, exonerated from the goons' boss from whom he lost a large bet, and get back his wife and his life."

Hilfy took a long whiskey swallow. "So you're hinging your life on a miracle."

Jack shot back, "Yeah, and you're going to win the Cowboys the Super Bowl."

Before Hilfy passed out at the table, Jack had some leads to Molinski's whereabouts.

"I remember this guy." Cathie, the barmaid whom Jack had flirted with a couple nights before his fateful trip to Houston, took a pen from her apron and filled in Molinski's face with black ink on the photograph. "He had beard, but that's him."

Cathie said Molinski was a regular and one of the few neighborhood bums they allowed in the bar. "He didn't bother anyone. He just sat there like your boyfriend over there, drinking whiskey, watching football, and moaning about how he could have been the star quarterback in the Super Bowl."

Jack was thankful Cathie didn't recognize him in drag but realized he wasn't the only person who has flirted with her since the start of football season. "Why did he stop comin'?" Jack said in his best female voice.

Cathie put her hand on her chin and looked at the ceiling. Then she remembered.

Molinski had passed out one night at the bar early one evening, and Cathie asked him to leave. Molinski awoke and staggered toward the broom closet instead of the exit. The bartender, Milt Johnson, tapped him on the shoulder and said, "Wrong way, pardner."

Molinski stopped, broke a beer bottle on the bar, and lunged at Johnson's throat. "Don't know what came over him," Cathie said. "All he said was 'wrong way'."

As blood dribbled from Johnson's throat, two bouncers corralled Molinski, threw him out onto the pavement, and kicked him in the stomach.

"The cops came but the bum disappeared," Cathie said. "We never saw him again."

Jack looked over at Johnson, still tending the bar while pointing to his watch – signifying closing time – and thought, "So that's why Milt's neck was bandaged. It must have happened the night *I* was thrown out of the bar."

Jack shook Hilfy's shoulder and said, "I gotta take a leak, then let's get out of here," without noticing his purse on the table.

Consumed with thoughts of Molinski's whereabouts, Jack forgot he was a woman. He walked into the men's restroom, pulled down his slacks, and peed into the urinal. At midstream he realized what he had done and that the man peeing next to him was staring at him from his fake eyebrows to his exposed penis. Jack turned his head and they immediately recognized each other.

"Repert!" Grog screamed as he tore off Jack's wig.

Grog looked bigger and meaner than ever. Jack turned his entire body, sprayed him, and sprinted out the door and into a winter storm. He was into the snow-covered parking lot before Grog zipped up and motioned Hog for another wild chase for the man who owed them money.

Jack flew around the Dippity Donuts and down Main Street with the goons blowing cold smoke and in pursuit. His recent runs in Geburtville proved productive as, even in his long black overcoat, he easily outran the two men who wanted to kill him. He tried to flag down a cab, but none stopped. He heard snow-crunching footsteps and turned around to see Hog charging toward him.

Jack sped down the road toward the rundown neighborhood of Repert's apartment on Beacon Road. He slipped momentarily, regained his balance, turned into a dark alley behind bars and brothels and ran and puffed and started laughing as a spent Hog stopped and grabbed his knees.

Jack kept running and smiling and looked back one more time at Hog retreating into the distance. Then Jack ran into what felt like a brick wall. He slammed the back of his head into the icy pavement. Jack now knew what it was like to be hit by a Mack Truck.

Or was it Methuvius the Magnificent? It was worse than either of them, and there were no referees in this dark alley. Grog lifted Jack's neck with a chokehold, turned him upside down, and pile drived him into the concrete. Broken glass cushioned his head-first fall.

Jack gagged and spit blood onto the snow. Grog yanked him up by his hair, crunched his fake glasses like they were a beer can, and drove his fist into the side of his face. Jack covered his face with his arms, so Grog drove his knee into his stomach and expelled the air out of his lungs. Jack struggled to breathe and staggered from one side of the alley to the other until Grog grabbed the collar of his black overcoat with his meaty left paw, clenched his teeth, and pushed his face up to his victim.

"OK, Repert," Grog said, pulling a German Stiletto from his pants pocket and twisting the shiny blade at Jack's throat. "This is what happens to punks who don't pay up."

Jack dropped to his knees and said, "Oh, no, no, please, no."

Grog pulled the knife behind his ear and as he thrust the blade downward, he was struck in the back of the head by a snow shovel. The monster dropped the knife and toppled onto the pavement like a felled gum tree.

Clutching the shovel and shivering in his black hoodie next to an empty whiskey bottle was Jack's old cellmate. He helped Jack to his feet and then swung the shovel back like it was a baseball bat.

"Now gimme my coat back."

Jack staggered forward, wiping blood from his lip. His cellmate followed him, "Gimme da' coat."

Jack broke back into a run and trotted up the alley. He held his side and ran with a limp, just quick enough to keep ahead of his inebriated and shovel-wielding former cellmate. Jack ran faster and faster. "Come back here!"

The next word from the old man that echoed off the brick buildings along the dark alley made Jack stop.

"Molinski!"

PART FIVE

Sudden Death

50

The words of Molli Glass' debut column in The Dallas Star leapt off the newspaper, through a Dippity Donut, and into the eyes of the Sawed off Sack of Shit sports editor.

The Dallas Cowboys' unlikely path to the Super Bowl was cleared by a more unlikely pass.

Ray Myles' decision to allow his punter to fling an Aussie Rules style shovel toss into the end zone on the final play of Saturday's NFL Wild Card Game was either ingenuity or insanity. If it worked, Myles was a genius. If it failed, he was a laughing stock and on the unemployment line.

The real author of those words sat five booths down in the donut shop. Soss' view of the presumed dead columnist was blocked by a bartender from the nearby Kazbar, several inebriated Cowboys' fans, and a bum. Jack was no longer in women's garb. Now he was disguised by faded lipstick, a bloodied forehead, and a puffy, purple eye. No need to worry.

Soss was to into his jelly donut and Molli's ghost-written column to notice anyone or anything else. The more he liked the lead column the slower he ate his donut and sipped his coffee. He often had burned his mouth and practically gagged while reading Jack's columns. Jack figured that was because Soss hated him and looked for anything possible he could hate in his column. It was personal, not professional.

Soss ate and drank never more slowly on Molli with an I's column, which detailed the difference of throwing an Aussie Rules football to that of an American football. Jack even detected a hint of a smile in the corner of Soss' glazed and jelly-covered lips. The Ex-Lax he had snuck into his press box cuisine obviously had worn off.

A few of the donut patrons kicked out of neighboring bars at closing time had arrived when Jack flung his former cellmate into the booth and poured hot coffee down the old man's frozen throat. He had talked the bum into dropping the snow shovel by offering him the black overcoat Jack thought belonged to Graham Repert, the man whose identity he presumably had assumed, and a bottle of 90 proof whiskey.

First, the bum had to tell him why he yelled, "Molinski," as Jack fled from him. It took several cups of coffee and a few cinnamon twists to sober him up enough to get the story and convince him that Jack wasn't Molinski without the beard and long hair.

The bum explained that everyone looks the same on the street, especially at night, but "me knows me overcoat anywhere." When asked why he didn't recognize him from the jail cell, the bum said, "Which one?"

Jack soon had what he needed but needed to leave in a hurry. Grog staggered into the donut shop with Hog's assistance. Grog's vision was likely too blurred to see the bruised and blood-splattered man he nearly stabbed to death. Jack wasn't taking any chances.

He told his trusting old cellmate he had to go to the bathroom. "OK, lad," he said. "Then hurry back with me coat and da bottle."

The bum got neither. Jack slipped out the backdoor and sprinted for Molli's Chrysler Sebring, which he had parked at the Kazbar. He was out of downtown before the bum noticed he was gone and before Soss finished reading Molli's column.

JACK WAS STILL panting when he drove past the Dallas city limits and fled to the dark, desolate highway en route to Geburtville. It was here that Jack put together the pieces from the discussions with his former cellmate, Ghost Bowl players, other acquaintances, and the events that occurred since The Dallas Star staff car crash and discovered who Graham Repert really was.

The lights on the Sebring did more than illuminate the highway. They shone the light of a fated quarterback.

Johnny Molinski likely drove up the same highway in his escape from his embarrassment at Lone Star State and his father's disappointment. He couldn't escape who he had become: "Wrong Way" Molinski.

He knew nothing else but football and failed at every venture and in every relationship in every town. He turned to drinking and gambling and soon was living out of his van. The man who could once hit receivers in stride 60 yards downfield couldn't even hit a dart board from across the local pub.

Jack's old cellmate met Molinski on the streets of Dallas, where he returned with a most delusional dream. He told him he wanted to bet his way out of the gutter. "I'll make enough money," he said, "that I'll be able to train all day and then try out for the Cowboys and lead them to the Super Bowl. It will be the resurrection of Johnny Molinski. I'll show everyone."

The cellmate burped. "The first thing you, uh, Molinski, uh, could buy would be scissors, shaving cream, and a razor."

"You and me both," Molinski said.

Molinski organised pick-up football games with fellow bums at tent city underneath the highway ramp near downtown. The "Down and Out Bowl," he called it. During a freak cold front in late September, Molinksi offered Jack's old cellmate a bottle of whiskey to let him borrow his coat. The cellmate didn't realize his wallet was in the pocket. There was no money, no credit card. The driver's license had expired several years ago.

Molinski found a local bookie at the Kazbar. Unbeknownst to the dim witted barmaid, he came there more to bet than to drink in the long black overcoat he refused to return its owner. He placed small bets for or against the Cowboys every weekend, mainly based on what Jack had written in his pre-game column while rejecting the advice given by The Dallas Star's NFL beat writer Jay Verona. His weekly winnings earned him enough to rent an apartment in a seedy part of downtown but not enough to pay the bills.

So Molinski bet the big one – $40,000 on the Houston Texans to beat the Dallas Cowboys. Based on his winning streak and what Jack wrote about the Thanksgiving Day game, this was a sure thing. The bookie wasn't as thrilled with Molinski's growing fortune or having his henchman attacked with a broken beer bottle. He decided to have Molinski rubbed out even before the game was played. Winning streaks weren't good for business.

The goons chased Molinski out of his apartment and into his van on the coldest November night in Dallas history. He fled downtown and kept driving until he ran out of gas.

As he approached Geburtville, Jack pulled to the side of the road and walked to the bridge he had peered over on Christmas Eve. He stared at the icy river below as the inevitable revelation spilled into his brain.

Jack remembered the Armadillo key chain, the column in the Beacon Road apartment, and the hitchhiker they picked up en route to Houston.

Jack took out the wallet from the overcoat pocket. The headlights glimmered off the driver's license photo of the bearded man named Graham Repert. Jack never really looked at the photo until now. Johnny Molinksi not only had taken the man's coat; he had taken his identity.

A brisk wind smacked into Jack as he leaned against the rail of the bridge. He never felt more cold or more lonely.

51

Lying, cheating, stealing, fornicating and so many other sins had been whispered into the plastic screen in the small, musty confessional at St. Blaise Catholic Church for so many years. But murder?

"What do you mean you killed your brother?" The Voice was more inquisitive than indignant.

Jack thought for a moment about the priest's question, then said, "I consider all my fellow football players – especially quarterbacks – my brothers."

Jack confessed what had been bothering him since falling asleep on the field house high jump mat the night after the Cowboys' Wild Card victory and his wild romp and stomp through downtown Dallas.

The real murder almost occurred in the wee hours of Sunday morning in an alley in downtown Dallas, and Jack felt close to death when he woke up the next afternoon.

His left eye turned from purple to black and so swollen it would take a crowbar to jar it open. His head and stomach felt like his former cellmate hit *him* with the snow shovel. The hair of his scalp was twisted in knots by dry blood.

Jack, wrapped in the black overcoat, staggered into town without anyone noticing him. That's because Geburtville was a ghost town on Sundays, also. People only came out for church in the winter and for picnics in the summer. No stores were open, a devastating discovery for a man in desperate need of painkillers. Jack reckoned he would use a gun if he had one and even wished Grog had finished him off with his razor sharp Stiletto.

Meanwhile, Jack witnessed another murder taking place at Ollie's Electronics. He sat on the sidewalk and watched the wildcard Minnesota Vikings flatten the NFC South Champion Tampa Bay Buccaneers more than the flat screen television in the storefront window. Jack wondered who could be in more pain, he or the Buccaneers. He lumbered back to the Gebbie Bowl at dusk, early in the fourth quarter with the Vikings leading 38-6 and privately predicted a similar demolition by the NFC West Champion Rams on the lucky-still-to-be-alive Cowboys in the next Saturday's Divisional Playoff game in St. Louis.

Jack sipped a bowl of canned soup and collapsed again on the cold high jump mat. The thought of Jeanie as he awoke the Monday morning warmed him up. He closed his unswollen eye and reminisced about clinging to her body as they awoke and kissing her tender cheek as he did on many Monday mornings that followed a Cowboys' game and a golf tournament. She brought him his coffee and the newspaper and they sat up in bed, reading in quiet solitude with a blanket wrapped around them.

When he opened his eye, no one was there. He rubbed his hand up and down the mat, helplessly hoping his love would appear. "Oh, Jeanie," he whispered, "I can't tell you how much I miss you."

Jack stared at the ceiling, listening to the soft voice of Gordon Lightfoot swirling inside his head:

If you could read my mind love
What a tale my thoughts could tell
Just like an old time movie
About a ghost from a wishing well
In a castle dark or a fortress strong
With chains upon my feet
You know that ghost is me
And I will never be set free
As long as I'm a ghost you can see

Jack lay there most of the day, getting up only to return to town for the painkillers and another can of soup. Then he flushed the pain pills down the toilet, wanting to be punished for what he had done to

Johnny Molinski. The priest on the other side of the confessional refused to give him penance.

"Why not?" Jack asked.

"Because you are already sorry and repenting for a sin you did not commit."

"But I killed him, Father. If I hadn't written those things, maybe he could have come back. Won his job back. Transferred to another school, taken Hilfy's route and played in Europe and his way into the NFL. Nobody wanted him after the hype I created. His father didn't even want him. There was no hope. He was a bum, a gambler, a drifter. What kind of life is that?"

There was only silence from the other side of the wall, so Jack continued.

"I figured he was in the Kazbar the night I got tossed out, but I never noticed. I was too drunk and too wrapped up in my own misery. I should be the one rotting in hell at the bottom of that hole, not Johnny."

Jack could hear the soft breathing on the other side of the screen. "Look above you." The Voice was never more clear.

As Jack stared at a small crucifix, the priest continued. "Jesus died on the cross to save us from darkness. He says if you follow him, he will show you the light. Perhaps Mr. Molinski would have become a football star and then lost his soul to fame and fortune."

"Not following ya, Padre?"

Padre explained by reciting scripture: "Whoever wishes to save his life will lose it; but whoever loses his life for My sake will find it. For what will it profit a man if he gains the whole world and forfeits his soul?"

"So you're saying Molinski is better off dead?"

"I am saying that if you live a good life, you will have a new life. Hang in there. You will see the light. You will have your miracle."

Jack returned to the field house more confused than when he left it. Maybe, he figured, it's no different from life.

52

The lights returned to the Gebbie Bowl the next night, but there were no miracles. Just grown men re-enacting their gridiron days by running and passing and tackling and celebrating after every score.

Jack was in no mood and had no glory days to re-enact. Only the bitterness and the fascination of what could have been. He was drawn to the sidelines by the car and pickup headlights that illuminated the otherwise dark and dreary field. Still, there was no desire to take part. He only wore a helmet and assorted gear to hide his identity.

"Why don't ya' come out here an' play, ya' pussy," one of the gridiron ghosts yelled from the field.

Jack watched them cracking into each other at the line of scrimmage or at full steam and staggering to their feet. "Not tonight," Jack said. "Bum hammy."

As he said it, he could hear Jeanie's voice in his head. "You never go for anything. You just sit back and watch and then run away. Just like you always do. Run away from your friends, from your family, from me. Go ahead, Jack, run. Run away."

"Well," the lumberjack of a man with a beard and a number 76 Lone Star State jersey said, "Did ya' find him?"

"Find who?"

"Molinski."

Jack remembered quizzing Molinski's former teammate the week before.

"Yeah, I saw him."

"Is he gonna play?"

"No."

"Why not?"

"Let's just say he's a little burnt out."

Jack was relieved when the man retook the field. A few more cries of "pussy" was not enough incentive to join them. He simply ran away, back to his safe house, just as he had done on that field 27 years before and as Jeanie told him what he had been doing ever since.

53

Molli and Jack were a hopeless and helpless pair.

Molli with an I didn't want to give up her column with The Dallas Star but didn't want to write it either. She had become an overnight sensation with her column on the Cowboys' upset victory. Readers skimmed past Dave Noonan's game-story about the David Cowboys slewing the Goliath Panthers and the "I feel good" quotes to Molli's column. Soss was taking triumphant pats on the back for finding another talent in an unusual place. Little did he know the column came from a usual writer he detested and demoralized.

Letters of praise to the editor flooded the office of the Sawed Off Stack of Shit sports editor, who called Molli on Monday afternoon to offer her a job. Or sort of. He had to sort through some HR details to get Penny Pettigrew transferred back to the library and then post an advert for a sports columnist which he promised Molli with an undisclosed contract.

Meanwhile, he would keep paying Molli on a freelance basis. Her next assignment was the Cowboys-Rams' Divisional playoff game in St. Louis.

"Sorry, can't go to St. Louis," Jack said on Thursday afternoon, knowing he would be spotted by a goon or a scribe en route or in St. Louis. He already had blown his cover in Molli's high heels.

Molli leaned back in her chair. Her soft permed hair was now straight and looked like it hadn't been washed since Cullen III said, "I don't." She wore jeans and an old plaid shirt and looked like a rodeo writer. "Well, I can't go. I can't write."

A writer Molli never was. Writers have imagination, intuition, and curiosity. Not once did she question Jack about who he was, where he lived, or where he came from. Little did she know of his plight and the potential blockbuster of a Pulitzer Prize-winner of a story that lay before her.

Her troubles were nothing compared to Jack, who didn't want to take his life but didn't want to live it either. He sat on the corner of her desk looking more apathetic than her in sweat pants and the old Gebbie's jersey he slept in the night before. Molli didn't notice his purple eye because she didn't look him in the eye.

She tapped her bitten unpolished nails on her desk that was topped by the sports pages laced with Jack's ghost-written stories.

"What am I gonna do, Graham?"

"Go to St. Louis. I'll watch the game on TV and dictate a column over the phone."

"But they saw you dressed up as me at a couple of games, and I'm a foot shorter than you."

"Only a glimpse. I was sitting down. And I was better looking than you at the moment."

Molli rolled up a newspaper and swatted at Jack, who blocked it with his forearm.

"I've got a better idea," Jack said.

Molli stopped swatting. "OK, I'm listening."

"Call Soss, I mean Schwartz, and tell him you want to write an in-depth feature on the Cowboy Express Bus and that you will ride to St. Louis and back on the bus."

Jack swore he would never ride on that bus again, but he had no other way there. He knew Soss would embrace his new protégé's story suggestion and take credit for the idea. Jack would make a few calls to find out in what bleachers these bums sit and have Soss pay for a seat. Jack could blend in with the fans and go unnoticed, bat out a column on Molli's laptop, and send it from somewhere in the stadium while the bus people were cheering – and likely yelling, "Better luck next year" – as the players in their leather jackets and mink coats marched to their luxury airport shuttle.

"I will do this on two conditions," Jack said. "One, you pay me what you owe me for the last two weeks' stories. Two, you write a column on Jeanine Pratt."

"Who?"

"Women's Pro Golfer. Just won the Christmas Classic and a berth in the opening LPGA tournament early next month. She's playing in a pro-am tournament in Fort Worth this weekend. Interview her on Sunday after the tournament. I'll write down the questions for you to ask. Use your tape recorder. Then I'll write the column for you."

"And why am I doing this?"

Jack hopped off Molli's desk and looked at the floor. He had his selfish reasons but gave Molli another one.

"Women's sports, especially golf, gets lousy coverage. Your stock, especially among women readers, will rise significantly and you'll be even more popular."

Molli laughed. "Yeah, right. You've got a thing for this Jeanine Pratt person."

Jack pointed his trigger figure. "Got me."

Molli glared at Jack, still not noticing his purple eye. "What am I going to do about Schwartz's job offer? If I agreed to write for the Star I would be deemed the worst writer in the history of the newspaper."

"Nah, that would be Penny Pettigrew and followed closely by Dave Noonan."

"So what am I gonna do?"

"I donna know. Go back to college and change your major to Home Ec?"

Jack ran for the door as Molli swatted at him again, trying to purple the other eye. Her voice echoed through the quiet Geburtville breeze as Jack darted down the road. "Make that bus ticket to St. Louis one-way."

54

Marjie Mason is your typical housewife. She cooks, cleans, pays the bills, takes care of her three toddlers and a golden retriever, and provides a comfortable home for her accountant husband in an affluent Dallas suburb.

She is the last person you would suspect wearing a mid-thigh length Jarmelle Beezley jersey with a belt buckle and no pants or panties aboard the Cowboy Express while sucking on the spout of a 20-gallon keg and then crooning "Mamas, don't let your babies grow up to be Cowboys."

The other 43 inebriated passengers, including the driver and a presumed dead sportswriter, sang in unison in the dark bus lit only by the butts of cigarettes and cigars.

Mamas, don't let your babies grow up to be cowboys.
Don't let 'em pick guitars or drive them old trucks.
Let 'em be doctors and lawyers and shit...

Marjie provided the perfect lead for a future ghost-written feature in The Dallas Star by a man with blue and silver face-paint and who blended in with the other Cowboys' fanatics. Between a succession of gulps and burps and an occasional outburst of, "Y-e-e-haw, Cowboys," she offered Jack her story.

"I'm in prison," she said. "I'm trapped in a luxury home and all I see is the damn washer and dryer, diaper pail, bath toys, and a butt-load of dishes. My husband/warden gives me a furlough every time the Cowboys play out-of-town."

"Does he know you're wasted and not wearing any underwear on a bus full of drunk horny bastards?"

"Nah, he just thinks I'm a big Cowboy fan."

What Jack discovered on his 11-hour ride on a bus so rowdy that the crowd noise drowned an engine that otherwise sounded like it was going to explode was that there weren't many true Cowboy fans on the Cowboy Express. This was simply a temporary escape from whatever hell hole they lived in.

They all grew up to be doctors and lawyers and such, as the real Waylon and Willie song goes, or wives of doctors and lawyers. They didn't grow up to be Cowboys or even Cowboys' fans. The Cowboy Express was their escape from reality, a reuniting of their college days when they had no responsibilities other than passing a course with a D-minus and making sure the condom fit. The Express passengers were ghosts of their former selves riding through a fog somewhere between Little Rock and Memphis.

Except for Stan "Pretty Boy" Sorrell, who looked more like a skeleton than a ghost. He sat in the front row with the earphone of his old transistor radio in his left ear and stared at the snowflakes smashing into the head lights. His gold and white teeth lit up the van and his face. He wore an old blue Cowboys' jersey with white plastic on the shoulders and the number 14. There was no name on the back. Jack presumed it belonged to Eddie LeBaron, the Cowboys' first quarterback.

"You probably stole ol' Eddie's jersey, 'cause they didn't sell 'em back in his day," Jack said, squatting next to him.

"No sir, I done bought dis one, in 19 and 63."

"Pretty," as everyone called him, claimed to be the first Cowboys' fan. He said he went to the first game in 1961 and never missed one since, claiming to drive, fly, or take the train. "Whatever it done took," he said.

Jack found it hard to believe that the former high school janitor could afford to go to all those games and even harder to believe that Pretty played some pro ball. He did believe that Pretty was one of the first passengers aboard the Cowboy Express, when the former school bus was driven to Washington, D.C. for the NFL Championship Game in 19 and 83.

"We done lost dat one," he said. "It was a l-l-long trip home."

Pretty said he didn't mind the drinkin', the smokin', and whatever might be going on in the back of the bus. The noise?

'I'm half-deaf and it get drown out by da transista radio. Da bus would have to blow up to hear anythins. I sleep most of da' time, anyways."

PRETTY WAS ASLEEP by the time the fog lifted, and the Gateway Arch glistened in the distance. He didn't wake up as the Express passengers greeted St. Louis with their traditional 10-moon salute. The letters, two spaces, and exclamation point on each cheek spelled out, "Dallas Cowboys Rule!"

He didn't wake up as the van rocked up to the Homer Dome – a stadium named for the Rams' founder, not for the multitude of four baggers from the baseball team. He didn't wake up as the passengers in their Cowboys' football jerseys poured out of the bus carrying a mini-keg they would smuggle into the stadium or when Jack tapped him on the back and said, "Let's go, pops."

Jack shook his shoulder. Pretty still didn't respond. He felt for a pulse around Pretty's neck and couldn't find one. Pretty wouldn't watch the 2006 Divisional Playoff game, but he would listen to it. Jack tuned the transistor radio, with the earphone still stuck into Pretty's ear, to the game broadcast.

All Jack heard as he walked through the parking lot was a group of Dallas escapees singing in the distance.

Mamas don't let your babies grow up to be cowboys.
'Cos they'll never stay home and they're always alone.
Even with someone they love

55

From Jack's perspective in the cramped Cowboys fans' section of the Homer Dome, Scott Hilfinger was the only one hitting his target. Button hook. Sideline route. Post Pattern. The ball spiralled out of Hilfy's rifle arm and every time smacked into the awaiting arms of the Cowboys' water boy.

When the water boy finally ran out of energy, Hilfy had him prop a water cooler on a table so he could fire footballs at it.

Hilfy resorted to amateur and fake targets in the NFL Divisional playoff pre-game warmup, because the real ones were too busy collecting the underthrown and overthrown balls from the Cowboys' first and second string quarterbacks. The Rams' cornerbacks stood on the sideline and giggled. They laughed and held their guts when the Cowboys' injured superstar Rex Fanning walked onto the field in his Rex Fanning number 7 jersey and jeans and, as if to show his replacements how to do it, threw a quail that had a hang time longer than a Colin Flanders' punt. One of the Rams' cornerbacks pretended to hold a shotgun in his hands and shoot down the helpless pigskin.

After the teams retreated to the locker room and returned for the opening kickoff, the Cowboys' strategy was certain: don't throw the ball.

The Rams didn't bother taking the Panthers' cue and try to hurt Jarmelle Beezley. They figured they didn't need to. They were the NFC West Champions with a 12-4 record. They won five straight games. They had an opening round bye. They had 2,000-yard rusher Racine Charles. They were playing in the Homer Dome, where they hadn't lost all season before a home crowd so noisy the opposing quarterback had to use hand signals to call an audible.

As Rams' defensive tackle Omar Fickens told a national televised audience before the game, "This here ain't no walkover, this here's a stomp-over."

Everyone in the stadium – on the field, in the stands, and in the press box – seemed to believe it except for the player with the sky blue number 50 stretched across his white jersey. Muta Falusa looked like a big boulder with a bulldog snarl beneath the silver bars of his facemask.

On the first play from scrimmage he cracked through a gap between the Rams' center and guard and smashed into Racine Charles a moment after he took the hand-off. On the second play he shoved Racine into a sideline yardage chain, and on the third drove his helmet into his gut on a screen pass he had snuffed out.

As expected, the Cowboys went nowhere with their constipated offense. Tailback slant. Fullback power. Tailback sweep. No draws, no option plays. Not even an end around. What few fans the Cowboys had in the stadium booed, and so did the cheerleaders. "I've seen better play calling by a middle school coach," Jack said to a fan, likely too drunk to pay attention to the game.

THE BOOS FOR BOTH TEAMS echoed off the Homer Dome as the players jogged to the locker room at halftime with the Rams leading 3-0. The Cowboy Express patrons in their white and blue Cowboys' jerseys with various numbers didn't boo anymore. They just drank. They drank the keg they smuggled into the game by the time the players jogged back onto the field. The patrons pooled their money and bought a fully stocked cooler from a stadium beer vendor.

Jack drank a few himself for camouflage purposes. Even wearing face paint and new fake glasses and on the road, he was paranoid about being spotted by what he figured was a "network of goons."

Jack wished he had bet the under on this game, especially after the Cowboys threw only two passes and had only one first down in the third quarter. The Rams and their listless offense, mauled by a Ram-eater of a linebacker, couldn't go anywhere either. Their biggest weapon was their punter Corey Leadbetter, who nailed the ball in the Cowboys' coffin corner and a nail in their coffin with four minutes to go in the game.

Three QB sneaks that accumulated the length of the football is all Beezley could muster. Flanders' right heel bordered the back line of the end zone when he received the fourth down snap. His hurried punt was a bullett that Rams' returner Raheem Rashaad caught at full speed and returned it to the end zone before Flanders realized it wasn't blocked.

The Cowboys were down 10-0 with 2:43 left and their season resting on a quarterback who had thrown three completions for 23 yards. Myles looked around at Brody Guthrie snoozing on the bench, Hilfy tossing the ball to the waterboy, and Fanning signing autographs and talking to a sideline reporter. He took off his headset and dropped it to the ground. "We're doomed," he said.

The only way the Rams could lose would be to kick the ball to Cowboys' return man Antonio "The Rocket" Crocket. So they squib kicked it to him. The Rocket, who wears number eight because he says "dats how long it take me to run from goalpost to goalpost," seemingly should have worn number 7.5. His runback cut the score to 10-6. Agberto Gerrone's extra point kick made it 10-7 until Myles took the point off the board.

"What the fuck is he doing?" Jack yelled.

The only other Cowboy Express patron somewhat sober and paying attention said, "The Rams were offside, so he's going for a two-point-conversion from the one-yard line. Gerrone looked so shaky in warmup, Myles isn't even sure he'd make the extra point."

"Good point," Jack said.

Falusa checked in at fullback and plowed behind his blockers like it was a rugby maul before finding the end zone and cutting the lead to 10-8.

Myles then made another unusual decision, kicking away instead of an onside attempt. When Falusa piled drived Racine for another third down loss, The Rocket stood at his own 40 with 37 seconds left for a punt that none of the 80,000 spectators or 80,000 television viewers doubted he would ever field. The Rams' punter Leadbetter practiced kicked an invisible ball in the direction of the Rams' bench.

The strategy would have worked had the real ball not gone off the side of Leadbetter's foot and into the playing field. The Rocket scooped it up and raced to the Rams' 24-yard line.

Beezley's ensuing kneel down, one of his biggest gainers, and timeout set up Gerrone with a winning field goal attempt of 41 yards. The crowd suddenly grew quieter than a Catholic congregation. Rams' fans held hands. The Cowboy Express patrons stopped drinking.

Some closed their eyes as Gerrone said adios to the football and the Cowboys' season with a wide-left boot. The referee interrupted the crowd's thunder by informing them that their Rams' head coach had called a timeout a fraction before the snap in an attempt to freeze the kicker. He interrupted them again after Gerrone's next attempt sprayed wide right to inform them that Fickens had jumped offside.

There were a mixture of boos and cheers when Gerrone sent his next missile from the Cowboys 27-yard line. This one was a pop fly with more hang time than Fanning's pre-game quail. One-hundred and sixty thousand eyes fixed on the crossbar as the football rammed it like a pinball and bounced higher than the uprights. Only the referees on the end line could tell which side of the bar it fell on.

They looked at each other and nodded. Their next gesture sent one team screaming and jumping, the other team firing their helmets into the turf.

56

The Dallas Cowboys' third string quarterback finally got the call from the head coach.

"Hilfigger," Ray Myles shouted as he looked inside the team's airport shuttle bus just before it departed from the Homer Dome.

Scott Hilfinger stood up. "Yes, coach."

"Grab your bag; you're on the equipment truck."

Myles needed Hilfy's seat on the Cowboys' charter flight for Rex Fanning, whose private jet was experiencing a technical problem. No "sorry" or "thank you" from the coach or the Prima Donna quarterback, who demanded an apology after Hilfy brushed him with his green gym bag on his hasty bus exit.

"Watch the shoulder, you prick," Fanning said.

The bus door got Hilfy in the butt before he could utter a lame apology. The next bus door he faced, on the Cowboy Express, had to be pried open.

Jack spotted Hilfy about to board the equipment truck and invited him to take Pretty's vacated seat. He explained that Pretty's corpse was stowed in the luggage compartment below, and its stench was overwhelmed by the beer spilt on the seats.

Hilfy stuck his green gym bag on the rack above him and plopped down. "I'd much rather ride in a dead man's seat next to a guy traveling incognito in Cowboys' face paint than on that crappy truck. Who knows when he'll get back."

Jack pulled his hand to his ear. "Listen to that bus engine. Who knows when *we'll* get back."

Jack pulled his index finger to his lips when Hilfy asked about the facepaint. "Shhh, they're looking for me all over the place. There could be a goon spy on this bus."

Jack dictated his column to Molli, who had refused to lend him her laptop, on a passenger's cellphone above the Cowboy Express celebrants:

Muta Falusa grew up wearing a skirt, the traditional Samoan lava-lava. In Saturday's NFL Divisional Playoff Game in the Homer Dome, he wore a Rams' running back.

Racine Charles gained 2,000 yards in the regular season. In the post season the Cowboys' middle linebacker made sure he didn't gain 2,000 inches. Falusa not only blocked Charles' path through the line but his team's path to the Super Bowl, setting up a dramatic come-from-behind win on a field goal attempt that pooped out a foot beyond the goalpost.

"Molli's a pretty damn good writer," Hilfy said, after Jack dictated his final word and pressed the disconnect button on the cellphone. "How long she been writing?"

"The real Molli can't write worth a shit. This Molli started writing at age 14, about the same time I stopped playing football."

Hilfy scrunched his face. "What happened little Jacky, daddy wouldn't let you play?"

Jack turned his head to the window and looked at the snowflakes pounding the dark highway. A few minutes later Hilfy pulled his whiskey flask from his gym bag, took a sip, and put it front of Jack's lips. Jack took a big gulp and handed it back.

"It was the first game of my freshman season," Jack said. "I trained all summer. Threw a zillion balls through that old tire hangin' from the oak tree and to my friends on Jack's Home Field. Spent hours and after-hours in the weight room. The coach made me the starter and said I would one-day lead Geburtville to the state title."

Hilfy took a swig and handed the flask back. "Your dad must have been proud."

"Huh," Jack said with a wry chuckle. "He didn't know I played. He hated sports, said they were waste of time; wouldn't even let me watch football on TV."

"He must have gotten pissed when he found out you were playing behind his back."

Jack took a longer swig. He stared out the window and to that foggy night in the Gebbie Bowl where the 14-year-old boy with Super Bowl dreams called the first play in the huddle, barked "On two," and trotted to the 50-yard-line. He looked over his center's helmet to boys twice his size, one with peach fuzz growing beneath his facemask yelling, "Come on, pussy, I'm gonna fuck you up."

Little Jack wanted to take refuge on the sidelines. Instead, he took a deep breath and stammered the signals, "D-d-down, s-s-set. "

"Spit it out, retard," the nose guard said, as Jack looked over his linemen's helmets.

"H-h-hut one. H-h-hut..."

Before he uttered, "Two," a man wearing work boots, jeans, and a plaid shirt marched onto the field.

The referee blew the whistle as the man grabbed Jack's facemask and pulled him off the field.

Everyone laughed – the players, the coaches, the cheerleaders, the parents – as the man yanked off his son's helmet and stripped him – pads, uniform, and all – in his team's end zone. Jack stood there in his T-shirt, jock strap, and cleats. The man grabbed Jack's hair and dragged him out of the stadium.

Jack took another swig on the whiskey flask and pressed his forehead into the seat in front of him. "I hated my father."

JACK DIDN'T SAY another word for three hours. By then, the whiskey flask was empty and everyone's bladders were full in time for the first PPP stop.

"What does PPP stand for?" Hilfy asked, leading Jack out the bus door.

Jack pointed to the Cowboy Express patrons running for the gas station toilets or the nearest trees. "Puke, Piss, and Petrol."

Between PPP stops, Hilfy got Jack's mind off football. "Gettin' any lately?" Hilfy asked.

"Any what?"

Jack finally got it. "Not that I know of."

"Huh?"

Jack told Hilfy about the night he spent with Molli. "I know I didn't do anything or else I would have remembered."

"Not necessarily," Hilfy said, filling up his flask from the remnants of the beer keg.

He recalled waking up in a barn with a naked fraulein in Germany and in the cry room of a church in Spain with the minister's daughter. They told him all of his antics of the evening and even showed him pictures.

"I was too drunk to remember any of it. How do you know that wasn't the same with Molli?"

"'Cause I'm still in love with my wife."

Jack stared back at the dark highway, ignoring Hilfy's laugh and the drunken chatter of the bus patrons still conscious. He could see Jeanie in her pink silk nightie that hung over the soft breasts and hard nipples he caressed on cold winter nights as this. He thought about it as the Cowboy Express chugged into Texas and made its final PPP.

HILFY CONVINCED JACK to wash off the remains of his face paint and questioned his paranoia as he took a football from the bus and threw it to Jack as the driver filled up the gas tank.

"There is nowhere to hide." Jack drilled a bullet pass at Hilfy's chest. "They are looking for me in every nook and cranny. They were probably at the Homer Dome and driving the same highway back to Dallas."

Hilfy grabbed the ball and rifled it back. "Nice pass for a DH. Now go long."

Jack bounded past the gas pumps and sprinted for the ball Hilfy lofted above the flood lights of the gas station. Jack stretched for the ball that hit his hands perfectly in stride and smacked into a concrete wall of flesh and muscle. Jack bounced like he had hit a padded wall and landed back-first on the concrete.

He didn't need to look at the person's face to know who had stopped his momentum and about to stomp the heel of his boot into his chin. He had stopped Grog previously with a cup of hot chocolate, a stream of urine, and a bum's snow shovel. This time he only needed a football.

Jack flung the ball hard and hit his little target between Grog's legs. He fled to the Cowboy Express before Grog's knee-first plant on the concrete and flopped into the driver's seat as the other goons were dragging Grog, who hollered "You're dead meat, Repert," to their Chevy pickup truck.

Hilfy hopped through the open door as Jack twisted the key, drove away from the pumps, and pulled onto the highway ahead of a drunken, frozen flock of bus patrons who begged them to return. "Ever driven a school bus before?" Hilfy asked.

Jack looked into the rearview mirror. "Ever been shot at before?"

"What?"

The bus engine roared as Jack shoved the floorboard stick into the highest possible gear and pressed the accelerator to the floor. Jack could see dim lights in his rearview mirror beneath a light fog and pulled off onto an access road and then down a dirt road. He turned off his lights hoping to lose the goons while trying in vain to see the road.

The bus wobbled back and forth like an out-of-control washing machine but was not running away from the red pickup.

"Can't this thing go any faster?" Hilfy shouted over the loud, scraping engine.

Jack pressed his right foot even harder. "It's an old school bus not a fucking Ferrari!"

Jack steered the bus onto a paved road that led to Geburtville. He heard a gunshot from the pickup as it closed to within 10 bus lengths of them. The Cowboy Express had an arsenal of its own – two cases of Coors Light.

Hilfy opened the back door and threw Silver Bullets at the goons. Each can smacked into the windshield, setting off clouds of beer foam that made the driver's visibility impossible. "Take that, mother fuckers!" Hilfy screamed above the screeching of tires and rumbling of engines.

The pickup, with the help of rapidly moving wiper blades, finally managed to pull alongside the bus. Grog shot out the windows with his semi-automatic pistol and sprayed bullets into the side of the bus.

Jack swerved, trying to knock the pickup off the road. The pickup rammed sideways into the bus. Grog aimed his handgun at Jack's head. As he was about to pull the trigger, Hilfy rifled a silver bullet through a shot-out bus window into Grog's wrist, dislodging the gun onto the roadway. The next silver bullet rammed Hog, the driver, in the head and splattered another beer volcano that rendered him helpless. The pickup truck skidded off the road and slid to a stop into mud so thick it would take a wrecker to yank it out.

Jack honked the bus horn and he and Hilfy saluted the goons with a one finger salute. They laughed until Hilfy started sniffing gas and Jack noticed the needle steadily dropping on the gas gauge. Smoke poured from the hood and billowed through the shot-out windows. Jack coughed. "We've been hit."

"Pull this thing over before it blows up," Hilfy yelled.

JACK FOUND a final resting place for the Cowboy Express – and for Pretty – on a little rodeo ground, where real Cowboys roamed, adjacent the highway. Hilfy grabbed his green bag and the last two silver bullets and yanked Jack out of the driver's seat. They sprinted past the rodeo ground just as a loud explosion shook the ground beneath them. They didn't bother looking back at flames shooting out of the Cowboy Express. They kept looking ahead at the distant lights of Geburtville as they ran through fog down the dark, desolate road.

"I think I was wrong," Hilfy said.

"About what?"

"I should have ridden back on the equipment truck."

57

Jack didn't have to see his beloved wife. Jeanie's words, soft and gentle and resonating from Molli's micro tape recorder, made Jack feel her. He could smell the sweet scent of her shampooed hair, taste the peachy gloss of her moist lips, touch the smooth texture of her warm, silky skin.

Jeanie may as well have been whispering into Jack's ear.

"I never imagined what my life might be without my husband. To wake up and find him not only gone from my bed and from my life but from this Earth has made me entirely sad. There are so many things I want to say to him."

Molli's next question should have been, what would you like to say to him? Being an inept reporter and not knowing her dead husband would be listening, Molli asked, "So how does it feel to make the LPGA Tour?"

What else is there to say? It feels good. The rest of the interview had Jeanie prattling on about her practice routine, her mental approach, and the many past tournaments Jack already knew about. He had what he needed for a column but not what he needed to bring her husband back to life – and back into her life.

Jack clicked off the tape recorder as Molli skimmed over her email and fan mail at her desk at the Geburtville Gazette. "Interesting interview," Jack said. "Did she say anything off the record about her husband?"

Molli didn't look up from the fan's email, praising her for the Cowboys' column Jack wrote for her on the Saturday following Molli's interview with Jeanie at the Forest Green clubhouse. "Nah. I hear she was married to some hack sports columnist from the Star. She seems to be doin' all right without him."

Jack wanted to see it for himself. Molli agreed to let him drive her Chrysler Sebring to the Cowboys' Monday press conference where Coach Ray Myles would say he feels good about his team's chances against the wildcard Minnesota Vikings, whose shocking 41-6 win over the NFC North champion Green Bay Packers gave the Cowboys at least one more home game, in the NFC title game.

Jack's real intention was getting Scott Hilfinger to the Cowboys Training Center in time for workout and then go spy on Jeanie.

Jack and Hilfy had arrived at dawn into Geburtville out of breath but out of danger following their four mile run from the Cowboy Express burial ground. They passed out on the field house high jump mat and spent the Sunday recovering from their high speed shoot-out with the goons and the alcohol they had poured down their throats. Hilfy now could see Jack's paranoia and that he was a wanted man in goon world. He knew that for Jack, Geburtville was only a temporary hideout.

Jack knew that Hilfy also was on borrowed time. It would take a miracle for him to get on the playing field in the NFC Championship game or the Super Bowl. "A shame," Jack thought as they tossed the ball around at Jack's Home Field. He was amazed at the accuracy of his Silver Bullets that eventually freed them from the goons and at the bullets he was throwing him so accurately and passionately around his special field.

"Football is all this guy knows," Jack thought as he tossed the ball back. "There is no life for him after football, especially in Deadhorse. He belongs in the NFL."

Jack denied Hilfy's request for a noon cocktail en route to Dallas. He looked over at Hilfy from the driver's seat. "Why don't you lay off the booze until the end of the season?"

"You mean until Sunday?"

"Whenever. You need to think of yourself as sperm."

"Sperm?"

"You need to be in top shape whenever you get the call, so you can sprint around the million other sperm and get to the egg first. You got to be ready."

Hilfy shook his head and stared at the Dallas skyline. "With my luck when the call comes, it'll be a hand job."

The advice Hilfy gave Jack was to get back in the game. "You're in pretty good shape for your age. I had trouble keeping up with you on our run. You throw the ball pretty well too."

Hilfy parted with his green bag, a smile, and final words from Jack. "Go make that Super Bowl."

JACK WHIZZED through a Dippity Donuts' drive-through and listened to Myles' press conference on the radio en route to the Forest Green Country Club where his sweet Jeanie would be practicing and then later attending the Annual Club Awards Banquet. He forgot that also attending the ceremony would be Dick Schwartz, that Sawed Off Stack of Shit sports editor who often played a Monday afternoon round at the club. In fact, the first two cars Jack drove past in the parking lot were his Mazda Miata with a for sale sign still attached to the back window and Soss' Black Lexus with the cracked tailpipe.

Jack sat in his car and watched Jeanie in her short pink skirt on the warm winter day smacking balls down the fairway to the orders of the Legend. Jeanie hit fades and draws with precision and concentration. Chad, her horndog caddy, simply held her golf bag and concentrated on her finely tuned butt cheeks with every turn and twist. Jack gripped the steering wheel and kept watching until he no longer could stand watching Chad watching his wife.

Instead he watched the cigar puffing Soss driving his golf cart down the 18th fairway, flipping his ball into the fairway with his "hand wedge" while his playing partners weren't looking, and launching his ball toward the green with a fairway wood. Jack gripped the steering wheel even harder and then followed Soss into the clubhouse locker room. He hid in the toilet stall until Soss walked his hairy, flabby ass to the shower.

Jack stepped out of the stall, checked to make sure no one was around, sprayed Soss' underwear with heat balm, and stuffed his shirt and slacks into the trash can. Hiding behind a golf bag in the pro shop, Jack heard a scream from the locker room and saw Soss marching out to his car with a towel and an agonizing grimace.

"That's for ruining my only chance for a spot on ESPN's 'Two Minute Warning' by fibbing to the ESPN producer that I suffer from memory lapses and long stuttering blocks," Jack thought.

Soss returned in time for the banquet, where he presented Jeanie with the year's most Inspirational Player trophy. The emcee talked about Jeanie's work outside the club – teaching handicapped children to play golf, setting up a makeshift course at an orphanage, and playing mini-golf with cancer patients around hospital corridors.

Jeanie looked more appetizing than the filet mignon in her light blue strapless evening gown with a cut front, pearl necklace, and soft braided hair.

"That's my beautiful wife," Jack whispered as he peeked from a closet in back of the lounge.

Jeanie smiled as she thanked the Legend and his son for helping her through a difficult time but failed to mention her husband among the others she credited for her success. What hurt more was the peck Soss laid on Jeanie's cheek and the lip-lock planted by Chad. The crowd roared, "W –o –o-o-o-a," until he finally released, wiped the lipstick off with his hanky, and slid his hand down her bare back to her firm behind.

Jack wanted to storm out of the closet. He stayed long enough to hear the emcee wish Chad luck. He would leave in the morning to caddy for players the next two weeks at PGA tour events in Hawaii before joining Jeanie in Las Vegas for the LPGA event. As he left the banquet with his arm around Jeanie, it was evident he would be joining Jeanie tonight.

JACK FOLLOWED Jeanie and Chad to the parking lot and beat them back to Magnolia Avenue. He used his old key to open the front door but had no devised plan to stop Chad from spending the night with his wife.

Chad also couldn't wait to arrive at Jack's house. He parked his pick up in the driveway, left his keys in the ignition, and escorted Jeanie into the den. Jack listened from his master bedroom to their giggles and clinked wine glasses as they sat by the fire and drank and snuggled until midnight.

Jeanie was a lightweight when it came to booze, a fact that Jack counted on for a foiled romantic interlude. When Jeanie passed out, Chad carried her like her golf bag down the hallway. What Jack didn't count on was Chad carrying her to the master bedroom instead of the guest room, where Jeanie lay the last time he had snuck into his house. Jack slid under the king size bed as Chad opened the door. He dropped Jeanie on the bed and kept kissing her on the neck until she woke up and kissed him on the lips.

They wrapped their bodies around each other and rolled around the bed to the chagrin of the ghostly intruder below it. Jack's heart pounded with every "uh" and "ah" and wanted to pound both of them with a pitching wedge.

The passion was interrupted when Jeanie went to the master bathroom and said in the same sexy and slightly inebriated voice she used before an interlude with Jack, "I'll be right back, big boy."

Jack could hear Chad lifting off his belt buckle and sliding off his pants and shirt. Jack peeked in the darkness from the bed skirt as Jeanie re-entered the room wearing nothing but a seductive smile. She slinked to the bed, slid under the covers, and whispered, "Won't you join me, Monsieur Chad."

Jack had had enough. As he heard Jeanie's lover pulling the sheet over their heads, Jack slithered like a snake from under the bed to bedroom door left ajar. The couple was too busy to notice or hear Jack tiptoe to the dining room and out the front door. As Chad began to slide off his white Fruit of the Looms, his car alarm blared from the driveway.

He ignored it until he heard his pickup truck starting and backing down the driveway. Chad ran out the front door and chased his truck down Magnolia Avenue in his underwear, making it clear that his pickup was more important than sex. He finally gave up the chase and retreated to Jack's house and hopped in Jack's Miata.

Jack waited for Chad to come within long par three hole before flooring the pickup and driving down several dark streets to a park with a small, shallow pond in the middle. He slowly drove the pickup down a slope to the edge of the pond, shoved the gear stick into neutral, and jumped out.

Chad sped to the park and stopped Jack's Mazda Miata in front of the pond. He left the car running and lights on and dove into the pond. Jack, who had hid under a playground slide, jumped into the Miata and drove off while Chad stood in waist-deep water and pondered how to move his truck to dry land.

"Come back here, you bastard," Chad yelled.

As Chad was calling the police on a nearby emergency phone to help fish his pickup out of the pond, Jack was driving home. He parked on an adjacent street and ran to Magnolia Avenue. He entered his house and tip-toed back to his bed. There, he found Jeanie asleep, the top of the sheet barely covering her nipples. Her naked body was outlined on the sheet. Her breasts rose up and down with every breath. Jack's sleeping beauty was shielded in an aura of sweet perfume.

Jack shut the door to a room so dark he couldn't see himself taking off his clothes. He slid under the sheets, wrapped his arm around Jeanie's waist, and kissed the back of her neck.

58

"Bless me father for I have sinned. I slept with my wife."

There was a pause in the pitch black confessional long enough to wonder if the majestic voice Jack anticipated every Tuesday would resonate from the screen he knelt before. Jack couldn't wait any longer.

"Father, did you hear what I just said?"

"Yes, my son. I was just pondering why someone would confess to sleeping with his own wife. It is clearly not a sin."

Jack knocked on the wall. "Hello. Remember me, Padre? The guy who faked his own death, running around town like a ghost? The guy waiting for a miracle?"

"Yes, yes, of course. But please give me more detail and why you think it *is* a sin."

Jack told him the story of the previous day, how much he yearned for his wife, how much he missed being with her and not just making love to her. He stopped at the part where he slipped under the covers in that room even darker than the confessional. His mind drifted to the early morning hours.

Jeanie slowly awoke – but never fully awoke – from Jack's kiss. Jack embraced her from behind and slid his hand up and down her smooth thigh and buttocks. She took his left hand it pulled it up her stomach, up her ribs, and onto her pillow-soft breasts. He cupped one breast at a time and lightly touched her nipples.

He planted little kisses on the side of her face and felt her heart and lungs beating faster under her breasts. He stretched his fingers down to her navel moving south until her fine pubic hairs gave way to an overflowing well of passion.

"Oh, yes," Jeanie whispered as Jack moved his fingers up and down and wet her nipples with the tip of his tongue.

Jack said nothing. His own arousal was heightened by that of Jeanie, who moaned with her every deep breath. She kept her eyes closed as she stretched her head back to the bedpost, rubbed her hands through Jack's hair, and said louder between breaths, "Oh, please, fuck me."

Jack rolled atop Jeanie and rubbed the side of his face against hers. She straddled him, digging her heels into the back of his hamstrings. Had there been candlelight, the shadows on the walls would have shown the slow motion of two bodies rocking in perfect unison. The dark walls only echoed the screams of ecstasy.

Jack delighted in the fragrance of Jeanie's shampooed hair and perfumed shoulders, the warmth of her body, and the sweet "uhs" and "ahs" of each lustful thrust. She grabbed his buttocks like they were melons and stretched her lips wide as he drove to a climactic and blissful finish.

Jack felt nothing but love for his darling wife as they swayed back and forth with her every contraction. Jack kissed her on the cheek and brushed back the front of her hair with his hand. His eyes welled. He wanted so badly to whisper in her ear what was in his heart and what he wanted to say for so long.

Instead he whispered it into the confessional screen, "I love you."

"Why didn't you say it to her?" The voice from the other side called.

Jack dropped his forehead against the screen. "I suddenly remembered that Jeanie thought she was making love to Chad. She was still drunk enough and sleepy enough, and it was more than dark enough for her not to notice that it could be anyone else. I never felt that much intense affection from her. It really hurts knowing she could feel that for someone else."

Jack paused for a moment, the tears returning. "I'm forgotten."

He had let Jeanie drift back to sleep and dream about a man who returned from saving his pickup from a watery death to find a locked door and a forged "Bon Voyage, Chad" note that sent him on his way.

Jack felt no comfort from the suggestion that maybe, deep down, Jeanie was making love to Jack and not her caddy – "Oh Chad" never was uttered during the love-making. It only helped relieve some guilt. No penance necessary for a man who had suffered so much from his own misguided deed.

Jack simply was left in the darkness of the small confessional on the other side of a wall from someone who knew him only as a man looking for the parting of the Red Sea. The Voice sent him back into the world that late Tuesday afternoon with a passage from the disciple John, the words of a man Jack still did not believe in.

"I am the Light of the world; he who follows Me will not walk in the darkness, but will have the Light of life."

59

A new ghost arrived at the Gebbie Bowl beneath the floodlights of cars and trucks, and this one was in a wheelchair.

Kody Keimer's football career was ended by a blood disease that threatened his life. But it didn't take his spirit. He wheeled himself to the Gebbie Bowl to watch some of his former Geburtville High teammates take part in this game of Has-Beens.

Jack, a Never-Was, took advantage of the Keimer sighting to interview him for a follow-up story to the one he wrote after the state semifinal game. Again, he said he was just getting some notes for Molli Glass.

When Jack was finished, Kody asked the questions.

"When are you gonna get out there, Mister?"

Jack looked down at his faded purple jersey and baggy football pants and oversized cleats. "Uh, I donna know?"

"Did you play for Geburtville?"

"Sort of."

"Then what's stopping you?"

Fear. But Jack didn't admit it. He looked at the field of pulverized players and recalled the shame he felt the last time he walked onto the 50-yard line in a football uniform.

"I'm not warmed up."

Kody stuck a football into Jack's gut and wheeled backward along the sideline. He and Jack tossed the ball back and forth. "You gotta pretty good arm," Kody said.

The more he threw, the more confident Jack became, and the more sorry he felt for Kody. Here was a talented, young man who wanted to play to the highest level but couldn't. Same as Jack, sort of. There was no excuse now not to go out there.

Then, the call came from midfield. "Hey, number 13, get yer ass in the huddle."

Jack turned to see the quarterback limping back to the sideline. "Now's your chance."

Kody said it, but Jack said it to himself.

He flipped the ball to Kody, slid the pad-less helmet over his head, and trotted onto the field.

"Hey, it's that guy asking the questions about Molinski," a guard yelled from the huddle.

"Did you find him?" a wide receiver asked.

Jack arrived in the huddle and stared at the grass. "Yeah."

"Tell him to come out and play with us," the guard said.

A defensive tackle, illuminated by the high beam of a pickup, interrupted from the other side of the 50-yard line. "C'mon. Stop talkin' and start playin.' I wanna crush somebody."

"That be you," the running back said. "Fake it to me and run a sweep to the right. On two. Break."

The offense, all except Jack, broke the huddle in unison with, "Break!" Jack stood five yards behind the center, who bent over and covered his hand on the ball. He looked around the stadium like he was looking for his father to emerge and yank him back to reality. He glanced at each lineman, twice the size of those he faced in his youth and even less cordial. "Step up and get your face smashed in, fuckwad," the defensive end said.

Jack obeyed. He looked over at Kody, who gave him the thumbs up sign. He straightened his shoulder pads and placed his shaking hands under the center. Stomach butterflies took away his breath on the grass and mud-scented field. He called, "H-h-hut one."

"Can't hear ya, freak show," the middle linebacker screamed, digging his heels into the turf and gritting his teeth.

The other linemen snarled like ruthless orcs as Jack's hands shook even more. He went to yell for the second "Hut," but the word froze in the back of his throat. Jack backed away, and the referee blew his whistle.

The defensive linemen laughed in unison. One of them said, "What's wrong, pussy got your tongue?"

The offensive players said nothing. They huddled as the starting quarterback limped back on the field to take Jack's place.

Jack took off his helmet and stared at the midfield stripe as he strolled back to the sideline.

"Go back to mommy," the corner back hollered with a chuckle.

Jack kept walking until he reached the high jump mat in the safety of the field house. He lay there, pads and all, staring at the ceiling as every car and truck drove away from the Gebbie Bowl until it was, again, pitch black.

60

It should have been the pinnacle in the journalism career for Molli with an I or for her ghostwriter – a 1A story in The Dallas Star.

Molli and Jack only glanced at the story beneath the feature headline, "Burning memories of the Cowboy Express" and the picture of the fallen bus below The Dallas Star masthead and the date, January 17, 2006.

The Cowboy Express found its final resting place, appropriately, in a desolate rodeo ground where real Cowboys roamed. The burned out vessel lies quietly with, aboard, the corpse of its most faithful passenger and the burning memories of those who accompanied him anonymously on their journeys to follow their favorite team to the ends of the Earth.

The guests were so anonymous on the Cowboy Express that the passengers had no clue which one was Molli Glass. Police had no clue who drove the bus from the gas station, and there were no bullet holes visible in the charred remains.

Police reports and pictures sent to Molli's email helped Jack write her a story that had Dallas readers and a Sawed off Stack of Shit sports editor buzzing.

Jack listened on the other line as Soss praised his newfound star writer. "Best feature written by a Star sports staffer in 20 years," he said. "The story is being syndicated nationwide, and the television networks are talking about doing a piece. You're famous, Molli."

More like infamous. She was becoming a bigger star in Dallas than Geburtville, where her local stories warmed the hearts of its readers. There was a story about a high school basketball center who played with a hole in her heart, a story about a woman who used Tae Kwon Do to cure her alcoholism, and a story about an 80-year-old competitive half-blind skier. The game stories also were featuristic, like the one from Tuesday night's big win by the Gebbie's boys basketball team.

Josh Richards says he plays the game for fun – that hitting 20-foot jump shots in a gymnasium packed with screaming spectators isn't much different from hitting them on an empty playground on a lazy Sunday afternoon.

Jack had accompanied Molli to that game and whispered the questions to ask Richards in the locker room. Jack didn't need Molli's tape recorder to remember the quotes.

"You're remarkable," Molli said two days later from her desk at the Geburtville Gazette. "What, are you like some escaped criminal who wrote for the prison magazine?"

"No," Jack said, sitting atop Molli's desk. "Just a simple ghostwriter trying to earn a few bucks. Just call me Casper."

"Casper, the Unfriendly Ghost?"

Jack had been more unfriendly to the players and coaches he slammed in his columns and surprised himself at his sudden knack for human interest. This was the kind of writer Jeanie wanted him to be, and perhaps the kind of person she wanted him to become. The Cowboy Express story, Jack figured, caught Jeanie's attention. He had told Jeanie about how he had wanted to write that story, and there it was on the front page with the byline of a woman writing in Jack's writing style.

If that story didn't give her a hint that he was still alive, the column Molli soon would pen on her certainly would.

"Not sure if I will be around next week," Molli said.

"Whattaya mean?"

"There's nothing for me here. I'm a phony writer. I should never have majored in journalism."

Jack stood up from her desk. "So what are you gonna do? Go to some island in the Bahamas, lie on the beach all day sipping margaritas, watching the sun go down."

Molli sat back in her desk chair and pushed a Bic pen into her lips like it was a cigarette. "Hmm, great idea."

"Then what am I suppose to do for money?"

"It's always back to you, Graham. Why don't you take over my job, permanently. The real sports editor is retiring."

Jack stood still, his mouth wide open. He escaped Geburtville as a teenager and came back only to hide from the goons.

"You've shown you can write, Graham. You must have some clips from the prison newspaper."

Jack couldn't tell her that he wouldn't live here as a ghost, because he was living here as a ghost. He was accumulating enough money from ghostwriting for a bus ticket north to a new life. Somehow he still wanted the old one back. Weeks living in an abandoned field house left him lonely.

"Is this what death is really like?" he thought, later that afternoon while staring at the field house walls. "You die and everyone in your former life forgets about you and goes on merrily without you?"

Jack felt like he was the only sad person at his funeral. No family was there. No kids. Jeanie had insisted she didn't want children, no matter how much her husband pleaded. Too busy hitting golf balls and pursuing her dream "to take care of some snot-nosed kid."

Jack didn't want to die. But, like the Cowboys' fan rotting in the Cowboy Express and the Cowboys' third stringer rotting on the Cowboys' sideline, maybe he already had.

61

A Jack Byrne pre-NFC Championship game column would have read:

The Dallas Cowboys don't deserve to be here.

This ridiculous run to the Super Bowl would have ended long ago had it not been for the demolition of a has-been quarterback who was leading them nowhere, NFC East divisional opponents weaker than a rest home grandma, and some ridiculously lucky plays that defy logic and imagination.

The Molli Glass pre-game column read:

The Dallas Cowboys have defied logic and imagination to put themselves one game away from the biggest game of them all in their own den.

A season that looked dead with the loss of their star quarterback on Thanksgiving has been resuscitated by a unified, hard-working team, an enthusiastic coach, and some innovative escapes that would have made Houdini proud.

Jack cringed as he typed "star quarterback." But he had to. His normal style even under Molli's mug would have tipped The Dallas Star butchers, the Cowboys fans, and the police that Jack Byrne is alive and well and body slamming their beloved team in print. He would be thrown into the slammer and executed by the only goons not free to chase him.

Jack had to write what Molli with an I with some journalistic skills would write. He found it boring but better than Dave Noonan's pre-game story:

The Dallas "Cinderella" Cowboys have a date with destiny on Sunday against the Minnesota Vikings in the NFC Championship Game. If the slipper fits, the Cowboys will find themselves back at Tom Landry Stadium in two weeks time for the Super Bowl.

Jack thought Noonan should be jailed or beat up for writing that dribble, though he knew that the goons can't read. He knew it was no coincidence they showed up at a gas station in the middle of nowhere, that their network masterminded by an evildoer had goons looking for him in every corner of Texas but Geburtville, and that he couldn't stay away from the one place every goon knew he would be – Tom Landry Stadium.

He had disguised himself as a Cowboys' fan, a Cowboys' mascot, and a woman. Now he had made his way into the Vikings' fans section of Tom Landry Stadium sporting a gold helmet with white side horns, a purple face, yellow braided locks, and a long blond beard. Jack guzzled a beer from a Viking stein and felt safe amidst a crowd of purple who would protect anyone in Viking garb and wearing Fran Tarkenton's number 10 jersey. Jack just had to make sure he didn't crack the slightest grin if – and when – the Cowboys scored.

He stifled the urge when the Cowboys' ace return man Antonio "The Rocket" Crocket took the opening kickoff from Cowboys' goal line to Vikings' goal line in a personal best time. The fake Vikings screamed at the real Vikings prompting Jack to fake his accent to further hide his identity. "C'm on, Minne-Soda! Jeez, you guys gotta play herder if ya wantta gO to the Super BOWl."

He booed with the other Vikes after they fumbled the ensuing kick-off, the Cowboys recovered it, and Jarmelle Beezley scored two plays later on an option play. He put his hands over his eyes when Darin Friese picked off a Vikings' pass. He hid his smile and watched between his fingers as Friese returned it 42 yards for a touchdown and did a chicken dance in the end zone.

"Soar-y, ass play dat was," Jack said, concealing his joy.

Unbeknownst to the phony Vikings, Jack was the only one in their midst not pouring down the Moosehead 12-ouncers to drown his sorrow – especially when The Rocket returned a punt 68 yards with a minute left in the half. The small Viking flock was stunned and overwhelmed by the unusually raucous Cowboys' fans, some scurrying to the Cowboys' ticket booth to get any remaining Super Bowl tickets.

The Cowboys' bench also was celebrating so much they rarely noticed the Vikings' last minute march that cut the lead to 28-3 as a grinning Ray Myles rejected Muta Falusa's and his linemen's pleas to carry him on their shoulders to the locker room at halftime.

The only Cowboys' player not high-fiving his teammates as they strode to the locker room was Scott Hilfinger, who sat on a water cooler with his chinstrap stuck to his palm and observed the halftime activities. Jack watched Hilfy watch a baton twirler in Cowboys' colors drop every baton she flung into the air and wondered if it is was a harbinger of the coming half.

62

The Cowboys returned from the locker room with a conspicuous player missing. Jack could see from his perch in the Vikings' fans section, Scott Hilfinger asking Jarmelle Beezley, "Where the hell is Guthrie?" and Beezley shrugging his shoulders.

Hilfy wasn't in the locker room celebration, when the Cowboys' second string quarterback was emptying his gut in a toilet. Brody Guthrie had met some friends at a tailgate party outside the stadium before the game. A bad combination of roast pig, nachos, chilli, old potato salad, warm beer, and first half excitement took its toll.

This was Hilfy's chance, and he knew it as he tossed the football back and forth to Beezley on the sideline. If the Cowboys could keep expanding their lead, the coaching staff would want to protect Beezley in the fourth quarter and put him in to finish the game. Announcers would talk about Hilfy (or whatever detail was listed in the media guide) to a nationally-televised audience and another team would give him a chance next season. He also would get his post-season bonus and could give a 24-hour notice to the Downtown Y.

Hilfy was lucky enough to be in this position. Rex Fanning failed a physical earlier in the week, and now Guthrie couldn't physically move his head from the commode. He had waited so long for a break, and finally this could be his chance.

Jack felt more lonely and vulnerable in the second half. Most of his newfound friends in Vikings' get-ups had either given up on their Super Bowl chances or passed out from Moosehead. None of them seemed to notice Minne-Soda's opening drive that consumed 16 plays and eight minutes of the third quarter and cut the deficit to 28-10.

The Cowboys' three-and-out was followed by a 14-play drive that culminated with a one-yard scoring plunge by Vikings' fullback Brock Zmenski on the first play of the fourth quarter to cut the lead to 28-17. Hilfy stood along the sidelines with his helmet secured on his head but his hands on his hips. He tore off his chin strap after Theunis Adkins was stopped a yard short of the first down on a third down play at the Vikings' 40-yard line with 11:27 beaming off the giant scoreboard above.

The Vikings' faithful started to sober up until Colin Flanders dribbled a punt inside the one-yard line and their punter, Neville Clarkson, planted his heels an inch from the end line a few futile plays later. As the Cowboys retreated at the center's snap to set up a return for The Rocket, Clarkson sent an end-over-end pass that tight end Thomas Westly hauled in for a first down on his 12-yard-line.

Hilfy ripped off his helmet. Jack made out the f-word from the lower lip thrashing from his upper teeth. The Cowboys went into a prevent defense. The Vikings stayed patient, running and passing for four and five yards each down and quieting the crowd more and more with every first down signal from the referee.

When Minne-Soda quarterback Warwick Glenn snuck over for the touchdown, three minutes and 27 seconds were still beaming from above. Glenn fumbled the snap on the two-point conversion try to leave his team behind 28-23 and needing one more touchdown to go to the Super Bowl. Jack's newfound buddies, like their heroes on the bench, had found new life. Jack smiled, but deep down he was as depressed as those fans in Cowboys' jerseys that surrounded them and hollered, "Ya'll sid-down, ya' purple pricks."

RAY MYLES LOOKED LIKE a deer staring into the stadium lights as day was giving way to night and his team was blowing their biggest chance at a Super Bowl in so many disappointing seasons. He whispered something in Beezley's ear just before he entered the Cowboys' huddle, took the snap, rolled around the end, broke a tackle, and stormed down the sidelines to a suddenly rejuvenated crowd.

Vikings' free safety Horace Felkins saved his team by lunging and grabbing the back of Beezley's shoulder pads, a horse collar tackle that resulted in a 15-yard penalty and an injured quarterback. Beezley was helped to his feet and staggered to the bench, where an ice pack was placed on his neck. Myles called time-out.

Hilfy strapped on his helmet and marched toward Myles, who already had made his decision. The Cowboys lined up in the Wildcat formation with Adkins taking the snap.

"The Wildcat?" Jack said under his breath. "The Cowboys don't know the Wildcat."

Adkins took the snap and didn't know whether to run it, pass it, pitch it, or punt it. He was dropped for five-yard loss at the Vikings 40. So they ran the play again and again until it was fourth down at midfield. Boos rang out from the crowd and from Hilfy, who tore his helmet off again and threw into the bench. The bench is where he would sit, arms folded, for the rest of the game.

Flanders then picked the wrong time to launch the longest boot of his career. The ball landed in the end zone seats, giving Minne-Soda 80 yards and two minutes to book a return ticket to Dallas for the Super Bowl.

The Vikings had no time and no timeouts for a sustained drive, so their quarterback went wild with passes over the middle and scrambling from defensive linemen and enough spikes to put the Vikings within Hail Mary range with three seconds left in the game. Every person in Tom Landry Stadium – the fans, the players, the coaches, the water boys, the cheerleaders, the announcers, the referees – seemed to simultaneously hold their breath after Glenn dropped back to midfield and launched a missile to the end zone.

Five Vikings' receivers and seven Cowboys' defensive backs stared at the ball as it floated in the cool air and descended to Earth. Two dozen arms lunged at once at the brown spiralling object, but the ball landed in the palm of a single player.

The referees sifted through the pile of players. A single gesture would erupt the crowd into a Super Bowl frenzy or a deafening silence.

63

Scott Hilfinger sat there on the bench with his mouth open and his helmet lying on the ground where he had flung it. The referee pointed his right arm toward the playing field, and one-by-one the Cowboys' defenders rose from the pile and started dancing.

Cowboys' free safety Martel Reefus, who had high jumped seven feet in high school, had outleaped the entire end zone crowd to make the game-winning interception and set the stadium crowd and Cowboys' sideline aroar. Soon there was another pile of Cowboys' players in the end zone. And throw in Myles, his coaching staff, water boys, cheerleaders, and – strained neck and all – Jarmelle Beezley.

Everyone but Hilfy, who sat on the bench shaking his head.

The Dallas Cowboys returning to Tom Landry Stadium for the Super Bowl did nothing to improve the mood of the Cowboys' third string quarterback. Nor did the pitcher of beer served to him at The Bar in Arlington by a Viking.

Hilfy sat back in the booth and stared with his mouth open just like he did after Reefus' interception. "So you were a Cowboys' mascot, then a woman, then a fan, and now Eric the Red?"

"Whatever it takes to watch you make the Super Bowl, hoss."

Hilfy poured a glass of beer down his throat as fast as he poured beer into his glass. "The Cowboys made it. Not sure if I will."

Jack sat in the booth facing the back wall and hiding from a potential goon swarm. He poured himself a beer and chugged half a glass. "Why wouldn't ya.?"

"Fanning still thinks he can be ready."

"For what, holding a clipboard and looking like the washed-up quarterback he's been for the past three seasons?"

Hilfy poured himself a beer and topped up Jack. "Man, that was my chance. But he puts in a runnin' back instead of a quarterback."

"Didn't Adkins play quarterback in high school?"

"Every one of those fuckin' guys played quarterback at some point in their lives. Even the center. So he has Adkins run the Wildcat, which we don't even have in the fuckin' playbook.

"Myles just winged it to keep me off the fuckin' field."

Hilfy downed three more beers before asking, "What kind of shit beer is this?"

"Moosehead," Jack said, raising his glass.

"Isn't that Canadian?"

"That's what my fellow Vikings have been pouring down them the past five hours. I told 'em they had Moosehead on tap here."

"They drink Moosehead in Minnesota?"

"You must have flunked geography, Hilfy. Minnesota practically is in Canada. That guy passed out next to us is from Moosehead, Minnesota."

Jack explained that the more fake Vikings that followed him to the bar the less conspicuous he would look. The goons would have to take out every fake Viking to find Graham Repert.

"So to get into the Super Bowl," Hilfy said, "You'll dress up like a Indian?"

"Nah, I'll have to think of somethin' else. Hard core Kansas City fans won't get tickets. Mostly corporations buy up all the tickets and give them to their shareholders. You might see some Chiefs' jerseys but no Chiefs, no chants, no chops, and no tomahawks."

The more they drank, the more Jack thought about it. Jack and Hilfy slithered out of The Bar in Arlington past passed out fake Vikings and any real goon still looking to make him walk the plank. En route to downtown Dallas, Jack pulled Molli with I's convertible into the 24-hour DrugMart and returned with a case of toilet paper rolls. Then he sped to Highland Park.

To honor Dick Schwartz, Jack and Hilfy went on a teepeeing spree at the mansion of the Sawed Off Stack of Shit sports editor. Jack pulled rolls out of his black overcoat and fired them on all the bushes and shrubs, while Hilfy launched them over the tallest oaks on the property. The white paper hung off the leaf-less branches like stringy ghosts fluttering in the darkness.

"That, you sonuvabitch," Jack yelled as he as he tossed the final roll at the chimney and ran back to the convertible, "is for earlier in my career when you demoted me to the copy desk for a month, because I didn't file my college game story before deadline on a game that didn't end until after the fuckin' deadline."

Jack sped through Highland Park, while Hilfy pointed to the row of mansions that passed his window. "Thought only doctors, lawyers, and Dallas Cowboys could afford to live here."

Jack never understood how a sports editor could afford a place with a turret, tapestry, manicured gardens, pool house, and a butler. Old money, maybe.

He wasn't worried about being caught in the teepeeing act. Soss predictably would be waiting for the first edition of The Dallas Star and the Fort Worth Express, bring it to Dippity Donuts, and gaze over Dave Noonan's story about how "the slipper had fit the Dallas Cowboys and now they had reached the Land of OZ...aka Super Bowl" while sucking the glaze off his donut.

That's what Soss was doing while Jack was once again watching Hilfy and his green gym bag zigzagging to the front door of the Downtown Y. Jack then marched through The Dallas Star parking lot and snuck past a sleeping security guard and up the stairs.

The newsroom had emptied of butchers who had swooned over Molli's ghost-written column about "the Hail Mary pass that was hauled in by a Leap of Faith." Jack opened the bottom drawer of his desk and found the disk he had left there. He pushed the water cooler out of the way and slid the disk into his old PC.

"There it is," Jack said, reading the feature he wrote on Hilfy, and then filing it into his email.

Jack then looked around and tip-toed to Soss' office and jiggled the gold door handle. Unlocked. He stared at the large oak desk to find what he was looking for: a press pass to the Super Bowl. The telephone ring echoed off the office walls and startled the intruder. Jack grabbed the ticket, stuffed it into his black overcoat, and darted from Soss' office before the gold door handle got him in the ass.

He was power-walking into the hallway, down the stairs, past the Morgue and the snoring guard, and into the parking lot as a scratchy voice from Soss' answering machine mumbled into the darkness of the sports department.

"Sorry, boss, we never done spotted Repert tonight. But if he show up at da Super Bowl, he dead meat."

PART SIX

Red Zone

64

Jack Byrne walking into the Super Bowl would be like Butch Cassidy walking into a Bolivian gunfight without a gun. But it would take a Bolivian battalion to keep him away.

Jack was born, though not bred, a Cowboys' fan. He spent so many Sundays in his youth looking through Oliver's Department store window, doing his own play-by-play in the absence of sound from the muted display while reading the roster from The Dallas Star. The glory years of his Lone Star State stint were replaced by years of frustration as a Dallas Star writer and columnist writing the epitaph on another dismal season.

He should have been writing the obituary on the 2005 Cowboys before his own after the Thanksgiving Day Game, but youthful hope overwhelmed the hopeless demure of the often cynical sportswriter.

Somehow the least likely Cowboys' squad to make the Super Bowl made the Super Bowl. And a Super Bowl on their home turf, albeit in front of more corporate out-of-towners who bought tickets as far back as training camp.

Jack had not missed a Cowboys' home game since he started covering the Cowboys, and was not going to miss one. No matter if he had to go as a woman, a fan, a mascot, or an Indian.

Soss and his mob were on the lookout for an Indian.

"Injan?" Grog said, as he huddled with Soss and Hog in the corner booth at the Kazbar after after-hours, long after the Cowboys' victory in the NFC Championship game.

"By all indication and sightings from our network, Graham Repert is a Cowboys' diehard," Soss said. "They now tell me he was likely dressed as a Viking yesterday."

Soss said he would dress one of the goons as an Indian and sit in the Kansas City Chiefs' section to locate Repert and have him scalped. Other goons would be dressed as fans, ticket-takers, merchants, ushers, and even sideline security officers knowing every freckle on

Repert's face from the mass Wanted poster of a sketch that looked nothing like Jack Byrne sent via email. "Until then," said Soss, who could not conceive of Jack without hair and a goatee, "we will search every bar stool and butt stool in the world to find the cocksucker."

No welsher had gone this long without having a knife in his back, a bullet in his brain, or fitted for cement shoes.

"How 'bout if he fronts up with the forty-thou?" Grog asked.

"He'd have to bet on the Cowboys to come up with that," Soss said, noting the 30-1 early Vegas odds in Kansas City's favor.

Soss paused and looked outside the Kazbar window, turned back to Grog and Hog, and gritted his teeth. "The Big Boss is coming down for the first time since he left Dallas to watch the Super Bowl and he wants Repert dead, D-E-A-D."

"I didn't graduates college but I can spell dead," said Grog, still humiliated by being blinded by hot chocolate, peed on, hit in the nuts, and knocked unconscious by the welsher at-large. "We find 'im."

Geburtville, that ol' ghost of a town, seemed the only safe haven. But for how long? The old high school, including the Gebbie Bowl and field house, was set for demolition.

Jack was a prisoner there and in his own mind. He could escape the field house to Jack's Home Field, but not his thoughts. Every football toss through the old tire yielded no plan to get back a life so quickly forgotten. He wanted to see what life was like without him. Life just went on without him. He never would have found that out had he dialled the last digit of his cellphone as his supposed remains burned beyond recognition in Nowhere, Texas.

The football smacked into the tire and fell to the ground with an even more painful realization. He would never find out what life was like *with* him.

65

"...I'm sorry for these sins and for all my sins."

Jack's first full confession was met with silence.

"Hel-lo-o-o." Jack knocked on the screen as Tuesday's confessional hours were coming to an end. "Anybody home? I'm asking forgiveness here."

"You want fries with that, my son?" The Voice was never more clear.

"No, just my penance. Some Our Fathers, some Hail Marys."

"Have you ever prayed an Our Father or Hail Mary?"

"No, but I saw a Hail Mary at Tom Landry Stadium on Sunday."

The pause made Jack realize the padre was not a football fan. "Look, I've done a lot of wrong in my life," Jack said, like as I just confessed. I thought it might make me feel better."

"Does it?"

"A little."

Jack looked through the light filtering through the screen and could hear breathing behind it but no words. "So are ya' gonna forgive me or what?" Jack said.

"I am not the one who needs to forgive. You do."

"Huh?"

"You claim so many people have wronged you. Your father, your wife, your boss. You need to forgive them the way Christ forgave. What they did to Him was nothing compared to what was done to you."

"What did they do to Him?"

"Hung Him on the cross."

Jack considered that. He felt his palms where the nails went through Jesus and touched his forehead where the crown of thorns pierced Him. Inwardly, Jack was hanging from the cross. "What miracle saved Him?"

"Eternal life."

"So I can get a miracle, get my wife back, my life back, by simply forgiving people?" Jack's tone was more sceptical than inquisitive. "How do I forgive my father? He's dead."

"Just follow the light, my son."

The light from the screen was fading. It was all too much for Jack to take in. "Can I get my penance to go?"

There was a slight chuckle from the other side of the screen. "Read chapter 13 of the Acts of the Apostles, verses 37-39. But for now, pray with me."

The Voice started, "Our Father who art in Heaven."

"But I don't know the words."

"Just follow along, my son."

Together they prayed, their words reverberating off the confessional.

"...Give us this day our daily bread and forgive us our trespasses as we forgive those who trespass against us. Lead us not into temptation, but deliver us from evil."

"Amen." Jack said, waiting for an echo. There was none. Only silence.

Jack knocked on the screen again. "Hel-lo-o-o."

There was no answer.

66

The words delivered in monotone resounded from the portable radio and reverberated off the walls of the Geburtville Gazette editorial offices.

"The Dallas Cowboys have announced that Rex Fanning has passed his physical and will be the starting quarterback in the Super Bowl."

Molli with an I sat at her desk and looked at emails while Jack sat on top of it and stared at the ceiling. His first thought was of the former third string quarterback. "There goes his dream; there goes any chance he had of making something of his life."

Scott Hilfinger tore the tape with his name misspelled in permanent marker off the wall of the Cowboys' training facility, turned in his helmet and shoulder pads, grabbed his green gym bag from his locker room space, and was out the door before the radio announcement was heard and before the door handle could hit him in the butt.

Fanning hadn't even served up his first practice quail as the Cowboys' starter before Hilfy and his duffel bag had checked out of the Downtown Y.

And what of Jack's story of the third stringer? The best story he ever wrote was sent from the disk Jack rescued from his desk drawer at The Dallas Star sports department to his email where it was slowly rotting away. The story he thought that would make him realize his Sports Illustrated dream or at least propel him back into his old life was gone.

Jack looked down at Molli. "We have to get him back."

"Who?"

Molli was too consumed with her own dilemma to be concerned with the never-was quarterback. Bored with a profession she did not want to pursue and a job someone was doing for her, Molli was ready to go back to school and continue her pursuit of an MRS degree.

Then her cellphone rang Wednesday morning. ESPN called and said they wanted to interview her for a position as a sideline reporter.

"Melissa Parsons is having complications with her pregnancy, and doctors have ordered her to bed," Molli said. "Isn't that great?"

"For who?"

"Me, silly. The ESPN producers saw all the great stories I wrote."

"You mean the stories I wrote."

"And they want to interview me this afternoon over lunch at Ritz Tower."

Jack shook his head. "Do you even know where the sideline is?"

"I'm sure they'll show me."

"They'll also tell you where to point the microphone and what questions to ask through an earpiece. With your legs and your blonde hair, you'll be perfect for the job."

Molli said if she got the job she would show Graham her appreciation by telling the Gazette editor how much he had helped her and suggest she make him the new sports editor. That would make Jack no longer a ghostwriter but a writer in a ghost town. He had grander plans his contemporaries once considered delusions of grandeur.

THE GRANDEST DELUSIONARY was somewhere wandering around downtown Dallas with a green gym bag, a duffel bag, and a bottle of whiskey waiting for the next bus to Deadhorse, Oklahoma. Jack caught a ride with Molli, whom he taught a Football for Dummies course on the drive to her interview.

"So is the football field 100 yards or 100 feet?" Molli said, as the Dallas skyline loomed in the distance.

"Wouldn't worry about overwhelming them with your football knowledge," Jack said. "You'll already have overwhelmed them with your perfume."

Molli parked her Sebring in front of Ritz Tower, applied another layer of lipstick, took a final glance into the mirror, and handed Jack her car keys. "Hope you find your quarterback," she said.

"Hope you find the sidelines."

Jack hoped the goons didn't find him. He bought a half-dozen glazed donuts at the Dippity Donuts drive-through and then snuck into the Kazbar with a newspaper covering his face. Sitting in the corner, next to his green gym bag and his own Dippity Donut dozen, was the former Dallas Cowboys emergency quarterback.

"Heard the big news," Jack said. "Whattaya gonna do next, hoss?"

"You mean after I slam down a dozen glazed and a dozen Coronas?" Hilfy said.

"Yeah."

"I gotta seven o'clock bus that will put me Deadhorse at midnight," Hilfy said with a burp. "Guess that'll make me the Midnight Cowboy."

Jack didn't echo Hilfy's laugh. "You're in no condition to go on a bus," Jack said, noticing Hilfy was halfway to his Corona goal. "Why don't I drive you there?"

"Already bought the ticket and a bottle with all the money I got left in my rotten stinking life."

Jack helped Hilfy exit the bar just as a group of Super Bowl-bound Cowboys, including the new third-string quarterback Brody Guthrie, entered it. He shoved Hilfy into the backseat of Molli's Sebring and drove to Ritz Tower, where a smiling Molli was descending on a glass elevator. Jack didn't have to ask if she got the job.

Molli talked faster than a horse racing announcer as Jack drove back to the Kazbar. "Are we stopping for a celebratory drink?" she asked.

Molli would have that drink, or four, with Guthrie. Her final Dallas Star interview, as a favor to Jack, was intended to make the inebriated braggadocio spill his guts of his disgust at being an emergency quarterback to the sexy lady with an ESPN-loaned earpiece hidden behind her right ear. Jack asked the questions while hiding behind a steering wheel in the Kazbar parking lot, and Molli repeated them to an unaware Guthrie.

By the time the interview finished Guthrie had bragged about his career to the sexy blonde and told her the Cowboys didn't have a chance in hell of winning the Super Bowl, that Rex Fanning was an overrated pissant, and that he'd rather be hanging dry wall in Albuquerque than wasting his time on the Super Bowl bench.

"Great job," Jack said, as the words flew off Molli's micro tape recorder as he steered the Sebring back onto the freeway. "Hope you don't mind my passed out friend and his duffel bag going back to Geburtville with us."

Molli looked back at Hilfy cradling the backseat. "Just as long as he throws up in the bag."

67

Hilfy waited until he got to the field house to throw up. He was still ridding his stomach of donuts and Corona right up until game time.

Jack found more gear in the field house and ordered Hilfy to suit up. Hilfy was still too drunk not to comply or put on the number 13 Manitoba Mooses' jersey Jack found in his duffel bag. Hilfy's only request as he zigzagged onto the cold Gebbie Bowl turf lit by car and truck headlights was that Jack take his place when he passed out.

"You'll be fine," Jack said, staring eye-ball to eye-ball with the former Dallas Cowboys' – Manitoba Mooses' and so many others' – quarterback while holding his arm to keep him upright. "Think of this as your Super Bowl."

Hilfy looked around at the pot-bellied players in various uniforms. "Super Bowl? More like a Toilet Bowl," Hilfy said. "Gimme a fuckin' football and let's see what I can do."

What he did was launch missiles over the out-stretched hands of middle-aged defensive backs and into the arms of middle-aged receivers. He fired bullets into the soft guts of truck drivers-turned-tight ends as soon as they cut over the middle or to the sidelines. He eluded bouncers-turned-blitzers with quick, subtle side-steps and dropped perfect lobs over the shoulders of once fleet-footed running backs, giving them a clear path to the end zone.

There was not a smidgen of dirt on his Manitoba jersey or a dribble of sweat down his neck as Hilfy jogged off the field to the triumphant claps of his teammates and the awe of his opponents following a late fourth quarter scoring strike to the corner of the end zone.

Hilfy could have thrown for more than 500 yards had he not passed out on the bench. "Your turn," he said, as Jack tried to shake him back to consciousness.

Fulfilling his agreement, Jack jogged to the huddle and snapped his chin strap onto his helmet. "Where's the other guy?" a lineman said.

"Takin' a break, so you got me," Jack said.

"Fucking great," said another lineman.

As Hilfy slept, Jack marched to the line of scrimmage in front of defensive linemen who grew at least a foot since the last time he put his hands under the center's cheeks. They dug their heels into the ground, and their eerie silence told him they wanted revenge from the scoring rainbows delivered by the uninvited ghost.

Hilfy never awoke in time to see Jack finally take a snap from the center, drop back to the 50-yard line, and take a knee. Or spike the ball with their team up by 40 points and all their timeouts left. Or quick kick from the shotgun formation. Hilfy also didn't hear the opposing players and his teammates flap their arms like chickens and pelt him with, "Baw-w-w-k, bawk-bawk-bawk, baw-w-w-k," as Jack tore off his helmet and retreated to the bench, his head staring at the damp grass.

Jack sat on the bench next to the snoring Hilfy as one-by-one the cars and trucks were driven away and ultimately leaving the Gebbie Bowl again in darkness. Still, Jack stared at the field.

"Next week." Jack said, blowing breath-like smoke into the frigid air and clenching his teeth. "Next week I won't be such a coward. I'll show ya'. I'll show everyone.

"And I mean everyone."

68

Jack didn't wait for the radio announcement that likely would follow Molli's column in Thursday morning's sports section of The Dallas Star. He needed to get Hilfy back to Dallas and back in the huddle where he belonged.

Brody Guthrie didn't belong in the Super Bowl after what fans, players, coaches, and owners read below the headline "Super Bowl not home for Guthrie" over their hot coffee or morning dump.

While Scott Hilfinger was rifling footballs at moving targets in a remote gridiron pasture somewhere north of Dallas, Brody Guthrie was pouring down shots at a downtown bar and seeking greener pastures.

"Country home, take me home, to the place, I be-long," Guthrie sang while John Denver likely rolled over in his grave with his hands covering his ears. "Albuquer –que, that's where I'll be after the Chiefs crush our Big D."

On that flat note Guthrie was likely headed as far away from the Super Bowl as Ray Myles could send him. That's why Jack had to rush Hilfy back to the Cowboys' camp.

"We don't want to give Myles or the Heywards any ideas about finding another third stringer, " Jack said as he stuffed Hilfy's duffel bag and green gym bag into the trunk of Molly's Chrysler Sebring.

"Drop me at the bus station," Hilfy said as Jack hurried him to the car. "It'd take a miracle for me to play in the Super Bowl, much less win it. I'd rather go to Deadhorse."

Getting Hilfy back to camp was like dragging a dead horse. He showed Jack no appreciation for boosting his confidence with a Ghost Bowl appearance, for warming his frozen fingers on Molli's laptop and sending the bye-bye Guthrie column on deadline the night before, or for giving him a ride to the Super Bowl.

Hilfy said he barely remembered playing in the Ghost Bowl, throwing five touchdown passes, hitting targets all over the field, and eluding blitzers.

"Too much in the zone to remember the game?" Jack said as he drove into Dallas alongside his front seat passenger, Molli, who had to report to her new ESPN bosses in time for the Cowboys' Super Bowl photo shoot at Tom Landry Stadium.

"Too drunk," Hilfy said from the backseat, reminding Jack of the other forgotten performances he played high on alcohol in Europe.

He didn't respond when Jack suggested playing in the Super Bowl could cure his alcoholism.

Hilfy sobered up by the time Jack entered the stadium parking lot and the monotone radio announcement rang in their ears: "Brody Guthrie has been released from the Cowboys, a team official has told the press this morning. No reason was given for his dismissal, but referring to his team as the Chiefs' 'unworthy' opponent in a local sports column likely didn't help his cause."

GUTHRIE TURNING UP for the Cowboys' team photo would be like David Duke showing up for a Black Panther rally. Instead, Hilfy showed up in his torn blue jeans and vomit-stained Manitoba Mooses' jersey. Myles and Royce Heyward conferred outside the camera crew, who were focusing their lenses and telling the players where to stand on the field.

"What's that fuckwad doin' here?" Myles said, pointing his forehead at Hilfy.

"You mean Hilfudger, or whatever his name," Heyward said.

"Thought we cut 'im."

"We're required to have an emergency quarterback and I ain't got time to find anyone else unless you do. You ain't gonna play him any, are ya?"

"Not as long as I'm conscious."

"Maybe we could dress up a mannequin in a Cowboys' uniform and prop him on the sidelines."

"I'd rather play the dummy."

"Which dummy?"

Heyward ordered Hilfy to the dressing room. Minutes later, Hilfy returned to the field with silver football pants and his number 13 white jersey managers were about to donate to Goodwill. He stood in the far right hand corner of the photo, where his face would be obscured by an exclamation point on the poster graphics.

Unlike his teammates, when the photographer hollered "Say, Super Bowl Champions!" Hilfy did not smile.

69

Jack felt frozen dirt under his fingernails. His naked body was strapped in shackles and laid belly-down on a mud floor surrounded by concrete walls and rusty bars in the lone window hole. There was no glass to protect him from the winter blast that blew a swirl of dust.

There was no toilet. The cell must have stunk of vomit and urine. But you don't smell anything in a nightmare. You just feel – in this case cold, tired, lonely, hopeless.

Jack looked around and saw only darkness. No Soss dressed in warden garb. No father guarding his cell. No Jeanie standing there with her arms draped around Chad and laughing. Nothing but fear and a line from Simon and Garfunkel's Sound of Silence that thumped over and over in his brain, "Silence like a cancer grows…Silence like a cancer grows…Silence like a cancer grows…"

The concrete walls started to crack and creep in on him. Jack tried to move but couldn't no matter how hard he tried. He was nobody in nowhere. He couldn't even scream.

When he awoke, darkness prevailed. He wasn't lying in cold dirt. He was wrapped in fine white linen and a fluffy duvet in a heated room that smelled of sweet lilac.

He turned on the bedside lamp and squinted at the 50-inch flat screen, the mini-bar, and the white robe with the Ritz Hotel insignia hanging on the bathroom door.

"How did I get here?" he thought.

Then he remembered.

Jack drove Molli to the airport after the Cowboys' photo shoot on Thursday for her first assignment, the Pro Bowl in Honolulu, and she asked him to drive back from Geburtville to pick her up on Monday afternoon for the Super Bowl Media Day. Jack rarely watched the Pro Bowl, which he once wrote was a "Hawaiian holiday for overpaid stars whose vacation started when their season ended."

Jack did watch this game from outside Ollie's Electronics but was more interested in Molli's debut performance. He couldn't hear what she was saying but didn't need to. The Pro Bowl is a party atmosphere, and Molli simply had to stand there with a microphone, smile, and with a flowery lei dangling from her bronzed neck ask questions she would ask at a party. Like, "Have you tried surfing here in Hawaii?"

Molli was not intimidated by the football celebrities, because she didn't know who any of them were. She thought an All Pro was someone who no longer plays for free in college. She wrapped up her day's work by staring into the camera with, "This is Molli with an I saying, 'Aloha,' from the Pro Bowl."

Jack greeted the new ESPN fluff reporter with "Aloha" outside the airport terminal without her realizing the word could be used to say, "Hello" or "Good-bye," and without a thank you for picking her up or ghostwriting the stories that had landed her a job she never dreamed about. She did offer him to sleep on the sofa bed of the one-bedroom suite at the Ritz Hotel, compliments of ESPN, because she needed a ride to the airport early the next morning for her flight to New York.

JACK DROVE MOLLI from the airport to Tom Landry Stadium for Media Day. Molli walked through the gate with Jack and flashed her new ESPN badge at the security guard and said, "He's with me."

While Molli was going from player to player while sticking a microphone before their flapping lips, Jack walked up the end zone seats to a player who wanted no part of Media Day.

"No one wants to interview the third string quarterback," Scott Hilfinger said, leaning back in the upper end zone seat and watching the reporters buzzing like gnats around star players with Oakleys and an "I feel good" quote.

"I'd be standing around like a dodo, just like at practice," he said.

"A dodo is the appropriate animal to characterize yourself," Jack said.

"What is a dodo?"

"An extinct, flightless bird."

Hilfy took a flask out of his green gym bag beneath his seat. "I am on a flight out of here the moment the Chiefs hoist the Lombardi Trophy," he said, taking a long sip of whatever deadly potion he poured into the flask. "It's Greyhound Airways, non-stop to Deadhorse."

"One way," Jack thought.

AN HOUR OR SO LATER, as dusk settled, Hilfy was on a bus back to the Cowboys Training Center to hear Coach Myles' secret Super Bowl game plan he would be no part of. Jack was about to leave when the stadium lights came on and stars appeared in the hole in the roof and on the field.

Bob Griese. Dan Fouts. Terry Bradshaw. Fran Tarkenton. Joe Montana. Lynn Swann. Steve Largent. Charlie Joiner. Howie Long. Randy White. Eric Dickerson. Marcus Allen.

These were the players Soss assigned Jack and other reporters to write their obituaries in case of sudden death. Many were there to cover the Super Bowl for a media outlet or an annual Super Bowl trip to catch up with old teammates.

The Hall of Famers took to the Tom Landry Stadium turf for a private old old-timers game in their gray sweats or Lycra attire. The skills were there, but they played like what they showed their audiences in slow motion replays. They didn't sprint; they floated downfield, hauling in perfectly lofted passes from the rusty-armed quarterback, and making one-handed grabs on the rare errant toss. The running backs lost a step or two or three but still cut up field with precision to escape the grasp of once quick-footed defenders. A light fog drifting from the turf made it look like they were playing in a graveyard.

Ghosts of the Gridiron

They turned Tom Landry Stadium into a field of dreams, and Jack had a front-row seat. He thought he had gone to football Heaven. He also imagined himself or Hilfy or Molinski out there after a legendary career. They all had the ability, he thought, but didn't get the breaks.

Finally, the game ended. The players shook hands, some hugged, and together they vanished into the night. Jack drove to the Ritz Hotel without Molli, who went to dinner with an ESPN producer and likely stayed in his suite across the hall.

Jack couldn't go back to sleep after he awoke from his nightmare. Like Hilfy, he had a dodo flight path but one with no bus ticket out. The walls – and not just the field house walls – were caving in.

Jack worked up a do-or-a-die plan on Ritz Hotel stationary in the wee hours of that Tuesday morning. He drove Molli's Sebring into the Dippity Donuts' drive-through and sped to Geburtville and back at dawn with Molli's micro tape recorder and a bag with every last cent he had earned, two items that would either make him soar to the heavens or crash into the Earth.

70

Jack no longer could hide in his long black overcoat but was willing to give it – and the money-filled envelope in his pocket – for a 40-1 shot at freedom.

The Cowboys' odds of winning the Super Bowl rose from 30-1 after Rex Fanning was named the Cowboys' starter. No NFL team had carried such horrific odds going into the Super Bowl much less winning it. Jack knew that, but he did not know what was going on in the office of the Executive Sports Editor of The Dallas Star.

Soss, that Sawed Off Stack of Shit sports editor, had conjured up a plan to make him and his network of goons millionaires. He had staff writer Jay Verona write positive stories about the Cowboys, glorifying their much-maligned veteran quarterback and how their recent inspired play was enough to pull the biggest upset in the history of sports. He also disclosed injuries to key Chiefs' players, although team officials said the team was in perfect health.

He recalled Penny Pettigrew from the Morgue, because he knew Miss Sunshine would write only bright, cheery columns on the Cowboys' chances. "Remember, folks, our Cowboys are at home," she wrote." Home fans. Home cooking. Home field advantage. The crowd will root, root, root for the home team."

Miss Pettigrew did not know the game was almost sold out long before any rooter knew who would be playing, and that most people would rather throw beer bottles at the Cowboys than cheer for them.

Low-life gamblers looking to make their fortune also did not know that. They could put their last 1000 bucks on the Cowboys in hopes of earning 40,000 bucks. Stories in the Star made it seem like not so much of a gamble.

The gamble for Soss and his gang would be if the Cowboys actually won. They promoted their 40-1 straight up (no point spread) odds and had a mountain of takers on the Cowboys. Soss and Verona witnessed Fanning's quails and his teammates' lazy, just-happy-to-be there attitude in training. For insurance, Soss' mystery associate found a rogue referee willing to call an interference penalty on Cowboys' defenders anytime the ball was thrown downfield. The referee would receive a cut of the profits.

What Jack did know, based on comments about Molinski's whereabouts, is the action was going down in the back room of the Kazbar. He drove a sleep-deprived Molli to the airport on the Tuesday morning and pulled her Chrysler Sebring in front of the Kazbar to see a line of gamblers walking in with an envelope and walking out without one.

Jack needed a delivery man and found one passed out next to the dumpster in the Kazbar parking lot. His old cellmate was too drunk to remember Jack's welshing on the overcoat and the whiskey bottle he had promised him. So he offered the coat and bottle again to deliver the sealed envelope with his life savings and a note that read: "My debt is cleared if the Cowboys win. If they don't win, don't bother hanging me from the goalpost. I will do it myself. Regards, Graham Repert."

Jack waited in Molli's car outside the Kazbar for his old cellmate to come out. He didn't come out alone, likely threatened to be tossed inside the dumpster if he wouldn't tell the goons where Repert was hiding. Five or so goons, including Grog and Hog, marched into the parking lot only to see the Sebring speeding away from them.

What Jack did not know was that his bet prompted a call from the goons to the Star sports office, where Soss told them, "Bet's off for that prick. He now owes us $39,000. I want him hogtied to seaweed on the bottom of White Rock Lake before the opening kickoff."

Jack retreated to Molli's hotel room, called the front desk, and asked in a female voice for a 2pm checkout time. That gave him enough time to script the quotes off the tape recording of Molli's interview with Jeanie and write a column on Molli's laptop she had asked Jack to return to the Geburtville Gazette.

Jack needed very little of the interview, batting out Molli's feature by checkout time. It was more of a personal message to his wife than a sports column:

Everyone knows Jeanine Pratt's story: Caprock State star golfer moves to Dallas to be coached by the Legend, struggles through years of frustration and near-misses at earning her LPGA card, loses her husband in a fiery crash, and ultimately triumphs on her home course to earn a spot in this weekend's LPGA opener, the Las Vegas Women's Classic.

But how many know that Pratt can repeat every line of Happy Gilmore. That she spends most of her free time whacking golf balls in her backyard net with a Big Bertha, that her favorite love song is 'How long will I love you,' that she hates jelly donuts and being stood up at the airport, and that she can throw a Titleist the length of her block.

Only Jack would know that, and Jeanie would know that only Jack would know that. Reading Molli's column would be a call from the grave. Or did Jack's spirit take over Molli's body like Patrick Swayze did with Whoopi Goldberg in the film Ghost? Would Jeanie recognize Jack's writing style, though she seldom read his columns?

This all went through Jack's head as he drove the lonely road to Geburtville on the cloudy Tuesday afternoon. Certainly Jeanie would realize Jack was alive and help him recover his life without going to prison. Or would she be so angry that she would make sure he was put away for life, sharing a cell with inmates named Grog and Hog?

Jack was busting to tell someone his plan, and the only confidential someone was in a little box at St. Blaise Catholic Church. "Wait till I confess my miracle plan," Jack thought.

Jack rushed through Geburtville, kicked up dust on the dirt road leading to St. Blaise, and was almost in the confessional before the engine died.

"Boy, I got something to share with you," an out of breath Jack whispered into the screen. The reply was not the tender voice of an orator but the screech of a Leprechaun.

"In da name of da Fotter, da son, and da holy goat."
"Huh?"

71

Jeanie skimmed through the sports column ghost written for Molli Glass early Wednesday morning without considering how a writer whom she had never met could discover secrets only known by the ghostwriter. She was too consumed with getting to the airport.

She left the newspaper open to that page next to her half-filled coffee mug on the dining room table on the first honk. The Legend drove her to the Forest Green Country Club en route to the airport. He wanted to work on her short approach shots as final preparation for the Las Vegas Women's Classic.

Jeanie dumped a bucket of balls a full wedge shot in front of the 18th green and began pelting the balls to within birdie distance of the flagstick. She lofted one right at the stick as she heard a "whack" from the nearby first tee followed by, "Look out!" from the Legend, who stood a few yards from Jeanie. Neither heard anyone holler, "Four!"

Jeanie also never heard the Legend saying, "Jeanie, you all right?" after the Titleist struck Jeanie on the side of her head with more force than she had used to fire them at Jack. Jeanie crumpled to the cold bent grass like a ragdoll.

As the blaring siren from an approaching ambulance neared the golf course, the culprit and The Dallas Star execs abandoned their morning round and fled in a Black Lexus with a bent tailpipe without an apology.

While Jeanie was being rushed to St. Luke's Hospital, Jack was returning Molli's computer to the Geburtville Gazette.

"Who are you?" the managing editor said.

"A friend of Molli's," Jack said. "I've been helping her out the past couple of months."

"Hope you learned something; she's a brilliant writer. Hope she does well with her new ESPN gig. She's earned it."

Jack laughed inwardly and pointed to Molli's column on Jeanie in The Dallas Star. "She wrote a brilliant column on that golfer Pratt this morning."

The editor shook his head. "She should have written an obituary."

"Pardon?"

"Just got a police report that said Pratt got hit by a golf ball and is in a coma."

JEANIE WAS STILL in a deep sleep when Jack arrived at her bedside. She lay in a hospital bed in ICU with tubes strapped to her arms and monitors beeping around her. She slept like the angel she soon might become, her soft breathing barely lifting the light blue blanket that covered her hospital gown.

Jack held Jeanie's hand with his left and brushed her forehead with his right. Tears formed in his eyes. "Jeanie, my love, it's Jack. I am so sorry for being such a crappy husband, for being so unsupportive, so uncaring. You deserve better. I love you with all my heart."

Jeanie's heart monitor sped up but she did not wake up. A bloated nurse tapped his shoulder. "Who are you?" she said, not noticing the tears welling up in his eyes.

"I'm her husband."

"Jeanie's husband is dead. Get out."

Jack got out of the room but not out of the hospital. He roamed the hallways, peering occasionally through the glass in ICU to see if Jeanie remained unconscious. He distracted himself by reading the name plates on patients' rooms. He stopped when the name on one door read, "Jozef Molinski."

Jack poked his head inside to see an old man lapsing in and out of consciousness. The same bloated nurse, apparently the hospital Nazi, pulled him out. "You gonna tell me you're Mr. Molinski's son?"

"I am."

The Nazi nurse shrugged. "He doesn't have a son or none that we know of. He's been blithering on and on about some Johnny dude. Let the ol' man die in peace."

Jack walked to reception and then snuck back to Jozef's room. The wrinkled up man had more tubes and monitors than Jeanie. The man's eyes creaked open. He squinted at Jack's face, his vision blurred. His hoarse breath gave way to croaky speech.

"Johnny, my son?" the disoriented old man said.

Jack played along. "Yes, dad, I'm here."

"I'm sorry, son. So so sorry." Tears dribbled down the old man's face.

Jack thought telling the dying man what a horrible father he had been for abandoning his son when he needed him most would be sweet justice for the awful life Johnny had lived. His next thought was of the last words he had heard from the Voice in the St. Blaise confessional.

"Forgive us our trespasses as we forgive those who trespass against us."

He had received no such wisdom the afternoon before from the Irish priest, likely a substitute and likely the same guy who presided over his funeral service.

"You did what?" the priest screamed loud enough to be heard by the penitent waiting in line, when Jack told him about his faked death.

"Say 10 Hail Marys and 10 Are Fotters and beg our Holy Fotter for forgiveness."

The only one begging forgiveness was Johnny's fotter. Jack stared at the old man, struggling to breathe and thought of his own father and how he dragged him off the football field and never supported him in the first place. He wondered if his father would have begged forgiveness had Jack visited his deathbed.

Jozef took Jack's hand with a literal death grip and squinted into his blurry eyes. "Whatta say, son?"

Jack focused his eyes on Jozef's, but he was thinking about his own father. "I forgive you," he said.

A warm smile came over Jozef. His hand slid off Jack's, and rested his gray head on his pillow.

"Good."

It would be Jozef's last word. He went back to sleep as Jack left his room and never woke up.

Jack dined on an Almond Joy he bought from a vending machine with the few coins he had left. He wandered back to ICU and peered through the glass at Jeanie's bed.

Empty.

THE BLOATED NURSE said she had no authority to tell Jack – a stranger, she surmised – whether Jeanie was dead or alive. Instead, he followed Chad through the hallway.

He stopped when Chad ducked into a private room outside ICU with a rectangular glass window at eye level. He waited several minutes before spying into the room.

Jeanie was awake, groggy but smiling at her new visitor. Chad held her hand and stared into her eyes.

"Honey, I'm so glad you're all right." Jack could hear Chad's words trickling through the open door.

He then heard how Chad jumped on a plane in Las Vegas, where he was waiting for Jeanie, as soon as he received a call on his cellphone from The Legend, and came straight to the hospital.

Jeanie didn't say anything. She just stared into Chad's eyes.

"Never," Jack thought, "has she ever looked at me that way."

Jack couldn't take it anymore. He sprinted to Molli's Sebring he had parked in front of the emergency room. He didn't even bother to remove the parking ticket from the windshield wipers as they swept the cold rain off the glass.

He disregarded the slick highway on his return to Geburtville where the Ghost Bowl awaited. Jack gritted his teeth and gripped the steering wheel tighter than Jozef Molinski gripped his hand. "I'll show 'em," Jack said.

He would show "them", referring to his father and Jeanie and anyone else who doubted his football ability, how he could perform on the gridiron. He thought about all the practicing and dreaming at Jack's Home Field, all the juking and sprinting on his escapes from the goons, all the times he took the coward's way out on the field or in life.

Jack sped through Geburtville looking for the lights surrounding the Gebbie Bowl. All he found was darkness.

There were dump trucks, not pickup trucks, along the banks. There were diggers and tractors, not receivers and defenders, on the field. Yellow danger tape was strung around the field and the field house. The goalposts had been removed.

Jack abandoned Molli's car and stared at the field as rain and sleet pelted his black overcoat. "Game over," he mumbled.

72

Jack's wake up call on the Thursday before the Super Bowl was a wrecking ball.

The nightmare about the legion of Jack haters declaring war on him was real. This war was not fought with bazookas and bayonets. It was fought with sledge hammers, bulldozers, and dynamite. The army was composed of demolition experts and a battalion of workers wearing orange vests and hard hats.

The wrecking ball smashed into the far wall of the field house with a massive bang. The field house shook like it was in an earthquake. The brick wall crumbled and knocked Jack off the high jump pad. He had only enough time to grab his VW keys and a bag of his belongings he had filled in anticipation of the blitzkrieg and flee to the locker room door before the second blast flattened the building.

Jack crawled through the rubble and the thick dust fog to the exit just as the bulldozer rammed into what was left of the field house. Jack used the VW as his escape pod. He twisted the key in the ignition. He wasn't sure if the awful grinding noise was his deep cough or the engine.

It was both. Jack backed the VW van out of the car port just before it collapsed. He swerved onto the football field, dodging massive diggers and excavators on his final burst downfield past workmen who cheered him with raised shovels.

Jack was safe but had nowhere to go. Molli's father had taken back the Sebring the night before and had it delivered to Molli at the DFW airport upon her return from her work orientation in New York. That arrangement meant that Jack could not collect from Molli the final $440 she owed him for ghostwriting. Now he was down to his final $4.40.

Jack couldn't afford the much needed cold and flu medication to combat the hacking and sneezing worsened by his three-hour sleep in a damp overcoat. He couldn't risk driving the rusted out VW into Dallas, where it could be spotted by goons.

So he hid it on Jack's Home Field. "I am going to die here," he thought as he shivered in the night as a cold winter blast shook the van. It wasn't until dawn Saturday, Super Bowl eve, until he gathered enough strength to stagger into town in search of stale Bryson Bagels discarded into the alley dumpster he hoped would calm the storm that raged in his stomach.

He retreated to the van, a mere windblock from Old Man Winter, with the Saturday Star sport page he pilfered off a delivery truck. Jack browsed the hyped Super Bowl coverage, including another story about the Cinderella Cowboys, and stopped his eyes on a headline buried at the bottom of page 12d between tire and oil change ads.

Brave golfer makes cut in Vegas.

Appearing on the black and white photo beside the story was Jeanie collapsing into her caddy's arms, her fingers wrapped around his neck. Barely visible on one finger was an engagement ring.

73

Jeanine Pratt barely had enough time to put on her golf shoes and kiss her fiancé before knocking her drive down the fairway on the first hole of the Las Vegas Women's Golf Classic.

Waking up with a migraine in Dallas on Thursday morning and to a neurologist who said she would be hospitalized over the weekend while subjecting her to a brain scanner did nothing to deter Jeanie's determination to be on the first tee at the Las Vegas Golf and Casino Club at 9:31am the next day.

Nothing was going to keep her from realizing her dream – not even her caddy, who wanted to keep her in bed. He figured marrying her was the only way to ensure screwing her. He claimed the emotion he had experienced after Jeanie's brush with death led him to the jewelry box of his long-deceased grandmother.

Jeanie's eyes didn't sparkle in the rectangular emerald of the tainted-gold ring, and she did not say yes to his "Will you marry me, babe?"

"I'll tell ya' what," Jeanie whispered, glancing around at the room. "If you make sure they don't scratch me from the tournament and help me make the cut, I'll marry you in Vegas."

Chad slid the ring on the wrong ring finger. "Deal."

Chad returned to Las Vegas on Thursday night with Jeanie's clubs and golf shoes. Jeanie followed him Friday pre-dawn, sneaking out of the hospital to a getaway taxi and catching a dawn flight.

Jeanie arrived onto the first tee just as her name was announced. She had dressed into her tournament garb in the hospital, napped on the plane, and put on her golf cap and glove in the taxi en route to the first round of the 54-hole tournament.

"From Dallas, Texas, Jeanine Pratt!" The announcer's words echoed off the adjacent club house and large gallery as Jeanie stuck her tee into the soft turf and grabbed her driver from Chad. No one noticed her hospital slippers, which she replaced as she stepped onto the tee. She staggered down the fairway and almost fainted before walking to the wrong ball.

"Mine."

The blurred grimace of the world's number one-ranked player, Ko joo-Yang, woke Jeanie to the reality that she finally was playing in a LPGA event. She also realized the spectators weren't there to watch her. Anna-lise Joubert, her other playing partner, wasn't ranked in the top 100. She had white compression socks stretched up her lean, tan legs and yellow bikini briefs visible under her short purple golf skirt every time she bent over.

No one noticed Jeanie in her red golf skirt and white sweater wobbling from tee to green, almost collapsing as she leaned over the putter. Chad handed her club after club and aspirin after aspirin, everytime saying, "You can do it, babe."

The golf writer at The Dallas Star and Jack seemed the only ones who noticed Jeanie finished with a two-over 74, a shot ahead of joo-Yang and three shots behind the leader. Jack used the rest of The Dallas Star sports page to line the paper bag and absorb his vomit. He lay there shivering in his black overcoat wishing after every spew that Chad was there to hand him a gun he could use to blow out his brains. "You can do it, dude," Jack thought.

Instead, Jack was set to endure a long, lingering death. It might take weeks for someone to discover his cold corpse in the van hidden in the oak trees on Jack's Home Field. He needed a warm home, and Jeanie having made the cut in Las Vegas left his former Dallas home vacant.

Jack pulled himself into the driver's seat. He barely had enough strength and mobility in his wrist and desire to live to turn the key in the ignition. He drove out of Geburtville and to the side streets of Dallas to make sure no goon recognized the rusted out van. He parked in the alley of his Magnolia Avenue home, slid over the fence into the backyard, and crawled to the backdoor.

Jack probably would have froze to death on the back porch had the spare key been removed from its hiding place under the only potted plant on the property. Jack stood long enough to let himself in and turn the heater on full before collapsing on the living room sofa where he had slept after so many Monday Night football games. He was so exhausted he did not notice the sports page opened to Molli's column on Jeanie next to the half-filled coffee mug.

AS JACK SLEPT, Jeanie was shooting an 88 in the second round of the Las Vegas Women's Classic. "That's a fucking double snowman," Chad said, lugging his fiancee's golf clubs off the 18th green and sounding more disappointed than Jeanie that she was in last place by four shots going into Sunday's final round.

As Jack slept, Soss was meeting with his boss at the Kazbar about his plans to nab the elusive Graham Repert should he come anywhere near the Super Bowl. The Sawed Off Stack of Shit sports editor received a nod from the man so infuriated by his abandonment by the Cowboys that he created a network of illegal betting consortiums around the country.

The corrupt business left Bill Kazmeer wealthier than his ex-Cowboy teammates and welshing clients buried in a Pennsylvania coal mine where he pretended to work.

Jack slept all afternoon, all night, and all morning until a doorbell woke him up on Super Bowl Sunday.

74

Jack answered the bell like a prizefighter who had been cold-cocked by a left uppercut. He picked himself off the sofa and staggered to the front door as if in need of smelling salts. All he could smell was the bile that fled from his stomach from a day of vomiting and underarms in urgent need of deodorant and change of clothes.

After peering into the peephole, Jack realized there was no time to brush his teeth. There were goons out there. These goons were dressed in neatly pressed blue uniforms. They wore a badge on their shirt pockets, a night stick on one hip, and a revolver on the other.

The door was the only object blocking his true identity. Jack hadn't shaved in several days. His hair had grown out, and he left his fake glasses in the now demolished field house. He was a dead ringer for Jack Byrne. He would be opening the front door to a man who faked his death and subjected himself to prison time.

So he opened the back door and fled to the VW van, the object of the police enquiry. A curious neighbor, who hadn't heard any backyard ball-whacking in a few days, had alerted the police to the rusted VW and a potential prowler. The cops likely noted the expired license plates and inspection sticker.

Jack slowly drove down the alley until he looked in the rearview mirror at a distant but rapidly approaching squad car with lights blazing and siren blaring.

"Here we go," Jack said, pressing the accelerator to the floor. He spun the VW out of the alley onto Magnolia Avenue with now two police cars in pursuit and fleeing faster than the night Jeanie flung her golf balls. He reversed his path of the last time he was chased by cops, winding through the same strip mall and between rows of parked cars at the Bag 'N Save and hiding behind a brick wall at a Dippity Donuts drive-through.

Jack scraped all the change out of his pocket and the ashtray and said to the teenage clerk, "Gimme as many donuts as you can for this change."

It was a half-dozen, and the girl threw in a cup of hot chocolate and agreed to let Jack eat them in the drive-through until another car came. Jack munched and sipped for 30 minutes while listening to Super Bowl pre-game commentators telling radio listeners how the Cowboys were in for a Super whipping. Jack motioned to the clerk inside the store. "Where is everyone today?" he asked.

"It's Super Bowl Sunday, silly," she said. "The game starts in two hours. Aren't you gonna watch?"

Jack felt the Super Bowl press pass in the pocket of his black overcoat. "I'm watching it live."

He sounded doubtful. There were police goons and regular goons looking for him in and out of the stadium. A goon of each brand was polishing off a pre-game donut inside the shop when they spotted Jack and his VW in the drive-through window.

Jack heard a siren, chugged the remnants of his hot chocolate, and drove back through the strip mall with a police car and a goon pickup truck in pursuit. He drove down a one-way road the wrong way, ran a red light, and soared up a freeway entrance ramp.

He whizzed past downtown to the Tom Landry Expressway, zigzagging through Super Bowl traffic as if his life depended on it. It did. The pursuit was relentless. Police and goons radioed for support and soon two other police cars and two more pickups – including one transporting Kazmeer and goons disguised as security guards to the game – gave chase. Jack's only ammo was the donuts, hot chocolate, and butterflies he spewed out the window.

"Deadmeat!" Kazmeer screamed out the window as his pickup rammed into the back of the VW van.

The van spun and lifted on its left tires, but Jack managed to gain control and swerve into the HOV lane. He sped away from the chasers, blocked in traffic, and thought he had escaped until he heard a loud pop on the left side of the van. The bald tire on the left rear wheel blew out from the friction on the road, and rubber exploded onto the freeway.

Jack could see Tom Landry Stadium on the horizon and that he was not going to get there. He slammed on the brakes, forcing the car into a spin. The van slammed into a Pepsi truck, bounced off the guardrail, and flipped onto its top. Sparks flew off the road as the van skidded along the pavement still faster than the speed limit and screeching louder than its driver before ultimately coming to a screeching hault a football-field width from the first exit ramp to Tom Landry Stadium.

Cars and trucks braked while drivers and passengers turned their heads for a glimpse at the wreckage beneath a cloud of smoke. Police goons and regular goons exited their vehicles and sprinted around stopped cars while pulling out their guns. They surrounded the crunched van. Kazmeer echoed a police officer, "Come out, you scum."

Pistols drawn, they waited.

There was no movement. There also was no body.

Except for the keys dangling off the Armadillo-shaped key ring in the ignition, the VW van was empty.

75

Jeanine Pratt sat in her wedding dress at the Caesar's Palace bar while her fiancé shared a round of beers and chicken wings in the next room and watched the Super Bowl pre-game on a cinema size screen with his fellow caddies.

Not even a horny toad like Chad would give up football for sex. He left his bride-to-be in the next room, sipping a margarita while watching on a small Sony screen a high school band with a mistimed honk in the brass section march into Tom Landry Stadium and garnering the courage to say, "I do."

Jeanie's wedding dress was a knee-length pastel she tossed into her suitcase the morning of her golf ball beaning to wear at the LPGA Awards Dinner. There was no award for Jeanie, only a made-the-cut prize cheque that barely would cover her bar bill.

Like her first Christmas Classic, where she met Jack, Jeanie teed off alone at dawn. Only Chad and an elderly official in a golf cart followed her down the fairways. Unlike Jack, Chad did not find the solo pairing amusing.

He had hoped they would put Jeanie in a threesome that included Anna-lise Joubert, so he would have something else to look at other than Jeanie's errant drives. Jeanie hoped for a "Wow, you got a hold of that one, babe," or another Happy Gilmore quip after her tee shot on the seventh tee had a longer hang time than a Rex Fanning pass.

All she got from her head-shaking caddy was, "Shit."

Chad had never seen Happy Gilmore or even Caddyshack. He *had* seen all of the Terminator movies at least twice. When Jeanie jumped on back of the official's cart on the 15th fairway, Chad yelled, "Get your ass down off there, babe. He might give ya' a penalty stroke."

That would have left Jeanie with an 81 and tied for last place. Her birdie on the 18th hole kept her out of the cellar but without a high-five from her caddy.

"Let's go find an Elvis Impersonator, get married, and fuck," he said stomping to the clubhouse.

"Maybe, I don't want to marry you," Jeanie said.

Chad stopped, gritted his teeth, and pointed at his fiancee's face. "Hey, babe, we had a deal."

The deal and Elvis and the caddy shagging would have to wait until after the "Super Bore," as referred to by the maragarita sipper who pondered the birdies and bogeys and a life that was about to take a mulligan.

The honking that echoed from the band to the bar continued until the horn blowers marched off the football field and cleared a green-turf path for the gridiron gladiators who trounced onto what each hoped was a field of glory.

76

Scott Hilfinger on his unlikely path to the Super Bowl had seen Jack Byrne disguised as a woman, a Cowboys' mascot, a Cowboys' fan, and a Viking.

But a tuba player in a high school marching band?

Jack gave a little honk and a wink as he passed Hilfy leaning against the tunnel wall amidst a mob of white, silver, and blue-clad players with stars on their helmets and in their eyes after a barrage of camera flashes blinded their path down the tunnel to Super Bowl XL.

The light Jack wanted to see was at the other end of the tunnel. It was blocked by goons searching for a welshing, compulsive gambler named Graham Repert and by police looking for the man who kidnapped a high school tuba player.

It wasn't a miracle that Jack and Hilfy – and the Cowboys – made it to the Super Bowl. In the least, it was a fluke.

Jack had squeezed through the crumpled windshield of his mangled VW van as it stopped dead on Tom Landry Expressway. Battered and bruised and bleeding, Jack limped through the honking and swerving traffic on both sides of the freeway and climbed over a concrete wall, shielding himself from those who wanted to imprison or pulverize him.

He followed the distant sound of a marching band to an abandoned outdoor drive-in with lines drawn to shape a football field. He yelled to a hipster band director above the pounding and blaring of drums and horns, "What's goin' on here?"

"They rehearsin, man," he said, scratching his chin fur. "This here's the high school all star band. They about to march into the Supa Bowl."

"Cool, man," Jack said.

The hipster sniffed at Jack's clothes and stared at the blood dripping from his scalp. "You stink, man."

Everyone marched the three blocks to Tom Landry Stadium but the tuba player. Jack had lassoed the Port-a-John the tall boy they called "Chubster" was using next to a construction site with an old rope and wrapped it around and around and tied it to a pole.

Jack slipped the band uniform the boy had discarded outside the Port-a-John over his black overcoat, fitted his blue furry hat over his bloody head, and strapped the tuba over his sore right shoulder. Jack blew into the instrument to drown out Chubster's cry for help, and fell in line with the band.

A large plastic chin strap covered Jack's whiskers as he synchronized his steps with the other tuba players and marched down the Tom Landry Stadium tunnel. The baggy band pants covered his bloodied Nike sneakers as he high-stepped in agony over the turf field while occasionally blowing into the mouthpiece. Jack figured Chubster had called 9-1-1 on his cellphone while sniffing fresh urine. He also figured the police who rescued Chubster would not interrupt the pre-game performance to arrest a tuba player.

Jack was more worried about the goons. He peeked at the sidelines to see Grog dressed as a security guard and Hog disguised as a chain crew member not far from Molli with an I, who tested her microphone in front of a television camera. His view of fans and non-fans filling the seats of the massive stadium was blocked by the bill of Chubster's hat.

There were a few pity claps as the high-skipping majorette marched the band off the field to the drum rolls. Jack's eyes rolled ahead from Hilfy to the police officers waiting at the tunnel exit for the tuba-playing impersonator and behind to Grog following the band up the tunnel. Jack dropped his tuba and ducked into a side door that he knew all too well from his reporting days. It was the door to the Cowboys' locker room.

HILFY WAS LUCKY to find that door after missing the team curfew at Ritz Hotel, where every player but the third string quarterback spent the night. The hotel ran out of rooms. Instead of bunking in his bed at the Downtown Y, Hilfy passed out next to Jack's cellmate beside a dumpster after being tossed out of the Kazbar.

Hilfy woke up with a Super Bowl hangover not cured by a half-dozen Dippity Donuts. He somehow found the Cowboys' shuttle bus and then meandered to The Bar in Arlington. As his teammates were being taped up, Hilfy was getting liquored up.

Few people at the bar believed him when he said he was playing in the Super Bowl. "More like spectating from the bench," he said between burps.

Hilfy had spent more time at The Bar in Arlington than on the stadium playing field in the aftermath of constant snubbing by Rex Fanning and Ray Myles at Cowboys' pre-Super Bowl practices. One session, he was the opposing quarterback used as a tackling dummy for blitzing linebackers. Another, he was Fanning's PA – driving him to and from the locker room in a golf cart, handing him a towel between quail tosses, pretending he was him and signing autographs for kids outside the gate. Everything but shining Fanning's cleats or wiping his ass.

Hilfy tried to wipe the memory of the worst week of his life by pouring whiskey down his throat. He hoped he was so drunk he wouldn't remember the humiliation he would suffer standing along the sidelines while Fanning served up another duck to Chiefs' defensive backs.

Jack watched on a locker room television as number 13 waddled to the sidelines 20 yards behind the water boy as the Cowboys trotted onto the field to a few hopeful claps from the few Cowboys' fans lucky enough to get tickets in their home stadium. Jack was disappointed he would be watching the game like he had all the other Super Bowls – at Oliver's department store, his university apartment, his house, or the Kazbar. With goons and police searching the stadium, he would have to come up with a more clever disguise than a tuba player.

Still, Jack could hear the crowd on top of him and smell the heat ointment players had used to lather their nervous muscles. He could hear the national anthem and jets flying over the stadium. Suddenly, there was quiet.

He stared up at the television screen to see Agberto Gerrone slipping to his silver-padded butt as he approached the teed up football and, to a collective groan of 100,000 spectators, striking a dying dribbler that skidded like Jack's VW van to midfield.

The Super Bowl had begun.

77

Had Jack been covering the Super Bowl instead of hiding in it, he would have been writing the Cowboys' obituary after Rex Fanning's first pass.

He would have typed something like:

Was it a bird?

Was it a plane?

No, it was an end-over-end quail from Rex Fanning almost fair caught by the Chiefs' free safety on their way to the biggest annihilation in Super Bowl history.

Fanning's pass – more like an "Oh, Dear Lord" than a Hail Mary – was followed by the red-clad Kansas City Chiefs' opening 50-yard, eight-play scoring drive that culminated in Sexy Lexie Allen's Fosbury Flop over the Cowboys defensive line and two Cowboys' rushing attempts that smacked into a brick wall named Marvin Mallard, the Chiefs' incredible hulking tackle, and another up-for-grabs toss by the Cowboy king.

Cowboys' tight end Heath Garrett, who sprinted downfield to break up the pass, would have been whistled for offensive pass interference had the rogue referee not been arrested in the Minneapolis Airport for concealing a handgun in his carry-on bag. Soss, that Sawed Off Stack of Shit sports editor, wasn't too worried about Kaz's abandoned insurance policy after the Cowboys' offense lumbered, eyes staring at the turf, to the head coach with his hands on his hips and a death stare that said, "What the fuck was that?"

ESPN announcers Sid Langdon and Colt Renner implied "What the fuck is this?" during a first half in which the Chiefs dominated the line of scrimmage en route to time-consuming, multi-play drives that led to two short field goals for a 13-0 lead. The spectators were too busy exchanging stock tips to boo after every Fanning pass skidded off the turf five yards in front of a receiver, fluttered five yards over his head, or smacked into the helmet of Mallard or another lineman charging in for the kill. The Cowboys only saw red.

Jack was more excited by the Super Bowl commercials and chunked tape rolls at the television. "Get Fanning out of there," Jack yelled, just quiet enough to not be heard by security guards outside the locker room. Myles, who had strict orders from the Heywards to leave Fanning in for the duration, would not take him out. Instead, Mallard did.

After another dying quail into the Chiefs' secondary, Mallard drilled his helmet into Fanning's chest and drove him like a nail into a coffin into the cold backfield turf.

A collective "Uhhh" was uttered from the nine-hundred dollar stadium seats to the Rich Bastard's nine-thousand dollar luxury box to the lone viewer in the Cowboys' locker room to the beer chugging and back slapping caddy in the Caesar's Palace bar and to his margarita sipping fiancée in the next room.

Mallard got a 15-yard penalty and Fanning a cart ride to the x-ray room. Mallard also got a scold from Chiefs' head coach Randall Tubbs, who barely could see Mallard's smirk through the gray bars criss-crossing his helmet that sunk to his elephant-size neck.

"Sorry, Coach. I wanted ta do da star quarter-a-back a favor."

"A favor?"

"Put 'im out of his misery."

JACK THOUGHT it might be an opening for Hilfy should Fanning's replacement Jarmelle Beezley suffer the same fate until Molli and her pearly white smile flashed onto the screen with an injury report.

"This just in, Sid." Molli listened to the call from her earpiece and echoed the statement from the producer in a nearby television truck. "Rex Fanning will not return to the Super Bowl. The Cowboys' team doctor has reported that Fanning suffered a broken collarbone, wrist, and a sprained neck after being drilled by Marvin Mallard. Molli with an I reporting from the Cowboys' sideline."

Ghosts of the Gridiron

Jack squinted to the background to see Hilfy drinking from a flask he had smuggled under his football pants and nearly falling off the bench. "He's lost all hope of playing in the Super Bowl, no matter who Mallard crushes," Jack said to the lonely locker room walls. "Maybe I can slap him back to reality at halftime."

The Cowboys were lucky to make the locker room alive and back to the field following Ray Myles' tongue-lashing that started with, "This is the Super Bowl, you mother fuckers, not a Powder Puff League Final," and ended with "Now go out there and eat their butts, rip their jocks off."

Hilfy didn't hear a word. He sat on the metal chair above the white athletic tape with his misspelled name scribbled with a magic marker. He didn't have the strength to take the helmet off his head, which rested against a hook with a spare number 13 Cowboys' jersey hanging from it.

Hilfy didn't move when his teammates and coaches stormed out of the locker room and trotted back to the bench following the ageless, bell-bottom jeaned Mick Jagger's belting of his final line of Start Me Up, "You could make a dead man c-o-o-o-me."

Jack, who had been hiding behind a whirlpool tub, patted the side of Hilfy's helmet. This four-fifth's dead man didn't know if he was coming or going. He let out a little moan and closed his eyes. His whiskey breath could make a dead man come back to life.

Jack stared at the spare jersey hanging from the hook, looked up at the television screen at the Cowboys gathering on the sidelines and slapping each other's shoulder pads, and snapped his fingers.

Five minutes later, Jack stood in the middle of the locker room in full Cowboys' attire – silver padded pants, silver helmet with a blue side stars, black cleats, blue and white socks, black chalk under his eyelids, white wrist bands, and shoulder pads beneath a white jersey with blue stripes fronted with the number 13 below a little NFL insignia and backed with the number 13 below the proud letters that spelled out "Hilfigger."

Hilfy's left eye creaked open for a split second. He must have been thinking, "A woman, a Cowboys' mascot, a Cowboys' fan, a Viking, a tuba player.

"And now, a Dallas Cowboys' quarterback?"

78

Jack Byrne fantasized his entire life about being right where he was on February 5, 2006 – on the sidelines at the Super Bowl with his silver helmet and blue numbers 13 glistening off the stadium lights.

The reality was quite different and not too kind. This was war, and the weapons were an artillery of 300 pounds of muscle slamming into an opposing 300-pounder at full speed. Jack stared through his silver facemask and winced with every bone crunching tackle and every flesh crackling block. Jack's crash outside Tom Landry Stadium was nothing compared to the collisions in it.

Every tackle, every catch, every run, every snap was captured in a click from hand-held and tripod mounted cameras that flooded the end zones. Television cameras were everywhere, sending every moment of the world's biggest game around the world. Photographers, reporters, doctors, trainers, ball boys scurried about doing their jobs as the warriors staggered off the field and took refuge and a blast of oxygen or a shot of painkiller alongside their battery mates on an aluminium steel bench. The noise from 100,000 spectators blasted through Jack's ear holes like a train, and a mixture of heat bomb and perspiration whistled up his nostrils.

This was real football – nothing like what he played in Geburtville – and you don't come close to experiencing it through a department store or press box window. You also can't hear the players screaming at each other after a hard take down.

"I gots you mudda fucka," Chiefs' linebacker Reginald Simmons hollered at Jarmelle Beezley as he tried to escape to the sidelines after another wild scramble.

Beezley rose to his feet and yanked Simmons' facemask against his. "Suck my dick, man," he hollered as gray-haired referees pried them apart

"You'd like dat, faggot," Simmons said, smirking and pointing his index finger.

No one was more profane than the Cowboys' head coach, who fired either his clipboard or his headphones to the turf after every missed tackle, every dropped pass, every errant throw, and even after Agberto Gerrone's line drive 37-yard field goal attempt rammed the crossbar and bounced over it to cut the deficit to 13-3 early in the third quarter.

"What was that, you mother fucking greaser?" Myles screamed at the former soccer player as he jogged off the field with his teammates patting him on his little shoulder pads. "If there would have been a fuckin' goalie down there, there'd still be a big fuckin' goose egg on that big fuckin' scoreboard."

Gerrone pulled off his helmet and looked up at the grimacing head coach. "Como?"

As much as Jack wanted to be there, he didn't want to be there. "What happens if that linebacker pile drives Beezley into the ground and Myles has a brain fart and orders the emergency quarterback into the game?" Jack thought. "I'd freeze into the stadium lights."

Jack wanted to crawl into a foxhole. But he had nowhere to hide. He was safer on the sidelines with a nearby Grog in his security vest roaming his eyes at the crowd, Hog placing the yardage chains directly in front of him, and cops searching for the tuba player's kidnapper. The facemask hid his face, but what happens when the helmet is removed and his face is revealed?

"There is no way out," Jack thought.

All he could do was continue pretending he was Dallas Cowboys' quarterback Scott Hilfinger, patting players on the back as they left the field with a "good job," and twirling a football with his fingers.

If the Cowboys could somehow pull off a miracle comeback, he would win his bet and could plead with the goons that his debt was cleared. Maybe they would just break his arm or leg or a few ribs or cut off a finger for all the trouble the two phony Graham Reperts caused them. Maybe the only way he was leaving the Super Bowl, seemingly like several of his battered teammates, was in a body bag.

Jack put all negative thoughts out of his head as a referee's whistle blew through the cool night air, and the players pulled off their helmets and retreated to the sidelines. There was only one quarter left in Super Bowl XL and his beloved Cowboys were trailing by 10 points to a team that hadn't given up 10 points in one quarter all season.

"Come on you guys; let's win this thing," Jack yelled as the starters assembled around their head coach.

Myles gritted his teeth but didn't look at Jack. "Shut the fuck up."

79

Jeanine Pratt's dead husband and soon-to-be second husband were in the same room, and she didn't even know it.

The IMAX-size television screen at the Caesar's Palace All-Sports Room illuminated Jack's sideline image, while Chad sat before it with a Bud and his buddies barely paying attention. The Cowboys were unable to make a dent in the Chiefs' immovable defensive mountain as the massive scoreboard clock, about as big as the Caesar's Palace screen, ticked the final minutes off the underdog's improbable dream.

It was really more of a Super War, and the Cowboys were the victims. One-by-one the players either limped or were carried to the sidelines by trainers who looked like Army medics scurrying on and off the battlefield. The opposing players were nothing but a red blur. Ray Myles-turned-General Patton hollered at his wounded warriors to limp or crawl back into the action.

"Put a Band-Aid on it, and get your ass back out there you pussy," Myles yelled at tortured tailback Theunis Adkins, after Marvin Mallard drove his helmet into his knee cap and severed ligaments off the bone.

"There goes the Wildcat offense," Jack thought, watching Adkins pounding his fist on the sidelines turf. "Unless they cream the punter, I should be safe here on the sidelines."

The real number 13 was safer in the locker room, sitting upright in an alcohol-induced coma, while his team withered on the adjacent field. Jeanie had joined Chad in the All-Sports Room and watched her first Super Bowl like she was watching a war movie. She didn't notice the third string quarterback hiding behind third string linemen, also fearing a call to battle or the blonde sideline reporter who had slept with her dead husband and racked up airtime with her constant injury reports.

Ghosts of the Gridiron

"Stop the fight," giggling television analyst Colt Renner said. "The Cowboys will be playing their water boy if this gets any worse."

"The one person they should send in," play-by-play man Sid Langdon said, "is a priest."

AFTER THE REFEREES stopped the clock for the two-minute warning, Myles tried one final time to revive a team that, by the grace of Chiefs' fumbles and personal foul penalties, were still only down 13-3. The Cowboys were out of timeouts, out of luck, out of hope, and almost out of players. Jack eavesdropped on a flea-flicker play that Myles instructed to Beezley on a third down and forever from the Cowboys' 45-yard line.

Beezley took the snap from under the center and fired it backwards to Antonio "The Rocket" Crocket, who fired it backwards to Beezley. Chiefs' defenders, not realizing Crocket's pass went backwards, chased the scrambling Beezley to his own sidelines. Beezley launched a pass to the opposite sidelines just before Mallard rammed him into a line of players and coaches.

Neither Beezley nor Myles were awake to see Crocket haul in the pass at the 20 yard line and dance into the end zone. All 357 pounds of Mallard had smashed into Beezley and then into Myles, who was staring at the airborne missile. All three men crashed into a metal bench, and only Mallard got up.

Trainers and doctors rushed to the sides of Beezley and Myles, neither one responding. Television replays did not do justice to the vicious hit that didn't even result in a penalty. Instead, the Cowboys were whistled for delay of game after the assistant coaches argued – like when Myles was thrown out of the Redskins' game – about who would take over the team.

Defensive line coach Alvin Baines again won the argument, reminding the other coaches he had been with the team the longest and he was still the meanest. He sent Gerrone out to kick the extra point and back out to try an onside kick with the Cowboys trailing 13-10. Baines demonstrated what he wanted the Mexican to do.

"Amigo, you kick ball, uh, diez meters. Then fall on it like you is da goalie.

"Si," Gerrone said, trotting back to the field.

This would be like a chip shot for Jeanie, whose eyes were glued to the huge screen like Chad's and so many others around the world. The stadium grew quieter than the Cowboys' locker room as Gerrone trotted toward the ball and slipped again as he did on the opening kickoff.

"Chinga," Gerrone yelled and repeated in English by Cowboys' fans, coaches, and players.

The football bounced through the hands and between the Chiefs' front line of sure-handed receivers and running backs. The Cowboys' special teamers charged past the front liners and dove for the loose ball that was swatted into Chiefs' territory.

It took referees five minutes to remove the pile of white and red-clad bodies. At the bottom was a lone kicker who cradled the pigskin like it was the last chimichanga on the Chiefs' 40-yard line. The referee pointed to the Chiefs' goal-line, igniting a roar by Cowboys fans' in Tom Landry Stadium, Caesar's Palace, and homes across the world.

Baines patted Gerrone on the helmet. "Good job, amigo."

Baines turned around and around until his eyes caught the numbers 1 and 3 glimmering off the stadium lights and a player staring at the turf. It was the unlucky number worn by the player he clothe-lined as the team ran out onto the field in Houston. Baines' superstition was overwhelmed by his desperation.

"One-three, gets ya'lls butt over here," Baines said.

Jack turned in the other direction like he didn't hear him. Baines marched over to the trembling player and looked at the name on the back of his jersey.

"Hilfigger, Hilfudger, whatever yo's name, didn't you hear me call ya'lls number?" he said. "It's ya'lls time to shine, man."

Jack pointed to his chest. "M-m-m-me? B-b-but Coach Myles said..."

"I don't give a rat's ass what Coach Myles said. He out cold and I'm da coach now. You're da emergency quarterback, and this here's an emergency."

Jack stared at the Cowboys' players waiting in the huddle and the players on the sideline ready to pounce on him. He looked at Grog in his orange security vest and Hog on the chains. No NFL player would refuse his dream shot, and Soss and Kaz and every goon in the stadium knew it. A refusal would blow his cover. His teammates would yank off his helmet before the television cameras, and he would be Graham Repert to the goons and Jack Byrne to the cops.

All his life, this was Jack's wish. Now it was a death wish. Either he would be murdered, incarcerated, or flattened by an angry 357-pound tackle.

Then he thought of Hilfy, who would have given anything for this chance had he stayed sober for one more game. And of Molinski, whose dream he shattered years ago. He looked at Baines and the Cowboys he had trashed in the press for so many seasons and realized he was the only player on the Cowboys' bench who had ever taken a snap. "Maybe I deserve to die," he thought.

Jack closed his eyes, took a deep breath, and buttoned his chin strap. Jeanie stared at the huge screen as a player broke away from the sidelines and headed for the Cowboys' huddle.

"Now playing quarterback for the Cowboys," called the stadium announcer, "Scott Hilfinger."

Every spectator in the stadium and in the world but Jeanie let out a collective and curious sigh. "Who the hell is Scott Hilfinger?"

80

The first thing Jack noticed as he stood in the middle of the blue star on the 50-yard-line of Tom Landry Stadium was the lights.

They were everywhere.

Beaming from the massive light poles attached to the stadium roof. Glowing from the press and luxury boxes. Flashing from spectators' cameras and cellphones. Blinking from the rows of photographers. Illuminating from a scoreboard, the boldly lit letters and numbers that told the Super Bowl story: Chiefs 13, Cowboys 10 with 42 seconds remaining in the game and 0 timeouts left.

Jack stared past the goalpost to the light of the end zone tunnel, his passage to freedom that seemed farther than the stars that shined above him. Everything was bright but him. Jack must have been in a shadow, a dark shadow cast by the monsters who circled him in the huddle or glared from the line of scrimmage with large teeth sparkling from their charcoal skin.

His Ghost Bowl teammates were midgets compared to Cowboys' offensive linemen. The Chiefs' defensive linemen were more than giants. They were red fire-breathing dragons who melted the air without saying a word. Their piercing eyes spoke for them.

"We should be celebrating our fucking Super Bowl victory on the sideline instead of standing here before a twerp, no-name third stringer who wants to steal our glory. We are not only going to kill you; we are going to bury you."

His teammates weren't much kinder.

"C'mon, man, call a fuckin' play," reserve tackle Rolando Freidrich said.

Unable to speak, Jack shook his head. He didn't know the plays and neither did the interim coach. Ray Myles' headset also was a casualty in the crash with Marvin Mallard. Alvin Baines couldn't hear Sterling Heyward cursing at him from the booth to get Hilfinger out of there or from the offensive coordinator, whose instructions could not have been repeated in the huddle even if Jack wore Hilfy's helmet. No one bothered to wire it up.

Heath Garrett called his own play. "Look guys, we only need 10 yards to get into realistic field goal range. Just chunk the ball over the middle linebacker and I'll grab it. On two."

The Cowboys clapped in unison, "Break," and trotted to the line of scrimmage. As the 40-second play clock wound down the final 10 seconds, Jack twisted his head back and forth to see the red dragons digging their paws and cleats into the turf. Trying to disguise his fear, he swaggered up to the five-ass salute and put his trembling hands under Friedrich. "Wrong butt, you idiot," Friedrich whispered before the gnarly grin of the opposing tackle.

Jack scooted over to the center, Clay Washburn, and stammered, "S-s-set." barely loud enough for Washburn to hear over a crowd now bracing for a dramatic finish.

"Louder," Washburn screamed.

"Set, hut!"

The center pumped the ball into Jack's cold palms as the play clock struck double zeros and almost broke his fingers.

Jack somehow held onto to the ball. He tip-toed backward a few steps and looked at nothing but massive claws and biceps charging toward him with a ferocious growl. He closed his eyes, cocked the ball behind his ear, and tried to fling it. The ball slipped out, and the Garo Yepremian-style toss was more of a shot put. Mallard drove his helmet into Jack's stomach and drilled him like a spike into the Cowboys' turf star. The ball caromed off the back of Friedrich's helmet and into the air for a few helpless moments before landing a few inches short of diving linebackers.

Jack coughed blood and held his aching ribs as he staggered to his feet and television analysts and spectators worldwide snickered at the replays.

Antonio Crocket grabbed Jack's facemask in the huddle. "What da' fuck was dat, man?"

Jack stared at the ground, now feeling a fraction of the humiliation Johnny Molinski must have felt. He wanted a bottomless pit like the one in his nightmare or the one that swallowed The Dallas Star staff car to open beneath him. This would be the only way to escape the gridiron grunts and sideline goons who wanted to grind him into extinction.

Garrett called another play for a quarterback whose only appearance in a pro game was in his wildest fantasy. "Everyone go long and simply hand it off to Mertz on a draw. Do you even know what a draw play is?"

They broke the huddle again and this time Jack put his hands under the center's behind the first time. But he failed to get the snap. The ball dropped to the ground, and Jack couldn't find it underneath his linemen's size 16 cleats. The clocked ticked as referees moved bodies off the pile, and Cowboys' receivers rushed back to the line of scrimmage.

Washburn pushed off Chiefs' players, who tried to pin him and run out the clock, with the pigskin he had recovered. Washburn shoved a referee out of the way and slammed the ball on the ground, "Hurry, you turd. Spike it."

Jack hollered over a barrage of boos and jeers, "Set-hut," and this time held on and hit his first target – the turf a foot below his outstretched fingers – as linemen crunched their shoulder pads against each other.

Jack looked up for a moment to see the giant number 13 on the scoreboard. There were 13 seconds left for a team given little chance before the season or this game to be in with a chance at a Super Bowl title in the final 13 seconds. It was fourth down, and there was only one final chance to put the ball in Agberto Gerrone's range.

Garrett made it clear as the players assembled at midfield and with the play-clock and their hearts ticking that they couldn't be tackled in-bounds. The only hope, as the Cowboys and the Chiefs knew it, was a Hail Mary fling to the sidelines. Neither they nor Jack were sure if the turd-stringer could heave it that far.

Jack looked behind and to the side for an escape route as soon as the Chiefs would intercept or bat the ball down. He looked over to the sidelines where Myles, who barely had regained consciousness, almost fainted again at the sight of him. It was too late for Myles to reclaim his head coaching throne.

The play clock ticked but couldn't keep up with Jack's fast-beating heart. Hopeless teammates crossed their fingers alongside the bleary Myles and his fully-conscious coaching staff and players. Spectators stopped booing and grew deathly quiet along with those who watched on screens all over the world.

Soss, that Sawed Off Stack of Shit sports editor, grinded his teeth in the press box. The Rich Bastard clamped his beer bottle in his luxury box. Hilfy creaked open his eyelids for a second before the small locker room television and fell back into a drunken slumber. Jeanie slid her hand on Chad's shoulder and stared at the giant Caesar's Palace screen.

Jack stood a few yards back from the center in a shotgun formation, not risking another fumbled snap. The play clock clicked the final seconds 3 – 2 – 1 as a million flashes went through his scrambled brain. His father pulling him off the field. His wife flinging golf balls. The Dallas Staff car exploding. Goons chasing him down alleys and highways.

Then he heard the Voice calling from a quiet confessional in the only place he felt peace. "Go to the light, my son. Go to the light." A sudden calmness came over Jack. He closed his eyes and breathed in the cool night air.

He opened them as the play clock struck zero, and the snapped football smacked off his facemask. The crowd roared. Receivers sprinted to the sidelines. Defenders burst into the backfield. The game clock counted down, "12...11...10."

Jack bent down and picked up the football as Marvin Mallard hurled his 357 pounds at him in one all-out final crunching blow. Jack closed his eyes again and ducked just as Mallard flew over his helmet and crashed behind him. "9...8...7"

Jack reopened his eyes again, glanced at the 50-yard-line below his feet and ahead at nothing but the light shining from the end zone tunnel to the goalpost and a parting of a red sea of defenders.

A massive hole opened as pass rushers swept to Jack's right and left. Defensive backs followed receivers to the sideline creating waves on opposite sides of the field and a vast pathway to the end zone. In a fleeting moment three quarterbacks came together – one foiled by a father's distaste, one by a writer's pen, and the other by the coaches who had abandoned him. High on adrenaline and fear, Jack shot out of the pocket with the football tucked under his arm.

He blew past the line of scrimmage before anyone realized it. The red tide was sidelined until Jack reached the 30 and stormed toward the goalpost, sucking him in like a magnet. He ran as if the green turf was a cushion of air, bounding him downfield with legs churning and arms swinging and head swaying in rapid synchronism. It was as if his spirit had taken over his body, and he was watching himself burst toward glory propelled by a thunderous roar that echoed off the stadium.

As he reached the 20 and the clock three, Jack's only concern was the wave of redshirts rushing behind him, their footsteps growing louder with every stride. Ten yards from triumph he ran even harder and only looked ahead at the goal line rushing toward him through the bars of his facemask. Within five yards of glory he sensed a hand lunging for the back of his jersey.

With one giant leap for immortality Jack soared into the air, reaching the ball at the line. The crowd's roar hit a crescendo as the clock stopped on zero. The pursuer's hand swiped only at the air and the unknown quarterback, running like a gallant gazelle, sped into the end zone without stopping.

Jack's real goal line was the stadium exit, and he had no time to wait for a victory hug. He sprinted toward the great light of the tunnel ahead of the red men spilling to the ground in anguish and men in white, silver, and blue raising their arms in absolute ecstasy. He ducked his head, shielding his true identity from the photographers who aimed their cameras at his face and took one more stride before going helmet-first into the thinly padded goalpost.

The crowd let out an awful, "Ooh," as Jack crumpled to the ground, the game ball still tucked into his arm. All those lights radiated on top of him as players, coaches, trainers, photographers, and camera crews rushed to his side.

All Jack saw was darkness.

81

After interviewing the triumphant players and coaches on their home turf and awaiting the presentation of the Lombardi Trophy, Molli with an I was hurried to the Cowboys' locker room.

"Hilfinger is starting to come to," the ESPN director said through Molli's earpiece.

Molli and her cameraman pushed through the swarm of writers and photographers to a groggy number 13, who sat on a locker with his football helmet still strapped on his head. He looked from side to side at the mob armed with notepads, tape recorders, and television cameras ready to send his first insightful words around the world.

Their hero's eyes wandered to the small television screen and a replay of the glorious dash to Super Bowl infinity and the helmet-to-goalpost collision that knocked him out cold. Cowboys' PR men helped number 13 to his feet and onto a small platform where he could be seen. People worldwide, including a bride-to-be golfer in Las Vegas, glued their eyes to a screen for their first glance at the face behind the helmet. The writers stretched their tape recorders to within inches of his chin. Camera operators and photographers focused their lenses on his facemask.

Molli joined the quarterback and the PR men on the platform. She listened for the first interview question in her earpiece, looked at the camera, and asked, "How does it feel to have scored the most dramatic winning touchdown in Super Bowl history?"

Number 13 unbuttoned his chin strap. He grabbed the ear holes of his helmet, and slid it upward. A silence prevailed in the locker room and in living rooms around the globe. Jeanie, wide-eyed, stared at the massive Caesar's Palace screen until the mask was lifted and his face was revealed to the world.

It was, indeed, the face of Scott Hilfinger.

Hilfy let out a curious smirk and said, "It feels good."

AS HILFY UTTERED his only sentence, Jack hid in the Morgue at The Dallas Star and rewrote a lead he had written two months before.

Scott Hilfinger's unrealistic dream of playing in the Super Bowl, much less starring in it, began in Deadhorse, Oklahoma. If it hadn't been for a miracle the magnitude of the Red Sea, that's where the third string quarterback and his old green gym bag would be headed right now.

Jack took the the greatest story he ever wrote wasting away in his email and brought it back to life. One click on the period key that followed the untouched last line – *he made his father proud* – and one click on the send button beamed the story of Hilfy's remarkable journey to the Super Bowl to every major newspaper around the world.

Except The Dallas Star.

Jack only had been unconscious a few seconds before trainers reached his side and pushed smelling salts to his nostrils. He kept his eyes shut, because he knew he had a better escape plan than running up the tunnel. Instead, he would be driven up it in an ambulance with flashing lights and a loud siren.

Paramedics placed him on a stretcher and lifted him into the back of the ambulance where he had stowed his black overcoat before taking the field in the Cowboys' number 13 duplicate jersey. One paramedic attached wires to the patient's body and looked at a monitor, while the other revved up the engine. The paramedic in the back of the ambulance dialled the emergency room at St. Luke's Hospital in downtown Dallas.

"His vitals look good," he told the doctors through his cellphone. "He's in no danger, but we'll bring him in for observation."

The paramedic was so confident of the patient's health, he joined the driver in the front seat and left the patient alone in the back as they drove up the tunnel with Cowboys' teammates patting the sides of the ambulance and wishing a speedy recovery for their newfound fallen hero.

The driver sped down Tom Landry Expressway faster than Jack drove the VW bus in the opposite direction that afternoon. The flashing lights and sirens prevented him from having to dodge traffic until driving into a mass of Cowboys' fans running and yelling or driving and honking through the downtown streets. When the ambulance stopped and waited for a clearing, Jack tore off the wires and slipped out the back door with the black overcoat wrapped over his jersey. Consumed with the panic of carving through traffic and deafened by the loud siren, the paramedics never realized their patient had escaped.

They realized it when they heard Hilfy talking on the radio as they pulled up to the emergency room and figured he had slipped out before they left the stadium tunnel and staggered to the locker room.

Jack stuffed the Cowboys' helmet and uniform in a dumpster in The Dallas Star parking lot and snuck past security en route to the Morgue wearing nothing but a long black overcoat, blue knee-high socks, and football cleats. He barely had enough energy to bat out the replacement lead on the Morgue computer before passing out in the chair.

A FULL DAY'S EFFORT of running away from goons, cops, Chiefs, and paramedics took its toll on Jack as the adrenaline finally wore off and the pain of his bruised ribs and bumped head took over. When he awoke, one of the greatest Super Bowl stories was being printed all over the world.

Jack limped to Dippity Donuts and soothed his soreness with a dozen glazed and a cup of hot chocolate courtesy of a Cowboys' celebrator. He waited a little later than usual for Soss, that Sawed Off Stack of Shit sports editor, to arrive with his Dallas Star and Fort Worth Express Super Bowl issues hot off the press.

Jack noticed that Soss looked dejected, like he had just lost a million dollar bet without knowing Kaz had sacked him as his Dallas booky and told him when they met at the Kazbar, "Because of your bright idea and that squirrelly third string quarterback, I'll have to get my goons to kill off hundreds of winning bettors so we can break even."

Soss suspected another sacking if the Star's Super Bowl stories didn't measure up to their competitors. Soss sat in a corner booth at Dippity Donuts and between several empty booths to Jack, who peeked from behind a donut box. Soss dunked a jelly donut into his coffee and huffed as he read the Super Bowl column by a former Morgue librarian that thrice contained "Cinderella Cowboys" and "Nike Glass Slipper" in the same paragraph. Cowboys' beat writer Dave Noonan managed to get "David and Goliath" into his lead.

Soss took a big bite and turned to the Express newspaper and to a front page story with the byline "Jack Byrne" glaring off his wide-eyed pupils.

"That's for killing my original Hilfy story and dispatching me to the rodeo," Jack mumbled under his breath.

Soss gulped as he read the magnificent lead and then stood and held his throat.

"He choking," hollered the Arab donut clerk. "I call 9-1-1."

"He'll be dead by the time they get here," Jack said, glaring at his red-faced nemesis bending over a chair without the slightest hint he would try to save him.

Jack thought of all the harsh treatment he endured over the years, all the humiliation. Soss deserved death by donut, and Jack enjoyed watching him gag and his silent, desperate plea for help.

Finally, Jack walked over and grabbed Soss from behind. Jack stuck his fist into Soss' pudgy gut and pressed upward. The donut chunk flew out of his mouth and hit a goon in the forehead. Jack turned for the door but the jelly-faced Grog grabbed him by the waist and shoved him into Hog, his fellow goon. "Gotcha, Repert."

Soss took a few moments to regain his composure and then focused his squinty eyes on his most hated and assumed dead columnist who had haunted him for the past two months.

"You?" he said in a scratchy voice, while pointing a well-groomed finger at Jack's face. "You're Graham Repert?"

"The one and only," Jack said, resisting without success from Hog's chokehold. "The one who stuffed a donut in your tailpipe. The one who re-directed your golf balls. The one who tee-peed your house.

"The one who just saved your miserable life."

Soss pointed again. "The one we been chasin' all over tarnation for the $40 grand you owe us."

"Can't read your own sports page, Dick? Cowboys won; I don't owe you a damn thing."

Hog tightened his hold. "What do we do with him, boss?"

"Kill him."

Grog threw Jack into the wall and caught him by the throat on the rebound. A siren and flashing lights ordered by the 9-1-1 caller interrupted the goons as they carried Jack into the lit parking lot. The same two police officers who apprehended Jack before at Dippity Donuts rushed in. The one staring at Jack said, "What's going on here? Don't I know you?"

Soss smiled and grabbed Jack's arm, leading him to the police officer. "We just found Jack Byrne, the world's worst and not-so-dead sports columnist."

The officers wrestled Jack to the ground, one hitting his sore ribs with his night stick and the other slapping hand-cuffs on his wrists twisted behind his back and dragging him to the flashing lights of the police car. Jack heard Soss in the distance as they spun out of the parking lot. "Don't let the paddy wagon door get you in the ass on the way out."

BOTH OFFICERS threw Jack face first into the same cell he landed in the night before his faked death. He also had the same cellmate, the real Graham Repert.

Jack was in too much pain, physically and emotionally, to sleep. He thought of Hilfy, who was likely celebrating with his newfound teammates. Of Molli, who was likely enjoying a well-deserved nightcap in her Ritz Hotel suite. And of Jeanie, who was likely humping her caddy for the third time at a Las Vegas resort.

A few hours later, at dawn, Jack crawled over to the cellmate's bunk and felt an arm colder than refrigerated meat under a thin gray blanket. The man's wrinkled eyelids creaked open to the blurred vision of the man still wearing his coat. With heavy liquored breaths, the old man's tired, hoarse voice cracked his dry lips.

"Did ya' find the meaning of life, lad?"

The old man closed his eyes and stopped breathing. Jack felt his wrist but not a pulse. He let him lay in peace until a police guard opened the jail cell and led Jack to a little room with a black telephone hanging on the wall.

"Ya' got one phone call," he said.

Jack pulled the telephone off the hook and stared at the numbered buttons glimmering off the light that filtered through a barred window. He pushed the receiver to his left ear and pointed his cold, trembling forefinger at the telephone buttons.

He pressed the area code and then six numbers one at a time at careful intervals and then paused. He closed his eyes and slid his right hand over them. Tears mixed with blood dripped down his fingers and splattered on his cleats. He pulled his hand off and focused in on one button and pressed it hard.

The guard escorted Jack back to his cell and slammed the door. Jack stared at the old man's body lying on the hard, cold slab and started crying again. Jack took off the long black overcoat and draped it over him.

Then he knelt before him and prayed.

EPILOGUE

February 4, 2018

Thirteen seasons passed since that day a number 13-clad player dashed down the Super Bowl gridiron to ultimate glory. The Dallas Cowboys had three winning seasons and four head coaches and no playoff victories.

Ray Myles was fired after the Cowboys' 2-14 season in 2008 and never coached again. One of his big criticisms was how he named Jarmelle Beezley the Cowboys' quarterback for the 2006 season without giving Super Bowl hero Scott Hilfinger a chance to compete for the starting position.

That didn't deter Hilfy. The fame over the winning touchdown run and the accompanying story Jack wrote and sent world-wide attracted interest by several NFL teams. The New Orleans Saints, in particular, noticed Hilfy's amazing arm at a mini-camp and signed him in the spring of 2006. Hilfy won the starting job in training camp and quickly developed into an elite quarterback.

He led the Saints from obscurity to the playoffs within three seasons and broke about every Saints' game, season, and career passing record. He was twice named the NFL Player of the Year.

In his final season Hilfy returned to the Super Bowl, back in Tom Landry Stadium for the first time since the Cowboys' dramatic victory. Down 28-24 to the Baltimore Ravens and backed up on their 10-yard line with 1:52 left in the game, the Saints called on their 42-year-old quarterback.

What the 100,000 stadium fans saw from the man with the black number 13 emblazoned on his pure white jersey was no different from what Jack watched during Hilfy's first practice with the Cowboys, in pre-game warm-ups, and at the Ghost Bowl. Pinpoint passes over the middle and to the sidelines. Perfectly executed screen plays. Beautifully-lofted passes downfield.

As he marched his team down the field there were no thoughts of his lingerie model wife and their twin daughters watching from the stands or the 30-acre ranch outside Deadhorse, Oklahoma that awaited them after the final snap. Total focus on a playing field lined with players, coaches, and photographers.

Hilfy propelled the Saints to the Ravens' 13-yard line. With four seconds left on the massive overhead scoreboard, Hilfy had only one play to regain the glory from the dramatic run 13 seasons before and send himself out in, what Dave Noonan and other Internet bloggers would write, a blaze of glory.

There was no running this time, no race for the goal line – simply a wonderfully arced pass to the corner of the end zone over a Ravens' cornerback and into the outstretched arms of tight end Garth Mueller.

Tom Landry Stadium erupted. Saints' players swarmed the end zone. Offensive linemen lifted Hilfy on their shoulders and carried him to the sidelines. Hilfy was named the Most Valuable Player, and he thanked the Saints' organisation for giving him a chance and "another unnamed person" who made it all possible.

Hilfy walked to the 50-yard line where he was mobbed by reporters, who drilled him with question after question, and camera crews, who focused their lenses on his face. Finally, Hilfy said, "I have time for only one more question and then I have to go celebrate."

A voice rang out from the media masses: "Pretty good shootin' out there, hoss. What would your father say about your performance?"

Hilfy smiled. Tears streamed down his face as he looked up at the sky. "I'm sure Dad was up there watching, and I am sure he is very proud."

Hilfy looked back at the sportswriters clearing from midfield. "Thanks for asking, DH."

The two men then stood alone in the glimmering lights, eyeballing each other. One with black paint under his eyes and carrying his helmet and the other with wrinkles under his eyes and gray streaks on his hair and goatee.

"Been a long time," Hilfy said.

"Since the Cowboys' last Super Bowl," Jack said.

"Thought maybe you were dead."

"I've been working as a ghostwriter. Mostly, autobiographies for athletes who rose from obscurity and inspire younger athletes to make the most of what they have."

"Whose book are you writing now?"

"Some guy who started in Deadhorse, Oklahoma and worked his way up the ranks."

Hilfy had requested his agent find someone who could write his autobiography and the agent heard about this highly sought-after ghostwriter who knew more about him than anyone else. Jack followed Hilfy around that season without him knowing it.

"You must have it already written."

"All but the final chapter, and you just wrote that yourself."

"What's title?" Hilfy asked.

"*Who the hell is Scott Hilfinger?*"

"Perfect."

The two men walked toward the goal line with their arms clasped around each other and en route to a victory drink at The Bar in Arlington, this time hiding from fans but not goons. There, Jack would tell him his story. He would start from the moment he was thrown into jail.

JACK STILL REMEMBERED the voice on the telephone a few rings after pressing the telephone button on his one and only call from the little room outside his jail cell.

"Hello."

Jack swallowed after a short pause and a deep breath. "H-h-hi, Jeanie. It's me."

Jack wasn't sure if Jeanie would faint or hang up. She did neither.

"Jack?" Jeanie sounded more hopeful than curious.

"Oh god, Jeanie, how I've missed you."

"Where are you?"

"Dallas County Jail."

The next sound Jack heard was a dial tone. He retreated to his cell wondering if those were the last words he would hear Jeanie speak. He lay on the slab where the body of his former cellmate was removed and contemplated his punishment for a faked death, a likely lengthy jail sentence and pummelling from prisoners, and defamation of his character from the local media.

That afternoon the guard escorted him back to the little room, where he was met by a well-groomed man wearing a three-piece suit and holding a leather brief case. He said his name was Martin Hennessey and he was hired to defend him.

Jack told Hennessey about how and why he faked his death, the goons who chased him over a bet he did not make, and Soss' likely involvement. The next morning Jack was summoned again to the little room and this time met by Hennessey and Dallas County District Attorney, James R. Foley. If Jack were to tell him everything he knew about Dick Schwartz and whatever he witnessed at The Dallas Star, Foley told Jack he would drop all charges against him.

Within a few hours, arrests were made all over Dallas and the culprits were being processed at the Dallas County Jail. A massive bust would lead to the extermination of America's biggest illegal gambling operation and the successful prosecution of its kingpin, Bill Kazmeer, and his goons who battered and murdered their clients.

Jack was led to freedom as Soss was being escorted by two police officers bigger than his goons down the hallway to his cell. Soss turned to Jack and gave him an evil look that said, "I wish *you* would have burned to a crisp in that Dallas Star staff car."

"That's for all the Super Bowls you didn't send me to," Jack said. "For all the lives you destroyed. And for Yo-Lo, for Lanny, for Johnny."

Soss turned around one last time when Jack yelled, "Hey, you Sawed off Stack of Shit."

Jack smiled: "Don't let the jail cell door get you in the ass on the way in."

On the way out, Jack asked Hennessey who had hired him. He told him the person was waiting outside.

JACK WALKED DOWN the sidewalk outside the county jail at dusk and saw someone walking toward him. She wore a white overcoat and makeup that covered her angelic face and carried a box of Dippity Donuts.

"You're not gonna throw them at me?" Jack said.

Jeanie smiled.

"I'm so sorry," Jack said, looking at the concrete.

"No, I'm the one who's sorry," Jeanie said. "I'm the one who turned you into a golf widower. I'm furious for what you put me through, but it made me realize how much I love you."

Jeanie slid her head under Jack's chin. He wrapped his arms around her and felt the warmth that he missed so intensely for two months. He wanted to hold her for another two months.

Jack said she didn't seem surprised when he called. Jeanie said she had put the pieces together from the column written about her in The Dallas Star. Her memory of the intimate details of the column that "no one but you would know" faded when she was struck by the golf ball but came back when a quarterback was running to the winning touchdown in the Super Bowl.

"He possessed the same running style as the man who dodged my golf balls," Jeanie said.

Jeanie also had noticed a wedding ring on the quarterback's finger as he was lifted into the ambulance. The man who pulled off his helmet in the locker room wasn't wearing a wedding ring.

"I never felt you were dead," Jeanie said. "I always felt you as I walked down fairways and hallways and as I lay in my hospital bed. People said I was in denial, but deep-down I knew it was more than that."

Jack pulled away from Jeanie. "Then why were you going to marry your caddy?"

"Funny story," Jeanie said.

Before Chad came to the hospital, the doctor told Jeanie she was pregnant even though she only had had sex once in the past four months. Jeanie already knew she had to marry Chad even before she made the deal with him.

"I had to have a father for my child, no matter who the father was."

Jack, now awed, said, "You realize now who the father is."

"Only you could make love to me like that, Jack."

Jeanie left Chad at the Elvis Impersonator at the Happy Hills Wedding Chapel "when the piped in music was playing our song, the song we first made love to. I knew you were still in my heart and in my life."

Jeanie sang softly, with Jack closing his eyes and hearing the music in his head.

How long will I want you
As long as you want me to
And longer by far
How long will I love you
As long as the stars are above you
And longer if I may

They hugged again, Jack kissing Jeanie on her soft hair and taking her hand and walking to a red sports car that would take them home.

"Are you happy?" he asked.

"I will always be happy if I am with you, Jack."

"Then you will always be happy."

JACK WALKED WITH HILFY toward the stadium tunnel without any mention of Jack's glorious run and without knowing if Hilfy knew if it was Jack impersonating him or if Hilfy thought he was too drunk or too knocked out to remember doing it himself. The truth would have made them infamous, not famous.

As they walked, Jack would reveal that his momentary lapse of life had taught him the meaning of life. "Sometimes you have to die to live again," he said. "That held true for you, me, and for Johnny."

Jack, fearing repercussions from his squealing on the goons, would not reveal the place where he had moved. He wouldn't tell Hilfy that it was a place with thick trees and old street lamps lining the roads. A place with quaint shops and friendly people, who always asked how you were doing and not who you were doing. A place he could throw a football to his son in a grassy park where a football stadium once sat. A place with a Catholic church he could worship in peace with his family every Sunday morning and sing carols every Christmas. A place where the bagel shop was bought out by Dippity Donuts.

It was a place where he was called "J.B." without anyone asking what the initials stood for, where he could watch a good high school football game every Friday night in the fall, and where he could relax by the fire in his den and watch Monday Night Football while his wife, the club pro at a nearby country club, whacked golf balls into a backyard net. It was a place where Jack's Home Field was replaced with his dream house, and he could look out over his town with joy and contentment and with an old tire still hanging from a massive oak tree.

Jack would drive away that Super Bowl night in his red Mazda Miata with a half-dozen glazed and a cup of hot chocolate through the fog northeast of the city to his home, a place no one would look for him.

ABOUT THE AUTHOR

Greg Lautenslager's passion for writing was ignited in Mrs. Gregory's sixth grade class at St. Pius X School in Dallas, Texas. He since has written thousands of stories for newspapers and magazines around the world – including 10 years as a sportswriter for The Dallas Morning News. *Ghosts of the Gridiron* is his second novel. His debut novel, *Following the Flame,* was published in 2005. Mr. Lautenslager lives with his family in Nelson, New Zealand.

Lightning Source UK Ltd.
Milton Keynes UK
UKHW011525011221
394872UK00003B/917